P9-CDB-220

Los Angeles, CA 90025

TWENTY-SEVEN

NOV 0 8 2017

VANGUARD

ANN AGUIRRE

A RAZORLAND COMPANION NOVEL

2310 80970

FEIWEL AND FRIENDS
NEW YORK

NOV 0 8 2017

A FEIWEL AND FRIENDS BOOK
An imprint of Macmillan Publishing Group, LLC
175 Fifth Avenue, New York, NY 10010

VANGUARD. Copyright © 2017 by Ann Aguirre. All rights reserved.
Printed in the United States of America.

Our books may be purchased in bulk for promotional, educational, or
business use. Please contact your local bookseller or the Macmillan Corporate
and Premium Sales Department at (800) 221-7945 ext. 5442 or
by e-mail at MacmillanSpecialMarkets@macmillan.com.

Library of Congress Cataloging-in-Publication Data is available.
ISBN 978-1-250-08982-3 (hardcover) / ISBN 978-1-250-08983-0 (ebook)

Book design by Rich Deas
Feiwel and Friends logo designed by Filomena Tuosto
First edition—2017

10 9 8 7 6 5 4 3 2 1

fiercereads.com

For Karen and Fedora.
Their love fires up my word engine.

one

shadows deep

When you are old and grey and full of sleep,
And nodding by the fire, take down this book,
And slowly read, and dream of the soft look
Your eyes had once, and of their shadows deep.
                    —William Butler Yeats, "When You Are Old"

Ash and Bone

Morning crept across the floor in buttery streaks, sunlight warming the wood of the cottage Tegan shared with Dr. Wilson. Normally he would've shouted her awake by now, loud with speculation about the latest round of tests. The silence scratched at her, so she clambered down from the loft, curious but not alarmed. When she found him pale and breathless, clammy in his bed, she touched his forehead.

Cold, too cold.

His lips were tinged blue. Cyanosis. *So what's the diagnosis, girl?* Wilson asked with his eyes, not his voice. She considered the possibilities quickly: pulmonary embolism or coronary failure. Either way, she had no medicine for him, and she lacked the skills to operate, as he'd said they once did, correcting broken hearts with a facility so advanced that it sounded like magic. He reached out, and she curled her warm fingers around his, noting the brittleness of his bones and the age spots on the back of his hand.

"I won't last," he wheezed.

"You promised to stay the winter."

"Can't. I'm . . . sorry, dear." Such rare affection. It thickened her throat as she clutched his hand tighter.

"What can I do?"

"Find . . . find the . . ."

"Who?"

"Catalina. Go to Rosemere. Ask . . ." But Dr. Wilson failed to finish his final request, as the last breath shivered out of him.

A rap on the door jolted her upright. She hurried to answer and found the mayor, Agnes Meriwether, pacing with an agitated air. "Get Dr. Wilson. I have to—"

"He's gone," Tegan cut in.

The older woman stilled, her face falling into desperate lines. "Then I'm too late."

This woman had made the doctor's existence a living hell, tormented with guilt over what he'd done trying to save the town. Instead his research nearly destroyed it. Tegan scowled. Even now it was about what Mrs. Meriwether needed, not that someone clever and wise had passed.

"Indeed," she snapped.

Whatever crisis she'd come upon this time, Mrs. Meriwether put it aside. "I'll organize the services. Quickly, wash him and get him ready."

The mayor left, and within moments the bell sang out, tolling Dr. Wilson's departure. Tegan counted. *Sixty-four.* That was a good age in these times, but she wished he had stayed longer. Grief came at her like a determined enemy. With grim fortitude, she filled a pail from the pump outside and hauled it in. Normally the family performed these rites, but Tegan considered this service the last she could offer. His flesh felt cool and waxy as she cleansed the world's cares from him. Next came the anointment with scented oil. There might be some significance to this, but she reckoned it really just helped with the burning.

Once she finished, she closed his eyes and knelt beside him, waiting for the bearers. "I don't know what I'm supposed to do. Is Catalina a person or a place?"

The question burrowed at her until the men arrived, shuffling outside with awkward uncertainty. She let them in before they knocked, and they were efficient about getting Dr. Wilson onto the board that would take him to eternity. Tegan finally put on her good dress and tied her hair back. By the time she got to the center of town, everyone had already assembled.

News travels fast.

The holy man read from his little black book. Then the bearers delivered the scientist's body to the flames.

Tegan wept alone.

The rest of Winterville sighed over seeing Dr. Wilson reduced to ash and bone, but his service passed with no other exclamations of grief, for he'd left no relatives behind. Only one apprentice, who hid later in a stand of balsam fir trees, needles sere as straw beneath her feet. A crisp breeze carried the distant scent of dried herbs sparking in his pyre, as the town had stopped burying their dead after the days when they rose and ate. Now bodies went with more haste than seemed human. *Just in case.*

Tears streamed down Tegan's cheeks and she swiped at them with an impatient hand. It was time to pack up the laboratory, as this marked the end of her studies. The knowledge that had died with Dr. Wilson left her hollowed out with a regret so ferocious, it felt like sickness. *I didn't learn enough. Not nearly enough.* When people greeted her as Dr. Tegan, the title scraped her raw; she felt more like a quack, her mentor's word for a bad physician. She cried a little longer and then squared her shoulders.

During the war, when she'd served as field medic for Company D, she'd seen her share of loss, and she'd mourned for each fallen comrade, each soldier she couldn't save. Nobody had thought they could succeed, starting with only twelve volunteers, but they proved themselves to everyone in the free territories by rallying a proper army and defeating the horde—with unexpected aid from the Uroch and Gulgur. If such an unlikely alliance could thrive, well . . .

I'll get through this, too.

When she headed back toward town, she met Millie in the road. Millie's family had left Otterburn some time ago, finding the honors the villagers bestowed burdensome. The girl's skin was burnished brown, and her hair fell in waves, black like a raven's wing, past her shoulders. In truth, Millie was pretty enough to have town boys falling over their feet, but she showed little interest in them. Most days, Tegan had to chase Millie away from the lab to get any work accomplished. Millie craved stories about what Tegan had seen and done, the places she'd gone. Sometimes Tegan felt as if she had a filigree tattooed on her forehead, with letters that read DOES NOT BELONG in ornate script.

"Are you all right?" Millie asked.

Tegan tipped her head back to study the sky. *Rain, just past nightfall.* Both the pattern of the clouds and the dull ache in her thigh promised as much.

With a sigh, she shook her head. "There's a lot to do yet."

"Will you stay and do the doctoring in his place?"

It was the first time anyone had asked that directly. Maybe it was what Dr. Wilson had wanted, but he'd died without saying so. Now she had only a word: *Catalina.* And an oblique request.

That's my answer, she realized.

"Once I finish at the lab, I'm going to Rosemere."

"Take me with you," Millie said.

She hesitated. "Can you fight?" And then she remembered her friend Deuce, known as the Huntress to the rest of the territories, handing her a weapon—without asking. So she waved the question away. "Never mind. Have you talked to your folks about this?"

"No. But they won't stop me if I choose to go. They already think I'm too good to stay in Winterville forever." A hint of pride brightened her tone.

As well it might, since Millie was famous throughout the territories as being the girl whose kindness had saved the world. Tegan beckoned her on. The wind was kicking up, whirling leaves at their feet as in a game of chase. Millie fell into step with a merry skip that made it seem like she was dancing. Tegan hurried toward the laboratory, half-afraid she'd find the townsfolk burning Dr. Wilson's things, too.

If they try, we'll fight.

Tegan's mouth flattened into an angry line. Dr. Wilson had so many important documents, reams of data and information it would take her a lifetime to unravel. Inside the lab, it was dark and still, cold as Dr. Wilson's hands had been. Millie followed close behind, nearly bumping into Tegan when she stopped, riveted by the sight of Agnes Meriwether pawing through a stack of papers.

"Those don't belong to you."

The mayor jerked like a criminal caught in the act. "I loaned Dr. Wilson a couple of novels last week. I only wanted them back."

"He never read anything but research material." Tegan's voice rang flat and cool. "Get out. And don't let me catch you here before I've finished packing."

She'd hide all the important resources at the cottage. It wouldn't be long before Winterville purged this building and dedicated it to some other purpose. When she left, she'd take the most valuable book, the one that had curled pages and meticulous drawings of the human body. The cover was black with embossed letters, and though the thing weighed almost as much as her staff, she'd carry it with her always. Maybe with sufficient time and effort, she'd grow into her title like a sea creature that scuttled from shell to shell.

"You don't like her," Millie said.

Tegan nodded. "She wants easy answers, quick fixes. And that ends badly."

To the terminus of his life, Dr. Wilson had been troubled by what he'd done to save Winterville. He'd performed experiments on a live mutant and created a pheromone solution that repelled the monsters, but it also drove people mad, resulting in carnage that haunted the living. Winterville still bore the scars, and the scientist had died with all that guilt still weighing on him.

"I've heard about what happened," Millie murmured gravely. "Where should I start?"

"Those crates, if you don't mind. The townsfolk should stay out of the cottage while I'm away."

With Millie's help, it took only a couple of hours to ferry over the things she meant to keep. Exhausted, she prepared a simple meal of toasted bread covered in soft yellow cheese. She ate with Millie in silence, grateful that she didn't have to stay here alone. With Dr. Wilson gone, this didn't feel like home anymore.

Afterward, the girl touched her shoulder. "If you'll be all right, I'm going. Are we leaving in the morning?"

Tegan nodded. "I'll gather the supplies we'll need to reach Rosemere."

"Can we make the journey alone?"

Once, she might've hesitated. But she was stronger now, confident in the skills she'd learned from Morrow and in the peace Company D had forged.

"If we're together," she said, "then how can we be alone?"

Millie flashed a bright smile. "Thank you. For taking me seriously. It's not that I don't like it here, but . . ." She paused, likely gathering her thoughts. "I want to be more . . . *see* more. In Winterville, they still know me as the girl who was so, so good in Otterburn. But that can't be the *only* thing I'm known for, my whole life."

Tegan understood. Just as she hadn't wanted to be labeled a former captive, Millie didn't want to stay on the pedestal people had built for her. "You'll love Rosemere. When I first saw it, I couldn't believe there was anywhere so pretty in the world."

"I can't wait." With a wave, Millie bolted.

Tegan got to work immediately. Though she'd been in

Winterville for a while, she hadn't forgotten how it felt to wander. Dry provisions, cook pot, walking stick, waterskin, the most accurate territory map in the doctor's collection, two changes of clothes (including socks), and finally, that precious book. *Ready.* As dusk ripened into full darkness, she climbed into the loft. Soon the rain she'd predicted earlier fell, tapping against the metal roof. Apart from Millie, she hadn't made friends here, devoting all her time to supporting Dr. Wilson.

It doesn't matter. In the morning, I'll be gone.

Millie met Tegan at the appointed hour, and they set off with minimal fanfare, though a few townsfolk waved and others called out greetings. Travel wasn't as hazardous as it had been, and they'd likely see traders along the way. Tegan set a pace she could maintain, amused to see that the other girl had a staff as well, raw cut and in need of smoothing. But she didn't tease. In fact, pleasure swirled through her like milk spreading in a cup of tea— that Millie admired her enough to emulate.

Me, not Deuce.

All over Winterville, girls sparred with twin wooden blades, reenacting the battle at the river. They always made the boys play the horde, much to their dismay. The clacking faded as the two friends put the town behind them. For a while they proceeded in silence. For some reason, Millie was collecting small stones in a pouch, but Tegan didn't ask about that.

"Have you ever traveled before?"

Millie shook her head. "Not really. Unless you count the trip from Otterburn."

That was only a few days, not like the odyssey to Rosemere. "Where you infamously cared for the sick Mutie." One act of kindness—that was why the Uroch had betrayed their forebearers and fought with humanity at the river. When she thought about it, the free territories owed Millie Faraday more than they could repay. But it was also fitting. She recalled Ma Tuttle, her foster mother in Salvation, quoting, "A little child shall lead them," from her holy book.

"Please don't mention that," Millie said, sighing. "It was so long ago. Did you know people bring things to our house sometimes? An old couple came all the way from Otterburn with a basket of vegetables."

Tegan bit her lip against a smile. The pure vexation in the other girl's tone made for bright amusement, but she managed not to laugh somehow. "It must be awful."

"You're mocking me. At least you *know* things."

"Thanks to Dr. Wilson."

"Even before, you studied under another doctor, right? In Salvation."

Yes. That's two healers I've outlived. It's hard not to think it would be unkind to accept a third teacher. "Doc Tuttle, my foster father. He saved my life and took me in when we first came out of the ruins."

"It was terrible there, I hear." The statement rang like a question, but Tegan had no plans to talk about what her life had been like before.

Even when her mother had been alive, there had been too much fear and uncertainty. Afterward, it was all shame and violence. While she'd told Deuce a more sympathetic version of the truth, she'd fought to make damn sure she wouldn't add any cubs to the Wolves' number while clinging to such a miserable life. Blood and pain and—

No.

Deliberately, she snipped that thread of thought and tied it off in a mental suture. "The world is better now. It might be there, too."

But I doubt it.

"Do you know lots of people in Rosemere?" At the moment, Millie was all eagerness.

Give her five days on the road, washing up in rivers and eating burned porridge. She'll lose that bounce soon enough.

Tegan thought for a moment. "Deuce and Fade are there, along with her family. Stone and Thimble and their boy, Robin. Gavin. You might remember him. And James, of course."

She'd have to be oblivious not to understand how he felt, but like Millie, Tegan wanted a lot of things more than romantic attention. James was handsome, clever, and kind; she supposed she *should* love him, but so far she could only muster the same pleasant warmth she felt for Deuce and Fade. Yet she'd nearly broken her own heart trying to save James's life, so maybe she did care a little more.

Never mind that anyway. I'll be seeing him soon enough.

"It is so incredible that you say their names like that."

"Hm?"

"As if they're just . . . people."

"That's how others see you, too," Tegan pointed out.

"I suppose. But that's just . . . strange."

Tegan understood why the other girl felt that way. The Huntress and her partner were famous in the free territories, as ferocious fighters and the leaders of Company D. They'd come from down below to change the world, and that was fairly intimidating. Yet she'd traveled with them long enough to understand that they were human.

She fell quiet and kept walking. Around midday, they took a break to eat beneath a stand of trees, basking in the sweetness of the shade. Tegan brushed her hands back and forth, the grass prickly beneath her palms. The summer had been long and dry, so it needed more rain than had fallen the night before. But the growing season was nearly done anyway. Soon the yellow would yield to brown as the leaves brightened like a weaver laying out her liveliest swathes of cloth.

"How long will it take?" Millie asked eventually.

"It depends how fast we walk. When I was with Company D, sometimes we covered twenty miles in a day. But there's no reason to push so hard." At the other girl's disappointed expression, Tegan estimated the number of days, doubling what it would've taken on an offensive march.

Assuming we don't run into trouble.

"I've never slept outside before, but I packed a bedroll. I heard Trader Kelley say he sleeps underneath his wagon."

"Some do," Tegan allowed. "If you're done, we should move along. The distance between us and Rosemere won't shrink from discussing it."

Millie leapt up and packed the remains of lunch without being asked. Tegan dusted herself off, checked the map to make sure she was on the right track, and then resumed the trek. Now and then they met travelers on the road, but nobody showed signs of wanting to pass the time with gossip or trade, so Tegan just waved and kept moving. It was a little unnerving to spot Uroch in the distance, and once, she thought she spied one of the small folk scurrying into a burrow. But Millie didn't seem to have noticed, and Tegan didn't care to spook the girl.

So she said nothing.

As the shadows lengthened, she scanned for a good campsite. Perhaps a mile on down the road, she found a spot someone had used before; it even had a fire pit left from the last tenants, charred ground surrounded by a good ring of stones. The area had been cleared of small rocks and branches, so it would be fine for sleeping.

"This looks perfect," Tegan said, dropping her pack with a sigh.

Her thigh burned with a low ache that never quite went away. Constant pain was a small price to pay for her life, after all.

With Millie's help, Tegan built a fire. Squirrels and birds complained overhead, chattering about the girls' intrusion. Ignoring this, Tegan made a simple stew from fresh vegetables and dried meat. They took turns eating from the pot while she hoped the smell didn't draw anything dangerous from the woods nearby.

The darker it got, the more alone she felt . . . and yet not. Around her, the woodland creatures fell silent. Her skin prickled from the weight of unseen eyes. Scooting closer, Millie seemed to sense it, too. Tegan tilted her head and froze at the unmistakable crack of feet breaking a branch nearby. *Close. How close?* But woodcraft wasn't her specialty, so she couldn't be sure.

On a bracing breath, she jumped up and readied her staff.

Into the Unknown

"Who's there?" Tegan called.

A cloaked figure emerged from the tangle of branches, brushing dry leaves away, surely not the act of a violent intruder. She couldn't determine who it was, however, so she kept her weapon high. Millie clutched her own walking stick. Later, Tegan might critique the girl's stance.

"Did I startle you?" The low rumble belonged to Szarok. He was the vanguard of the Uroch, which meant "the People" in their native tongue.

He pushed back his cowl, and she let out a relieved sigh. Millie showed no such relief, however. She probably hadn't seen any of these creatures since she was a little girl tending what she thought was a wounded animal in the woods. His skin gleamed silver-pale in the firelight, and the shadows elongated his claws and fangs. There was a beautiful ferocity about him, Tegan thought, measuring the slant of his cheekbones and the golden gleam of his eyes. He was all precious metals, smelted and forged in the dread furnace of fate.

"A little," she admitted.

"Where are you bound?"

"Rosemere."

"You know him?" Millie ventured to ask.

Quietly, Tegan performed the introductions, and the other girl recovered from her nerves enough to offer her hand to shake.

But Szarok bowed instead. Deuce had told Tegan that the Uroch could share memories with a touch and that they inherited recollections from their ancestors. She had a thousand questions, but it seemed impolite to fire them at him like a cannon of inquiry.

"Are you hungry?" Millie offered Szarok the pot.

"No. Thank you. I paused to warn you to be careful. When we broke the horde, the threat was quelled, but the territories are not entirely at peace yet."

Tegan appreciated the warning. "I'll be alert. Our allies are still wearing armbands, yes?"

"Since your people cannot tell us apart. Not by appearance or smell or—"

"*I* can," Tegan said with a touch of asperity. "Your skin is healthy and free of lesions. Your eyes are a different hue. And the Uroch generally do not run about naked or clad in filthy rags. The rest of my folk will catch up in time."

"I wonder if I'll live to see that day."

Millie glanced between them. "Are you sick, sir?"

She could've answered that his people died young, a curse from stepping onto an expedited evolutionary track. But it would've been rude to pretend to be an expert before someone who knew better than she.

Szarok only shook his head. "Now that I've spoken my piece, I'll go."

"Stay." The offer surprised Tegan, but she didn't retract it. Instead she gestured at the fire. "The night is cool—and three shadows on the ground are better than two."

"You hope my presence will deter marauders." His amusement came across low, laughter like a snarl in his throat.

"Is that wrong?"

"No. I'll stay. As it happens, I have business in Rosemere. I carry a message for Morrow's father."

Tegan wondered what it could be, but if he meant for her to

know, she'd find out soon enough. "Then we may as well continue together in the morning."

As Tegan spread her bedroll, Millie nudged her. "This is *incredible*. Is this how all your adventures begin?"

She repressed a laugh. "No, there's usually a talking horse."

"What?"

"Never mind. Get some sleep. There's a lot of walking ahead."

With minimal chatter, Millie tucked into her bedroll and Tegan eased onto her pallet, favoring her bad leg. It hurt more than usual, so she rubbed it and hoped sleep would bring some relief. To her surprise, Szarok knelt beside her and watched her fingers with apparent fascination.

"Can I help you?" Her whisper carried a faint bite.

"I might ask the same of you. This old injury, it healed poorly?"

"I'm lucky I kept my leg." She should probably hate and fear him, as one of his kind had inflicted the damage.

Yet she couldn't see him as one of them; they were clearly different species, much as the feral humans who had risen in Winterville weren't the same as those who raised vegetables and hauled water from the well. So she didn't withdraw when he leaned closer to inspect the site she was massaging. He didn't offer treatment, either, which she appreciated.

"It doesn't seem to inhibit your ambitions."

"Should it?" she snapped.

He gestured with two spread hands, talons unfurled, which somehow read like a shrug. "Some of the People are intolerant of physical imperfection. But . . . I think this prejudice did not originate with us."

"That's ours." Her sour tone indicated what she thought of that mind-set.

"Go to sleep," Millie begged.

That was good advice, so she nodded to Szarok and rolled into her blankets. He settled on her side of the fire pit. With the embers smoldering nearby, it wasn't cold, and the sky through the dark lattice of branches shone crisp and clear, the full autumn bloom of stars like a crystalline bouquet overhead, each spark of light raying like stray petals.

The Uroch was silent so long, she thought he must be sleeping. Then she caught a rustle of movement. "I'll stand guard," he whispered. "Dream well."

To Tegan's surprise, she did.

In the morning, she and Millie split the remaining stew and cleaned the pot with a hunk of bark. Though they offered Szarok breakfast, he declined. Millie bombarded him with questions and he was patient, keeping pace as he answered. In the sunlight, he kept his hood up, rendering him a mysterious figure. Around noon, they met Trader Kelley, who had fresh bread and ripe apples. Tegan would've bartered—she had arnica salve that was good for burns and minor injuries—but he gave them three rosy reds as a gift, along with a crusty golden loaf.

"What news?" she asked.

"Lorraine is having some kind of festival in the spring to commemorate the treaty. They're planning on sending an emissary to Appleton." Then Kelley took a second look at her hooded companion and added, "I guess I told the right person."

"We've already established trade agreements. I'm sure delegates will be sent when the time is right," Szarok replied.

They chatted over the meal, and then Tegan signaled the break was over by getting to her feet. She wished she could ride in a wagon all the way to the Evergreen Isle, but this caravan was headed in the wrong direction. So she saluted Trader Kelley with two fingers, as she'd learned in Salvation, and then continued the journey. It was a hot day, and the Uroch leader must have been sweltering in that cloak, but Tegan didn't suggest he shuck it. There had to be reasons beyond vanity or camouflage for wearing it; intuition suggested it would be impolite to pry.

"At this pace, it will take two weeks to reach Rosemere," Szarok said that night as they made camp.

"I'm aware." Tegan didn't glance up from her flint and tinder, focused until the tiny golden sparks became a little fire. "But any faster and I'll suffer. So will Millie, as she's not trained for a long trek."

Already, her own muscles protested, sore from her uneven gait. Though she had good boots made by Deuce's father, Edmund, they'd rubbed two new blisters by the end of the day. One of them felt puffy and tender while the other had burst, leaving her stocking sticky. She needed to peel out of her clothes and cleanse her wounds, but the Uroch's presence left her shy. Still, Tegan was a doctor—or so they claimed—and it was nonsense to allow timidity to prevent her from treating herself. If another girl had come to her with such foolery, she'd have whacked her patient on the back of the head. After dinner she set aside some clean water and stripped out of her boots and stockings. Millie was entertaining their guest anyway, so she started when Szarok came to peer over her shoulder as she examined her own feet.

"You're bleeding," he said.

His evident surprise aggravated her. "I got soft studying in Winterville."

She washed, then made short work of dotting the broken blister with salve. The other one, she decided not to pop. Though the skin felt puffy, it was better to let it split on its own. Still, she wrapped it, too, so that her stockings wouldn't take any further damage. It would be a while before she could wash and dry them properly. She hung them up nearby to air out and headed back to the fire, where Millie was feeding thin, dry branches to the flames.

"How are your feet?" Tegan asked.

The girl glanced over with a dismayed expression. "Can you tell . . . ?"

"No, but it's common sense. Let me see."

Millie had three blisters, two on toes and one on a heel, so Tegan repeated the treatment. Out of habit, she glanced over at

Szarok, but his feet were bare and clawed, probably tough enough that he didn't need shoes unless the weather got considerably colder. Curiosity pecked away at her like a hungry bird, but still, courtesy kept her quiet. Treating him as Dr. Wilson had Timothy—the Freak he used to create the pheromone spray that once protected Winterville—would be unforgivable.

As she packed up her supplies, in the distance she heard a clacking, grunting snarl. *Not Freaks,* she told herself. And even if it were, the old ones might veer away since they were traveling with a Uroch. The noise got louder, almost like a challenge, and within moments Szarok was on his feet, poised for action.

Eventually a black bear rambled into view. It stood up on its hind legs and called out; Szarok responded with a growl. The two eyed each other for a long, tense moment. The bear sniffed the air, probably drawn by the smell of food. Tegan lifted her staff, but it was ridiculous to think of scaring the bear off that way. Yet she had no skill with a rifle, so there had been no point in hauling one. Better for her to bear the weight of supplies she could use.

Szarok can't fight that thing with his bare claws. Can he?

The Uroch didn't seem to know that. Without looking away, he said, "Get to safety. I'll drive it off."

Tegan wrapped a length of cloth around her palm, grabbed the pot, and ran, beckoning Millie as she went. The distraction lured the creature, but now she had a wild animal chasing them through the dark woods. Behind them, Szarok swore—or at least she guessed he had, from the guttural sounds—and a struggle crackled the undergrowth. Stones and branches bit at the soles of Tegan's feet as she dashed headlong. She might not be a great fighter, but she was clever. Running wouldn't save them, but a tree might.

"Here," she panted out.

Bears could climb, but she hoped Szarok would drive the beast off before it found them. For good measure, she left the pot at the base of the trunk. *Better to feed it leftover stew than human flesh.* She and Millie scampered up, breathing hard. *Blast. Now I have to rewrap our feet.* That seemed a fairly mild concern, however.

Hope there's nothing worse.

In the dark, Millie clutched Tegan's hand, leaning into her. "Will he be all right? Should we have stayed to help?"

"Have you fought a bear before?"

The girl shook her head.

"Then no. Sometimes the best we can do is follow instructions."

Countless moments later Szarok came for them, a dark shadow at the base of the tree. "It's safe. Come."

Millie climbed down first and Tegan after. Szarok reached for Tegan too suddenly for her to recoil. One moment she was perched on the lowest branch, preparing to jump, and the next, he had her in his absurdly strong arms. Nobody had ever lifted her unless she was wounded, and even then, she'd wanted to fight. Generally she didn't enjoy being touched. Szarok didn't seem to register her resistance, and as he set her down, it faded.

But he smelled of copper, a sign he must be wounded. Tegan waited until they got back to camp before demanding, "Where are you hurt?"

"It's not serious."

She leveled a cool look on him, some of its impact doubtless lost in the dark. "*I'm* the doctor."

"Tend to your own ills first."

Sighing, Tegan did that, annoyed over the supplies wasted in wrapping their blisters a second time. She wrestled with putting her boots on and decided it was better to air the skin overnight. Finally she sat down beside Szarok to check the damage to his forearm. It looked as if he'd blocked a claw swipe, so it was incredible he'd only received a four-striped gouge.

"You don't need stitches. I'll clean and wrap it for you."

His physiology fascinated her. His blood was darker than a

human's, and she analyzed possible reasons, based on what she'd learned. *Venous blood is darker because it's deoxygenated. So does that mean the Uroch have evolved to survive on less oxygen? That would mean they could thrive in high altitudes, and they would be able to hold their breath longer. Yet they're not good in water, which probably has to do with bone and muscle density—*

"You're staring," he said.

"Sorry. Am I hurting you?"

"No." His eyes remained fixed, tracing her movements as she washed away the blood. It smelled a little different, not just like copper, but something else, like wet earth after a rain. She had no specific word for it, but it wasn't unpleasant. His flesh was cool and completely smooth, but it felt thicker than her own. She suspected the lack of hair made him vulnerable to the sun.

That explains the cloak.

With careful hands, she coated the wound with healing salve and then wrapped his forearm in a bandage and tied it off. "How's the pain?"

"Bearable." He put his hand over hers for a few seconds, and she stared at the long fingers, silver-pale and topped with claws.

I'm not afraid. I should be, maybe. But I'm not.

"Thank you," Millie put in from across the small campsite.

Szarok shifted, seeming uncomfortable. Since Tegan couldn't see his face, she wasn't sure why she thought that, but his flinch confirmed that impression. Briskly, she stood, put away her doctor's bag, and hung the troublemaking pot from a high branch. Provided there was no more excitement, they could eat the leftovers in the morning.

Millie went to sleep first, and if Tegan had any sense, she'd do the same. But instead Tegan lay awake in her bedroll, listening to the other two breathe. It wasn't adrenaline keeping her awake; she'd survived much bigger battles. While she didn't love fighting like Deuce did, she didn't fear it, either.

With a curse, she rolled over to find Szarok awake and watching her. Her heart skittered. "You didn't sleep last night, either. Is something wrong?"

There had to be some reason he'd been sent to Rosemere. Maybe the rest of the Uroch didn't like the treaty terms? *If they want more, the free territories will go to war again. And this time—* No, there couldn't be worse lying in wait. It had to be behind—with hope and brightness shining on the horizon.

But his whisper surprised her, stole her breath, in fact. "Could *you* rest at ease among your enemies? You've killed so many of my kind."

"*You're* afraid of *us*?" The idea seemed laughable. And yet . . . "Then why did you approach Deuce and fight alongside us?"

"Fear does not change what is right or my grief over what I've done. Maybe this decision was for the best. Or maybe I've betrayed my own people for nothing. Only time will tell."

With her heart sinking like a stone, Tegan remembered the sea of carnage after the War of the River. "Sometimes you don't know what's right until it's far too late to change it. You just do the best you can, moment to moment."

"You are wise," he said at length.

She shook her head wryly. "Hardly. But I'll tell you something else." It seemed right to whisper confidences in the dark.

"What's that?"

This was something she'd never shared before. "I'm afraid of my people, too."

Against the Grain

hy am I still here?

On the fifth day, Szarok asked himself this. Moving at his regular pace, he would've reached the river in a day or two. To guard these frail, slow creatures, he'd gotten wounded and delayed his mission by over a week. *Rzika will not be pleased.* The others rarely left Appleton, occupied with crafting policies that would govern their people going forward. Such work was rarely easy, as there was a wide range of intellect and outlook among them.

One female rarely stopped talking. Her questions were endless, and she granted respite only when he slept—or pretended he did. As for the other, she studied more than she spoke, her amber gaze keen as a blade. They smelled different as well. Millie must have sewn dried flowers into her clothing, because her movements carried a faint sweetness, whereas Tegan radiated a medicinal tang, likely from the salves and tinctures in her doctor's bag. Both lacked the richness of layering pheromones that would make them attractive, though the longer they traveled without scrubbing away natural musk, the more tolerable they became.

Neither had asked about the message he carried for the governor of the Evergreen Isle, and Szarok appreciated that discretion. Their company wasn't disagreeable, even if it was odd. This was the longest he had ever spent in close contact with humans.

His ears and nostrils hadn't stopped twitching under the bombardment of aural and olfactory input. They even *breathed* louder than the People, particularly when he tried to move faster.

"You need to rest?" he guessed.

They had only been walking for half a day. It was difficult to be patient when time meant such different things to their species. But he tried not to show his need for haste, as his ancestors had harmed Tegan in the first place. While he might not have injured her directly, he carried some of that responsibility by way of the rage-fueled memories he'd inherited.

Tegan nodded. "We should pause for a meal anyway."

Efficiently, she passed out equal shares of food. Szarok found it easier to chew through the tough dried meat than they did, so he finished first and tried to quell his distaste and impatience. Not well enough, evidently, for Tegan gave him a sharp look.

"You needn't travel with us the whole way. Since your arm's healing well, you have no further need of me, and we'll be fine on our own." There was no hint of hesitation in her voice, or countenance, either.

Not a bluff.

"Are you so eager to part company?" he asked, mostly to test her.

A lie will smell sharp and acrid.

"No, but I'm not the one constantly staring down the road, either."

A fair and honest response.

"Apologies if I pressured you."

"It's all right," Millie said cheerfully. "I think she's going easy since this is my first trip."

Tegan didn't deny that, so it must be true. *Interesting. She would push herself harder, but not this girl. They must be close kin.* It was a trivial fact that might prove useful, so he filed it away and let them enjoy the break until Millie's sweat had dried. By that time, she got to her feet on her own and didn't need to be prodded.

Now and then he broke and ran ahead to check the path for potential threats, but for reasons he couldn't articulate even to himself, he always circled back. The females were steady if not swift, and they were good at combining random ingredients to create edible meals. Tonight it was dry grain mingled with fresh fruit, and while he wouldn't call it delicious, it filled him up with minimal effort. The texture revolted him, but humans seemed to prefer softer food. He noticed they rarely cracked bones with their teeth and sucked out the delicious marrow. Their offerings wouldn't suffice for long; already he had to throttle the desire to hunt.

"Thank you for the food," he said once they'd eaten.

Millie chased away a couple of nighttime scavengers without even realizing it. Her voice carried well through the trees. He listened, wondering if the burrowers he'd smelled a mile back would approach. A few moments later, they did. Szarok spotted their eyes first, shining in the darkness, but he didn't move. Too warm a welcome and they'd be gone; the same for a show of force. *The Gulgur must be coaxed.*

He didn't expect the healer to follow his gaze and pinpoint what had commanded his attention. Though she didn't shift, she whispered, "What should we do?"

"Nothing. Unless you want them to run."

She stilled then, and the other female followed suit, though he suspected she was reacting to cues more than comprehending what was about to happen. The girls hardly breathed for what seemed like ages, and then at last one Gulgur stepped out of the shadows. The firelight was sufficient for his features to be visible: strong chin, large nose, wide forehead, sparse hair. Szarok hadn't seen enough of the small folk to be sure if this one was young or old.

"Am Haro," he said.

Tegan performed the introductions, much to Szarok's amusement. *She considers herself our leader, then.* Millie sat quiet, perceptibly trying not to startle the small folk. They exchanged a few pleasantries, and the visitor made it clear why he'd emerged.

"Care to trade?" Haro asked.

"Yes, please," Tegan answered.

Apparently judging it safe, two female Gulgur emerged from the undergrowth and opened their packs next to the fire. He'd seen only males before. The group had jewelry, old-world oddities, bits of leather, and all kinds of useless junk. He didn't need anything, but it took the humans much longer to make up their minds. Millie swapped for a leather strap while Tegan haggled for an impossibly small pair of scissors. The Gulgur accepted a pot of healing ointment, the same stuff she'd rubbed on his arm. Without meaning to, he touched the bandage and smelled the infusion of herbs, and beneath that the sweetness of the oil and beeswax she'd used to create the salve.

When the transactions were complete, Tegan offered their guests the remainder of the food. After some private discussion in a tongue Szarok didn't speak, the Gulgur dug in. It surprised him that they seemed willing to share the camp, not only with two humans, but with him as well. The small folk tended to be wary and insular, rarely straying from their burrows until necessity demanded it.

"What's your name?" Millie was asking the smallest Gulgur. "Chi."

Millie glanced at the other female, who had her hands in the cook pot. "And you?"

"Dia."

They don't speak much.

But he smelled the wariness rolling off them in waves strong enough that it skirted fear. Yet he didn't think anything in the camp warranted such a reaction. He raised his head and scanned the perimeter, seeking threats, and found none. Puzzled, Szarok studied the Gulgur.

"It's you," Tegan whispered.

Because he didn't care to admit he couldn't guess her meaning, he held silent.

"You're making them nervous. You didn't look at their things or offer hospitality. All you do is watch. While I understand you don't mean any harm, the Gulgur find it intimidating. You're not giving any cues that you're friendly."

"Friendly is not a quality the Uroch cultivate," he said with a chill in his tone.

"Exactly. And we haven't been at peace that long. It's an uneasy truce in some ways, and they don't know if they'll offend you somehow. It won't hurt to make an effort."

Stung, he demanded, "How?"

"Talk with them. Don't study them."

She doesn't understand. As vanguard, it is my duty, *my honor and my obligation, to learn as much as I can.* Only recently had the People realized how critical it was to take in information as the one service they could provide to their descendants. *If only my ancestors had known, perhaps I would be wise. Perhaps I would not be so uncertain if such memories had been given to me instead of so much hate and violence.* Certainly she couldn't understand that each moment he chose not to lash out, he repressed the tide of loathing that surged from breathing human stink; that required a choice, control over impulse.

My instincts tell me it would be better if you were dead, healer, that I would enjoy the taste of your blood in my mouth.

Szarok imagined speaking the words aloud, Tegan's cries of terror startling the birds from sleep in a frantic panic of beating wings. But no, the Uroch had chosen peace; they had chosen not to join with the horde to annihilate their distant ancestors. Even if humans were dumb and slow, heavy like clay boxes, their bones had provided the foundation that brought the People to life. Rzika had put it best:

If we destroy the last of our distant kin out of blind hate and fear, we may as well be like the old ones. We may as well live and die without Awakening.

Beside him, Tegan stirred. She touched her throat. For some reason, it pleased him to make her uneasy.

Though he remained unnaturally aware of Tegan's discomfort, Szarok addressed Haro. "I saw another trading party, half a day from Appleton. Would you know them?"

"Definitely." Thus encouraged, Haro launched into an explanation of how the bravest of the Gulgur were being tested. The ones who survived and returned with anything of value—objects or information—would be promoted in clan hierarchy.

"Interesting." Szarok knew little about the structures of Gulgur society, so he asked questions as long as Haro would indulge his curiosity.

It proved to be longer than anyone else cared to listen, as the females began settling in for the night. Eventually Haro tired as well, and Szarok relaxed enough to let exhaustion trickle in. *How many days has it been since I slept well?* He couldn't recall, certainly not since he'd joined company with the humans. Szarok thought everyone else was asleep, so he startled when he turned and found the healer far too close. Somehow he swallowed the instinctive snarl. *I don't hate her. I barely know her.* Breathing deep, striving for calm, only drove her scent deeper into his lungs, an unpleasant tangle of smoke and sweat.

"What?" The guttural exclamation shamed him.

I should be better at feigning courtesy.

"We got interrupted before I could change your bandage earlier." She spoke so softly, he could barely make out her words.

Since he could smell the fluids on the cloth, other predators probably could, too. So he nodded in mute acceptance and didn't protest when she unwound the fabric. But she didn't discard it, merely folded it over and tucked it into her bag. There shouldn't be any sinister reason why she would want traces of his blood, but . . . it troubled him. Szarok had heard how her mentor had tortured one of his people until the poor soul had died, mad with loneliness.

Stung, he demanded, "What will you do with that?"

"Scrub, boil it until it's clean, dry it, and use it again," she said, as if that answer should be obvious. "But not until we get to Rosemere, so be careful. Between our feet and your arm, I'm already running low on supplies. Don't move."

She rubbed her palms together briskly so that her hands were warm when she touched him, so much that it was a shock to his cool flesh. He fought the urge to pull away; her fingers were soft, like creeping slugs. *She's helping you. Be grateful.* But anger boiled up because her kindness likely carried a hidden sting in the tail.

She will hunt you, too. Humans can't be trusted. They shoot and stab and kill. Those, the last words his sire had snarled at him on the battlefield, on a bloody plain before the river. Szarok had taken his memories as blood surged over his claws, spattered on his skin. *One day my offspring will know everything I have done.* The People were too young to consider this a crime, but he sensed the wrongness in his bones. *I went against the one who gave me life. He died on my claws.* The warning troubled him still, more now that there was dissent in Appleton. His sire had been speaking of the Huntress, of course, not this healer.

And yet . . .

Not noticing his tension, Tegan pressed up and down the scabbed wound. "This looks good. It's sealed, no signs of infection. I'll put more salve on it, but it doesn't need to be wrapped. Just be careful not to break it open."

"Very well," he said.

Holding still proved excruciating torture. First she tugged on his arm, angling it toward the fire, and then she painted delicate stripes on each individual wound. He wondered briefly if she meant to torture him, or if this was some test sent to measure his patience. By the time she finished, he'd broken out in a cold sweat and his jaw ached from clenching his teeth to swallow the snarls. *Human hands, ugh, human hands.*

"You don't like me."

It took him a moment to realize she'd actually spoken those words. *I should be polite. I should be tactful.* Somehow the truth came out instead.

"Not only you."

"You don't like any humans?" She seemed surprised to hear this for some reason.

At first he didn't answer, as it seemed like a stupid question. How many did she think he knew? There had been the Huntress and her mate, the storyteller and his politician of a sire, and the soldiers who'd slaughtered his people like beasts. Even if the old ones were monstrous and mindless, they had no hand in their own creation. Humans only ever saw them as a threat or monsters to be put down. If any had ever pitied the elders, other than the talkative girl they called Millie, Szarok had never heard. It was her actions, after all, that changed everything, so he tried to be patient and respectful. That might count as liking, he supposed.

"Millie," he said finally. "She's flowers and sunlight."

Tegan's hands stopped moving on his arm, so there was only pressure. Finally he yielded to the urge to shake her off, and then he scratched at his skin, trying to dislodge the sensation of insects crawling. A good rake of his claws made it better.

Scowling, Tegan bristled. "So you did this for one girl. That makes no sense. You helped us. You sided with us. Yet not only do you fear us, as you said before, you also actively dislike us. Except for Millie. So why not destroy us then?"

Szarok wondered if it would do any good to have this conversation, yet he didn't turn away. "Have you destroyed everything you hate and fear?"

A shudder rolled through her, so hard that she doubled over, and for a moment he thought she might be sick. The sour stink of her sweat sharpened, and he hesitated, unsure what he was supposed to do. But whatever had triggered such an extreme reaction, she controlled it, as he so often did. Eventually she straightened and lifted her chin, daring him to comment on that momentary weakness. *She may be a healer, but she is a warrior, too. I would do well to remember.* Reluctant respect lanced through him, bright as a blade.

Tegan breathed audibly through her nose. "No. But I wanted to."

"Then you understand my feelings precisely."

"Do I? How intriguing." She let out a mirthless laugh that sent a chill down his spine. "But now I wonder whether I should be afraid of *you*."

"Possibly," he said.

"I'm too tired for that. I only have the energy for certain threats." With that, she rolled into her blankets and gave him her back, impressively unconcerned.

Unwillingly, his ire melted into amusement. *Even with all the old ones who ever lived and died shouting in my head, I will not hurt you.* He didn't mean that stray thought like a promise, but it sank into the center of him like a vow. Some of the contention slid away, too. For tonight, he would set aside all his questions and the issues of right and wrong. Szarok listened to her breathing even out, the snorts and snuffles from the Gulgur huddled together across the fire.

This, this is a good moment, a memory worth passing down.

When Dreams Come True

James Morrow had been watching the horizon for months.

That longing stare had become part of his routine, in fact, and it didn't matter how many teasing remarks it mustered. Every day, without fail, rain or shine, he had his breakfast and then went to the dock to stare out over the water. If he waited long enough, Tegan would return to Rosemere. He had good reasons for believing, because she had friends so close here that they might as well be called family. He didn't waste more than five minutes this way, but each time, it felt like a promise in good faith.

That morning his patience bore fruit as, instead of empty river, he glimpsed the blossoming white sails of a boatman heading for the Evergreen Isle. At the hour, it could only mean he'd spotted hopeful travelers on the shore. Nearby, a fisherman checked his net with careful eyes while sparing him a smile.

"Think this is your lucky day, lad?"

"Could be. If it is, buy me a drink." Morrow flashed a smile, trying to hide the wistful ache square in his chest.

If she loved you, she wouldn't have gone.

But love didn't always grow at the same pace. For some, the feeling shot up like a determined vine after a hard rain; for others, it sprouted by increments so tiny, you wouldn't notice at all until the minuscule green shoots finally broke through into the light. He hoped Tegan was the latter, and when she caught up, he'd be waiting. The graceful boat surged closer until it tapped up against the dock and its owner leapt lightly onto the boards to tie it up.

Eagerly, Morrow skimmed the passengers for Tegan's face . . . and found it. She was sunburnt and weary, but her eyes held the same bright, beautiful gleam. She had always been beyond clever, seeking patterns, striving to understand the inexplicable. Her craving for knowledge matched his thirst for stories, so he'd always thought they would make perfect partners. More than once, he'd imagined continuing his quest to replenish Rosemere's library, Tegan beside him, but she'd left to study in Winterville before he could ask.

Now she's back.

"You couldn't stay away," he said, smiling.

Her head came up, and she grinned. "Have you been waiting here all that time?"

Wiley the fisherman decided to weigh in. "It's powerful sad, miss. He doesn't even go home. We have to bring him a bit of bread and fish now and then to keep him from dying. I think his feet have rooted to those planks."

"Wiley," Morrow scolded.

But in truth, he didn't mind her thinking he had waited with such single-minded devotion. He'd never made any secret of his courtship, silly to complain now. But Tegan only laughed and accepted a hand from the boatman. Despite her slight limp, she was sure and graceful. A girl Morrow didn't recognize came after her, and a cloaked figure who could only be Szarok. A chill ran through him as he considered what this visit portended.

"You must be James Morrow." The girl had a pretty face, brown skin, and thick black hair, tied back with a simple leather strap. Her eyes rounded as she peered up at him, and he almost took a step back at the delight that flared bright as a signal fire in her expression. "You are, you're him."

"Er, yes," he said.

She seized his hand and shook it with great enthusiasm. "I'm

Millie Faraday. I was born in Otterburn, but I moved to Winter-ville last fall."

"Nice to meet you."

Somehow Tegan slipped past while he was greeting the rest of the party. This reunion wasn't going at all as he'd hoped. Mil-lie stuck close, asking about the island, and soon he lost sight of Tegan altogether. But based on the way she was headed . . . *She must be visiting Deuce and Fade.* Millie spun in a slow circle, tak-ing in the bright houses and the cheerful chatter in the distant marketplace.

"It's remarkable," she breathed. "I mean, Tegan told me this was the prettiest place she'd ever seen, but I couldn't picture it. I don't know what to do first."

With every fiber of his being, he wanted to chase Tegan, but that would be beyond rude to a first-time guest. "If you'll give me a moment, I can show you around."

He turned and bowed to Szarok, for he'd noticed that the Uroch didn't make casual contact even among themselves, let alone with humans. "It's good to see you again."

That was courtesy, not strictly truth, but he'd been raised too well to greet anyone with a blunt inquiry into their business. The Uroch leader returned the bow, matching his manners.

"Is your father at home? I bear a message for him."

Morrow nodded. "Do you remember the way?"

"Don't trouble yourself. I can find it."

That was easy to believe, since James and his father lived in the largest house on the island, three bedrooms instead of a cottage with a loft. In a moment more the Uroch headed away from the dock, threading behind the storage sheds on the shore. His chosen path would keep him away from the townsfolk, probably for the best. There was nothing to gain in rousing anxiety. Which left him with an excited girl, currently bouncing on the balls of her feet.

But she wasn't oblivious to the nuances of his mood,

apparently. "Are you positive you want to guide me around? It's all right if you have other things to do."

"I'm sure," he said with a persuasive smile. "Who knows the best stories better than me?"

And so, the first four hours of Tegan's return Morrow spent with Millie Faraday. They covered every inch of the market, pausing every five feet for her to exclaim or admire. She couldn't be that much younger than Tegan, but her enthusiasm felt childlike, possibly because she'd seen so little of the world. He bought her some fresh fried fish and vegetables for the midday meal, and she got tipsy on a mug of hard cider.

Finally she stumbled a little, ready to rest. "Do you have any idea where Tegan went?"

"I have a guess," he said.

Sure enough, he found her ensconced in the stone cottage on a rise at the far end of the village. Voices came from inside, jokes and laughter, and he followed the sound all the way in. Millie seemed less sure of her welcome, but Morrow had supper here at least once a week and sometimes he spent the night in their loft, so he had no doubts about his reception, no matter who else they might be entertaining.

"It took you longer than I thought," Deuce said.

"I figured you'd be her shadow," Fade added, tilting his head at Tegan.

With his eyes, he pleaded for them to shut up. His affection wasn't a secret, but did they have to be so obvious?

Tegan only laughed. "Unless I've underestimated our James, he's been playing host with Millie, demonstrating Rosemere's charm."

"That's true." Millie bobbed a curtsy to Deuce and Fade in succession.

Though Morrow doubted she realized, the girl shrank back against him, trembling in the presence of such great heroes. *Lord, that must be tiring.* He set a steadying hand beneath her elbow and she threw a look over one shoulder, such melting gratitude that it astounded him. But he supposed their legends had grown larger than life, so maybe it was hard being confronted with the reality. He tried to imagine how the scene looked to Millie and couldn't superimpose her perception over his own.

The stone cottage with its hand-sewn cushions and simple furniture was basically his second home. From the herbs drying on hooks in the kitchen, to the pans and dishes stacked on the shelves, everything about this place was familiar and dear. The rafters had been polished recently, so the house smelled clean. There was a pot of something bubbling in the hearth, adding to that air of warmth.

"Come on," Deuce said. "It's not that cold yet, but we shouldn't leave the door open."

Fade grinned. "You say that like you'll be the one chopping wood."

"She can't cook, either," Tegan added. "Do you smell that? It's awful."

Deuce shook a fist. "That's *your* laundry."

At first Morrow suspected she was joking, but when he peered into the pot, they were definitely simmering strips of pale cloth. Millie let out a nervous laugh and settled on a pile of cushions near the fire. Since there weren't enough chairs for everyone, he guessed she was showing respect with that gesture, and he did the same, not wanting her to feel less than everyone else.

Fade poured mugs of spiced ale and sat down in a chair big enough to hold him and Deuce. It helped that she curled into him the moment he nudged in, and Morrow glanced away from the sweetness of their comfortable intimacy. By contrast, Tegan had a seat to herself across the way, and he only wished she wanted him close. Millie swirled the liquid in her mug, watching the foam boil up.

"Do you want something else?" he whispered.

"No, it's all right. I've had cider and ale before." But she didn't seem enthusiastic.

Not my concern.

"How are you, really?" Deuce was asking.

"It's hard to imagine that Dr. Wilson's gone," Fade added.

Oh. That's why she came.

It shouldn't hurt—why did it?—but of course, it made sense. If her mentor were alive and well, Tegan would still be in Winterville. He didn't realize he was leaving until he unfolded to his feet. "I should make sure Szarok found our house. Please, excuse me."

He hurried off without waiting to see if anyone would call him back. If anything, his steps moved faster because she wouldn't . . . and it would be worse if someone else did. Running, it took him only fifteen minutes to race through the village and up the winding path that led to the spacious house he'd grown up in. Funny, a girl who didn't love him had driven him away from Rosemere, and on his travels, he'd met Tegan. Now when he saw Clara, happily married to the town smith, his heart no longer clenched.

Morrow let himself in quietly, breathing in the familiar scents of home: oil and beeswax, dried lavender, and a sachet of sweet herbs, given as a gift by one of the widows who hadn't given up on tempting his father to remarry. With quiet steps, he headed for the governor's office, but loud voices halted him in his tracks. *I thought Szarok would've already been and gone.*

"You've done nothing but hint at a second war for the past hour," his father shouted. "How am I supposed to react? I have no authority to—"

"But you permitted my people to camp at the other end of the isle. Why is a permanent settlement too much to ask?"

A long, fraught pause followed. Finally his father sighed. "It's too soon. Give us time to acclimate, and then we'll talk again."

"My people already question your rights to decide what ground we hold, where we rest, and where we're allowed to live.

I came to you because I judged you a man of reason once. I'm trying to prevent further bloodshed." From the Uroch's impassioned tone, Morrow guessed all of this must be true.

But it's alarming.

"I understand all of that—I do. But only last year we were slaughtering one another. You think people are ready for Uroch neighbors? The villagers will rise up if I grant permission for you to found a colony here."

Ferocity gave power to Szarok's reply. "Because the Evergreen Isle is pure? Because you want to keep it that way? You'll leave us the places you don't want, force us to live in your ruins, and hope we don't get sick from mechanisms we don't even understand."

Though eavesdropping was beyond rude, Morrow couldn't tear himself away.

"It's not about purity; it's about keeping the peace."

"Then this is your final word?"

His father sighed. "I'm not saying no. I'm just saying . . . not yet."

"How long must we wait? Do you understand that our lives burn at a different pace? While you wait for the perfect moment, you may be explaining to my offspring why you denied such a reasonable request. Or perhaps there will be no talk at all by then."

"Are you threatening me?"

"We are a warlike people inexperienced in the pursuit of peace. If you refuse our good faith offers, I can't guarantee the truce will hold. I can smell your fear, even now. You are uneasy at having me in your home. The rest would feel the same over allowing us to settle the other end of the island, yes?"

Another pause, then the governor confirmed, "Yes. Can you give me some time to think? I understand your position, and you're not wrong. I don't like myself for being so afraid."

"Acknowledging fear is the first step to overcoming it," Szarok said.

"Perhaps. I haven't even thought about integrated towns, but that would be the next step, wouldn't it?"

"It's one that frightens us also, but we don't want to be left behind, and there is much we can learn from one another if we're brave enough."

"Well spoken."

Both parties seemed calmer now, so Morrow relaxed a little. He leaned against the wall, wrestling with the idea that he should go before he got caught. Yet there might be a little more to learn here, and curiosity flickered like a candle that couldn't be blown out.

"To answer, yes, I can give you a while to consider. I'm not eager to return to the elders with a firm rejection. The situation was . . . volatile when I left."

"They're not content with Appleton?" the governor asked.

"It is a ruin. We don't have the resources to rebuild, and we squat in filthy houses that are falling down around us."

Morrow imagined the conditions must be awful. The horde might not care about corpses or hygiene, but the young ones, the Uroch, were doubtless overwhelmed by the squalor they had inherited. Cleaning and rebuilding an old-world city? No. It was too big an undertaking, so no wonder they wanted better land upon which to start fresh. But his father was right; the prospect of a Uroch town on the Evergreen Isle would terrify the townsfolk.

"I hadn't even thought of that," his father said heavily.

"What is not given must be taken." Szarok sounded firm. "I don't mean this as a threat, only a truth. I much prefer for you to choose generosity. But understand, this request is only a courtesy. You cannot claim all this land."

True, the Evergreen Isle had a history of welcoming anyone who wanted to stay. Nobody quibbled over ownership; they just made room. *But the immigrants were all human.* It troubled Morrow that he made the mental distinction. He hadn't realized he nurtured such prejudice until this moment, but they were only a year or so past realizing that the Uroch weren't mindless monsters.

"You don't have to settle here," the governor snapped.

"So you prefer if we struggled elsewhere, where trade is difficult and we have no one to ask for help."

"I can see we've reached an impasse for today."

Movement from the office alerted Morrow to the imminent exodus, and he leapt away from the wall, backtracking until he could dart around a corner. Shamefaced, he felt about five years old as they passed his hiding spot. His father watched until Szarok left the house. Afterward his shoulders slumped and he retraced his steps.

Without thinking, he went after the Uroch leader, who was unaccountably waiting just outside the front door. He raised a brow. "You were expecting me?"

"Yes. I smelled you as soon as you stepped inside."

"Why didn't you say anything?"

"It seemed impolite. You must have had your reasons for skulking about."

He clenched his jaw, ignoring the heat that washed his cheeks. "I'll speak to my father for you. You made good, sound arguments."

Szarok sighed. Despite the cowl, the slope of his shoulders hinted at great weariness. "Even if he agrees, this will be no easy task."

"Maybe I can help with that, too. The villagers like me, so they might—"

"A pale thing such as 'like' will melt away when you request a terrifying favor. A kind offer . . . but stick with your stories." With that, Szarok strode away.

Morrow might well feel the sting of that rejection for days.

Questions and Answers

fternoon ripened into night before Tegan finished catching up with Deuce and Fade. For as long as she'd known the girl, Millie had never been quiet so long. Instead of questions, she had only admiring stares. But over dinner and two cups of ale, she loosened up enough to quiz the two about their time down below.

That suited Tegan fine. She'd already asked if they knew anyone named Catalina, and since they were newcomers, it didn't surprise her to learn that they didn't. *I ought to ask James*, she thought, but he'd taken off so fast that she didn't have a chance. In the morning would be soon enough, however. Tonight all she really wanted was to feel clean. She hated to ask, since Fade looked so comfortable, but she couldn't stand going to bed this way.

"If you'll point me in the right direction, I want to draw a bath."

With obvious reluctance, he pulled his hand from Deuce's shoulder. "There's a cistern out back. I'll haul the water for you."

That spurred Deuce into action, and she fetched a cauldron large enough to stand in. "This is what we usually use, and here's the dipper for rinsing."

"Would it be too much trouble for me to wash up as well?" Millie asked.

Tegan smiled. "We might as well do it together. I suspect they'll be happier when we scrub the stink off."

Laughing, Deuce said, "It's been a while since I lived so rough, but the smell has *not* gotten better."

After he brought in several buckets, Fade took off. Tegan appreciated his discretion, since the house didn't offer much privacy. It might be fine for Deuce to strip off in front of her man, but as for Millie and herself, this was best. Deuce heated the water a little at a time, enough to wash and rinse. Tegan grimaced at how cloudy and scummed the water was by the time they'd finished. Sighing with pleasure, Millie put on clean clothes. While Tegan did the same, Deuce dumped the dirty water onto her kitchen garden.

"Careful you don't kill your vegetables," Tegan teased.

"Eh, they're already growing in dirt."

This made Millie laugh, but then she clapped both hands over her mouth as if she weren't sure she was allowed to find the Huntress so entertaining. Tegan encouraged her with a smile. Though these were her comrades, they had to seem larger than life to Millie. She tried to imagine what it would've been like to live quietly in Otterburn and then suddenly have the greatest heroes in the free territories show up and pronounce that she'd played a role in saving the human race.

It's no wonder she's nervous.

As a distraction and out of real curiosity, she asked, "What was that we used to wash with? It wasn't the same as what they use in Winterville."

Soapmaking was a huge undertaking, and half the town turned out to cooperate. They used a mixture of ashes and animal fat with enormous vats for stirring and cooling, and the end result was tan and soft, given out in cups to everyone who participated. But Deuce had shaved what looked like a chip of wood directly into the washing water and then agitated until it turned white with suds. Tegan had never seen anything like it.

"It's some root that grows around here. You can dig it up in the fall," Deuce answered.

"And it requires no processing?" After Tegan asked, she read the impatience in her friend's expression. *Yes, I did forget who I was asking. Sorry.* If it wasn't a weapon, Deuce had relatively little interest in learning more about it. Or at least, that used to be the case.

But she answered anyway, indulging Tegan's spectrum of curiosity. "No. It's not easy to find, though, and it grows deep. There's a man in town who makes his living on searching for it."

"They had so *many* things at the market," Millie put in. "Life must be easier here. In Otterburn, we didn't make anything that wasn't useful, and it was like that in Winterville, too."

She must be talking about the jewelry and scrimshaw. Tegan recalled her own first impression of Rosemere, how she'd marveled at the beautiful bone carving of a fanciful creature that James had told her truly existed. *Dolphin.* From that day on, she'd longed to see one, just once, leaping in the sea.

"It's like a dream," Deuce admitted, cleaning up after their bath. "You can't imagine how it was down below. The sun scared me half to death when I first came topside with Fade."

"You truly grew up under the ruins of Gotham?" Millie ventured to ask.

"So they tell me. Our elders told us the above world was all poison and death. We thought being exiled was the same as an execution."

Tegan considered this, comparing it to her own childhood. Her mother had lived with a small pocket of survivors in what they'd called a university. Teaching her to read while they hid from the gangs and the occasional monster had been the best gift her mom had been able to offer, despite her physical weakness.

Tegan couldn't remember ever seeing her mother fight; she was all bones and eyes and fear. Once, she'd asked about her father and received only sobbing in response and such a look of heart-rending grief that she never dared again. She remembered uncles, one so old that he looked like a statue, and aunties as well, but dying came so easy.

By thirteen, she was alone.

And at fourteen, the Wolves found her.

She clenched her teeth against a wave of rage. When Tegan lifted her gaze, she found Deuce watching her with a worried expression, but she couldn't bring herself to force a smile. Some things were beyond forgiveness, and some evils left only poison at the bottom of the well. She glanced at Millie, relaxed now before the fire.

"I hear you came with Szarok," Fade said some while later. He smelled of cedar smoke and liquor, but he wasn't drunk.

"He's here?" Deuce asked, perking up.

She clearly liked the Uroch leader, but Tegan suspected she didn't know him well enough to hold that opinion. He'd done his best to make a good impression on the great and terrible Huntress who had slaughtered so many of his kind. *Apparently he cares less about influencing the company healer.*

"He said he had business with James's father . . . and before you ask, no. I don't know what kind."

A wry grin quirked Deuce's mouth. Even when she smiled, she wasn't attractive. Living underground had left her sickly pale with skin that never took color, only peeled and burned and peeled again. Likewise, her eyes were a milky gray, and her teeth uneven. But she was fierce, loyal, and lethal in a fight. Tegan would do her best never to cross her.

"It's not my business," the Huntress muttered.

"*I'm* your business," Fade said, settling beside her.

Tegan mumbled something as she headed for the loft. It was impossible to talk to them when they were like this. Since Millie was a smart girl, she followed Tegan up, where two pallets were already spread. The space smelled smoky and sweet, cozy because of the hot air wafting upward from the fire. Sighing, Tegan snuggled into her blankets.

"They're not what I expected," Millie whispered.

"Nobody ever is."

That seemed to settle the conversation. Fade and Deuce quieted downstairs and eventually retreated to their room. Lying in the dark, Tegan stared up at the rafters, wondering why she felt out of sorts. Aggravated at herself, she closed her eyes. They snapped open when she realized she was worried about Szarok, where he might be sleeping, if he'd eaten, if he was cold, and whether his errand had gone well. James *should* have offered hospitality, and he had ample space to play host. Yet such thoughts weren't like her.

Odd. But I suppose you can get used to anything.

In the morning, she woke, still wondering, so she slipped out of the loft before anyone else awakened. The sky was still pink and gold, light creeping over the water and painting the treetops. They truly had a lovely view from here, and she paused long enough to savor it before putting on her boots and hastening toward town. Market vendors were barely stirring, though the boatmen had already taken to the water, and fishermen were casting nets from rowing boats closer to the shore. Awed, she watched one woman's impeccable balance despite the rocking of the water, momentarily distracted from her errand.

"I consider myself to possess reasonable courage, but I'd rather be burned alive than try that," a deep voice rumbled at her shoulder.

Tegan turned and found Szarok, hooded as ever. His brown-clad figure created a little chaos near the pier where they stood, townsfolk giving second and third looks and a wide berth. That unnecessary caution sparked an urge to scold, but Tegan restrained it because she reckoned he wouldn't welcome her interference.

Still, she understood all too well how it felt to be alone among your enemies.

"You hate the water that much?"

"I believe you already know the answer, healer. Did I not make my discomfort plain during yesterday's crossing?"

She *had* noticed that he crouched in the center of the boat, his claws dug into the wood as if he could prevent the craft from flipping through sheer determination. "I'm teasing. Don't the Uroch do that?"

"*We* do," he said with gentle stress. "But that presumes a certain degree of kinship."

"I'm sorry. I didn't realize." Genuine regret pierced her.

"Presumption sometimes reads like kindness, if it's well meant."

"If you say so. Did James take care of you last night?"

It was impossible to see more than a hint of his features, given the angle of the rising sun and the shadow of his cowl. "Was he supposed to?"

"Then I guess not. Where did you sleep?"

He paused, probably weighing whether she needed that information. In the end, he gave it, though Tegan didn't know why. "I made camp outside the village. It seemed . . . safer."

"Than what? Staying with James or asking for a room at the tavern?"

"Either. Take your pick."

"Deuce and Fade will put you up. There's a space in their loft with Millie and me." Tegan made the offer on impulse, but she had no doubt her friends would back it up.

Szarok stared at her in silence.

If not for the Uroch joining their side and negotiating with the Gulgur, they would've made their final stand at the river. *None of us would even be here, so I can't believe they're treating him this way.* With a ferocious scowl, she tugged at his sleeve.

"Come, they'll be fixing breakfast. Don't dawdle."

Without waiting to see if he'd follow, she led the way through town, back to the cottage. Though sometimes she felt wistful about not having such a place of her own, she also understood that meant being unable to pick up and go on a whim. Roots in the ground equaled personal business to tend, and she wanted no part of that. There were dolphins in the world, after all, and they were only the first of many wonders.

When she stepped through the front door, Szarok in tow, Deuce waved from stirring something in a pot. It smelled like burning. Laughing, Fade took the spoon from her and whispered something that made her hit him. Millie was sitting at the table, wearing a shy smile. Her visible relief at recognizing Tegan made her feel bad for sneaking out.

"I brought someone," she murmured somewhat unnecessarily.

"You shouldn't have needed bringing," Deuce said to Szarok. "Take off that cloak. It's plenty warm in here, and we all know what you look like."

Fade echoed the greeting as he served somewhat charred porridge. There was also bread, cheese, and fruit, along with baked fish left from the night before. Fade brought a chair from the back room, so everyone had a place at the table. Tegan served herself a little of everything, letting the conversation wash over her; she noticed the Uroch didn't eat much. Deuce and Fade carried most of it as they offered Szarok news related to the Evergreen Isle.

And eventually Deuce asked so Tegan didn't have to. "I hear you had business with the elder Morrow. Anything serious?"

"It's not your worry," Fade muttered.

Tegan had the sense he said that a lot. She stifled a smile.

"I'd rather not discuss it until I have an answer from the governor." It was a polite refusal, but Szarok definitely had no desire to involve Deuce in his affairs.

That quelled the talk a little, so Tegan did her part to liven things up again. "I need to speak with him myself. He might know something about Catalina."

"Can I go with you?" Millie asked softly.

"Certainly. Unless I don't know him as well as I think, James should appear shortly and he'll escort us."

Before the breakfast dishes were put away, Morrow proved Tegan right. Deuce laughed as she answered his knock and called, "Good thing I didn't bet against you."

"I'm so predictable?" The storyteller hung his head in mock despair.

Quietly, Szarok followed Fade out to help with some household chore. Tegan had already gathered her bag, as she didn't like to move without it, just in case someone needed treatment. Her time with Doc Tuttle had persuaded her that preparation was half the key to saving lives. As she set out, she noticed that Millie practically glowed over seeing James again. She tried to hang back and let the girl monopolize his attention, but James caught on and slowed his pace, putting himself between them.

You are too kind, truly.

Passing the docks for the second time, Tegan didn't expect anything of note, but a larger ship than she'd ever seen had its sails unfurled, streaming toward Rosemere. She stopped and got jostled from behind. James drew her smoothly out of the path of some merchants lugging a crate of wares, and she pushed his hand away half-heartedly, her gaze locked.

He laughed quietly. "The long-haulers don't come often, but when they do, you can expect some excitement."

"Who are they? Where are they from? What *kind* of excitement?" The questions tumbled out of Millie and, for once, Tegan shared her enthusiasm.

"By their colors, this ship's out of Antecost, an isle north of here. They've got goods to trade, for sure. About twice a year they stop to see if anyone wants to sign on for a long voyage."

"To where?" Tegan demanded.

James furrowed his brow, seeming troubled. "You'd have to talk to their captain to learn more. They'll be docked for a few days, laying in supplies."

"Ah, there's no rush, then. I do have a question for your father. We should take care of that first."

"Maybe I can help?" he offered.

"Do you know of anyone or anything called Catalina?"

"Hm. That's familiar. Why . . . oh. I'm positive that was the name of an island in an old book. But it's across the world. I don't know of anyone who's ever traveled so far. At least, if they went, they never came back."

Dr. Wilson wouldn't have sent me on an impossible quest.

With a final look at the impressive ship still some distance away, she turned. Millie seemed just as riveted, so Tegan tapped the girl's arm. She practically stumbled over her feet as they moved away from the docks and toward the market. The back-and-forth of haggling villagers contrasted sharply with the solemn atmosphere in Winterville.

It's like a different world, here.

"Is that all you can remember?" Tegan asked, disappointed.

James took her arm to guide her around a wagon stalled in the road and then paused to ask if the man fiddling with the wheel needed any help. "Do you have your tools, Cedric? I can run to your workshop—"

"No, it's fine. I'll be done in a jiff."

Millie smiled as they went by, seeming charmed by everything Rosemere had to offer. In fact, the other girl opted out of visiting the governor in favor of chatting with people in the market. James watched her, evidently concerned about leaving her behind, and Tegan nudged him when he didn't appear to realize he'd left her question dangling.

"James," she prompted.

"Yes, right. Well, there *was* a woman," he said, teasing her with a bright spark of hope that foundered when he frowned. "Wait, no. She might've been Catarina. I'd need to confirm with my father. I was pretty young when she died."

"Then let's ask him."

Silence Answered

The conversation with Morrow's father revealed no new information, and it was nearly lunchtime by the time they finished with lengthy pleasantries. Frustration simmered like a soup at low boil, but she didn't know who Dr. Wilson had wanted her to talk to. *You taught me so much . . . yet I can't do this simple thing for you.* James stood as she did, but he wasn't done with his tea, so she waved him off.

"I know the way back," she said. "Please don't rush on my account."

But she should have known that wouldn't discourage him. She refused his arm when he offered it, and he walked her back toward town while she stewed in frustrated silence. Millie met them on the outskirts, visibly excited by something she'd heard.

The girl grabbed James's arm. "Is there really a library in Rosemere?"

That was exactly the right distraction, because James lit up like a storm lantern. "Yes, there's a building in town. I've been bringing back volumes from my travels, oh, for the last four years."

"Would it be too much trouble for you to show me?"

Quashing a flicker of amusement, Tegan left them to sort out their plans for the afternoon. Doubtless James would be irritated when he realized she'd slipped away, but he loved books enough for that to count as compensation. She enjoyed the solitary walk back toward Deuce's cottage, bathing in the silence as one would a big copper tub. Peace washed over her and eased some of her impatience. Perhaps Dr. Wilson wouldn't blame her if she couldn't solve the riddle he'd unintentionally set forth, but she would always feel unworthy as his last student, should that eventuality occur.

She passed the tavern first, low trills of smoke puffing out the chimney, and then the market. The stalls were open now, though only a small number of vendors came every day, mostly fish and produce. As for the wares Millie had admired, they only showed their finery a couple of times a week, as it was impossible to earn a living on beauty alone. Tegan stopped at the dock, because the ship she had admired from afar had dropped anchor and they were rowing their party ashore.

A sailor nearby turned to her and likely guessed her next question. "The water's too shallow for a ship that size. They'd run aground."

"Thank you," she said, smiling. "I did wonder."

"You're James's girl, aren't you?"

That claim pricked her like a needle left in a cushion. "He is my friend, yes. We fought together in the war."

The man's gaze went to the polished staff she carried, and his smile brightened. "You're the healer. I'm sorry to ask, but would you mind checking out my shoulder?"

Oh dear.

Tegan tried not to make a face, but this was the most common response when people recognized her. *I'm lucky it's not worse this time.* Yet she always carried her bag for just this sort of request, so she glanced around and found an empty space in the shade. The sun shone surprisingly bright for a day so late in the fall, but the blue sky made up for the heat.

"Come, I'll have a look."

The sailor whipped off his shirt with no concern for who might be watching. She noticed the lump on his left shoulder immediately, and he flinched when she applied pressure. A few moments later she felt reasonably sure of her diagnosis.

"Is it serious?" the sailor asked.

"I think not. This is most likely a boil. It needs to be lanced and cleaned. At some point, it may rupture on its own, but it will become considerably more painful and swollen before then."

"I'm supposed to set sail in a few days. I promised Captain Advika. Will I be hale enough for a long voyage?"

"I don't see why not," she said. "It isn't a life-threatening condition, but I can't take care of it here."

"Oh." The sailor seemed disappointed that she wouldn't take a knife to him on the pier.

Tegan didn't feel comfortable offering Deuce and Fade's cottage up for medical services, either. If this man told anyone else, soon she'd have a line out the door, and her friends would have no peace as long as she remained under their roof. A glance around didn't suggest an immediate solution, either.

"The tavern has a storeroom. Would that work?"

"Let's take a look."

It was better than she'd hoped. When he heard what she needed to do, the proprietor helped the sailor stack the crates, clearing one half of the space. Then he offered a set of clean sheets for her use. Her patient sat down on a crate and waited for treatment to begin.

Half an hour later she had a bowl of bloodstained cloth, a fresh bandage tied around the sailor's shoulder, and a line outside the door. The tavern owner must have let it slip that she was treating ailments, so it wasn't surprising that this would be the result. Doctors were few and far between in the free territories, so she worked willingly through lunch and beyond. Some just wanted someone to listen for a moment while others truly needed help. One old woman with a persistent cough didn't like hearing she needed to give up her pipe.

By the time Tegan emerged from the back room, carrying her

sack of tribute offered in exchange for medical care, the main hall was full of farmers and sailors. She'd seen most of them in passing, but she didn't recognize the tall, brown-skinned woman with a mass of black braids. Like Deuce, this woman preferred pants to skirts and hers fit well, belted around the hips, heavy with pouches and weapons. Her tunic gleamed with bits of gold, lending her an audacious charm.

"You must be Dr. Tegan," the tall woman called with an infectious smile.

She offered a cautious smile in response. "Do you know me?"

"Everyone in Rosemere's singing your praises. You must've seen twenty malingerers today. Buy you a drink?"

She realized she was both tired and thirsty, so she nodded. "Yes, please."

"Barkeep, another mug!" In response, the owner slid a cup of cider, which the woman caught neatly.

Tegan accepted it and clacked it against the woman's in a casual toast. "They weren't pretending to be ill, you know. I'm just glad I didn't have to deliver any terrible news."

"I imagine. Give me the open sea any day."

"You're the long-haul captain?" If she hadn't been so tired, she would've already guessed as much.

Deducting points for stating the obvious, Dr. Wilson whispered.

"Pleased to meet you. I don't suppose you're interested in signing on for a voyage? I'm always looking to add a doctor to my crew, but they're hard to come by. Anyone who's spent so much time learning isn't usually willing to sail off into the unknown."

Tegan paused, her mug midway to her mouth. "I've always wanted to travel."

"I'll be in port for four days. I'm staying here until then, so if you decide to take me up on it, stop by anytime."

"Thank you." After draining the mug, she set it on the counter and nodded a weary farewell to her new acquaintance with the intriguing offer. Belatedly it occurred to her. "Have you ever heard of an island named Catalina?"

"Of course," the captain said. "Never been. It's beyond even what *I've* attempted."

The subtle stress implied that Advika was well-known for daring trips, and that made Tegan pause. "I'd love to hear more about your travels."

"I'll look for you tomorrow."

She threaded through the crowd, and though a few drinkers took a second look, her staff made them reconsider. Tegan wasn't sure if it stemmed from respect for her profession or the fact that she could crack their skulls if they aggravated her. Possibly it was some combination of the two. Outside, the sun had crept across the sky, throwing shadows as the day died. The light went faster here for some reason. In a heartbeat the colors faded and then dropped into deepest night, spangled with stars.

"There you are," said James.

Turning, she found him approaching from the east end of the village, Millie still at his side. *They must've spent all day in the library.* She'd done the same when she first arrived, but based on the sparkle in Millie's eyes, Tegan suspected it was more James's charm than any overwhelming adoration of the written word.

"You had a productive day?" she asked.

Millie tipped her head with a frown. "Why do you look so tired?"

Can't accuse her of being tactful.

"I've been seeing patients. It's rewarding but not precisely restful."

"Oh. Now I feel bad," the other girl mumbled.

"For playing or insulting me?" Tegan teased.

Millie laughed, as Tegan had intended. "Both, I reckon. Do you think Deuce and Fade are looking for us?"

"By now? Probably."

"I'll walk you back." James fell into step between them, offering his arms for escort.

Though Millie accepted, she couldn't. Tegan already had her staff in one hand and doctor bag in the other. Maybe it frustrated him that she found it impossible to lean, but it was a fact that wouldn't change. Soon enough he'd force a personal conversation on her, and she didn't look forward to it. If only he could content himself with friendship, life would be much simpler. Yet he'd already decided that she was the heroine of his dreams, and in her experience, it rarely mattered what a girl wanted when a man set his mind on something. The people of Rosemere would doubtless protest if they knew she thought of their favored son that way, but whether his courtship was cruel or kind, one thing was unassailably true:

Love is a burden when you don't want it.

"You seem to be thinking hard about something," Millie observed.

Rather than deal with that today, she mustered a smile. "I am, in fact."

"Don't be stingy." The other girl nudged her with a friendly shoulder.

That was one of her favorite things about Millie Faraday. She never treated Tegan like a careless misstep would leave her floundering. So many people took one look at the hitch in her stride and assumed she had been broken once and would be again, when it was the opposite—that the pain reminded her she was strong enough to survive and always would be.

"Remember the ship we saw earlier?" At Millie's nod, she shared her news.

While Millie asked her usual plethora of questions, James went lukewarm, his steps slowing to the point that even the other girl noticed. "What's wrong?"

But James only gazed at Tegan steadily, his heart in his eyes.

"I thought . . . Do you remember that *I* offered to take you to sea? I was going to show you the dolphins."

It has to be you? she thought. *The dolphins don't exist otherwise?* But she didn't say it aloud, for he was a good man—he just wasn't *hers*—and it would be unkind to wound him for her own amusement.

"I remember," she said.

But I was hoping you'd *forget.*

James seemed to sense her reluctance, and he brightened up, that effort like pulling a sore tooth. "If you decide to go, tell me. I've fallen behind in my quest to fill Rosemere's library, and I'm always game for adventure."

Tegan surveyed him with an assessing eye. When he'd almost died, she realized she loved him dearly—as a friend—but he seemed hearty enough now. He probably thought traveling together would wear her down, like a shoe against the road, but they would see in time who was leather and who was stone.

So she nodded. "I've a couple of days to think it over. But I'll tell you: I'm drawn to the idea. I've always wanted to learn more about the world."

"I wish I could go." Dejected, Millie kicked a rock that bounded along the path and eventually skittered into a ditch. A splash of water followed.

Tegan bit her lip. She held no sway over the captain, and it seemed unlikely that the woman would consent to taking on deadweight. "She might consider you if you're willing to work. Do you have any useful skills?"

"I'm *ever* so kind," Millie said with a wicked grin, her eyes wide as soup bowls.

Tegan laughed. "You're welcome to try that look on Captain Advika, if you wish."

"My ma always says I'm the fastest at cleaning that she ever met. Do ships need scrubbing as much as houses?" Millie wondered aloud.

"In fact, they do," James answered. "And some captains will take on passengers if the price is right. I'm sure my father could help us come to terms."

It was hard not to hate him when he said things like that. The hardship and terror that had swept over everyone else in the free territories—that was an *adventure* to him—or rather, a choice he'd made. He'd only suffered because he wanted to save books, not people. The fact that he didn't seem to grasp what pure luxury his prior existence had been . . . That lack of awareness separated them more completely than a chasm. Before he decided to go out and face monsters, he lived here in perfect peace and security, the world open before him like an oyster with its pearl, and that was a creature she had only seen in books.

Millie whispered to Tegan, "Did you know his father was so powerful?"

"I knew."

A long pause and then the girl said, "I'm glad nobody spelled it out for me, then. I probably would've been too nervous to speak."

"Secrets are rude," James reproved.

"We're plotting against you. Don't take it personally." Tegan smiled and pressed ahead, quickening her pace through town.

She greeted a few people as she went, not pausing or looking back until she reached the cottage yard, where Deuce was talking to friends from down below. Stone and Thimble were a lovely couple, the only known survivors from Deuce's enclave. Before Deuce and Fade's house was built, they had stayed with Stone and Thimble. Today Stone and Thimble had their little boy, Robin, with them, and they seemed to be having a party, gauging by the laughter.

Tegan's palms went damp as she stared at Robin, and suddenly she wanted to be anywhere but here. She didn't regret what she'd done, but when she saw his fat, rosy face, emotions tightened into a knot too complex to be termed one thing or another. Her head melted under the chaos, and she turned with a mumbled excuse. Before anyone could question her, she hurried north along the shore. Tegan put quite some distance behind her and for the longest time, she concentrated on breathing, not feeling. She ran until the dull pain in her thigh screamed like a whistle, shrill and undeniable. Slowing to a walk, she rubbed her leg. If she sat down now, it might be difficult to stand up again.

I always get up again. That's what you learn from falling.

Eventually her heart stopped racing; she strolled along the promontory, counting the different kinds of birds. From here, she couldn't see the village at all, only the spiky green tops of trees behind her, and the silver gleam of water ahead. It was hard to imagine what lay beyond the river, which was supposed to open into the sea, an expanse so wide, it took weeks to cross.

And what's on the other side? Uroch? Gulgur? Or something entirely new?

With a groan, she plopped down on a rocky overlook. She'd left the tavern in search of food, but now it didn't seem likely she'd eat anytime soon. What sounded like her name echoed some ways off, which meant James was probably searching. He wouldn't give up until he knew she was safe. *I should be moved.* Wearily, she fell back into the flax and stared up at the sky. Seabirds circled, swooped, and fought for food nearby, providing a raucous chorus for her respite. She didn't close her eyes, though; she sailed the blue, free as any gull.

Tegan imagined boarding Captain Advika's ship.

Maybe I won't ever come back.

Maybe that would be for the best.

But . . . she had ties here. Deuce and Fade were the closest she had to family, and one day she might want to bounce their babies on her knee. Sometimes the impossible came to pass, creeping on such quiet feet that you didn't even notice the world had changed. Around her, the birds quieted. When that happened in the wood, Szarok stepped out of the dark. Tegan sat up and glanced about.

"I know you're there," she said to the silence.

And the silence answered.

The Sweetness of Her Trying

"How did you know?" Szarok asked.

She was a mysterious creature, this human. In the twilight, there were others searching and calling her name. To his eyes, it seemed that she'd fled from her own kind, only to invite his company. Yet she didn't seem to find it odd.

"I'm not inclined to share my secrets." Tegan patted the ground beside her, her gaze returning to the water that bedeviled him.

"I'd rather not," he said.

"Oh. I'm sorry. Should we move closer to the trees?" Rising, she left the view she had been enjoying and chose a different spot. "Here?"

So many words crowded his mouth, they tasted like meat and tried to come out in a jumble of sounds that would be intelligible only to his own people. He swallowed them back, breathed, and tried again. "Yes, thank you."

"So polite," she teased.

He ignored her words. Today he was tired in a way that he never had been before, his heart overflowing with the silent surety that no matter how long he waited, the answer would never come as his people needed: *Yes, we trust you. Yes, we will help you.* No matter what promises had been made, humans would always view the Uroch as the terrible threat lurking in the dark. Being surrounded by the enemy might well drain the life out of him, for it was a constant struggle to bow and smile and not seem menacing. For some, his mere presence was enough to make them cross the road.

This is why they made me the vanguard. I can do this. I am patient.

"You're not well," she said eventually.

His gaze swung to her. It was nearly dark now, so he could see her better. In the light, the shapes lost their cohesion, and it was hard to tell humans apart. Szarok did better identifying them by smell. Today she was sweat and medicine, an unpleasant combination, but he could find her with his eyes closed, unlike that idiot still shouting her name. His ears prickled.

"What makes you say that?"

"I'm a doctor, remember?"

"So I seem sick to you?"

"A little. Tired, at least, and homesick, I think."

"What does that word mean?" Nobody had used it to him before.

"That you miss your home."

"For me to miss it," he said slowly, "I would need to have one first. Appleton is the place the old ones took. We Uroch had no say. Now that our time has come, we hope for better, but I don't—I don't see how. . . ." The human words dissolved again, under the weight of a despair so profound that it must sink him in the ground, like the mass graves they had dug for his ancestors.

"Oh." That round little sound was a rope, and it let him climb up to sit beside her, blinking in the starlight.

"I am sorry."

"For what?" She didn't look at him, and it helped.

He closed his eyes and listened to the water he hated. As long as he couldn't see it, the sound almost soothed him. "Troubling you."

At that, she laughed, and the vibration rang in his ears like a happy growl. "You're keeping me company while I vex those who love me. Don't you think I'm awful?"

"No."

"You'll feel lighter if you tell me," she said.

Szarok's eyes snapped open and gazed at her in wonder, trying to figure out how her eyes worked. Could she *see* the weight on him? From his own observations, these creatures were nearly blind and definitely dense to smells, but maybe she was different. *Better training?* He didn't even mean to answer her, but the words flowed out of him, hesitantly at first, and then in a torrent, until she knew everything. Shame and chagrin should be overwhelming him by now, but in the silence that followed, he only felt hollow, and in that space, a kind of relief. Full night had fallen as he talked, and it was cold enough that he could see his breath when he exhaled. She was shivering, trying not to show it.

Why won't she go back?

Tegan blew on her hands and then tucked them into her sleeves. "Does the answer have to be yes or no? Is there no room for maybe?"

"I don't understand."

"I understand why you can't stay in Appleton, but do you *want* to come here, where you'd have to fight for acceptance? Wouldn't it be better to find somewhere that's all your own?"

"We learn quickly," he said without looking at her. "But we have never built. The People are not patient. Without guidance—"

"You're afraid it will go wrong. That the Uroch will decide it's easier just to kill and take, like the old ones did."

Yes.

He didn't say it aloud, but she knew. It would be natural if she hated him, if she *feared* him, for those feral impulses not wholly settled. But instead she leaned against his arm, a minute but unmistakable shift. That small and subtle warmth reminded him of simpler times, before he understood the burden Rzika had handed him.

"Maybe won't save us," he said quietly.

"It could. Listen, I've been invited on a long-haul voyage. . . . Maybe you could come and scout potential settlements? Near enough that you could trade and request help, but not so close it makes either side uneasy. And . . . if you made that offer—to settle on a neighboring island—Governor Morrow might round up some men to help with the building." She peered at him, *so* pleased with herself and *so* earnest.

Szarok laughed. The sound startled her, but she didn't shift away. To her, he must have sounded like a barking dog. "That's the worst idea."

"Why?" she demanded.

"My people *hate* water. Yet you propose an extended sea journey? Rosemere on the river is bad enough. The only reason we came here first is because we have no relationship at all anywhere else."

That wasn't the only reason. It was impossible to put into words how the island made him feel. Crossing the water, that was a necessary trial to reach paradise, so pure because blood had never been spilled here. Humans expected that beauty as their birthright; it wasn't wrong to want the same for his people. Though the other towns had reason to be grateful, Szarok had made first contact here. But possibly he had been too hopeful in his estimate of Rosemere's tolerance.

"Then find your own solution." Her outrage was . . . pleasant, somehow.

"I shall," he promised.

"Do you think they've given up on me yet?"

"No. Your friends are the kind who will be out until dawn."

She sighed. "That's what I think, too. We should go back." They stood, and began to walk. "But . . . do you feel any better?"

"If I don't, will you prescribe some medicine?"

"Talking was the cure," Tegan said. "If it didn't work, I have more words."

"Oh?"

The moment she smiled, the moon came out from behind a cloud so it turned her face into a blob, all strange eyes and open horse-mouth, and she was so awful, he couldn't look directly at her. Szarok narrowed his eyes until it was tolerable.

Then she spoke, slow and measured. "You're my friend. And I'm here for you."

A low breath seeped out of him in an aching rush. Szarok growled a reply in his native tongue, but when she pressed him to translate, he only laughed and shook his head. Her voice went shrill, for it appeared the quickest way to aggravate this girl was to deny her knowledge. Tegan quickened her pace, demanding answers, and he increased the length of his stride, doing his best to outpace her. It seemed like a poor idea for them to return together, but she ignored his unsubtle hints and practically ran alongside him.

"Tell me," she panted.

Only when she stumbled and fell did he pause. She landed on her hands and knees, muttering words he recognized as curses. The human captives in the pens had taught him a wide variety of these words. Szarok took a step toward her, but she stopped him with a snarl worthy of a Uroch.

"I can do it. Don't help me. Don't *ever* help me."

So he stood by as she struggled to her feet and dusted her palms off. He caught the coppery tang of her blood, but since she said nothing, he found it best not to ask if she was hurt. This one should have been born with claws and fangs; she had the anger hidden, same as he. After that, he stopped trying to shake her, matching his stride to hers.

The other guests had long since departed, Szarok supposed. Near the path that led to the cottage, the governor's son paced alone, reeking of anxiety. When he saw Tegan, he melted a little and lost both height and dignity. Hands outstretched, he came toward her, and she backed up a pace so that her shoulders brushed Szarok's chest.

"Do you have any notion how worried we were?" The storyteller tried for a light tone and failed, a stern measure of scolding beneath.

"Is there some reason you should fear for me on Rosemere?" Anger radiated from her in a peppery wave. Too bad the human male couldn't smell it.

"You could have fallen . . . or gotten lost." He was very gentle in his reprimand, but he didn't seem to realize he was making it worse.

"I did fall," she bit out. "Then I got up again."

Szarok had no idea why he spoke then. "And if she got lost, I would find her."

The words provoked more of a reaction than he expected, as the human male fixed him with a sudden sharp look, and the intensity felt like a challenge. "Why?"

Puzzled, he cocked his head. "Because I'm good at it."

"It's true," Tegan said, not reading the nuances. Or not caring. With her, it was hard to be sure. "Come, let's find some food and go to bed."

With that, she dragged Szarok by his arm into the cottage, the first time such a thing had ever happened to him. Her fingers bothered him, and once they got inside, he swatted her away. She frowned and rubbed her hand.

"Don't do that," he said.

"What?"

"Handle me. I don't like it."

"I'm not allowed to tease you . . . or to touch. I'm sorry." Though her voice was soft, she seemed sincere, so he tried to understand her.

"You just . . . He was making you impatient?"

"Yes. I'm tired and hungry, and I wanted him to go."

The cottage was dimly lit, with just the flicker from the dying hearth fire. The others must not be worried about Tegan, and the storyteller was overprotective. But they had left crocks of soup and half a loaf of bread on the table. Since the stew was still warm, they must not have retired too long ago. He heard Millie's even breathing up in the loft.

"This is so good," Tegan mumbled, raking the vegetable mash into her mouth with a spoon.

Meat. I miss meat.

In truth, he preferred it raw, directly off the bone, and sometimes, his people enjoyed downing prey while it was still squirming. But humans would find that as revolting as he did this stuff. Eating this way for long periods seemed like it might kill him. He tore at the bread and pressed it with his fingers.

His stomach gurgled.

She paused.

"Sorry," he whispered.

But to his surprise, her expression softened. "I treated a fisherman today who promised my pick of tomorrow's catch. If you go with me in the morning, you might find it's exactly what you need."

"That's food you earned with *your* work."

"And you are my friend."

In all honesty, though he'd heard the word, he didn't truly grasp what it meant. But now she'd used it twice, and apparently it included listening to his troubles and feeding him when he hungered. She'd also come searching when he had nowhere but the woods to sleep. So then . . . by friend, she meant kin?

"I understand now how precious that is," he said.

She ducked her head. "Don't be silly. They're only fish."

As she ate, it was the most peculiar thing. Though he had no taste for smashed plants or dough, her pleasure filled him up. When she finished her meal, his stomach wasn't rumbling anymore. *Perhaps we are kin.* In a place where nobody spoke his tongue, where there were enemies all around, that possibility wrapped him in comfort.

"I should sleep here. Millie might be frightened if she woke and found me there in the middle of the night."

Tegan seemed unconcerned by this as she went up the ladder to the loft. "As you like."

The blanket he had carried with him didn't smell like his people any longer, and it was ragged and badly in need of washing. He didn't want to take it out of his pack in this human house. In the morning, they would see it and judge all the Uroch on what he lacked. But as he lay down in front of the fire, Tegan crept back down with a sweet-smelling quilt and a pillow.

"Here. It's a bit colder since you're on the floor. Sleep well."

A human wouldn't have known, but this was what she'd used the night before. He smelled her skin on the fabric, the remnants of her breath where she had rested her cheek; even the smoke from her hair left scented wisps as he nestled in.

She's given me the warmth of her own bed.

Szarok growled his answer. *If we're kin, let her learn the language of the People.*

This time, she didn't press him for a translation. Her footsteps crept away, and soon he heard her moving about overhead. Due to her measured breathing, he'd thought the other girl must be asleep, but her whisper proved otherwise.

"Where did you go?" Millie asked.

"For a long walk," Tegan answered with a faint sigh.

"James was frantic." Millie shifted, possibly adjusting her covers.

A sigh. "I know."

He wished he could close his ears, but it was impossible. Rolling away from the loft didn't help. The conversation continued, including him as an unwilling audience. But they did lower their voices to the point that the words turned into meaningless sounds, and the susurrations lulled him to sleep.

His dreams came broken but sweet, shards of memories that didn't belong to him. In the morning, he woke nearly light-blind with someone squatting over him. He scrambled away, claws out, only to realize it was Tegan. His heart thundered in his chest, and he had no idea what he might do if she drew closer.

"Did I startle you?" She didn't move.

"It's . . ." The words stuck in his throat.

It's not all right.

I'm not all right.

"Don't come so close without warning me. It's impolite." That was the least of what he wanted to say. Rage-snarls nearly throttled him.

"Humans wake each other up in a variety of ways. Just tell me what I need to do."

He couldn't focus on her expression, and fear rioted in his head, giving way to uncertainty. *How did I sleep so well among my enemies?* The last time he'd gone down so deep, he had been protected by his kinfolk, secure in the fact that nobody would come with guns or knives. Bewilderment tickled like a bug in his ear. Without meaning to, he jerked his head to shake it out. His breath galloped away from him, hard and fast.

He couldn't speak to answer.

"Szarok? Breathe. Just breathe. I'm truly sorry I scared you."

He dug his claws into his scalp until the pain cleared his head. "This. You say this."

Then he made the *wake and rise* sound, without expecting she'd ever attempt it. *We're animals to you. You won't.* To his astonishment, she did, deep in her throat. It wasn't right, but it was so close that he squeezed his eyes shut and almost, almost begged her to do it again.

Her tone drooped, a flower too wet with dew. "Was it that bad?"

The sweetness of her trying tightened his throat until he couldn't breathe.

"No," he said eventually. "Please, wake me that way tomorrow. Though I'd like to know why you've roused me so early today."

Nobody else in the house was stirring. The embers of the fire were dead and cold. Yet she was bright-eyed and eager, practically dancing in her desire to drag him into the daylight. As he stared up at her awful dollop of a face, he had the strange idea that if she woke him enough, days on days, that maybe he *would* get on that hell-boat with her.

Because she was kin? Because she was Tegan.

Just . . . because.

Fellowship of the River

That morning, Morrow left home early.

He bought sweet buns fresh at the bakery with a handful of chits, good only on the Evergreen Isle. Trade with the wider world was proving to be a challenge for his father, but fortunately he didn't have to worry about that. But he spotted Tegan much sooner than he expected, already on the dock, talking with Wiley, who was gesturing with a bucket. He recognized the brown-cloaked figure with her as well, but he couldn't fathom why they were together. Again. Possibly it was arrogance that made him think she'd miss him once she went away. But now that she was back, he felt like a glove made of thumbs, badly sewn and no use at all. Still, he pinned on a smile and hurried toward them with his paper-wrapped present.

Tegan smiled when she saw him, but she also beamed at bone carvings, sunsets, and unexpectedly gruesome stories. "Good morrow, James."

At least she still made a joke of his name. "I come bearing gifts. Are you hungry?"

"That's exactly why we're here," she said.

"I didn't think you were especially fond of fish."

Shaking her head, she accepted the pail of water from Wiley, and then handed it to the vanguard. "These are quite small, but you might be able to eat them whole. I'm not sure if you'd have problems with the bones?"

"Thank you for breakfast," Szarok muttered.

The Uroch took the offering from Tegan and rushed away, his head bowed. Morrow found the entire exchange odd and he said so.

"You embarrassed him," she said.

"Me?" That seemed unfair, no matter how he weighed it. "You were the one quizzing him about bones."

"He wouldn't have minded, except that you were listening."

Her statement stung like a slap. Morrow had the sense that she had drawn a line upon which she meant to build a wall, and when she finished, he would be standing alone on the other side of it. Truly he had no notion what to say.

The fisherman cleared his throat, and Morrow realized belatedly that they had an audience. "Can I take it that we're square now, Doctor?"

Tegan nodded. "But . . . if you don't mind, could you keep the little ones like that, just in case he enjoys them?"

"Done. Normally I throw them back, but I don't imagine one person's appetite will ruin my fishing," Wiley said, cheerful as a sunrise.

"Have you eaten?" Morrow asked.

"Not yet."

Trying to recover lost ground, he teased her with the sweet rolls. "Still warm, gooey, delicious. Would you like one?"

"Please," she said.

She still has a sweet tooth.

He got out a bun and broke it in half, his fingers honey sweet with sharing. The sun felt warmer on his head as she took the first bite, eyes closing in pleasure. Her strength was the first thing he had noticed about her, second her cinnamon-brown eyes, next her determination, and afterward, the smooth curve of her cheek, until her beauty and her resilience plaited around his heart with silken skeins. Now it was a joy merely to stand beside her.

She crammed the rest of the pastry into her mouth with such

delight that he had to laugh. "What shall we do today? And please don't make me entertain young Millie again. That would be exceedingly unkind."

"She's a sweet girl," Tegan protested.

"With boundless curiosity. I deserve a rest."

"I suppose that's true. But don't hurt her feelings. She already thinks we're all members of some private club that she could never join."

"The Fellowship of the River?" he suggested.

It disappointed him a little that she didn't seem to understand the joke, pale as it was. But she had spent much more time learning anatomy than reading old stories. When he thought about it, nobody in the world cared as much as he did about preserving old-world legends. Still, he wanted her to love what he did, not necessarily as much, just to love it.

Even a sliver of your heart would be enough, he thought. *A corner? A crack where the light can shine in?*

"We're *not* a secret club." Her stern look did yield to a twinkle, however. "But if we were, I'm sure we'd have a better name."

"Company D?" he offered.

"It has a certain ring to it."

They all had the patches Mrs. Oaks had sewn. He'd had his stitched onto his best jacket, though he didn't wear it around town. It seemed wrong to boast of his involvement when it was only a trick of timing that he had been at the right place at the right time. And too, he carried some misgivings, because it wasn't that he'd fought because he was strong, or it was right. His reasons seemed small, now that he examined them in depth.

I was curious.

Curiosity didn't make him stay, of course, when things were at their worst. But it wasn't a very heroic reason. *Some people are not heroes. We only write about them.* That, too, was a little embarrassing, the way others had taken his words and copied and recopied, so now what had been meant as a private gift for Deuce was making its way all over the free territories, mostly in the hands of traders who were peacock-proud to have their names in print.

"I'm in your hands," he told Tegan then. "What would you like to do?"

"Go see Captain Advika."

She really might go, then. He'd thought that when she came to Rosemere, it would be to stay. But it was also impossible to imagine Tegan keeping house as Deuce was learning to do. The Huntress didn't seem to regret turning her knives to chopping and slicing instead, but Tegan . . . Even if she stayed, she would be a healer first.

"At this hour, I'm sure she's still sleeping. I hear there was a fight at the tavern last night, and she was in the center of it."

Tegan grinned. "That sounds wonderful. She doesn't strike me as the sort of woman who starts what she can't finish."

"Truly spoken."

Instead of the tavern, they went first to the potter's house, mostly because Morrow thought she would be interested to see the work . . . and to learn. As he'd guessed, Tegan found the process fascinating. Like Millie, she had questions, but she paced them better, not distracting Artanno from his work. He wished he could be the one to reach around and shape the clay with his hands over hers, but he had no such skill. Her enjoyment was reward enough, though.

When it came off the wheel, her bowl was imperfect, but the potter put it in the oven anyway. "Come back tomorrow. You can take it as a memento."

Tegan's eyes widened. "Really? That's incredible."

They talked a little longer, and when they left, it was past noon, late enough for it to be feasible to talk with Captain Advika. "To the tavern, then?"

"Unless you're busy. I can go alone."

That offer pleased him as much as a kick to the shins. "No, I set aside the whole day. I missed you."

"You're sweet," she said, but her tone was more like, *Oh dear*.

Morrow swallowed a sigh and led the way to the tavern. When they arrived, Miwan, the fellow who owned it, was still cleaning up from the night before, fishing shards of crockery out of the floorboards. Morrow waved and glanced around, quietly hoping that the long-haul captain might have changed her mind. He found her in a dark corner with a mug of something.

The tall woman perked up when she saw Tegan. "Ahoy, Doctor. Did you come to sign on? I have a slice on my thigh that might need stitching."

"We should tend to that first, then talk," Tegan said.

Without further discourse, the two women adjourned to the back room. Miwan followed their exit with his gaze and then shook his head. "That woman is trouble in breeches."

"What happened exactly?"

"You know how it is with fishermen and sailors. Get a pint in them and they start telling tall tales. Advika claims she's been across the big drink, sixty days at sea, and nearly been pulled down to the depths by something as big as a house with eight arms and—"

"A monster?" Morrow cut in.

His enthusiasm for a long voyage kindled. *This time, I can pen a true-life sea epic.* To his mind, sharing a second adventure with Tegan culled all the disadvantages and dangers down to nothing. His father would probably squawk, but if he was so worried about his only son dying in a horrific and interesting way, he should probably marry again.

"That's what she said." The barkeep swiped at the counter. "But she had four pints in her by then. She said something about giant suckers as big as your face, and someone called her a liar, and a tankard got thrown. All downhill from there."

Morrow could see that some of the mugs had fresh dents. The tavern was usually a safe place to drink a bit, warm up, and eat some mediocre stew. But when the long-haulers put into port, life got more exciting. Before he could ask Miwan anything else, the storeroom door opened and the two came out.

"How many stitches?" Morrow asked.

"Five. It wasn't as bad as I feared." Tegan set down her doctor's bag, wearing a satisfied expression.

"Another fine scar for my collection," Captain Advika said.

"You mentioned before, about signing on?" Tegan seemed eager to bring the conversation back to the job offer.

"What I said still stands, and now I know you've got a calm manner and a steady hand. You might find it challenging to do the same work on board, though."

"I have a few questions," Tegan said.

"Let's hear them."

To Morrow's great delight, she had clever queries that elevated her in his esteem when he'd already thought it was impossible for him to admire her more. Tegan grilled Captain Advika about their route; asked to see navigational charts; requested a complete itinerary of planned stops; asked what sights they might see along the way; and then, of course, inquired about food and lodging, working conditions. The conversation carried on well into the afternoon. Now and then Morrow made an occasional comment, but mostly it was a pleasure watching Tegan work.

As they wrapped up, Millie popped her head in, seeming relieved to find a couple of familiar faces. Politely, he raised a hand to beckon her over, and she smiled so bright that he felt like the sun had come out. *It's too much for so little,* he thought. But her joy didn't waver as she sat down beside him and smoothed her gray skirt. He couldn't remember if he'd seen her in Otterburn, and she said she'd moved to Winterville to be near Tegan. Morrow guessed they must be close, if Millie wanted to follow the other girl to sea.

Oblivious to his scrutiny, Tegan was saying, "That sounds tremendous. But I'm wondering, how long would we be gone? Counting the return trip?"

"Half a year, most likely. Unless something goes horribly wrong. In that case, I couldn't say. So far I've always come back, but that's the way it goes until the time you don't. There are no guarantees on the high sea. I'll say this, though, having a good doctor could make all the difference in a bad situation."

"Then . . . I want to go," she said. "Do I need to sign something?"

Millie glanced at Morrow, her eyes wide. "This is happening?"

"For her. I haven't asked about us yet." It wasn't such a great service, but she touched his arm, quick like a butterfly, in a gratitude that looked so profound, it made him squirm.

Captain Advika shook her head. "Show up day after tomorrow, bright and early. As long as you're there when we leave port, your word is good with me."

"What if I have second thoughts?" Tegan asked.

"Then I'll send my boys to bring you aboard in chains," the tall woman said, grinning.

Millie leaned close to whisper, "I'm not sure if she's joking."

Morrow grinned. "Neither am I. That's the best part."

"Something funny?" the captain demanded, fixing dark eyes on them.

"Not a bit. But I am wondering if you'd consider taking on a couple of unskilled hands. Millie's willing to clean, and I'm largely useless except in a fight, but I'm sure my father would give aid in the cost of provisioning the ship."

"Are you trying to bribe me?"

Morrow tried for a charming expression. "A little?"

"Lucky for you, I love free trade, emphasis on free. I hear you're a storyteller and you wrote about the War of the River. If you have a copy, I'll read it the next two nights and give you an answer. I can't have some fool on my ship who's going to make me look bad." With that, she turned to Millie. "As for you, girl, as long as you're willing to do exactly what you're told, I don't mind taking on another deckhand. No pay, only rations, and no cut of any valuable salvage we run across. Is that a deal you want to make?"

Since Millie didn't seem to realize how bad an offer that was and seemed about ready to agree without haggling, Morrow stepped in. "You're asking for a half of a year with nothing at all to gain? That hardly seems just."

"She gets a free trip," Advika snapped, "and a wealth of experience. Plus, once it gets out she spent that long on *my* ship, she can take her pick of vessels."

Morrow surprised himself by wanting to fight. "So you say. But unless we see proof of that, she should get half a cut on any salvage. Her work matters."

The captain scowled, but Morrow suspected it was just for show. "Fine. Get me that copy of your rotten book. I think I'm in the mood for some critical reading."

He pretended to wince. "Focus on the story, not my poor skill."

"Worried now, are you?" His discomfort seemed to fill Captain Advika with glee, and he didn't mind, as long as it meant Millie wouldn't suffer on board.

"A little," he said cheerfully. "Well, then, this has been delightful, but I need to visit the library. I think they have a spare copy of the Razorland saga. My apologies in advance."

As he got up, the captain was starting to repeat some of the stories she'd shared with Tegan. That must have felt like her cue to leave, because for once, Tegan followed him instead of the other way around. Morrow paused just outside the doorway with an inquiring look.

"Did you want to browse some books? They won't let you take them to sea."

She smiled up at him, eyes bright and clear as sunlit whiskey. "I saw what you did back there. And I just want you to know, it was wonderful."

Pleasure rushed through him in a heady heat, until he realized it was nothing to do with her. She was just praising his simple decency in looking out for Millie. He tried not to show that it hurt, but damn and blast, sometimes even her praise stung like nettles. Because she only liked it when he turned to someone else.

"It was nothing," he said with an empty smile.

Madness and Drowning

"You can't go," Deuce protested. "There're a thousand reasons for you to stay."

"I know." Smiling, Tegan hugged her, wishing she didn't feel conflicted about doing so. She didn't like long goodbyes, as that seemed like asking for trouble.

Her bags were already packed, and Millie was pacing outside with nervous excitement. Amused, Tegan watched the girl's agitated stride carry her back and forth in front of the door. Quietly, Fade picked up Tegan's things and carried them out. If she didn't miss her guess, he wouldn't be heartbroken to have an empty house again, not that he'd ever been anything but polite. Still, there was a shadow in him that had never gone away, not after he was taken. Deuce had risked her life to rescue him after the old ones snatched him as prey and held him in their food pens as human livestock. What he'd seen and survived, it must have been monstrous.

Tegan understood better than anyone how some things changed you.

"I'll be back. Look for me in six months or so."

"Always," Deuce said with an angry sort of warmth.

"Take care of each other." With those words, she joined Millie, hoisted her belongings, and refused to turn around to acknowledge Deuce's frantic waving.

Walking quickly, they made it to the pier at the appointed

time and found James already waiting. "Good morrow," she called.

"At your service." He swept a bow, and she wished, slightly, that she found him as dashing as Millie did.

"You're just in time!" Captain Advika wove through the crowd to clasp Tegan on the shoulder. "The oarsmen will be making a few more trips yet, so feel free to head out."

"Thank you," she said. "I'm . . ." *Excited* didn't seem quite the right word. *Overwhelmed yet delighted* seemed like the best match.

But the captain had already lost interest, stomping down the pier to shout directions at dockworkers who were failing to load crates to her satisfaction. Bemused, Tegan traded a look with Millie and James, then the three of them set out to secure spots on the next little boat being rowed out to the larger ship. The heady scent of the river swept over her, and she breathed it in, trying to identify the separate smells.

Damp earth, peat, something green, a hint of salt or fish . . .

She wished she had James's affinity for words, because he could probably make it sound lovely, poetic even. Tegan gave up as an oarsman raised a hand, beckoning from the end of the pier. He caught the bag that held her clothes and personal items, but she held on to her doctor's bag. She'd carried it away from the ruins of Salvation, and they'd pry it from her cold, dead hands.

"Mind your step," the sailor said.

Tegan accepted his help in stepping onto the tipsy little rowboat, then Millie and James climbed in after her. Tegan settled in the center, gazing toward Captain Advika's ship. "Does it have a name?" she asked.

"The *Catalina*."

Stunned, Tegan stared at the man as he began to row. "Truly?"

"Why would I make it up? You'll see; it's etched on the prow."

Sure enough, he was right. She made out faded letters spelling the name as they approached. *It has to be a sign.* In passing,

Tegan wondered why the captain hadn't mentioned the name of her ship when she asked about the island, but . . . *I did ask specifically.* She made a note to ask the woman if she knew Dr. Wilson the first chance she got.

"Be careful going up."

A little shiver ran through her when she realized the sailor expected her to scale a rope ladder dangling down the side of the ship. Her bad leg shouldn't slow her down too much, but she had no idea how she'd make it with medical supplies in one hand. The mate solved that problem, at least, by tossing her bags like they were made of feathers. Another sailor at the top caught each neatly and set them on deck.

"Come on up, Doctor!"

She didn't hesitate further. On a deep, bracing breath, she lunged for the ladder with both hands, and got her feet tangled. Another moment sorted her out, then Tegan started climbing. Going slow like this, she wouldn't set any records, but she didn't fall into the water, either. Once she reached the top, a couple of hands drew her over the side and set her on her feet.

"Thank you."

Millie came up next, faster than Tegan, and then James swaggered onto the deck. He seemed more at home on a ship. He'd mentioned traveling to sea once, but it was hard to know what he'd actually done and what might be exaggeration for the sake of spinning a good yarn. Still, he wasn't the sort to craft outright lies, so she guessed he'd taken a short journey anyhow.

"We need to learn the names for everything," Millie said.

"Definitely. But I wonder who made such a beautiful thing." Tegan touched the smooth railing, awed by how the wood shone.

"There's a shipyard on Antecost," Morrow informed her. "In my experience, the mainland is bad; ruined cities are worst. Overall, the isles fared better during the dark times."

Probably because the Uroch don't swim. There were probably islands where the violence and madness had spread, but not these little havens. Enough people kept their wits and stayed alive that it was possible to start over.

"They called them the pride plagues in Salvation," Tegan murmured.

Since both James and Millie looked blank, Tegan guessed that wasn't the official name. Likely most of what she'd learned at school in Salvation would get her mocked by more educated folks. Tegan's mother had taught her what she could, but most days, their lives were driven by two principles: run or hide. Belatedly she sympathized with Deuce, who had gotten so frustrated wasting her days in a classroom. *At least what I learned from Dr. Wilson can't be judged and called wrong.* But as if he'd known his time might be limited, he didn't waste any of it on what he considered extraneous subjects.

Like history.

Yet it was hard to swallow, knowing that on the islands, small pockets of humanity went about their business, not knowing or caring how awful it was to eke out an existence elsewhere. In a way, though, it was also good. Because now that the tide had turned, people could join hands again, slowly, and learn about what they'd lost.

A sailor cleared his throat at her shoulder. "Doctor? I'm the first mate, Sung Ji. I've been with Captain Advika almost five years. It's a pleasure."

"Is she as fantastic as they say?" Tegan wondered aloud.

"If 'she' is the captain, then yes. I'd never dispute a word she said." The man grinned, showing a gap in his front teeth.

He was a tall man, lanky, with deeply weathered skin. He had permanent smile lines, probably from staring into the sun, but his corded arms said he was strong enough to handle any emergency. Though she knew precious little about such matters, Tegan figured the captain had chosen her second-in-command well.

"Good to know," she said, smiling.

"I'll show you to the cabin."

Happily, she followed, eager to find out where she'd be living and working for the next half year. The space astonished her—in that it was minuscule—and everything was built into the wall. Tiny drawers, medicine chest, bunk attached with rope that folded down for the end of the day. There was hardly room to turn around, and if she had more than one patient . . . but Tegan forced a smile.

"Thank you. I suspect you have work to do, so I can get settled on my own."

Nodding, Sung Ji dropped her bags and left with a final smile. Millie hovered outside, and it seemed to be sinking in that once they left Rosemere, *this* would be their home.

"I'll probably be sleeping on deck," the girl whispered.

James shook his head. "The regular crew have hammocks in the hold."

Tegan winced, as that sounded worse. "You can bunk with me, Millie. We'll have to squeeze, but it'll be better for both of us."

It wasn't that she thought Captain Advika had ruffians on board, but just in case, it seemed wiser not to risk it. James stepped past Millie and began inspecting the facilities, like he'd know a well-appointed exam room if one bit him on the behind. Exasperated, Tegan gave him a shove.

"This isn't yours," she snapped. "I'll organize it myself."

"I was only looking."

Lovely, he sounds hurt.

"Shouldn't you make sure the captain got all the provisions your father donated?" Yes, that was unkind, but it did the trick nicely.

James straightened, his cheeks hotly flushed, and he ran an aggravated hand through his hair. "I suppose I'd better. It would be terrible if I got put ashore on a rock in the middle of the sea." He tried for a light tone and failed, but Tegan smiled as if it was funny.

"Don't even joke," Millie said soberly.

Once he'd gone, Tegan took inventory and added her own supplies to the ones already on hand. A few articles made her gasp in wonder, clearly old-world salvage. Dr. Wilson had told her about such fine tools and shown pictures when possible, but certain things were hard to find in Winterville, like these gloves. They were stretchy and snapped right back into place, unearthly resilience, but they looked as if they'd boil clean immediately.

From just inside the doorway, the other girl watched in silence. Eventually Tegan glanced over, startled to catch a speculative look shot her way. "What's the matter?"

"I'm just wondering, is all."

"About . . . ?"

"Why you're so mean to James." Biting her lip as if she wasn't sure she should go on, Millie added hastily, "Well, you both laugh afterward, even when it's not funny, so I guess you two are playing some kind of sparking game? Where you run and he chases."

That's one way to look at it.

Tegan regulated her tone with some effort. "Not exactly. Sometimes when you run, it just means you need to get away, not that you're asking to be followed."

"That's what I think, too. It's pretty backward to do the opposite of what you want." The other girl's expression shifted to pensive shadows.

Tegan didn't pursue the conversation, preferring to finish her inspection before the ship got under way. With any luck, there wouldn't be major problems until she found out if she suffered from seasickness or not. *That would be an auspicious start, somebody needing to care for me while I puke in a bucket for days.*

Eventually Millie got bored and went up to watch them set sail. A bit later Tegan did the same because she didn't want to miss the departure. Deliberately, she went to the other side of the ship, leaving Millie and James alone. A twinge ran through her over not finding Szarok to say farewell, but he hadn't been anywhere she looked. Delaying further would've seemed . . .

obsessive, or like she thought—she didn't know what. But as she stood at the railing, gazing back at the Evergreen Isle, she searched for him among the faces in the distant crowd. They all blurred together, sadly, and she couldn't find his familiar figure.

Overhead, it was all a tangle of ropes or wires and billowing fabric. Sailors climbed up like it was nothing to tighten and adjust; staring up at them made her dizzy. She tried her best to stay out of the way as deckhands ran to and fro, doing things expertly. They snapped orders to one another that didn't even sound like words she'd heard before, but Dr. Wilson had told her more than once she caught on quickly, so Tegan figured she would pick up mariner vocabulary soon enough.

As the isle receded, she waved until her arm felt like it might fall off. The wind whipped her hair against her cheek, colder than she'd expected, and the rock of the river made it hard to stand without gripping the rail for dear life. Her shoulders burned with the effort, so she loosened her hands, hoping she'd learn to cope soon. So far her stomach felt all right, at least.

The first mate paused to pat her shoulder. "Don't fret; you'll find your sea legs."

She smiled and let go of the railing. "I'll put my faith in your word."

Cautiously, she picked a path back to the steep steps that led down to the lower deck. With only one wrong door, she made it back to the tiny clinic where she would live and work. But to Tegan's surprise, someone was waiting. *My first patient . . . ?* But no. Though it seemed impossible, she recognized that brown cloak. In conjunction with those tense, hunched shoulders, it could only be . . .

"Szarok?"

He jerked but didn't face her, curled into the smallest possible space. Even from here, she saw the shivers that worked through him in uncontrollable waves. Tegan flipped the sign so that it read CONSULTATION IN PROGRESS, then shut the door behind her. He seemed worse now than he had the morning she'd woken him. Controlling the urge to ask a slew of unproductive questions, she focused on treating him like a patient. Mental issues weren't her specialty, but . . .

There's no one else. He has no one. Only me.

"It's the water?" she guessed.

He shuddered, emitting a sound so miserable that she didn't need words to understand that he was suffering. Carefully, Tegan sat down beside him on the floor. "You might feel better if you talk. It helped before."

"What . . ." He struggled in shaping the sounds. "What should I say?"

"Well, I'm curious. You said this was a terrible idea, remember?"

Szarok leaned his head against the cabinet and the current jostled them so his skull rattled, but he didn't react to the pain. "It is. But I don't have a choice. The Uroch . . . sent a messenger. It's getting worse in Appleton. And Governor Morrow said he'll help, but only if I choose a site to build—"

"Somewhere else," she finished.

"I'm the patient one. I promised I would do this. So I sent the envoy back, and I got on this . . . hell-boat."

Poor Uroch, she thought.

Explanations did seem to be calming him, so she pressed for more, teasing a little, though he might be too terrified to notice. "That doesn't clarify why you've come to see the doctor. You're not sick."

"I didn't come for the doctor," he said. "I came searching for my friend."

Oh.

"Well, then. You found me. Am I helping?"

"Yes."

"If you were with your kin and you were frightened, what would they do?"

"When I was young, they covered me so I couldn't be found. But no Uroch stays small for long." He sounded . . . wistful, perhaps.

Without hesitation, Tegan reached for the blanket tucked into her bunk and pulled it down, then draped it over him. She didn't let an inch of him show, and though it was a silly solution, he relaxed as if the darkness and warmth formed an impenetrable cocoon. When she set her hand gently on his back, he didn't recoil. That permitted touch, even through layers of cloak and blanket, struck her as . . . special.

"Why are the Uroch so afraid of water?"

He hesitated, shivering in small bursts. "Because our first memories, the oldest ones, are of drowning, madness and drowning."

"But . . . how?" She'd thought the passing of memory had an air of ritual about it—that the Uroch chose who would receive their collected experiences.

"We can control it now. But before . . ." Szarok fell quiet, either unable or unwilling to explain how it used to be.

She didn't ask again. Instead she patted his back in a steady cadence akin to a heartbeat until his trembling subsided. Eventually he came out from under the blanket and up onto his knees, facing her, so she got unprecedented access to his face. His bones were sharper than a human's, too prominent at chin, brow, and jaw. The differences would probably be even more distinct in skeletal structure. His eyes had inhuman irises, rapidly flowering pupils, and the sclera was the same as the iris, not white at all. He had no hair, not brows or lashes, and his ears were larger yet fused to the skull and flat, not curled like a seashell. Certain sounds might even cause him pain.

She would've continued cataloguing the differences if he hadn't shifted away like her gaze hurt him. "What's wrong?"

"I'm not a specimen."

"No," she agreed. "But I was *learning* your face, not studying it. Is that wrong?"

"I don't understand the difference."

"Learning is just . . . wanting to know something. Studying is more scientific." In truth, her impulse had been a bit more complicated, but she couldn't say she wanted to know him well enough that she could picture his features at will.

"Then," said Szarok, "fair is fair. Let me learn you."

Pure Determination

egan stilled as Szarok leaned forward, but he stopped a foot away and just stared until her skin might crawl off her bones. Heat washed her cheeks; she dropped her gaze and scooted away, until her back met the cabinet behind her. If he meant this as a lesson, it was an effective one. *If this is how I made him feel, I owe him more than an apology.*

"Sorry," she whispered. "The difference between learning and studying doesn't seem important anymore."

He sat back. "As long as you know."

"Well . . . you don't seem panicked, at least."

Perhaps she shouldn't have said anything, because his eyes darted, like he'd just remembered about the ship. "It won't change anything."

"You can do this," she said. "Your people are counting on you. Antecost isn't too far north, and we're stopping to collect the rest of the crew."

"Thank you." Just then the ship lurched.

His skin was always gray, but judging by his tortured groan, he didn't feel well. Collecting her professional acumen, she touched his brow. Clammy with sweat. It wasn't hard to diagnose this as a case of seasickness, exacerbated by his fear. The passage didn't even feel that rough to her, though she had to steady herself occasionally as she opened her bag and rummaged for the right medicine. With a triumphant smile, she opened the pack of ginger restorative and added the powder to a cup of water.

"Take it. This will help."

He sniffed once and regarded the medicine with a dubious air. "How do I know your treatments won't poison me? You're a human doctor."

"Smell it. I'm sure you've had this before."

For a moment he stared, then he snatched the cup and downed the contents in a grimacing swallow. Gratified by his trust, she leaned over and let the bunk down from its vertical placement on the wall. The ropes bounced, but the bed seemed stable. She wasn't sure if she was supposed to let patients rest here or not, but since this was Szarok, she decided the answer was yes.

"Come and lie down."

He didn't argue, which spoke volumes on how awful he must be feeling. Once he did, she covered him again, then she wet a damp cloth, folded it, and rested it on his forehead. Tegan wanted to do more, but as a doctor, there was no further treatment to offer. She hated the fact that she wanted to put her hand on him, as if she had some healing touch. Instead she busied herself with putting away her supplies. As she worked, she hummed, and at some point, his breathing evened out. It might be polite to leave him in peace, but she feared it might send the wrong message, one of indifference rather than good intentions.

At one point she heard footsteps outside the door, but they only slowed in passing by, so it must not have been urgent. *Possibly James or Millie wondering where I've gone.* When the dinner bell rang, she decided she couldn't let him sleep any longer, at least not here. With some regret, she made the sound he'd taught her, feeling self-conscious. Yet his eyes snapped open immediately, so she must not have gotten it wrong.

"Do you feel better?" she asked.

"It no longer feels like my stomach will twist inside out."

"Good. I don't know what you should eat, if anything. You

don't like bread or vegetables, so maybe some broth if it's available."

Szarok sat up slowly, his expression sharpening into one she didn't recognize. At least, it was a look she hadn't seen on him before. "The fish . . . They were delicious."

"I'm glad."

With that, he went, and Tegan opened the office door to search for supper.

She didn't see him again before they made port, but she heard quiet complaints among the sailors that a monster had been given free run of the ship. As she stood watching the approach to Antecost, a rigger with a scarred cheek spat on the deck and muttered, "They ought to keep him caged. Safer for normal folk."

Thus goaded, she couldn't keep quiet. "The Uroch saved us in the war, unless you've already forgotten. They are our allies."

The sailor inspected her with eyes that left her feeling as filthy as his teeth. "It's nothing to us what you mainlanders do. We were safe enough."

"Then you're the monster," she said fiercely. "If it's fine with you that the rest of the world dies, as long as *you're* not bothered."

Before the situation could escalate, suddenly James was at her side. She didn't want to be grateful—hated that she was—but the look in this sailor's eyes was dreadful and familiar. Tegan took a step back, hands curling into fists. Smoothly, he set a hand beneath her elbow and guided her away from the brewing conflict. While she didn't want to be rescued, she couldn't physically fight every imbecile on the ship.

If there's one, he's bound to have friends.

"I see you're getting to know your colleagues," James said.

She shot him a baleful look.

"Enough of that. Admire the scenery."

While she was in no mood to appreciate natural beauty, when she focused, Antecost took her breath away. They were sailing toward the gentle side of the isle, but she could see that there were sheer cliffs topped with green forest. On the far end, a village sat like a bouquet of flowers and painted just as bright. She'd never seen houses that reminded her of butterflies before. As they drew closer, Tegan noticed that the paint was chipped and flaking away to reveal the broken plaster beneath.

"We don't know how to make the paint anymore." James sighed a little. "They're experimenting, but it never lasts intact past the first rain."

"But they keep trying." There was something sweet and hopeful in that.

He nodded. "We'll be in port overnight, or so I hear. After that, we'll be at sea for some time. The trip will be grueling."

So far there hadn't been any medical emergencies, just routine splinters and bruises, and she appreciated that respite from the intensity that would doubtless follow. "I'm ready."

Millie strolled along the deck toward them, her cheeks bright with wind and sun. She'd braided her hair so only dark wisps escaped to frame her face, and Tegan thought she looked uncommonly pretty. "Can you believe it? We're almost there."

"It's only the first stop," James teased. "You'd better pace yourself or you won't be able to handle the rest of the world."

They joked back and forth about possible sights and sea monsters while Tegan wore an absent smile. As before, the ship dropped anchor off the coast and they went ashore in small numbers, with a few men designated to stay back. She wasn't sure how they determined that responsibility, but nobody tried to stop her when she went down the ladder. James and Millie joined her. Above, the sun glowed orange on the horizons and the waves rocked back toward them in ripples of gold. The rower argued when James offered to spell him, but soon James had the oars in hand, pulling them toward the shore.

"You're good at that," Millie commented.

"This and fencing. That's all the sporting skill I have."

"Good enough," said the sailor, apparently enjoying his break.

The sky darkened, dropping from umber to purple. Soon the rowboat tapped the dock, and with some help, Tegan scrambled onto the weathered boards. From here she could see how stony the shore was before the village. In Rosemere, there was more of an embankment. But the water was different here, too, darker and rough with hidden rocks.

Seeming to follow her gaze, the sailor made an unfamiliar gesture, flattening both hands over his heart. "They call this Great Graveyard."

"Excuse me?" Tegan's eyes widened and she glanced at Millie, but the girl seemed more intrigued than frightened.

"There're ancient shipwrecks all around. These waters are famous for them."

Captain Advika was coming in on the next little boat, and she scoffed. "Are you telling ghost stories again, Bigby? If you scare off my doctor before she settles in, I'll make you the ship's surgeon, and somebody will kill you after you hack off a leg that could've been saved."

"I didn't make up the stories or wreck the ships," he muttered.

The captain fell into step as they headed for Port-Mer. "This used to be the size of Rosemere, but after the trouble, people flocked north in droves. Now there are little villages all along the coast, though there are only three ports safe for ships. This coastline's a bitch, plus, the weather's cold, plenty of rain. But you can eat venison forever."

"Good hunting," James added.

Briefly Tegan thought he was saying good-bye because that was how they'd parted in Company D. Then she realized he was making an observation as Millie said, "I love venison stew. Is there a place I can have some before we go?"

"There's a tavern," Advika answered. "Probably have a pot going. They usually do."

"I'm so hungry." Millie grabbed Tegan's arm and hauled her along in a fit of enthusiasm.

Tegan cared less about filling her belly than exploring before the light faded, so she shook free. "You two, go on ahead. I want to take a walk along the water. I'll be there directly."

"Are you sure?" James's gaze lingered, but he followed when Millie tugged his sleeve.

This time, however, he didn't look back when he strolled away. Instead of saddening her, she took heart in it. The captain didn't seem to have any pressing business, so she stayed with Tegan as she angled her steps toward the rocky beach.

"You're young to be a doctor," the other woman observed.

"It's better to say that I know a little about treating ailments." She didn't say that she was old where it counted—deep in her heart and down in the bone where it ached.

"Don't sell yourself short. Heaven knows you won't get the credit that you're due in this life with a soft voice and modest manners."

"I *have* seen a lot," she said.

"It shows. You carry yourself like you're walking over a deep well."

Though she didn't know what that meant exactly, she took it as a compliment. Tentatively, she smiled. "Did you always want to captain a ship?"

It was hard to tell how old the other woman was. She had an ageless face, strong but beautiful, yet her eyes hinted at grief. "No. In the beginning I just wanted to live." The captain picked up a flat rock and skipped it over the water in a sharp, skilled arc. "I'll tell you a secret, Doctor. I came from the ruins, too."

"In Gotham?" The startled question slipped out before she could stop it.

The older woman shook her head. "No. We called it Saint City. Before, it was something else, but you know what life in the old cities was like, don't you?"

Tegan nodded, choosing her own rock; she mumbled a curse when it sank instead of hopping. "Why did you call it that?"

"Where I lived, it was a city of the dead. Just graves as far as the eye could see. There were stone houses and carven statues and huge monuments. It must have taken centuries to build. But it was also safer than the rest of the ruins because there were so many places to hide, and it wasn't far from the river. I pinned all my dreams on that because sometimes when the weather was fair, I could see boatmen passing by."

"Someone stopped?" she guessed. That was what happened with Thimble and Stone, how they made their way from the ruins to Rosemere.

But Captain Advika gave a wry smile. "Not the first time I shouted or even the twentieth. It's funny when I think back on it . . . that my life depended on pure determination, and that in the end, my fate still hinged on somebody else's whim." Her expression lost that misty, faraway quality. "And so does yours. My crew . . . Some I only took on because they're smart or strong. But not good. Remember that."

"I will." Tegan wondered if the captain had heard something about her confrontation with the sailors complaining about Szarok, but she decided to accept the warning at face value.

"You coming to sample that venison stew?"

"I probably should. The food on the ship hasn't impressed me."

Captain Advika laughed. "Yeah, Cook's grub all tastes about the same, which is kind of an achievement when you think about it."

In companionable silence, they walked back from the pebbled beach to the packed dirt road that led to town. Here and there, Tegan saw signs that this was an old settlement, broken stone roads, layered over with newer attempts at paving. This patchwork process left the path uneven. Along the way, someone had lit lanterns for isolated circles of brightness, echoed by the silver moon hanging nearly full overhead.

The businesses were closed for the night, apart from the tavern, where almost the whole ship had gathered. James rose and beckoned; he and Millie had a table full of company, and Tegan sighed a little. His gregarious spirit exhausted her sometimes. She preferred to join a group quietly and just listen, but James always wanted to haul her to his side—at the center of attention.

"I'll get a pitcher of something," Advika said.

When she got to the table, James kicked a chair toward her. It wasn't discourtesy, since he was in the middle of a story. Everywhere he went, people asked him for words in lieu of payment. His ability to spin a yarn on demand was one of his most admirable qualities. This one was about a girl who thought she was a witch, and half the tavern quieted to listen. Grateful she didn't have to speak, Tegan ate her stew, pleased with the captain's recommendation.

Only half attending to the tale's climax, she peered around. There were unfamiliar faces in here, probably locals, packed tight and talking over one another. In quick succession someone started shoving, and darts went sailing around, slamming into the wall. Keeping low, Tegan hurried toward the door. Millie was shouting something, but she kept moving.

Outside, the air smelled crisp and clean, if cold enough to show her breath. Tegan realized she didn't know if she was supposed to go back to the ship, and if not, where she was meant to stay tonight. Going back inside seemed like a poor decision. She went toward the pier, but it was dark and still, not a place to linger with the captain's warning fresh in mind.

Turning, she nearly ran into a cowled figure. Relief dawned like sunrise, building into a brilliant smile. "Thank goodness it's you."

Szarok didn't respond to that. "Come."

Without touching her, he made it clear she was meant to follow. So she did. Some distance outside town, he'd made camp, well away from the water. It made sense that he'd take this opportunity to sleep on dry land, as it would be his last for a while. The fire crackled with cheerful disorder, wood popping and ashes tumbling, orange worms crumbling into gray. She breathed in the smoke and held out her hands, grateful to be away from so many people. Out here she didn't need to watch so hard, gauging potential threats from all angles.

"I'm glad you're here," she said.

"Why?" He sounded impatient, angry even.

It didn't faze her. "Because I know I'll be safe with you."

The Opposite of Enemy

"You are too trusting," Szarok said at last.

He intended to sound harsh, but Tegan only shook her head and smiled. "I have an excellent sense for when people want to hurt me. Have you eaten?"

"Yes." A wealth of information shaded that word, all of which he chose not to say.

She might understand that he'd hunted as soon as he could and savored the blood with all its delicious copper and salt. He'd eaten a hearty portion of deer before butchering the rest. Now one of the haunches roasted on the fire. Not for him. For her. Just in case. While she'd called him friend, after the way she had cared for him on the water, he considered her kin.

"Are you cooking that for tomorrow?"

He nodded because it was simpler, and explanations would probably confuse her. "You can sleep here if you wish. I'll be scouting all night."

"You're going?" For the first time, she showed signs of alarm, and it was hard not to reassure her in his own tongue.

It wouldn't help. They're only sounds.

But she'd woken him like one of the People today. "I'll be at the dock tomorrow. But tonight I must see if there's anywhere for us on Antecost."

Space and welcome were two different issues. But Antecost might be possible because there was no central party capable of making decisions for the whole isle. From what he'd gathered, each village had a chief or an elder, but they all operated separately. So if he picked a spot far enough away from everyone else, the Uroch might be able to come in quietly. Antecost didn't whisper of home like Rosemere, but it was significantly larger. That might be enough.

"You can't cover the whole island in a single night," she protested.

As he got to his feet, so did she. "Don't follow me. You'll slow me down."

She flinched and then sank back before the fire to cradle her staff like a reminder. "Go safely then."

Szarok snarled, for he hadn't meant to injure her pride. Only, the night was waning, and she couldn't move as he did. In the end, he turned and ran, ignoring how small a shape she made in her dejection. He'd already wasted too much precious time going to find her, yet he'd known instinctively that she would be miserable trapped in the tavern all night. What he'd done should be enough. Yet her shadow chased him as he ran, putting space between himself and Port-Mer. He ran along the gentle curve of the coast, and it wasn't long by his running speed before he encountered the next village, locked in peaceful slumber. Breathing hard, he realized he couldn't scout in a night, just as she'd said. At best he might see a few sites that were already occupied, but making his way down past the settlements would take time.

Maybe I should stay on Antecost and scout longer.

It would be good to cut the connection that had inexplicably formed between them. Since that move meant not getting back on the hell-boat, it seemed like an ideal solution. Making up his mind, he ran back toward Port-Mer. Now he had the time to say good-bye and to thank her for her friendship. It was halfway to dawn when he returned . . . and she wasn't alone in the makeshift camp. Szarok smelled the intruders before he saw them; his claws came up. But when he rounded the last bend, he found Tegan on her feet, staff before her in a warrior's stance. She didn't seem frightened or weary, just deliciously angry. He stilled.

"Take another step and I crack both your skulls."

"Don't be like that," an oily voice coaxed.

Both of these humans smelled unclean, beyond rancid. He considered killing them on principle, but so far they'd only offended his sense of smell. Tegan probably wouldn't thank him for interfering, either. *I've already angered her once tonight.* So he waited silently, just beyond their line of sight, in case she needed him.

The taller one lunged. In an instant she cracked him across the shins, the other in the chest, and followed with a flurry of swings. Each time she connected, someone cursed. Soon they were crawling away in a frenzy of begging. Afterward, he listened long enough to be sure they'd gone, then he ventured into camp, where she sat with her staff propped on her knees.

"Did you find your new home?"

You're fierce, he wanted to say. But praise made her squirm, and he would mean it that way if he spoke of it. So they both pretended bad men hadn't stolen her sleep.

"No," he said. "You were right. But I did find something I'd like to show you."

"Is it far?"

"I'm not sure. A little?" Humans didn't move as the People did, so the journey might wear her out. "But I promise you'll be back before the ship leaves."

"Very well."

Tegan stood and brushed off her breeches. She had one set of clothing like human women wore and one similar to what men did. When she held out her hand, he stared at it.

"This is how my people walk," she said. "When the road is long and dark."

He cocked his head. At first it didn't even seem possible, but her delicate fingers threaded through his, neatly avoiding his claws. "This way."

So joined, it was easier to lead her in the dark, and she stayed close, her feet falling where his trod first. The smell of water drove him away from this place initially, but it was a wonder *she* would treasure. This must stand as the best farewell gift he could offer. Szarok didn't speak until they broke from the trees some while later and the roar of a river spilling over jagged rocks sang an audacious tune. She glanced back and forth so the moonlight made of her face a swimming fish, all shimmering light and shadow.

"It's beautiful," she whispered. Letting go of him, she walked a few feet out into the water and bent down to let it trickle through her fingers. "Hard to imagine that the rest of the world is so devastated."

His hand felt light and empty.

"I won't be with you after this." Those were both the wrong words and the right ones.

"You're staying."

"This is our best hope. It will serve no purpose for me to continue on."

She nodded. "It's close enough to Rosemere that they can send supplies, and the governor said he would assemble a work crew to help you build. Maybe if the weather holds, your people can join you before winter."

"You think it's right, too?" For some reason, he'd hoped she would argue.

To wash away that feeling, he knelt and drank. Instead of turning her face away, she watched until he had his fill. He already knew that others thought he did this like an animal, but claws made it difficult to scoop it up as humans did. *Not to mention how inefficient that is.* Tegan came out of the pool and glanced back toward the horizon as the light rose.

"What am I supposed to say? You don't need my permission." The sadness in her soft tone struck him like a cluster of younglings all whimpering at once.

What she'd called homesickness before overwhelmed him, not for a place but for his people, and it was all tangled, for she smelled like him, where their hands had touched. She had hidden him from danger and fear, stood watch while he lay weak and sick. There were no words for this, not in any tongue he knew. Szarok could be sure of only one thing—whatever Tegan was, it must be the opposite of enemy, but none of the human captives had taught him that.

"We should go back." While he wished they could linger, there was no time.

"Not yet." She picked a flower blooming near the water. "I want to keep something to remember this place by."

"A stone would last longer," he said.

"You're so practical, it's tiresome."

Szarok took the first steps toward town. In the morning, she would get back on that hell-boat. When she sailed, he might never see her ugly face again. The pain startled him to the point that he had to hold on to a nearby tree. "It hurts. *Why* does it hurt?"

Instinctively, she turned to support him, but she appeared to remember his warning not to touch him. Her hands curled at her sides. "What's wrong? Are you sick?"

"You *did* poison me." It was a ridiculous accusation, and he knew it.

"I don't understand." In the dark, at least she couldn't see that he'd lost his reason.

A long breath steadied him somewhat. "Forget everything. Forget that we were friends."

"I won't and you can't make me."

Stubbornly, she walked on, evidently immune to whatever illness plagued him. But she couldn't see well enough to navigate the way back to camp, so he passed her and set the proper course. Other forest animals gave way before him; in silent deference they acknowledged him as a superior predator. *If only human girls had half the wisdom of a quiet tree squirrel.*

"The men who bothered you tonight, are they from the ship?" His breath singed the back of his throat as he waited for her answer.

She doesn't need me. She has her staff and that fine word-spinner.

"I think so. There's no reason for anyone in Port-Mer to look for me. I hardly spoke to anyone at the tavern."

"But you had a quarrel on board?"

She shrugged, an infuriating gesture. "Maybe."

That word gnawed at his resolve to sail no farther. This island might solve all his people's problems, and yet—

"I'll stay with you until sunrise," he said.

She seemed puzzled by the offer. "Why? It's strange. I only saw you briefly before the battle. You spoke to Deuce, not me. And after the fighting, my world was all blood and bodies."

Her pause gave him a chance to express gratitude, something he should've done long since. After the war, he'd taken everyone who could march back to Appleton, but there had been warriors too wounded to walk. "You treated the Uroch the same as human patients. Some of my people owe you their lives. They came home because of you, and I have not forgotten."

"Is *that* why you're kind to me?" Whatever she had been about to say, she forgot in a peppery burst of outrage. "I don't need special treatment for doing what I should."

"That's not what I mean."

"I don't care," she muttered.

Tegan stomped ahead, though it was no hardship to catch her. "It's not why I'm kind to you now," he finally said.

That got her to stop. "Oh?"

"It *is* why I offered to travel with you at first. I thought I might be able to repay a small debt if I kept you safe on the road."

Her brows drew together. "A debt tallied *only* by you."

"You wouldn't dismiss that record if you knew how few names are in it. And that's exactly why it matters that I keep track."

"Oh."

He was coming to like that little sound more than he should. "But that's not why I find you now."

If she asked, he didn't know what he'd say. Tonight he was tired but not hungry, and it seemed the words were speaking themselves. Swallowing hard, he said more in a few low growls, but her silence held like a tree branch bowing beneath considerable weight. Eventually she took a step toward him and flattened her palm over his heart.

Yes, he thought. *They're in the same place, more or less.*

Szarok wouldn't explain that he knew something of human anatomy from the memories handed down through his sire's line: bloody, gruesome explorations, and he remembered the pleasure of it, so her touch rocked him with a tremendous shudder. The impact resounded in his head like running top speed into a tree.

This time he didn't say, *Don't handle me; I don't like it.*

His heart said that for him, by racing until he couldn't breathe. If she had any sense of smell, she'd know—she'd *know*—and then she'd stop. Except his heart kept beating, and she kept touching, tapping, really, as if she were counting each thud of his heart. When he started, too, he forgot that she was human and about the bizarre pressure of her palm. It was just warm, and he got to one hundred before he realized he wasn't drowning in the old ones' memories.

He let out a slow breath. "What are you doing?"

"Learning," she said.

That was always her answer. Her consistency maddened him yet filled him with sweetness at the same time. Her interest . . . now it made him feel important, not different. The world was full of things she could study, but she chose him time and again. There was comfort in being known, especially by Tegan of the Staff.

"I won't tell you to stop."

"This is the last time anyway."

Hearing it stated so, he wished he could claw out of his skin and shuck his responsibility. But the People needed him. In taking Appleton, they had secured a foothold in the mainland, but it was a death sentence in the long term. The People were hunters, and they needed room to run. In Appleton they were still forced to wear identifying armbands, and there were hostile encounters on the road, humans with rifles and a long history of hate.

We hate you, too.

But not her.

Trembling, he put his palm over hers. *Stay. Scout the island with me.* But after that, what then? She couldn't live among the People for plentiful reasons, and he couldn't ask her to abandon her dream. *This is where our story ends.* So he swallowed the words and the sounds if not the feeling. The tiny point of contact said everything; it was brand-new and fragile.

Eventually she let go and he did, too. His feet felt heavy, and his impressions from the surrounding forest seemed to come from far away. All too soon the embers of the fire came into view, along with the lingering stench of the sailors. The horizon was lightening; now he could measure their time together in heartbeats. Soon Port-Mer would wake and everyone ashore must return to the ship.

"It's almost dawn." His throat hurt—tight and hot—despite the water he'd downed before.

"I'm glad we traveled together for a while," she said.

"As am I." Before they left, he kicked dirt on the smoldering ashes.

Together, they set out for the docks, but before they reached their destination, a clamor rang out from the center of town, screaming like he hadn't heard since the war. A woman sobbed; the scent of fresh blood rode the wind, great gouts of it. Human. Not animal. A cold chill crawled down his spine as hostile eyes pinned him.

"There's the beast," someone shouted.

"Malena . . . Malena!" The sobbing rose and fell like the waves that sickened him and rocked the boat so that he couldn't sleep.

"Seize it. Kill it if it fights."

In a heartbeat, armed men surrounded him and Tegan. Without thinking, he put her behind him, but she shouldered forward and raised her staff. Her glare might scorch them to death.

"What's going on?" Tegan demanded.

"My daughter . . ." The woman on the ground had misery in her eyes, rocking a body like the dead girl could get up again with so much blood pooled at her back.

"There was violence under the cover of darkness," a tall gray-haired man said, addressing Tegan, not him. "You think it's a coincidence that Captain Advika brought a monster to our doors and now poor Malena's dead?"

The mob seemed to be growing in size and ire, agitating toward violence. If they attacked, he would defend. And live. No matter how many of them had to die.

Tegan's cool voice rang out. "Impossible. Szarok was with me all night."

The Tide Is Rising

Morrow woke with a rotten head and upset stomach; he didn't even remember crawling off to sleep the ale away. When he came downstairs, he heard shouting, and the taproom was empty, so he went out to investigate. An angry crowd at this hour meant something dreadful must've happened. *Tegan.* He quickened his pace until he was running, arriving just in time to hear her offer an alibi to the Uroch leader. But . . .

She can't mean it like it sounds.

Others had plainly taken it that way, however, and now she was receiving scornful looks. He shouldered through the mob toward them, but Captain Advika beat him to it. The tall woman wore a ferocious scowl.

"I'm sorry as hell to hear about Malena, but do you have any proof? You can't go around accusing my crew willy-nilly."

A portly man with a handlebar mustache tried to take charge of the situation. "Rutger, fetch a blanket and cover the poor girl. As for the rest of you, if you saw something, come forward. No hearsay, mind, only what you directly witnessed."

The crowd rumbled, but then one of Advika's sailors, a short man with a wicked scar on his cheek said, "Are you sure you were with him *all* night, Doctor?"

From the bruises visible, he guessed the sailor had been part of the tavern brawl the night before. He had a rough look and an unpleasant gleam in his eye.

Plus, Morrow didn't like that sinister tone. But Tegan held her ground. "I'm certain."

She seemed to be daring him to call her a liar, but whatever their silent exchange meant, the crewman only let out a nasty snort of a laugh. She stepped closer to Szarok, and though she only came to his shoulder, from where Morrow was standing it seemed clear that she intended to protect the Uroch. *That's my problem,* he thought. *If the whole world stood against me, she'd probably take my side then.* But it was wrong to rail at a life that had given him so many blessings, and he shouldn't wish for misfortune just because Tegan would try to protect him from it.

The man with the impressive facial hair seemed to be in charge; he sent the girl's grieving mother home in the company of relatives, and he had two more men carry the victim off to be prepared for burial. From what Morrow had seen of the tears in her bloodstained dress, they could've been created by claws or a jagged knife. Nobody seemed to know how to react, but eventually the crowd dispersed, still muttering.

"Will this affect our departure?" Tegan asked Captain Advika.

The other woman lifted a shoulder. "They'll probably want to question everyone who came in with us. You and the Uroch should be fine, as long as you're telling the truth."

"That will take a while," Morrow added, joining them. "It's my guess that we'll miss the morning tide."

Advika sighed, staring at the spot where they'd found Malena. "Rotten luck, poor mite."

"I'd planned to stay on Antecost," Szarok said softly.

The local chief came up in time to hear that, and he shook his head. "That's a poor idea. With tempers high, once your ship leaves, I can't guarantee your safety. The men don't seem to believe your friend, and they're after some rough justice."

Those words had an ominous ring, but Morrow suspected the Uroch might not know exactly what the chief meant. "That means they'll come for you in the night and string you up."

"There are other islands." Captain Advika clapped Szarok on the back in what was doubtless meant to be a bracing gesture, but the Uroch flinched.

It was impossible not to notice that Szarok didn't withdraw a moment later when Tegan's arm brushed his, a gesture likely imperceptible to anyone who didn't watch with such care; his shoulders relaxed a little, too, so it seemed he took some comfort in her proximity. Despite racking his brain, Morrow couldn't name a time when Tegan had touched him if he wasn't sick or injured.

"I should stay," Szarok said to Tegan, low. "The mission—"

"Will fail regardless if you don't make it back to Appleton. Staying here is suicide. It's safer to continue on, try somewhere else." She glared up at him, not seeming to see Morrow, even in her peripheral vision.

Their conversation seemed almost . . . intimate. The realization hurt, and Morrow rubbed his chest as the throbbing in his head intensified. *I should probably do . . . something.* But he'd rarely been so conscious of how useless he was, and drinking the night before didn't help. Hazy didn't begin to describe his head.

Before long, the chief cornered Morrow to interrogate him about the night before. Fortunately, he had been spinning yarns for a full tavern until ridiculously late, and the owner could attest to the fact that he'd crawled upstairs to sleep off the drink in the dormitory. As he wrapped up his account, Millie came sprinting down the road, her skirt flapping.

"I didn't get left, did I?" she wailed.

Her full weight hit his chest, hard enough to rock him sideways. Morrow caught her out of sheer self-preservation, and he patted her back amid amused chuckles from the men who had been questioning him. He tried a rueful smile.

"She's impetuous."

"This is the one you drank with last night?"

He nodded.

She appeared to notice the dark stains in the dust nearby. "Did something happen?"

"That's why they need to know where we were," he explained.

They made inquiries of Millie, but nobody seemed to suspect her, and they softened when her eyes teared up over learning that a young girl had been murdered the night before. So far none of the villagers had spoken that word, but it fit. Whoever had done such a heinous thing, Morrow hoped the village men got a chance to string him up.

Once their small group was cleared, the village chief conferred with Captain Advika. "I'd prefer it that you return to your ship. I'll send your people back as we check out their accounts."

She nodded gravely. "I won't add to your burden by arguing. Take care."

With a gesture, she led the way to the pier, where a rowboat was already waiting. The captain took the oars herself, so there was room for the rest of them. But as she hauled across the water, her expression was grim and solemn. None of them spoke, as Morrow couldn't think of a single thing to say; sometimes he guessed it was best to hold your tongue.

Back on the ship, there was only a skeletal crew aboard. Tegan and Szarok disappeared belowdecks at once, but Morrow was in no hurry to lose the feel of the sun on his face. In a few minutes, maybe, he'd go see if she could give him a headache powder. If it didn't ease, the rocking of the waves would make him sick.

"You've got a terrible case of tankard flu," Millie observed, peering at him.

Startled, he laughed and repeated, "Tankard, what?"

Her smile went shy. "Don't they put it like that in Rosemere? It's what my ma says when my dad comes in jug-bit after a night in the tavern."

"I like it. I'll definitely put it in the story."

"You're really writing one? That's incredible. Will I be in it?"

"Definitely. But if you don't do something heroic, I'll have to make it up."

Though he was teasing, she seemed to take the joke to heart. "What sort of thing do you mean? I haven't done anything but walk and scrub since we left. Oh, and I went up a tree, because of the bear."

"B-bear?" he spluttered.

"Didn't anyone tell you?"

Millie launched into a surprisingly hilarious account, and she told it well enough that he felt like he was there, chasing through the woods alongside her, scrambling up the tree and clinging to Tegan. Before she finished, he rather wished he had his journal to make some notes.

"That's going into the book for sure. But . . . weren't you frightened?"

"Terrified. But afterward, kind of proud, too, you know? The way they talk about you—Company D, I mean—it makes me think you're all so special, and I'm definitely not, but there I was, part of an adventure." She hunched her shoulders in an inward shrug.

He'd noticed she did that a lot, and self-deprecation could be charming, unless it chewed away at person's sense of self-worth. Gently, he tipped her chin up so that her gaze met his. "Don't say that. You *are* special."

"Now you're just sweet-talking me. I won't be doing your laundry, Sir Storyteller." Millie gave his fingers a little tap, her eyes playful.

"I'm devastated."

"Idiot," she said.

"Feel free to enjoy the fresh air. I'm off to seek a flu remedy."

Morrow dragged his feet on the way to the medical cupboard, for that was how large the cabin seemed. It wasn't until he reached the threshold that he realized he'd thought he would find Tegan and Szarok together. But she was sitting on the bunk, her head resting against the wall. Up close, he noticed that her face was drawn with exhaustion, shadows beneath her eyes. Guilt surged through him for staring while she rested.

"It's bad when the doctor needs tending more than the patients," he said, smiling.

Her eyes snapped open. "Looks like I fell asleep on the job. What can I do for you?"

"Anything for a headache?"

"Certainly." She slid to her feet and rummaged through the drawers until she found what she was looking for, then she spooned it into a small portion of water. "Here you are."

Grimacing as he downed it, he gasped, then said, "This is punishment."

"That's how you know the medicine is working. It'll take a little while for you to feel some relief. You can rest here for a bit if you like."

"Is that all right?"

Her smile warmed him to his bones. "Of course. If you need anything at all, just tell me."

You, he thought.

But that was a request she couldn't answer. With a groan, he rolled onto the bunk and closed his eyes. The darkness provided such sweet relief that he let out a slow breath. *I'm never drinking that much again.* Last night had been the perfect storm of a dark mood combined with generous patrons who kept plying him with ale, and the more he swallowed, the happier everything seemed.

"James?" she whispered.

"Hmm?"

"Who do you think hurt that girl?"

"I don't know. Someone who hated her or . . ."

"Or?" she prompted.

"Or someone with a twisted mind. There are people in the world—"

"Who delight in pain." Her voice was clipped, and Morrow resisted the urge to steal a peek at her expression.

"I don't know what happened. Maybe nobody ever will. There are stories of investigators with nearly superhuman prowess at working out the truth, but they seem as far-fetched as the ones with gods roaming about."

She fell silent after that; he must've dozed.

The medical cabin was empty, door latched open. As he sat up, he rubbed his head. Most of the aching had subsided, so he swung his feet to the floor and got up. Upon reaching the deck, he saw that it was quite late in the day, and it seemed as if most of the sailors had returned to the *Catalina*. They were busy adjusting lines and sails, preparing to leave with the tide. Captain Advika was shouting orders, though she spared a smile for him. A few minutes later she joined him at the rail.

"We're behind and trying to outrun those clouds," she said, frowning at the horizon. "But I have a bad feeling about us lingering in Antecost."

"A storm or a hanging . . . That's a proper devil's bargain. I won't keep you. The sooner we're underway the better."

She went about her business, and he took note of the darkening sky; it had a strange yellow cast about the edges, and the air itself tasted heavy, salted on his tongue. The last of the crew came aboard then, and they raised the anchor. In a swoop of motion the *Catalina* came about, rocking away from Antecost. A chill wind blew across his cheeks, and he huddled deeper into his jacket, watching the land recede. Trees and bluffs blurred in green and gray; the ruined white towers that lined the coast dwindled into bony fingers.

For a time it seemed their luck had turned. With Advika and Sung Ji supervising the passage away from the isle, the ship caught a current. With the wind at their back, the sails billowed.

Though the sea was rough, they navigated the shoals and managed not to crack up on any of the wrecks already littering the relatively shallow waters. Behind them, the sky still loomed ominous gray with clouds as thick as coal dust, but eventually a cry went up among the sailors, and they slapped palms.

Morrow stopped a man at random to ask, "What're we celebrating?"

"We made it out of the graveyard, lad. Port-Mer is friendly enough, but they make half their living off salvaging wrecks."

Morrow's mood brightened a bit, so he uncurled his fingers from the railing and headed for the stern. The waves got rougher, adding a stumble and skip to his step. He would've denied that he was looking for Tegan, but his casual exploration bore no fruit. Morrow didn't blame her for wandering off while he slept, but he did wonder where she'd gone. A current of unease trickled over him when he remembered how the scarred sailor had glared at her.

Thunder boomed a few moments before lightning sliced the sky with silver heat. The water rocked up in response to the wind, whitecaps nearly tall enough to sluice over the side of the boat. *I should head below.* The storm broke in earnest before he reached the stairs, and he had to grab on and ride out the lashing of icy water that flooded over him. His vision went salty and white; no telling if he'd swallowed half the gulf. Rain stung his skin like nettles, cold and relentless. The wet wood made it hard as hell to keep his footing. Morrow inched toward shelter, one hand up to block the torrent.

Captain Advika was shouting something, too far away for him to make it out, but he guessed it was an order for all idiots to take shelter. Teeth chattering, he struggled to remember where the closest deck access was. Searching with his hands as much as his eyes, he found Szarok, hemmed in by three sailors. Everyone else was battening down, so this rang all his alarm bells.

Inching closer, he heard the scarred man say, "I know damn

well you weren't with the healer all night. Why did you let her lie for you, troll?"

Morrow barely caught Szarok's faint reply. "If you know that, it means you were watching her. That angers me."

"I couldn't give a goat bollock how you feel," Scarface snapped.

"You should. I'm practically a rabid wolf, or so I'm told."

"Yeah, but you got a soft spot. The bitch doctor who shamed us, for instance."

"Is that why you attacked the girl? To vent your anger?"

A tall sailor started. "How—"

"Shut your hole." His companion twisted his arm hard enough to make him cry out. "Should've said something before; now it's too late." Scarface took a step toward Szarok, and Morrow couldn't make out his expression in the driving rain. "Oh wait—they wouldn't believe you anyway because you're a filthy beast."

"I smelled you on her, all over her. But . . . that's not proof," Szarok said. "It's enough that I know. And if you give me a reason, I'll kill you."

That, James decided, was a promise. He shivered, and not from the water slipping down his back. Probably he should intervene, but the odds weren't good in this weather. It would be tragic if he made things worse.

"I don't think so. That doctor friend of yours? She'll get hers."

Szarok snarled, the sound audible even over the tremendous storm. "If you touch her, I'll make you plead for death."

"Now!" Scarface struck as the boat rolled beneath a massive wave.

The three shoved Szarok over the side and into the maelstrom of churning water. *Hell and damnation, he can't swim.* Morrow skidded on the wet deck, rain-blind and furious, but his hands closed on thin air and cold water. Now the attackers whirled on him, probably intent on sending him down next. He used the friction on the deck to slide away, anything to keep their crime from going unpunished.

He was five feet from the rail when Tegan blasted past him. In a heartbeat, she leapt into the churning abyss after Szarok. A cry ripped from his throat, but before he could dive after her, Millie grabbed ahold of his coat, her grip implacable.

She'd brought more sailors, who surrounded the culprits. Morrow tugged at her hands; she wouldn't let go, even when the pressure had to hurt.

"No," she said. Then more firmly and with finality, *"No."*

two

the pilgrim soul

How many loved your moments of glad grace,
And loved your beauty with love false or true,
But one man loved the pilgrim soul in you,
And loved the sorrows of your changing face.

—William Butler Yeats, "When You Are Old"

The Wonders of Being Stranded

Impact hit Tegan like a full-body slap; then the icy water stole her breath. She sank down, down, down. Her wet clothes became anchors, and it took all her strength to fight to the surface. All around her, the water churned, waves threatening to submerge her. Fighting free of her pants, she bobbed and went under, swallowing a mouthful of salt water. Spitting, she caught sight of a clawed hand sinking below the surface.

He must be so afraid.

Using her ballooning pants as a buoy, she fought the water and struggled toward him. By the time she got there, he'd dropped frighteningly deep. Tegan sucked in a breath and dove, terrified that she wouldn't be able to fight upright while carrying his weight. His movements were already slowing, oxygen deprivation combined with the chill. *The Uroch can last longer on less. Maybe it will be all right.* Her hand brushed his, the other still clutching the makeshift flotation device she'd created, and she latched on.

With all her strength she pulled, until his head broke the surface. *If he wasn't unconscious, he would fight.* She couldn't tell if he was breathing, but the cold would help. *I only have a few minutes.* The boat was a dark blur, rolling wildly on the waves. If Captain Advika was trying to come about, she couldn't know exactly where they were, and Tegan's hoarse cries sank into the wind and whistled away.

In the distance she glimpsed a rocky slice, not Antecost, but one of the small barrier islands that made navigating these waters so tricky. Tegan made the only decision she could as the rain poured down and the lightning cracked. Thunder boomed as she fought the water, sometimes going under, swallowing more, but she always floated up again, determinedly hanging on to Szarok.

Closer to land, she latched onto some deadwood and heaved him over it. That let her kick with some direction, and after what seemed like forever, she finally touched bottom and slogged up the sandy slope toward the stony shore. Her bad leg burned from overexertion, but she gave herself no quarter in dragging Szarok fully out of the water. Dr. Wilson had taught her rescue breathing, but she'd never used it. Without hesitation, she went to work and didn't stop until he choked and spluttered. Then she rolled him over so he could vomit up a ton of seawater.

He went a long time without breathing. . . . Is he . . . ?

Anxious, she leaned over. "Can you speak? Do you know who I am?"

"A foolhardy healer." Anger and asphyxiation left his voice even deeper, rough with the near drowning. "Why did you follow me? You could have died."

"So could you," she said.

Shivering mitigated the ferocity of his wrath, and he evidently decided to be practical. With some help, he sat up and took in the rocky outcropping, bounded by so much rough sea.

"Where are we?"

The storm ruined visibility, though, and a boom of thunder made her jump. "We should find shelter if we can."

When she stood, his expression shifted. "Where are your trousers?"

"Just a moment."

To her relief, they were still draped over the driftwood she'd used to save Szarok. With her back turned, she scrambled into them. The cold, wet fabric felt worse than nothing at all, and the rain just exacerbated her discomfort. It blew into her eyes as the wind tangled her hair. Yet she didn't regret the impulse that had led to this rescue.

An eternity of searching later, they found shelter along the cliff, where the sea had carved a narrow channel. From the mark on the walls, the tide would rise later, but for now they could scramble onto a shelf well above the waterline. At least they were out of the wind and rain. Once the storm stopped, they'd probably find the *Catalina* searching for them.

"There's no way to build a fire in this gale. Come, before we freeze."

It took her a moment to grasp that he was offering to share body heat. She crawled closer and nestled into his side. At first he was so painfully cold that it made things worse, but soon their skin reacted in physical magic, radiating warmth back and forth. She let out an exhausted sigh and stared up at the delicate stone teeth that rimmed the ceiling.

"How do you feel?"

"Half dead." He didn't seem to be joking.

"I'm sorry it took me so long."

"Save your strength. We don't know how long we'll need to survive here."

That sounded like good advice, but it was hard to relax in cold, wet clothes. At some point, she must have dozed because when she woke, they were tangled together like lovers. She froze, heart galloping in her chest. But he seemed to be sleeping, too, and the fear faded into an echo. Tegan already knew he didn't like being touched by humans, so there was no way he would've done this to get closer to her.

Outside, she heard no sign of the raging storm. The tide had come and gone, judging by the newly slick stones that she passed in slipping out of the cave. *Early morning,* she guessed, by the pink and gold fingers of light trickling above the horizon. In contrast to the dark torrent the day before, the sea was as calm and smooth as a mirror.

And I don't see the ship.

The situation wasn't good. *Time to see how bad it is.* Her pants crunched when she walked—not a good sign. This island was tiny, more of a skerry, but it did have trees, at least, which suggested some kind of life. Seabirds flew overhead now that the weather had cleared, and there were fish in the sea, provided they could figure out how to catch them.

Water will be our primary concern.

The sun felt good on her shoulders after a nightmare of a night. She followed the shore around until the land became a little more passable, and then headed away from the water, seeking higher ground where she could scout. Loose rocks slid underfoot and complicated her progress, but soon she reached the small summit. In the distance, a signal tower rose, painted with symbols she didn't recognize. The red paint made the sigils stand out against the pale stone; she guessed it was less than half a day's hike from where she stood.

Retracing her steps, she found Szarok outside the sea cave, examining the footprints she'd left. *A few moments more and he'd be tracking me.*

Tegan smiled. "I found shelter for us. We might be able to signal passing ships, too."

"You are extraordinarily capable."

That rang more like an observation than flattery, and for that reason, it settled into an empty space in her soul as the highest praise of all. "Thanks."

"I would like to understand . . . ," he started, then trailed off.

It was useless to press until he'd collected his thoughts. They walked for a while in silence, up the incline to the overlook, and then onward along the rocky path. The skerry held hints of green and scrubby trees, but it wasn't densely wooded like Rosemere or Antecost. *Because we're farther north?* So far she hadn't seen anything larger than sea fowl, though she'd noted two species she had never seen before anywhere else. Both were white and black, but nestled low on the rocks, there appeared to be a colony of birds that didn't fly. They waddled instead and dove into the water, possibly in search of fish. Even the wonders of being stranded fascinated her.

"Do you know what those are?" she asked.

Szarok studied the birds, then said, "Dinner?" Possibly this was a joke.

Maybe not.

Either way, she laughed.

Finally, about halfway to the signal tower, he tried again with the question he'd swallowed before. "Why did you lie for me?"

Oh. That's unexpected.

"It was only a tiny fabrication. We were together most of the night, after all, and I *know* you didn't harm her. There's too much at stake. Even if she had come at you with a knife, you would've taken the hurt for your people."

"You're so sure." He sounded bemused.

She stole a look. His eyes were distant, focused on their goal, but he seemed thoughtful as well.

"I am," she agreed. "And it was proven by your confrontation with those monsters."

"Monsters?"

"The sailors who murdered Malena."

"You say that so easily of your own people."

Tegan kicked a rock with a quietly vicious maneuver. "Humans are often the worst monsters of all. Besides, I know this about you. . . . Like Deuce, you're a hunter, not a killer."

"Yes." When he gazed at her in obvious pleasure at the description, his eyes glowed luminous and deep with darkening gold, somehow soft at the same time.

She'd never thought of him as warm before, but a little trill ran down her back and settled at the base of her spine, so that each step felt good and right, as long as she stood beside him. "Anyway, that's why."

"And why did you dive into the water for me?" This was the second time he'd asked.

Tegan sensed she wouldn't get away with deflecting this time. If she did that, he'd just ask again tomorrow, and the next day, and the next, until she got tired. "It was right." She struggled to find the answer that didn't give away too much. "And it would be too sad if you had nobody who would."

"My people would. My kin." Then he tipped his head with a ripening frown. "Rather, they would *want* to. But our fear runs deep. Even now it is hard for me to accept that I didn't die."

"What do you believe about the afterlife?" she asked.

He shook his head, seeming puzzled. "After life, there is death. Before we die, we choose someone to receive our memories. Thus, when we go, we leave what we learned."

So if something happens to him here, his memories are lost?

"If you want to know, ask."

Her cheeks heated, but . . . she did. *Hopefully this isn't painful.*

"Not lost," he said. "Diffused. I can choose to . . . let them go, uncontrolled, like it was in the days before we Awakened and learned we *could* choose. That is why all of us have memories of drowning. But if this happens, we consider it tragic. Much of my essence would be lost."

"Then I'll have to take good care of you," she said, teasing.

He paused. "You already do."

They were nearly to the signal tower when he spoke again. "What do humans think?"

"About what?"

"Dying."

"The afterlife? It depends. Some people think there's a paradise waiting for people's souls, and that bad ones, like the sailors who killed Malena, will go to eternal torment."

Szarok shook his head. "So you think there is a second life waiting? Is that why some of your people live as if this one doesn't matter?"

"Not everyone. I don't know what I think. Mostly I don't worry about it. I envy the Uroch for being able to pass down memories. The idea of preserving knowledge that way is . . ." She couldn't even think of a superlative strong enough.

"I never thought to meet one of your people who admired mine."

She didn't know what to say to that, so she let it be. Rising before them, the tower seemed even taller when they finally reached it. "Do you know what it means?"

Szarok shook his head. "I have a faint recollection of seeing these symbols before, but my ancestor could not read them. Nor can I."

The red paint seemed like a warning, but they couldn't afford to be particular. Yet the door was boarded over—from the outside—another discovery that chilled the blood in her veins. Szarok was examining the boards, half-rotten wood, somehow affixed into the structure itself, which was made of brick.

"I don't know of anything that could do this," she said.

"Some old-world machine, perhaps?"

She'd seen many things in the ruins. None of them explained this.

"Let's go a little farther first. There was something . . ." As she headed down the gentle slope, she spotted a cluster of metal buildings. They had similar structures in Winterville and Soldier's Pond, though these looked older still and half rusted into wreckage. But that wasn't what alarmed her most.

Tegan stopped walking.

"What's wrong? What is it?" While Szarok might be able to read her reaction, he didn't know enough about human customs to be frightened. Yet.

"That's a graveyard," she said.

Past the metal shantytown, row upon row of graves were marked with hand-carved crosses. But as the rows went, their quality deteriorated. The ones she presumed to be oldest were pretty, ornate even. But by the end, they were only rough hanks of wood or bone lashed together. She walked and counted. *Two hundred and seven people died here. Why?*

Squaring her shoulders, she came back to the metal box houses. One by one she inspected them, fearing the worst. They sat empty, save one. In that space she found two mostly decomposed bodies, their hands outstretched toward each other, and a smaller one curled onto its side between them. While she couldn't see what had hurt the two larger victims, the little one had a clear dent in its head.

"What happened here?" he asked.

She shook her head. "Whatever it was, they were the last. There was nobody left to bury them."

"We could, if you think it's important."

Tegan considered. Sensibility wouldn't save them. Once they took care of basic needs, they could revisit the issue. "We have other priorities. Let's finish our inventory."

The best discovery was an old well. Szarok drew up a bucket, sniffed, and proclaimed it clean. Tegan sighed in relief. While he might not be able to detect all bacteria, she felt safe in drinking anything he approved. The abandoned metal shacks yielded a meager store of useful supplies, including a lighter like Fade had. There were also some ancient, yellowed magazines, some dirty clothing, and medicines she wouldn't dare use.

If we get sick, we're in trouble.

"To the tower?" Szarok asked eventually.

"I think so. Just be ready."

It was improbable they'd encounter a live threat, as anything that might've been walled up in there must have long since starved to death. Still, she shivered as he pried the boards loose one by one, each thunk of wood echoing in her heartbeat. When he finished, it revealed an average door, painted red and touched with rust. It wasn't locked, and it swung open with a groan.

I'm not scared. . . . Why am I scared?

The rasp and crackle of her salt-stiff clothes sounded ridiculously loud. Tegan peered inside and found a round room with a metal staircase leading up in the middle of it. The walls were white-painted brick with moss or lichens growing in spots. Most of the furniture was broken, just a couple of intact crates here and there. Above, there was only silence.

"Come," said Szarok. "Hold on to me. The steps may be unsafe, and it's my turn to catch you when you fall."

The way he said it made everything all right. In Company D, she had always been the weak one, the girl who needed extra protection. No matter how hard she trained with James, she was always a step behind Deuce and Fade, who'd spent their lives fighting, and the professional soldiers with years of training. Even the poet who taught her first and later became her friend watched when he thought she wasn't looking.

James always acted like I was seconds away from horrible doom.

But with Szarok, it seemed natural to just . . . take turns. He took for granted that she was clever and competent, and he *trusted* her. A little breath almost became a hiccup because everyone always wanted to protect her, a completely separate impulse. In her deepest heart, Tegan had always feared the message she must be sending. Because nobody ever, ever—

Until now.

Her heartbeat quickened. Tegan remembered the strength of

his hand, how warm and firm it was when he'd led her to a water-fall in the middle of the night. She might well go anywhere he wished to take her, learn anything he wanted to teach.

She locked her fingers with his, staring up at the endless spire of ascending darkness, and she was not afraid. "Lead on."

Kinship

The stairs were thin and rusted, but they held. Tegan counted more than two hundred steps before they reached the top. Machinery filled the open space, a lot of ruined bits and broken things. Glass crunched beneath her feet from some kind of massive lens. However this thing had worked, it would be next to impossible to get it running again.

Yet . . . the wreckage spoke volumes.

Someone or something had slowly gone mad, alone in here. Gouges on the walls, scratches on the floor. Everything that could be smashed had been. The violence appeared to have escalated as time had worn on. Tegan followed an old blood trail until she found the source. Beside her, Szarok's breathing sounded hoarse and his fingers tightened until his talons pricked her. She didn't mind the pain; at a moment like this, it seemed right.

There could be no question that they were staring at the desiccated corpse of one of his ancestors. Time had not treated the old creature kindly, so the sunken features were even more monstrous. The most horrific aspect wasn't even the decay, but . . . this one had eaten part of its own arm, trying to survive, and then moved on to its left leg. Imagining the agony of a hunger that had driven such self-mutilation, she shuddered so hard, she almost fell over.

Humans don't do that. They just starve.

His voice was calm. "We should go. There's nothing of use here."

Somehow she descended all those stairs without weeping. But as they stepped out into the cool, clean air, she had to know. "How? How do you see that and not—"

"Not what?"

"React." She didn't mean for it to be an accusation, but it became one. That word hung between them like a pointing finger.

"You think I feel nothing? Everywhere I turn, there are reminders that we were horrific beyond belief. I have memories of my ancestors devouring themselves—and each other—in fits of mindless hunger. And that's why I have to be so much better than I want to be. Because every second that I'm alive, with every beat of my heart, I fear we could become that again. And if I changed, I wouldn't even mind."

His fear and rage hit her like a wave; she wobbled under the intensity, but in a way, it was glorious, too, like an unexpected storm after so many hot, still days. In the aftermath, he was shaking, just like her. But nothing else. And when he realized she hadn't let go of his hand, he regulated his breathing, shoulders slumped.

"Don't do that with me."

"What?" he whispered.

"Be better. Just be . . . you. If you're angry, tell me, especially if I do something wrong. Right now it's more important than ever for us to . . . cooperate." That wasn't the word she wanted, but it came out, serviceable but imprecise.

"You unsettle me." He drew in one deep breath, then another, staring up at the sky.

Tegan didn't ask why. She changed the subject.

"If we clean out the top floor, we can settle in downstairs."

Hopefully he wouldn't ask why that was necessary. She didn't relish explaining that she couldn't sleep with so much pain and tragedy above her.

He only nodded. "Let's bury them all together."

From what she recalled, his people didn't much care about funeral rites, but the body had to be removed from the signal tower for her peace of mind, and it seemed disrespectful to take care of only the human remains. She volunteered for digging duty, as she'd much preferred shifting earth to transporting the dead. Szarok lashed together some of the wood from the barricade and made a makeshift sled. Soon they were ready for a memorial, and it was hard to know what to say for these poor strangers. Tegan whispered a prayer she'd memorized as a child, and it took much less time to replace the dirt than it had to scoop it out.

When they finished, the sun had skated toward the far horizon, and her throat was nearly closed with thirst. She put her face into the rusty bucket as soon as Szarok pulled it up. In fact, he had to pull her away with a quiet shake of her head. *I'll get sick. I've gone without before.* Their clothes badly needed washing; her skin was starting to hurt, both from the stiff fabric and the salt crusted in her crevices. But she had nothing else to wear, and it was too cold to run naked while she washed and dried her shirt and pants.

"I took so many comforts for granted," she mumbled.

"Tegan," Szarok called.

She hadn't even noticed him moving away from the well. Hunger must be messing up her concentration, and she did feel a little dizzy as she hurried toward him. "I hope it's good news."

"I don't know what's in here, but I thought we should open it together."

"It" was a sturdy chest fastened shut with metal tabs. Szarok fiddled around until they popped up, one by one, and as he raised the lid, the trunk made a sort of *shhhh* sound, old air escaping. She held her breath as he pulled out the contents. Nothing edible, but this looked like military gear, similar to kits she'd seen in Soldier's Pond. Certainly there were uniforms, musty but wearable with some scrubbing.

"This will be useful," she said, playing with the various attachments.

Knife and fork, pick, a pronged implement she didn't recognize. *If need be, I could use this as a doctor's tool.*

Tegan found some cookware, a metal pan that could double as an eating dish. There was also a heavy cylinder that did nothing, but it had a lens like the broken one upstairs. *Flashlight.* Dr. Wilson had told her about them, but said it was rare to get them working. Finding a power source was problematic. This seemed a little different than the ones he'd shown her.

First, she couldn't open it to look inside. She shook it and nothing happened. Flipping the button offered no answers, either.

"Hm. This was a light, but it won't turn on."

His gaze flickered toward her discoveries, then he said, "You should wash up at the well and change your clothes. I can smell the sores. You'll be bleeding soon." His tone was matter of fact, but she squirmed over knowing he could discern so much just from standing nearby.

"What about you?"

"I'm going hunting."

Since she couldn't help with that, Tegan nodded and carried a change of clothes toward the well. *Best to get this over with.* She stripped, rinsed off with the icy water, and then put on the musty clothes. *Still better than what I had on.* Afterward, she used the cook pan and the bucket to wash out her sea-soaked garments.

If people lived here, there must be a better way.

But she wasn't so sure that was the right word. It was more like they had been confined here and left to die slowly. Like . . . Something about that seemed familiar. She searched hard for that tantalizing memory, and as she went back toward the signal tower to clean, it came to her.

Leper colonies.

As part of her studies, Dr. Wilson had told her stories about how doctors had failed, about the danger of superstition interfering with treatment. *Because we didn't understand the disease,* he'd said, *or how it spread, we feared it. Because we feared it, we failed our patients.* Long ago, in the old world, they used to send sick people away so they couldn't infect anyone else. The conditions were terrible, and people never got better. They just died where other people didn't have to watch. According to Dr. Wilson, it wasn't just the sick who ended up in places like that. Sometimes there were wars and people lost their homes, so they got on ships, not because they had somewhere to go, but because it was more terrifying to stay. But then other people wouldn't let them get *off* the ships, and then they got sick even if they weren't before. Then nobody would ever say, *Welcome; you're home now.* So they were sent off to places like this. Like the leper colonies. Where they suffered, hurt, and died . . . and nobody cared.

That's what this place feels like.

Tegan swallowed the tears that wouldn't help the dead. While Szarok got dinner, she had to do what she could to fashion some shelter. It took longer than she wanted to put all the shards in the crates from downstairs. Right now she couldn't decide how they could best use the glass, but they had so little, it was inconceivable to chuck it away. The crates had a brand on the side— PROPERTY OF—but she didn't recognize the last word. There were also more characters like the ones painted on the signal tower.

Trudging up and down the steps so many times left her woozy, but eventually the top floor was as clean as she could make it. Tegan stacked all the machine parts that looked like they might be useful and then went down for the last time today, she hoped. Down here, the brick floor was relatively clean and dry, but the moss and lichens needed to go. Wrapping her sleeve around her palm, she got a shard of glass and scraped the walls with meticulous care. Her arm ached as she went, but it would be worth it.

Someone clearly lived here at some point. They might be able to use the metal stove, provided the pipe wasn't defective. Exhausted, she put the glass back and organized the broken furniture according to what might be usable. By the time Szarok returned, she had the space beneath the stairs in decent condition.

"Dinner," he said.

Smells good.

Mouth watering, she followed him outside, where he'd built a spit and was roasting an enormous bird. That was a gift for her, clearly, because he didn't even like his food cooked. She smiled up at him in speechless gratitude. He returned the look with a sweet softness that made her heart quiver.

"You've done so much," he said. "Do you mind watching the food while I wash?"

"Of course not. I left the spare clothing in the chest."

"Don't forget to turn it."

Pointedly, she turned away so he knew she wouldn't spy on him. Tegan sank down with a muffled groan and tended to her meal. Szarok finished his bath before she was done, so he joined her as the sunset rioted in glorious colors overhead. If they didn't get rescued soon, winter would be difficult. There were tons of seabirds now, but they might fly away when the snow settled.

"Just a little longer."

He shook his head. "I've already eaten."

"Sorry. How was it?"

"Not bad. Not as delicious as the deer on Antecost. I think it's safe to eat now."

In her haste she burned her fingers and dropped the bird in the ash near the fire. It didn't deter her, however; Tegan only dusted it off, broke off some meat, blew on it, then crammed it into her mouth. It had a strong flavor, but it wasn't bad.

"Did you see anything else?" she asked.

"Foxes, plenty of them. They must prey on the seabirds. There's also a horned thing running around. They're fast."

"It could be worse."

Tegan finished her food and went back to study the metal

houses one last time. They contained pitiful rusted furnishings, nothing much of use, but she stared hard at those stained, foul-smelling mattresses. *Maybe . . .* She got out the knife and sliced them open. They were full of disgusting foam and dead insects and coils of wire, but the fabric might be salvageable. She slit two of them all the way open and shook them until her arms hurt, then she turned them inside out. The interior was much cleaner by comparison.

Szarok found her as the light faded. "What are you doing?"

"Making a bed. I hope. Were there lots of loose feathers where the seabirds nest?"

"Yes, a carpet of them."

"Bring back as many as you can."

While he was gone, she unraveled some thread from her shirt and stitched together the fabric. It was poor work, unlike when she closed a wound, but it would hold. Then she ventured out into the field past the tiny village and harvested the dry rustling grass, as much as she could carry. Another trip and she picked sweet-smelling purple flowers. When Szarok returned with a massive load of feathers, she was stuffing the mattress in great handfuls.

"Shove the feathers in," she told him.

The end result wasn't pretty as she stitched it up, but it looked more comfortable than the brick floor. At least the nights weren't cold enough to worry about blankets. With an exhausted sigh, she tilted her head toward the signal tower in silent invitation. He responded by lifting the mattress in his arms like it was his bride and arranging it near the ancient, potbellied stove.

"I cleaned the pipe," he said. "So we can build a fire if it gets cold."

"Let's just go to sleep."

As she moaned and rolled onto the mattress, he hesitated. "I can—"

"It's for both of us," she mumbled. "Don't be stubborn. We'll be warmer together, and it's not like this is the first time."

Mentally she wandered through the times they'd slept together. *In Antecost, on the ship, last night in the cave . . . This is the fourth occasion.*

"True." Careful as a feral cat, he tucked in behind her.

Someone else might have scared her so much, she couldn't relax, but this bed was lovely, all cut grass, wildflowers, and heavenly softness compared to the rock ledge. Paired with his heat at her back, she fell hard into sleep and woke only when he rolled away early that morning. Half awake and complaining, she rolled into the warm spot he'd vacated.

She found him later, skinning some prey. He'd prepared the meat and hung the skin in a way that she recognized from the fur and leather workers in Salvation. With their immediate needs tended, it was hard to know exactly what she should do, but reason asserted itself. Offering a tentative smile, she headed past him, down the rocky slope toward the beach.

"Where are you going?" he asked.

"To build a signal. We need to pile some rocks on the beach and hope a ship passes close enough to see it."

"A fire would do the same, but I fear wasting our fuel. To set a blaze large enough, we'd need to burn all the dry brush and—"

"We might not make it through the winter. Let's be cautious." Tegan agreed that approach was wise.

He nodded and set aside his task in lieu of working on hers. Together, they dragged enough rocks to form a V with the point heading out to sea. Szarok seemed puzzled by this idea, so Tegan explained, "I read this in a book. If you do this, it creates a tidal pool. Fish can swim in when the water is high but when the tide ebbs, they can't get out again."

"And we eat them," he said with apparent delight.

"That's the idea. We should also be able to eat the seaweed." She knelt to examine the swirling green stuff in the water.

"You want me to consume sea leaves?" His expression said that was very unlikely.

"Well, I will. I can't get all the nutrition I need from meat. This may not taste very good, but I need to swallow a little now and then."

"There are some plants," he said.

Tegan sighed, wishing she had more varied knowledge. "I don't know that much about foraging. We lived off the land some during the war, but I was never in charge of that."

"No, I'm sure these were planted on purpose. I've seen your folk digging them up."

She perked up. "Show me."

Szarok delivered them to a ragged patch behind the signal tower. When he churned up the earth with his claws, he produced an extremely lumpy potato. "There used to be more, I think. This is what survived."

"We should dig up all the ones we can find then. They'll rot in the ground if we don't."

"You know *I* don't want them," he said simply. "But since you're kin, I'll always get food for you."

Over the years she'd known James, he had said much sweeter things, so why did the simplicity of Szarok's words make her insides flutter? Truth be told, she didn't enjoy it; the feeling unsettled her. Then she realized she had chosen *his* word.

Unsettled.

"It will be a long, hard winter if nobody looks for us," she said then.

Szarok touched her shoulder, briefly. "We'll find a way."

The Last of Her Blood

The Isle of the Dead was inhospitable but not impossible to survive.

That was what Szarok privately called the place where they had landed. Sometimes he wasn't altogether sure that they'd survived the swim, but if not, he'd ended up in a human afterlife instead of releasing his memories. And that, that could *not* be true. So he helped Tegan fashion a relatively comfortable nest.

Between his hunting and the garden that had been left to grow wild, there would be enough food for a while. Down by the sea, the tidal pool they'd created did trap fish now and then. He savored them fresh and raw; she preferred hers cleaned and cooked.

The first few days, she watched the horizon as if she expected to see sails at any moment.

"They're looking for us," she said.

For you, perhaps. Szarok understood that she was a person of importance, a hero from the war and well educated. She knew how to heal the sick and comfort the heart when it ached. At first he resisted that gentling, but now that he'd stopped, it was easier to be with her. Sometimes he even forgot she was human, since they slept in the same bed and she smelled . . . familiar now.

"We have the resources to last for a while."

She nodded.

In the signal tower, she had a crate of tubers salvaged from that sad garden. *How many seasons did the vegetables grow untended, rot away, and go back to seed before we came?* There was nothing to explain who the bodies in the graveyard were or why they died here.

It had been almost a week.

Though he didn't say it aloud, the captain must have given them up for dead. *I would be, if not for her.* He had never owed anyone so much before, and the debt sat heavily on his shoulders. The least he could do was hunt and protect her with his life. So far, no serious threats had appeared, but this place echoed with sadness and pain, an ominous shadow falling across both of them. Each day they remained stranded, the People would be suffering. More than anything else, he hated being helpless.

"The sun is bright today. It won't always be. Come." She beckoned.

Already he'd grown too accustomed to her comfort and warmth. What he'd learned from Tegan contrasted so sharply with the pain and hate in his memories that his head ached with it. Yet he took the necessary steps toward her and let her link their fingers. She led him away from the signal tower, down toward the big brine. The only useful aspect of that aquatic terror was that it evaporated, leaving salt behind. Thanks to that salt, he was slowly curing skins to serve as their winter nest. While he hoped rescue came before then, it seemed foolish to bet their lives on it.

Silvered by the sunlight, the water lapped at the stony shore. A couple of fish swam lazily in their tidal pool, trapped but not alarmed by it. That wouldn't start until they left the water, flopping and desperate and choking. *That's how I feel in your world,* he told them silently.

"What are we doing?"

"No matter how it happens, we'll leave this island by water," she said. "So I'm teaching you to swim."

He bared his teeth. "My people cannot swim."

"That's because you've never learned. Even if there are some physiological differences, I refuse to believe you cannot learn to float. From a scientific perspective, that makes no sense. Rather, I suspect all the drowning memories you share as a species make you prone to panic in the water, and so it becomes a self-fulfilling prophecy."

Szarok stiffened. "You're saying we sink because we believe we cannot swim."

"That has to be part of it."

"But—" His protest terminated when she tugged him toward the water. Fear sealed his throat, so he could only snarl in word-less antipathy.

"We're only going this far today. You don't have to get undressed. Just let the water touch your feet. That's all." She stepped forward so that the waves washed over her toes. "Come on. I won't let anything happen to you."

Her smile drew him unwillingly. Once, he found her face so awful and strange, but now he saw only kindness. Before he realized his own intent, somehow he was standing in the icy water. His heartbeat spiked, and for the first few seconds there was only distant screaming in his head. When that cleared, he breathed a bit better. Her hand tightened on his. Today the waves were fairly calm, unlike the storm over the open sea. There was even a sort of terrible beauty about the emptiness where ocean met sky.

"I'm not afraid of drowning on land," he muttered.

"Then you should enjoy this. Just take a walk with me with-out leaving the water."

His claws dug into the sand, leaving divots that the water smoothed away. Over his shoulder, he watched this erasure. Tegan turned to look, too, but she was smiling.

"It gives you hope, doesn't it?"

"No."

"When I see that, it makes me think that no matter how bad it is, given time, things will eventually get washed away."

Szarok glanced at the water again, trying to see it with her eyes. "My feet are cold."

"Just a little longer."

That turned out to be the length of the shore, but she eventually let him retreat. Szarok prided himself on tolerating the lesson, and afterward, while they were eating the fish he'd speared with his claws in the tidal pool, he realized that he remembered the heat of her fingers more than the cold water on his feet.

"Tomorrow we'll do a little more."

"This is a waste of time. I cannot learn."

"Wouldn't you rather test if that's true? The Uroch never had a teacher before."

"Is that what you are?" he asked quietly. "My teacher?"

"In some ways. Just as you are mine. We're on a road nobody has ever walked before, and that means we can only learn from each other."

Reluctantly he smiled. "Learning again. You are obsessed."

"Is that a problem?"

"I can think of worse fates," he said.

Normally he stood watch for a couple of hours to make sure she didn't feel too nervous to sleep. But they had been on the island long enough that he felt sure there were no other predators. The foxes posed no threat and couldn't get through the door besides. So when she retired, he went with her.

"You're not staying up?"

"Not anymore."

The long look she leveled at him prickled a little, but it wasn't unpleasant. "Good night."

She fell asleep much faster than he. For countless moments longer he listened to her breathe. Perhaps she trusted everyone like this, but her ease with him seemed like a gift. Carefully, so as not to startle her, he reached out to touch the dark strands fanned out between them. Her hair was rough, but that might be because she couldn't wash it properly. It smelled a little, mostly of smoke, but there were also familiar echoes, likely reflected from his own skin. Slowly, he curled a lock around his finger and admired the ring he'd made.

Generally, the People didn't bond as humans did. Rather they cared for families as an extended clan, and heart-bonds waxed and waned freely. As vanguard, however, he had no such liberty. In human towns, he saw mated pairs cleave to each other long after breeding season passed. He had assumed it was just . . . different, but now—he fell asleep wondering.

At dawn, he stripped down and went hunting—not for seabirds or tidal pool fish, but for one of the horned creatures. The way the thing moved made Szarok believe it would taste similar to venison. It took him several hours, but he finally ambushed one and wounded it badly enough that it couldn't use the terrain to get away. With great delight, he drank down several mouthfuls of hot, delicious blood.

A noise nearby made him turn, and he found Tegan frozen behind him. *I must look terrifying.* But before he could decide how to react, she came forward. If she had been shocked at how bloody he was and the fact that he chose to stalk his prey in his bare skin, she didn't show it. But clothing could not be quieted, and it often carried smells that would give a hunter away.

"Do you need help getting the goat back to camp?"

Relief surged through him. "This looks different than the ones from the mainland."

"It's probably wild or inbred or both. Look at those horns." She leaned down to inspect the way they curved.

"I can carry it. But . . . how did you find me?" He'd thought humans weren't particularly good at tracking.

"Trade secret," she teased.

"It's unkind to reject my desire to learn." It felt . . . strange to joke with her while he stood bare skinned and covered in blood.

But it shifted things, too. The ache in his heart faded, as there was no reason to be wary. *Nothing I am will frighten her. Nothing of mine will repel her.* He felt this in his bones. No point in pretending Tegan of the Staff was just a human anymore. He had no way to express how clever, special, and wonderful he found her, but he hoped that she could feel it, even if the right human words never came. Covered in blood, he couldn't touch her.

But . . . he wanted to.

"I watched the birds," she said. "As they scattered and flew. Then the foxes. They all seemed to be running away from you, so I guessed. And got lucky."

Satisfied and impressed, he answered her initial question. "No, I don't need help. I'll eat my breakfast, then deliver yours."

"I'll head back then."

"Before you go . . ."

Tegan turned with an inquiring look. "Hmm?"

"I want to make a deal."

She narrowed her eyes. "I'm listening."

"If I continue with these swimming lessons, you learn more Uroch. I miss hearing it."

To his surprise, she brightened as if he'd offered her a present. "Done. I can't promise I'll be good at it, but I *do* want to learn."

"Thank you," he said.

She smiled and waved, heading back toward the settlement. In time, he'd feel comfortable eating in front of her, but being careful of human sensibilities had been ingrained in him as he trained to become the vanguard of the People: learning human ways, their speech, discovering what alarmed and frightened them. For him it had been just another sort of camouflage, useful for the hunt. Never could he have imagined that a human female would make him more at home in her presence than he had been anywhere else in life.

Later he met her at the shore, resigned if not excited. Tegan knelt and rolled his trousers up to his knees, then she took his hand. "We're going a little deeper today."

His expression must have said something funny, because she laughed.

"Why . . . ?"

"I've rarely seen such a sour face. Don't worry; you can do this."

When she walked out into the water, he planted his feet. "How did you learn to swim anyway? Who taught you?"

"Are you doubting my credentials?"

"No. I just want to know about you."

A shadow flickered behind her eyes, but it wasn't bad enough to steal her smile. "All right. One story, then we go out. Promise?"

"I promise."

She made him stand with his feet in the water while she spoke. "The first fourteen years of my life, I lived in Gotham. Most Uroch just call them ruins, I think?"

"We don't often remember names," he confirmed. "Impressions of a place are more common. Danger, fear, anger, pain, hunger . . . or rarely, kindness."

"Like with Millie."

"Yes."

Nodding, Tegan went on, "The part of the ruins I lived in used to be a school, or that's what my uncle Walter said. I had one mom, Teresa, and many uncles, and a few aunties. There were cousins, too, but they weren't all my blood."

"So you were raised like me. In a clan of kin." Suddenly intrigued, he puzzled over that. *Could that be why she's more like me than other humans?*

"Kind of. Mostly they were survivors who found each other and tried to hang on. But we had no doctors. So when people got sick, they died so fast. Illnesses I *know* I could treat now with minimal facilities and basic herbs."

"So there were humans who lived almost like the Uroch," he said softly.

"Worse than us, definitely. The worst dangers came from humans." She kicked at the water, sending splashes of it rippling outward. "When your people started changing, they began emerging from under the ruins. Before then it seemed as if they were afraid of the light or something."

"It hurt," he murmured. "And I still don't like it. At the brightest, it stings my eyes. My cloak is not only to keep me from human sight."

"So I'm torturing you doubly now, with sun and sea."

Szarok pressed her hand lightly. "Worth it. Now tell me how you learned to swim."

"Right. Well, at this school where we lived, there were big basins that caught rainwater. So when they filled up and the sun came out, somebody would stand watch while Uncle Walter gave me lessons. How to float, how to paddle, when to hold my breath. He even taught me the trick with my pants, twisting them into a flotation device. He said"—her voice shook, and she lowered her chin, probably not wanting him to see her tear-filled eyes— "knowing how to swim could save my life. And it has, twice now."

"Mine as well," he said gravely. "It sounds as if you cared for him deeply. Was he kin?"

"Only in the sense that he helped raise me. My uncle Tomas was my only blood kin, and he died before my mother."

Listening to her quiet account of how everyone she had known and loved had left her behind—without the comfort of their memories—it was impossible that his heart didn't twist and throb in his chest. Her old sadness swelled like the salt water lapping about his feet so that the two scents entwined, seaweed slipping about his ankles.

"I had no idea you are the last of your blood."

Tegan flinched so hard that he almost lost his grip on her hand. He'd meant it as a condolence of sorts. "Was that wrong to say?"

Mouth compressed, she just shook her head.

"You said I must tell you if you anger me. Is the reverse not also true?"

"I'm not angry. I'm just . . . not ready to talk. Someday, maybe. Which . . . I hope you'll accept for the compliment it is, since I swore I'd never speak of it again."

Szarok read the sincerity in her gaze and secreted away the promise of *maybe* and *someday*. Just when he thought he couldn't admire her more, he learned something that made her seem more wondrous. Any more brightness, and he would soon have no room inside for the warmth she kindled.

"I understand."

"But I can offer this instead. It's something I've never told anyone. When I was young, everyone died, one by one. Except for three, two of my uncles and me. One morning, I woke up and they were just . . . gone." She squeezed her eyes shut.

Szarok put one hand on her shoulder, unsure if that was right. When she leaned forward and rested her brow against his chest, he let that loose embrace stand. There could be no crowding her, but he wanted her to feel his skin and understand that even if she was the last of her blood, she was also the closest of his kin. Quietly, he rubbed his cheek against the top of her head, leaving his scent as a silent marker.

"They abandoned you?" he asked eventually.

She lifted a shoulder, not stirring. "I always secretly hoped that something terrible happened to them. Isn't that awful? But . . . the alternative is that after raising me for thirteen years, they thought it would be too much trouble to save me, too."

"I'm sorry." That was inadequate, but she seemed to take

some comfort in the slow tap of his palm on her shoulder, keeping time to their pulse.

Szarok doubted that she noticed, but her heart settled into rhythm with his, pounding a soundless message. She shifted a little now and then, but he remained steady and calm. *I will be home and shelter for you. I will be an island where the water never rises.* How long they stood that way, he had no idea.

Eventually she straightened and gave him a smile. "Well, this lesson is an unqualified success. You didn't even realize."

"What?" He saw only her eyes, her hair, her face. The rest of the world was gray and indistinct, unimportant even, in the face of her pain.

"Look how deep we've come."

Somehow, while holding her close, he hadn't even noticed as they waded into the sea, now swirling around his waist.

A Tale of Three Hangings

<hr />

Apall hung over the *Catalina*.

With the murderers locked away, they'd spent two whole days searching after the storm broke, but found no signs of Tegan or Szarok. The gulf was thick with skerries, some no more than a rock big enough for resting seabirds, while others could hide a whole village. Advika came to Morrow on the third morning, her face set in somber lines.

"Captain," he said.

"I'm sorry about your friends. But we've got to head for port now, or I won't get the supplies delivered before the ice starts forming. I won't risk these waters too deep in winter."

"We could just toss the culprits overboard and search a little longer." When she laughed, Morrow guessed that meant she thought he was joking.

Then the captain shook her head. "We have to deliver them to the family they wronged. It's the only justice that girl will get, and it's less than she deserves."

For a moment the sorrow receded enough to him to be drenched in shame. He wasn't the only person in the world who had lost someone, who was suffering. Sometimes Morrow suspected he might actually die of the tightness in his chest. *I should've saved her.* But Malena's family must be feeling even worse, because while he could cling to the faint possibility that Tegan had survived, they had no such hope.

"Do you think they'd like it if I wrote a song or a poem for Malena? I could dedicate it in my next book."

Her smile warmed her whole face. "I'm sure. That would be a comfort to any heart."

"Then I'll work on that on the way to Antecost."

She stared out to sea. "I wish I had a mirror that would let me gaze into a man's soul. That way, I'd never take on somebody who could do such an evil thing."

"It's not your fault," he said, a sort of rote assurance.

But the woman shook her head. "I feel the weight, no matter what you say. If they hadn't sailed with me, that girl would still be alive. They did the killing, but I judged wrong."

With a faint sigh, the captain strode away to confer with her first mate. Sung Ji was hard at work in the forecastle, a term Morrow had picked up along the way. He didn't pause to dip into their conversation. Instead he went below and snitched a bottle from the bags of one of the criminals currently confined. The rotgut tasted like evil and burning, but he downed it all anyway, then fell back into his hammock.

The next day, he woke with a pounding head and a knot in his stomach. Morrow staggered onto the deck without washing, and as he stood at the railing, he thought about leaning forward. Just a little, and a little more, until his feet left the deck, and the next wave, the next rough wave— But before he finished that thought, Millie dashed toward him, her eyes wider than usual. She grabbed his arm and jerked him toward the access to the lower deck.

"I can't do this; I need some help. He won't be still."

His mind felt like it was full of mud. "What?"

"Just come on," she said impatiently.

A moment later he understood. A sailor was pacing in the infirmary, blood soaking a cloth wrapped around his hand. Morrow was no doctor, but he could help by taking charge.

"Sit down," he ordered.

Since he must have looked like a drunkard and smelled like

one too, it surprised him when the deckhand complied. Millie settled then and started gathering supplies. Clean water, antiseptic, bandages, medicine. She must've seen Tegan work a little because she seemed competent, older than usual, as she prepared everything.

"This may hurt. Do you have a flask?" she asked.

"No." The sailor hesitated under the weight of her dubious stare. "Yes."

"Empty it, and I'll get to work."

The man knocked back the same foul-smelling stuff that had numbed Morrow the night before. Millie waited a moment. When her patient relaxed, she pried his fingers open to reveal a bloody palm with a ragged gash. She clenched her jaw, inhaled sharply, then started treatment. First she blotted the blood away and cleansed the wound with the mixture Tegan had left.

Millie's hands shook a little when she reached for the bag that belonged to their friend. But once she opened it, she found composure and cracked open the kit with needles and thread. Morrow's stomach twisted in time to his throbbing head, and he had to look away as she pulled the black thread through the sailor's torn flesh. The man whimpered like a pup, his eyes squeezed shut, and James held him still. Twice he tried to jerk away, but Millie kept going.

"There," she said finally.

When he looked again, she had a bandage tied neatly around the man's hand. The sailor staggered out, probably half drunk from the grog and blood loss. Morrow scraped a hand over his rough jaw, wishing he hadn't put himself to bed with a bottle. The infirmary was a hell of a mess, and he shouldn't make Millie deal with that alone. But damn, if she didn't have a cool head on her shoulders.

"You're good at this," he said, helping her to tidy up.

"I spent a lot of time doctoring animals. But you already knew that; I'm fairly famous for it. People aren't that different. Actually . . . they just complain more."

He laughed, the sound choking off when he realized.

I shouldn't. Not with Tegan missing.

She went on, "Thanks for helping. I've been taking care of little things, but this was more than I could manage on my own."

"I didn't do much."

"You always seem to think that, but you matter a lot," Millie said. "We'll be in Port-Mer later today. Sung Ji is worried that we won't make the next stop with all the delays. And some of the sailors are saying the ship's cursed now because we let a Uroch on board."

"That's superstitious rubbish." He considered knocking some sense into those imbeciles, but it would likely irritate Captain Advika if he caused additional trouble.

Smiling, she said, "I knew you'd feel that way."

When the *Catalina* sailed back into port, they didn't receive the same welcome as before. The townsfolk in the market wore grim and dour looks, until Captain Advika shoved the three men forward in chains. She grabbed a merchant seemingly at random and said, "Fetch your chief. He'll want to see to this personally."

"Take these louts and go," someone called.

"Malena's killers were among my crew," the captain said. "One of ours overheard the confession. I swear to you on my life, it was these three."

One by one, she kicked the back of their legs so they went down, kneeling in forced penitence. Morrow could tell by the way they bit the gags in their mouths, they wanted to curse. But Sung Ji and two men on either side of him held them down, and the chains prevented them from running or trying to fight.

Eventually the chief arrived. "You found the culprits?"

Captain Advika turned to Morrow and waved him over. "This is James Morrow. His father is the governor of the Evergreen Isle. I think you may have written to him now and then."

The chief nodded. "Good man, your father. I'm Byron Littleberry."

Morrow nodded, acknowledging the introduction, but it didn't seem right to interrupt.

Advika went on, "Mr. Morrow caught the sailors threatening the Uroch vanguard, and in the course of that conversation, he also overheard their full confession. This account is corroborated by Millie Faraday, another crewman."

"If that's true, we owe the vanguard an apology." With a sigh, the chief lowered his head.

Captain Advika's mouth curled down at the corners. "You'll have to find him first."

"Beg pardon?" That clearly startled Littleberry.

"While struggling with Malena's murderers, Szarok went overboard, and our ship's doctor followed him. They were both lost in the storm a few days back."

Now missing. Presumed dead. Morrow heard the words she didn't say. They twisted in him like knives. Even if he never got to be more than a silly clown who made Tegan of the Staff laugh now and then, it would've been enough. The idea that she might've passed from the world? Impossible. Untenable. It hurt to stand, to think, to *breathe.*

"I'm sorry," the chief was saying. "And our wrongs weigh even heavier since there's no way to make amends."

"Some things can't be changed. But regardless, there is no doubt in my mind that these men are guilty, and I am remanding them to your custody to do with as you will."

The sailors on the ground shouted, but their fabric bindings muffled the words, rendering them indistinguishable from mindless noise. That seemed to be enough for Littleberry. Quickly, he gave orders, and strong men hauled the criminals off. Morrow wasn't certain what came next, but Captain Advika didn't seem ready to depart quite yet.

"I have to see the family and offer reparations. Nothing I can say or do will fix this, but I have to try. Even if I was rushed, I should've made sure I could trust my crew."

Morrow inclined his head. Normally he'd offer to go with her, but today he felt acutely conscious of how bad he must look and smell. Shame percolated through him that he'd let himself sink to this state. The usual James Morrow would be welcome at a solemn service, but—

"Oh, take this with you. I did manage a poem for Malena. See if it's welcome?"

With a grateful smile, Captain Advika accepted the paper. "Unless I miss my guess, there will be three hangings today. I'm ordering *all* the men to remain on the ship with Sung Ji now, but I'd appreciate it if you and Millie would attend as our representatives, a gesture of respect."

"You want me to take Millie to an execution?" He didn't mean to bark it so loud.

At his exclamation, she came over. "It's fine, James. I lived through the tithes in Otterburn, so do you *really* think I don't understand how the world works? Sometimes awful things stop worse ones. They're not hanging those men because it'll help Malena. They're doing it to make any other mug think twice."

Her response rocked him. Somehow he'd gotten the idea that she was a beautiful child. But her eyes were wide open and clear as a summer sky with a quiet maturity that likely surpassed his own. *I shouldn't treat her like that. Just because she's cheerful, I figured she didn't understand.* But it seemed braver to choose optimism when you did know how grim the world could be—defiant joy that blazed a beacon in the face of adversity. Mentally, he was already writing the lines to describe her.

But he couldn't let on that she'd shaken him, even a little. So he teased. "Mug? Where did you learn that word?"

"My ma says it about anybody whose morality she comes to question."

"I like that," he declared. "It's going in the book. But your mother has an uncommonly colorful tongue. I'd like to meet her."

"Her tongue's pink, same as mine." She stuck hers out, and it was . . . he didn't know what. Not a childish taunt exactly, not with her knowing eyes. "But you can meet my ma, if you want."

For some reason, his cheeks fired, and he looked away first, fanning his shirt away from his chest. "I never knew an autumn afternoon to be so hot."

"You'll have the chills soon enough."

As Morrow took the poem back from the captain, he wished he wasn't so damn scruffy. He followed the crowd to the outskirts of town. They hadn't bothered to build the gallows like he'd read about in old books; from what he could tell, they'd chosen three solid trees. When the knots were tied and all witnesses had assembled, the chief dropped the nooses around the men's necks one by one.

Then Littleberry said, "We do this for Malena, may she rest in peace."

That was all.

The gags came off, and Morrow had never heard such hoarse pleading, sobbing, and praying in his life, a veritable babble of it, grotesquely silenced as the men of Antecost hauled each rope over a branch and strung each sailor up one by one. None of them died quickly, and that might come close to justice for the girl they'd murdered. Millie stood in respectful silence until the last of their feet stopped kicking.

"Please thank Captain Advika," Littleberry said with a formal bow. "I know it cost her time and trust to change her course this late in the year. I only hope no other settlements suffer because she did the right thing here."

"She's peerless and skilled or so I'm told," Morrow answered. "Here's a little memorial verse I wrote in Malena's honor. Would you pass it along to her mother for me?"

Littleberry nodded. "My pleasure, that's very kind."

Millie added, "Don't worry about us. Please send our condolences to Malena's family. I only wish we could've done more."

"You're always welcome in Port-Mer. In so many years, this is the first trouble we've had with the *Catalina*'s crew. Safe journey to you both." With that, the chief turned to his men.

As Morrow gauged Millie's impressive poise, he realized she was much tougher than he'd imagined, based on the stories about her legendary kindness. But a lot had happened since a little girl had saved what she'd thought was an injured animal. *Would she have helped the Uroch? If she'd known?* He decided never to ask, since she seemed to like animals better than people, even if she was determinedly merry around them. Finally she turned away, her mouth drawn tight.

"We should go back to the ship," she said in the flattest voice he'd ever heard.

"Are you all right?"

"Do you really want to know, or are you just asking because you're nice?"

"I care," he protested, stung.

"Since I'm feeling like pickled shit, I'll take you at your word." She set off away from the hanging trees, eyes on the ground. "I had a younger brother, you know."

"Sorry, I didn't."

"No reason to apologize. My ma and dad like to pretend he didn't exist. It's easier than admitting they just let him go. When Isaac won the lottery, they acted like it was an honor. He was so scared. We had a going-away party for him and everything like it was good, and I had to smile and eat cake. Never have wanted it since." She cleared her throat and swiped at the tears misting her eyes. "Now when I see . . . something like that, I always think of him. I wonder if he suffered, if he hated us at the end."

Morrow stopped. "Oh, Millie. If I'd known—"

"You can't fix me, storyteller. My hurts are my own. If you

want to hold my hand, I'd take some solace in it, but that's all I'll ever ask of you."

Such a simple thing. Without hesitation, he reached for her. Small hands, but rough. He could feel that she'd worked hard in her life, suffered more than he could've guessed. Morrow resisted the urge to put a sheltering arm around her, as he suspected he might get pummeled. Their hands swung like a lazy sailor's hammock as they walked. She didn't speak again for a while; he didn't, either, but the silence didn't boil with tension. Sometimes he chattered on for fear of that drowning quiet, but with her it was all right *not* to be a storyteller, too.

Just before they reached the market, she said, "Do you remember the first time we saw each other?"

It was an odd question, but she seemed intent on his answer. "When Tegan brought you to Rosemere?"

A little sigh slipped out of her. "No. There was another time, the first time."

"When was this?" Intrigued, he tugged on her hand, but she pulled her fingers free and set off at a quicker pace.

He matched it.

"Maybe we didn't," she said. "Maybe it was only me, seeing you. And from what I can tell, nothing much has changed."

"I'm sorry I don't remember. You won't give me a hint?"

Her smile was all the sweetness of summers lost, all the sorrow of loves left behind. "Maybe someday I will. You're not ready to hear it now."

Irrational Fits of Learning

Using salvaged bits, Tegan helped Szarok repair some of the furniture. Now they had a table and two chairs to go along with their makeshift bed. The furs he had been drying, he finished by smoking them. Just in time, as the temperature dropped after dark. In the heat of the day, it was still warm enough to continue his swimming lessons.

He didn't complain as much as he had before, and he no longer froze when they waded out into the water. She looked forward to holding him up, passing on what she'd learned from the uncle who'd disappeared. In turn, eventually Szarok would share these memories with his descendants, an unbroken chain of knowledge that transcended species. Tegan smiled.

"You're looking forward to another failure," he accused gently.

She shook her head as they went down to the shore. This had become part of their daily routine. Breakfast, some household work, swimming and language lessons, then he went hunting and she worked on the machines in the tower. So far he had much more success than she. Afterward, they ate together again and started a small fire in the stove, letting it burn down as they snuggled in to sleep.

"Of course not. If you don't swim before we're through, I've failed as a teacher."

"My success is yours?"

"Definitely."

"Then I'll do my best."

They waded into the water together. Though his hand tightened on hers, that was the only sign of his distress. "Today let's try floating."

Szarok mumbled something, but he leaned back into the water. He was so strong and so powerful out of the water—strange to find him so vulnerable here. Tegan recalled how Deuce had wanted to use the river to kill all of his people before he made first contact, and a shiver ran through her. He didn't notice, too busy battling the water. After sinking once, twice, thrice, he finally spat and stood up, his mouth pulled into an angry line.

"This is impossible."

"You just have to relax. And to trust me."

"The latter is always true. For your first request . . ." He sighed. "I can't. I don't know how. There is always the struggle in my head, the fear and the screaming."

Since she didn't have anyone else's memories—and sometimes dealing with her own was bad enough—she had no idea what strategy to suggest. Then an idea stirred, stemming from when they'd had the most success. *He was so focused on me, he forgot everything else.*

"Close your eyes."

"Why—"

"You said you trust me."

In response, his eyelids drifted shut. Gazing at his face always engendered this rare commingling of astonishment and delight. *He treats me like one of his own people.* Others might not take it so, but for Tegan, it qualified as the highest of honors. With some effort, she set aside her silent pleasure at being permitted unfettered access to . . . him, every part of him.

"The water is cold," he complained.

"Stop thinking about that. Focus on my voice. Now imagine it's all you can hear. No birds, no waves. Nothing but my voice.

You're listening to me . . . and you're breathing. Take a deep breath. Hold it. Now let it out."

She focused on that until he relaxed under her hands. His shoulders lost tension and he swayed with the water as it ebbed and flowed. Rather than rush it, she murmured breathing exercises until he seemed nearly asleep on his feet. *Time to take the next step.* Heart pounding with anxious excitement, she shifted until she stood behind him, hands still on his shoulders.

"Now it's time to prove your trust. Lean back and let me hold you." She'd never dared this much before, fearing he would panic.

But he fell back naturally and without hesitation, until his head touched her shoulders. His feet came off the sandy seafloor and his legs rocked on the waves. Tegan kept her arms around him, as she'd promised, still whispering. "See, I've got you. I'm holding you safe."

Szarok floated for a good thirty seconds before he realized what was happening. When he jerked upright, she suspected it was more startlement than true fear. With him standing, they were too close, but her eyes caught his, and she didn't mind his cold skin or the nervous press of his claws.

"I did it?" His tone was questioning, and then, "I did it!"

His pleasure burst like an overripe fruit, overwhelming her with sweetness. "You did. Now that you know you can, it should be easier."

"Hold me again."

This time he didn't need the slow induction. He just fell back into her arms and she kept them looped beneath his back, but with each rocking wave, his confidence grew, until he was floating on his own, riding the waves with a simple exhilaration that struck her as the finest thing she'd ever seen. Eventually she had to drag him out of the water because his gray skin seemed to be edged in blue, and now that the sun had gone behind a cloud, she was freezing, too.

"Let's build a fire at home. I know it's early, but we have to warm up before doing anything else. We can't get sick."

They held on to each other—for warmth, or that was what Tegan told herself—on the way back to the signal tower. Bits of scrub and driftwood went into the stove, and she nestled into Szarok as they had in the sea cave. For the first time, he wrapped his arms around her and then the cured furs. She waited, but there came no sense of choking, no innate panic. With the fire in front and Szarok at her back, she warmed quickly.

"Tomorrow I'll teach you how to hold your breath. And the day after, how to paddle. I'm not sure if the weather will hold long enough to finish the lessons, though."

He rested his chin on her shoulder, his face so close to hers that his features blurred. Somehow it felt right to tilt her head against his and close her eyes.

"That should be enough," he said softly. "But don't go to sleep."

She made the negative sound in his language, a little growl that was fun to trill out. Some of the sounds, she lacked the capacity to emulate. But since they had been on the island, she'd learned more than a hundred phrases. The Uroch tongue surprised her with its complexity, for they expressed complicated concepts in a relatively short series of sounds. She found *wake and rise,* which he'd taught her first, to be the easiest, but she could also manage *the hunting is good,* along with *we are feasting* and *what is ours, we protect.* Szarok claimed her version of *thank you, kinsman* was intelligible, but she had her doubts.

Without shifting or letting go, he spoke right by her ear, and she grasped maybe thirty percent of it. Embarrassed, she tried to bluff. *"Thank you, kinsman."* Tegan winced at how badly it came out, and her cheeks burned.

"You didn't understand," he guessed.

"I'm sorry. I wish I were better at languages."

"If I can float, you can learn Uroch." His tone was stern.

I deserve that.

"I'll try harder."

But actually . . . it was hard to concentrate with him so close, not because she feared him, but another sensation altogether, pervasive and new. He smelled wintry and fresh like the sea bath, smoky traces from the stove, and he was *so* warm. His body sheltered her; his breath on her ear sent pleasurable chills down her back. She recognized what she was feeling—in the abstract—but she'd never experienced it before. Knowing that he had hyperacute senses only increased her discomfort. *Can he tell . . . ?* Her one hope was that human girls didn't register in the same way that Uroch females did.

"You seem distracted." His tone told her little, but a faint thread of amusement, real or imagined, made her squirm away.

"I need to see your mouth and throat moving, for the most accurate practice." The heat of the stove seemed like nothing compared to the conflagration of chagrin burning up her face.

"Understood."

For the next hour, he spoke in Uroch and she translated poorly, attempting her own responses. By the end, her throat even hurt a little from making noises too deep for her usual register. She accompanied him as far as the well, sulkily hauling the bucket up with each grumpy tug of the rope. They both lowered their faces to drink at the same time, and her lips grazed his chin. Szarok stilled; so did she.

"S-sorry." Tegan snapped back and stumbled away so quick, her bad leg almost gave way.

Humiliated, she pressed her palms to her face, hoping she wouldn't actually combust.

He watched in apparent alarm. "That . . . I don't understand why you're so . . ."

She couldn't even find the right words to explain. Tegan turned to flee.

"If you're upset that you've forced something on me, shall I make it better?" Eyes curious, but not offended, he stopped her with a hand on her arm, a loose hold, not demanding.

If I want to, I can still run.

She didn't really want to.

"How?"

Gently, he leaned down and rubbed his mouth against her chin. Not a kiss, more of a nuzzle, but it was gentle and tender and so full of kindness that it made her want to cup his face in her hands and kiss him and just never, ever stop. But that would escalate the whole *forced something on him* issue, and there was the issue of his long, sharp teeth, along with the fact that she'd never actually kissed anyone before.

He clearly just wants me to feel better.

So she smiled.

"You're right. It's not awkward anymore."

Visibly gratified, he stepped back and went off for the day's hunting while Tegan sort of collapsed near the well and wished she wasn't still thinking about whether it was possible to teach the Uroch to kiss. *I could call it an experiment,* she speculated. *No, that's too scientific. Well, he knows I'm prone to irrational fits of learning—*

No. Stop.

Irritated with herself, she went to fiddle with the salvage items they'd found. Maybe it was her mood, but she gave the flashlight a vicious twist, and to her astonishment, it cranked, kept cranking, until it stopped. Then when she clicked the button, it lit up, far too bright to be natural, even in daylight. Elated, she switched it off.

I could use this to signal at night. A ship might see it?

Impatient, she ran back to the well and interrupted Szarok in the middle of his bath. He was oddly shy about letting her see him, and she'd always wondered why. Now it seemed there was no reason at all because he was lean and muscled and ferocious looking, even with bloodied water running off him in rivulets. He looked stronger than a human male with increased musculature, and he had natural weapons in the form of hands, feet, and teeth. But nothing about him struck her as monstrous.

He's splendid.

Hurriedly, he ducked to the other side of the well. "Is something wrong?"

"I . . . no." She growled out *sorry* in his tongue, couldn't remember how to say more. "I had news. Call me when you're done."

Tegan paced, too excited to let embarrassment take charge. A few minutes later he shouted, "Come, share your news."

She ran back toward him, waving the light. "Look!"

Szarok didn't require an explanation of how significant this was. His face lit with shared enthusiasm, and when she launched herself at him, he caught her. She'd never seen the Uroch play, but she experienced it firsthand when he tossed her up and then twirled her. Giggling, she held on and just savored the feeling, almost like flying.

But I don't need wings or wind or feathers. Just him.

"I think I can use the glass fragments in conjunction with this light source. There will need to be a ship in range, but . . ."

"It's a chance," he said. "More than we had before."

"I've been worried about how we'd make it through the winter. I even wondered if it would be possible to cross the ice, if the water froze. But while I looked at Captain Advika's charts, I didn't memorize them."

"It would be hard to carry enough supplies when we aren't sure how far we're going."

Sighing, she agreed. "If we signal a ship, they should be willing to drop us off at whatever port they're heading for."

"I need to get word to my people. It will not go well if they think I've let my memories go." A euphemism for a sudden, violent death.

All at once Tegan registered the enormity of his task. "If . . . if they hear you're lost, will it mean war?"

He closed his eyes. "Probably. There was already division among the Uroch about our decision to support humanity against our ancestors. A vocal minority calls the action I chose as vanguard 'a heinous crime.' And . . . there is part of me that agrees."

"Because even if they weren't Awakened, they were still your forebearers," Tegan said.

"Yes." His quiet resignation hurt her.

"We'll stop it."

Szarok leveled a look at her: puzzlement and something else. The muted sunlight that bothered him so also turned his eyes to molten gold, an eldritch beauty that grew the longer she gazed upon it. "You say that like my burden is yours, too."

She almost said, *That's what friends are for.* But she couldn't get the sentence out. Not anymore. So she growled the response in Uroch, one that he had spoken before in human words. Now it was time to say it so his heart could hear. *We are kin.*

A visible tremor shook through him, and then he pulled her close. Not in a hug, exactly, but chest-to-chest touching. He rubbed his cheek against her face, her hair, and then nuzzled into the curve of her neck. Breathless, she fought for calm, unsure how to respond, or if she should. He seemed so happy when he raised his face, such distilled joy. It faded a little when she didn't react as he seemed to expect.

"I don't know what I'm supposed to do," she whispered.

He understood then: luminous eyes, sharp features, and all of him inexpressibly dear. "If we're kin, you do it back. You put your scent on me, so others know, too."

With some part of her brain, she found that fascinating, but the rest focused purely on the raw pleasure of finally, finally having permission to do what she'd wanted for longer than she'd realized. She heard an echo of him saying, *Don't handle me; I don't like it,* and now she had an invitation. Her breath went in a rasp that was all anticipation.

It's so little by human standards, so why . . .

But her heart still pounded like mad when she rose up to press her cheek to his. The slow glide back and forth, skin touching skin. His felt incredibly smooth, different from a human's, but good. He had no hair for her to reciprocate with, and she couldn't easily reach the top of his head, so she improvised, pressing both of their palms together so his claws curled over the top of her fingers. The surprising intensity of their joined palms seemed to startle him. His eyes sparked, clouding with a confusion she shared. When she set her face in against his neck, he trembled, not once, but in waves.

"Am I doing it right?" she whispered.

That only made his shaking worse, but when she tried to pull back, he held on to her like she was the only solid ground in the world. "I don't know. Is this . . . Are we . . . all right?"

"I think so." Her voice came out husky, not just from language practice.

"If you're sure."

"We're only . . . sharing culture." *Why do I sound like that?*

"Yes." He curved his hands over her shoulder and ran his claws down her back. A shocking pleasure drenched her. "This is how we tease our young."

"It tickles." When she squirmed, he only did it more, until she was laughing, breathless, and just *melting* with delight.

He rested his chin on her head, where she'd nuzzled into the curve of his shoulder. "Now teach me something. You're not the only one who likes to learn."

Thank you, she thought. Tegan probably wouldn't have had the courage, if he hadn't phrased it in precisely that way.

"This," she said. "This is how we kiss."

Breath-Marking

Tegan cupped his face in her hands and leaned in slowly, giving him ample time to back away, if that was what he wanted.

But Szarok held still. When her lips were a heartbeat away from his, she whispered, "Close your eyes."

"Is this another test of my trust?"

"No, it's just how we do it."

He closed his eyes, seeming entertained by this custom. If only she weren't so nervous, she might be smiling, too. But since the pace and power all rested in her hands, anticipation and eagerness tangled until she shook as much as he had earlier. Her heart pounded so fast, it echoed in her ears as she closed the minute distance between them. Up close, his mouth was thin and delicate, a surprisingly pretty cover for his sharp teeth. Tegan wet her lips and then brushed them against his, soft as a whisper.

Szarok jerked, his claws nipping her shoulder. But he didn't open his eyes. "Is there more?"

"That depends."

"On what?"

Since she was the opposite of an expert, Tegan struggled with the explanation. "Families, blood kin, kiss like this."

Easier to demonstrate.

She pecked his cheek.

"But there are other ways?" he asked.

"Definitely. Between people who share a strong bond but aren't blood kin, there are lots of different kinds."

"Like the one you just showed me."

"That wasn't much. It was . . ." *Why did I think I could do this?* Her face blazed. "Well, a child might kiss his mother that way when he's young."

"But when humans mature, they save the mouth kisses for the one who holds their heart-bond." He seemed sure of this assessment.

And what a lovely way to put it.

"Exactly."

"Ah. Then . . . I would learn a little more, if you'll teach me."

He could've said nothing more guaranteed to fire her imagination. A little dizzy from the wealth of possibilities, Tegan studied his face and smoothed her thumb over the skin just beneath his mouth. On the third sweep, his lips parted a little to let out a soft breath. Then she went in for another kiss, pressing her lips first to his upper, then lower, and back again, emulating the way he'd scent-marked her. At first he only held still and let her do it.

She sat back. "Is it strange?"

"You're breath-marking me."

"A little, perhaps."

"Am I supposed to do it back?"

"It feels best when we do it together." She swallowed hard after saying that, but he didn't have the context to make it more than she meant.

"Can we try again?"

"Definitely."

This time, he met her halfway and instead of just kissing him, which felt good, he returned the pressure precisely as she gave it, lips sliding and sipping. Pleasure curled through her, sharp and sweet, especially when he exhaled against her mouth as if he didn't want to stop long enough to take a breath. She stroked his face as they kissed, luxuriating in the flex of his jaw and the smoothness of his skin.

Finally he pulled away and touched his mouth. Her own felt swollen and soft. "It's good. I like it."

"That's not all," she blurted.

Why did I say that?

She knew about tongue kissing, but she wasn't sure how that would work. His teeth might get in the way. But he tilted his head, apparently intrigued. Her entire body simmered, but for all she knew, he might just be . . . curious. It would be humiliating if he figured out how this affected her while he remained unmoved. Dr. Wilson would say there was nothing unusual about her reaction, and science couldn't predict how physical relationships developed.

All organisms are different, he used to say.

Szarok opened his eyes then. "I want more . . ." He trailed off, gazing at her mouth.

"But?"

"I'm not sure if I'm supposed to . . ." That statement trickled off. He seemed to be confounded over how to express his doubts.

"Just tell me. Whatever it is, it's all right." With her whole heart, she hoped that was true.

"This is not ours, not of the People. But . . . it makes me want," he said baldly.

Her smile broke the bubble of tension that had been rising steadily. "It's supposed to. Breath-marking is a prelude to more contact. If it doesn't make you . . . want, then we're doing it wrong. Or it means you feel nothing for me."

"I feel everything for you," he said. "So my mouth . . . you need it, too?"

"Yes." There was only simple honesty.

And somehow talking only deepened the ache. She could spend all day learning his lips and drinking his breath. They might starve, but it would almost be worth it. Tegan rubbed her chest and hoped she could survive these lessons. Life hadn't prepared her for desire; it was fierce, urgent, slightly terrifying, but also exhilarating.

She realized she had a question, and since he'd been honest, she owed him the same bravery. "Is it not like this between Uroch?"

He shook his head. "There is touch. And we play. But mouths are for eating. I think . . . we shy away from using them otherwise because . . ."

Because you used them to devour indiscriminately.

"Before, you said something about a heart-bond. What does that mean?"

He appeared to consider for a moment. "It's the one closest to you, not blood kin. Most often this leads to mating. Other times, I suppose you would call it friendship? To the Uroch, there are only layers of kinship. I don't know if I'm explaining it well."

"I'm so curious, but you got angry at me for 'studying' you."

His gaze lingered on her face, warm and gentle. "It's not the same now. My heart is open, and I choose to share. If you wonder, ask."

"Then . . . do the Uroch marry? That is, choose a heart-bond partner for life?"

"No. In the past, we didn't live long, so all our ancestors cared about was eating and breeding. We're still learning, as you would say."

Tegan had known that—of *course* she had—but the reminder that the Uroch didn't live as long as humans hit her like a falling rock. "You . . . How long?"

How long will you live? She couldn't ask, but he understood.

"I don't know. The young ones, the Awakened, are different in a number of ways. I hope that means we also have more time.

But . . ." Szarok flourished his claws, a gesture that she recognized as being similar to a human shrug.

"That must be hard," she said.

"There is no point dwelling on what cannot be changed, and what human knows exactly how long he has?"

"You make a good point." Her heart lightened then. "Can I . . . keep asking?"

"Insatiable. Yes."

"How does gender work among the Uroch?"

"Some are born male, others female. And some have both traits. If you mean for mating, the Uroch do as they wish. Sometimes we mate for pleasure, male to male, female to female. Sometimes it is from the need to get offspring. Or both."

"So that's not so different from humans, at least."

He shook his head. "Very different. No mouths. No breath-marking. We start and use our claws a little. It's . . . faster. You seem to know a great many frills and embellishments."

Tegan buried her face in her hands. "Don't ever talk to me again."

"No hiding. I like your kissing. Show me a little more?" A teasing gleam in his eyes told Tegan that he understood that this was a game between them, but also that it wasn't.

Should I . . . ?

Bold and a little reckless, she took his mouth as she had before. His eyes drifted shut on their own, a sign of his permission and pleasure. His lips worked against hers, and he parted them willingly so she could suck gently at each one. Surprised, Szarok growled deep in his throat, and it was beyond delicious that she understood the word *more*.

No longer worried, she teased delicately into his mouth, skirting his teeth. He didn't respond until her tongue teased his and then he licked, holding his jaw with such care that she could've devoured him. *You won't hurt me. I know your heart.* Then she showed him hers with the hungry-gentle glide of lips and tongue, pouring everything into the deepest kiss.

They were both breathless when she pulled back.

"That is . . . is so . . ."

She almost fell into him again when human words failed him, and then he lapsed into a deliciously heated tirade in Uroch that she only half understood. The bits that came through, however, set her on fire with blushing. But his reaction was flattering and precious, too.

Finally he managed, "Don't do that. To anyone else."

"I won't. I never have before."

He stared in evident astonishment. "Then how are you teaching *me*?"

Tegan grinned. "I'm amazing?"

"You are," he agreed.

"Kissing doesn't stop at the mouth," she told him.

Szarok only offered an expectant look, so she brushed her lips over his jaw, his chin, his cheek, his ear, the side of his neck. On the last point, he shivered and drew back. Since his eyes gleamed, she didn't think it was because he disliked it.

"Stop now, before the wanting becomes hurt."

Sensitive neck. Noted.

"Then we'll end the lessons here." Satisfaction thrummed through her, along with a ton of nervous energy.

"I am very interested to discover where the breath-marking ends."

She wandered some distance away before answering over her shoulder. "It doesn't."

His reaction was everything she could've hoped, shocked disapproval commingling with reluctant curiosity. She didn't linger for further questions. At this point, she could run the perimeter of the island and come back again without feeling winded.

Though it was relatively late in the day, she couldn't return to the signal tower yet. *I'd have to climb all those steps twenty times to simmer down.* Instead she walked through the old settlement and past it, toward the lowlands. She hadn't scouted this part yet, and the other settlers might have discarded something she'd find useful. Or maybe that wasn't the only abandoned camp. Szarok usually ranged where the animals foraged, so if he'd discovered anything, he would have said.

If I move quickly, I have time to walk to the southern rim and back before nightfall.

Tegan picked up the pace, alert for any sign of prior civilization, but she found only a beaten track that seemed to have been worn from many others walking this way. The lowlands were full of birds that scattered at her approach, scrub bushes, and green-brown grass. Native flora here differed from what Dr. Wilson had taught her in Winterville. What she knew of plants related mostly to the ones that could be used to produce medicine.

Soon the lowland gave way to rocks, some moderate in size and others so huge that she marveled at them. Strangely, five of them had been arranged in what looked like a ceremonial fashion, some upright and others fallen down. She paused to inspect the site, and guessed it must be incredibly old, far predating the metal huts and the signal tower. Here, she found fragments of pottery, too, and shards of bone.

They burned something here.

An unpleasant chill trickled through her, and Tegan straightened, returning to her original intent of checking the southern reach. It was hard not to be disappointed when the sea came into sight again, along with a mound of stones tumbling toward the water. Here, fat white-and-black seabirds with colorful beaks waddled about, scrapping over fish and diving into the bay with an awkward charm. She watched them longer than she meant to.

It's probably not wise to find something you've eaten this adorable.

The daylight got away from her, so by the time she started back toward the settlement, she'd lost the sun. Darkness dropped like a heavy veil, and she'd overestimated how clear the path back would be. She went slowly, not wanting to get lost. *He must be worried.* The island wasn't huge, however, and he had tracked her under worse conditions.

A shimmer of ice on her skin startled her into gazing up.

Snow.

But in that split second, as she marveled at the drifting white flakes, she tripped over a rock. Her bad leg gave, and she was closer to the edge than she'd realized. Tegan tumbled down an embankment, bashing against the rocks. She landed hard on the shore below, perhaps fifteen feet down, but it would be a difficult climb, bleeding and in the dark. Breathing hard and shaken, she took stock.

Gash on my arm. Contusions on right thigh and left side of rib cage.

Blood seeped from her wound, and she tore a strip from the bottom of her shirt without hesitation. She wrapped it and tied it off. *Remain calm. At least there are no large predators.* But she wasn't sure how far she was from the settlement, and the sea nibbled at this small slice of land. If high tide came in, she'd have to scramble to higher ground.

I can't fall again.

Her weak leg throbbed. Though Doc Tuttle had saved it, the pain lingered even now, exacerbated by exertion. She tried shouting for help but gave it up as the snow flurried around her, slicking the rocks and dissolving in the sea. By now she should be back at the signal tower, waiting by the fire. *He'll find me.*

He has to find me.

But . . . it was so cold. She couldn't wait to be rescued.

With great care, she searched for handholds in the dark. The wet rocks scraped her palms, but she hauled herself up, two feet, three. But on the next step, her shoe slipped, and she tumbled back, nearly smashing her head on a rock. Dazed, she lay on the stony sand, staring up at the spangle of stars while the snow drifted and melted on her lips, her cheeks, icing her lashes.

The reality crystallized.

I can't climb up.

Weakness ate at her, but she shoved it back. Despite the pain, Tegan hauled herself upright. *If I can't get out of here, maybe . . .* It was best to keep moving anyway. So she followed the sea ledge forward. Ideally, it might join and widen at the beach where she gave Szarok swimming lessons. It would be a long, circuitous walk, but she'd be able to climb the gentler incline on that side, even with these injuries.

With renewed hope, she set out, but five hundred feet or so along the rim, the land just . . . stopped, and the ground above was even steeper than where she'd failed to clamber out. Throttling a wave of terror that made her want to scream and scream, she retraced her steps. Damp through to her skin on her back, the cold worked down to her bones. At first it ached, and then she started to feel numb.

Tegan called out once, again. Then she heard rustling above. *There are no predators, except those foxes.* But if they came at her in a pack, smelling blood, she didn't know how it would end. *Don't panic.* Scant moonlight didn't grant much visibility, so she felt around for a weapon, and found only a rock. Hefting it, she decided maybe she could use it.

She paced.

When her hands went numb, she ignored it. Her feet lost feeling next. The urge to sleep washed over her in a comforting wave, and she pinched her cheeks, hard. It wasn't enough, so she gouged her fingers into the makeshift bandage on her arm. Tears streamed down her icy cheeks, but the pain also roused her a little.

Why wasn't I more careful?

There was no shelter down here that she could find, and huddling against the rocks only made her colder. It wasn't like the night in the sea cave. She didn't want to cry, but fear tapped, tapped, tapped at the doorway to her mind until she went half mad with loneliness and let it in.

Tegan had no way of knowing how long it had been, where Szarok might be searching. She had no doubt that he was, but—oh.

Oh.

What if the snow's like rain? Washing me away. Winter-fresh, so he can't find me.

And she knew—she *knew*—that he wouldn't give up. In the cold, dark night, he would search and run and *try,* until they both froze and died. The tears felt like lava on her cheeks, blessed relief from the cold, but also tasting of despair. This couldn't be the last thing she ever tasted, layered over the confection of his kisses like the doleful weight of graveyard earth.

No, please. No. Not this. Not because of me.

And the snow just kept falling.

Darkness and Thorns

The silence chilled Szarok, more than the dark and the cold. When the wind carried his voice away but brought back no answer in return, he ran from the signal tower. He'd last seen her heading for the metal houses, but as he crested the hill, he found no sign of her. Kneeling, he sought her familiar smell, and wisps of her sprang alive, faint but unmistakable. *This way.*

The scent trail beckoned and kept calling, yet it seemed strange that she would have gone so far. To his left, a curious fox kept pace, likely wondering if he might kill another goat. If so, there might be scraps to scavenge. *Not tonight,* he told it silently. Raw fear gnawed at him inside, as much as what he first felt in the water, as much as weighed on him when he walked into a human town, surrounded by his enemies.

He tracked her all the way to some strange ruins, but then great fat snowflakes flurried down. Szarok had rarely hunted in the snow—as vanguard, his training had taken precedence—and he found that it diffused the scent—not impossible just then—but the longer the weather continued, the fainter her trace became. In a few hours he'd lose all sense of her.

No, that can't happen.

She was small with thin, human skin. The cold would devour her slowly. Dropping to the ground again, he found her, only a whisper, past the frozen water melting on the stones. *She was here.*

She lingered. But from here, where? He snarled in frustration when he had to stop so often, checking and rechecking her path, only to find it ended at a bluff overlooking the sea. An icy blast of swirling snow stole his breath as he gazed down at the churning sea. Frost glimmered on the rocks below, and he roared at the possibility that she might have fallen. If that were true, he should already be diving, but a wave surged, breaking in a watery explosion on the stones.

Szarok threw himself toward the ledge, but . . . there was no trace of her. *She didn't go over here.* He crawled, inch by inch, searching, eyes closed. The fox went away, and the snow meant the seabirds didn't fly, so it was only dark and swirling sky ice, and the fear that escalated with every moment that he *could not* find her.

Not an echo, not a glimmer.

Just animal smells, but even those, apart from the sharper spikes of urine and scat, were fading, diminished beneath the inexorable flutter of the snow. So far, it only dissipated as it hit the ground. The day had been so warm, enough to swim without it feeling like ice torture, but past dark, after the sun slept, the weather seemed like madness. But none of his people had ever ventured so far north.

Szarok stayed low, checking for signs of her, aware that the longer it took to find her, the worse it would be. Even with his thicker skin, he'd started to feel the cold. Dread coiled into a knot in his chest, so huge that he could barely breathe around it. Now he smelled only wet earth, hints of clay and rotting vegetation.

Desperate, he snarled another wordless call. Though he couldn't catch her scent, and the snow was falling thicker and faster now, an answering cry rang out, so faint and wind-thrown that a human wouldn't have heard it. For endless moments he worried that snow devils might be plaguing him, sending him off on an infinite game of seek and repeat. But then, as he ran along the bluff, the distant sounds clarified into her voice. But she was obviously losing heart, likely wondering if she'd imagined him in the roar of the wind.

"Keep shouting!"

If she heard him, he couldn't be sure, but her voice rang out again and again. He'd never tracked by ears alone, and the wind was a tricksy beast. His eyes felt frozen by the time he uncovered signs of where she'd fallen. Her scent here had nearly dissolved, leaving only the shimmer of an echo, a touch of smoke and copper.

She's hurt.

Without hesitation, he leapt, though he couldn't see, could only feel the swirling cold on his skin and hear the dread crashing of angry waves. Szarok landed on a slick rock, but he dug in with his claws and kept his footing. Tegan crouched nearby, huddled in on herself for warmth. The smell of blood bit at him, but it was worse that she barely smelled of anything else. Questions boiled up, but they could wait until he had her safe and warm.

"Get on my back." Blinking slowly, she stared up at him with an uncomprehending look. Impatient, he knelt and drew her up behind him. "Hold on tight, understand?"

"Yes." The sound was faint, but she tightened her icy arms around his neck.

Without his claws, the climb would've been impossible in this weather. More than once, he slid and caught himself, spearing into the earth with his talons. He pressed forward without rest, without pause, and when he crawled back onto solid ground, he didn't stop moving. Szarok straightened and burst into a run. Her breath didn't sound right, too slow, too light. At any moment it seemed as if she might stop and topple from his back.

Snow blind, he ran with all his strength. Since he couldn't pause to warm her, he spoke, broken questions in human words and Uroch growls. She responded to nothing, and as he ran through the abandoned town, her arms loosened. He held her up, leaning forward so she didn't fall. The angle made it hard to control his dash down the hill toward the signal tower, and his feet slid over the icy ground, scraped but numb. He could smell his injuries but couldn't feel them.

Finally he burst into their little home and deposited her in bed. His hands shook as he stirred the embers of the fire to life and then fed it all the brush and dry leaves they'd gathered. Wasteful, but if they didn't survive this night, there would never be any need for more fuel.

Still Tegan didn't stir. He stripped away her frozen clothes without hesitation and then discarded his own. When he pulled her close, she didn't feel like a living girl at all, and a shock of horror pierced him. *Did she go while I was running?* Fighting panic, he set his head to her chest. *No. She's still breathing. I just need to warm her.* Her injuries didn't seem serious enough to cause such lethargy, so it must be the chill. He wrapped himself around her first and then piled all of the furs he'd cured on top.

Between the layers, close contact, and the fire, the feeling came roaring back to his dead limbs. Nothing prepared him for the agonizing flame and needles that prickled, a little at first, and then with an awful intensity that left him snarling. He threaded his claws through her hair; he'd found it bizarre and uninviting at first, but now her head fur seemed sweetly . . . wild, a remnant of the animals that humans had been, like a wolf or a cat.

Eventually the pain faded. He held on to her, helping the only way he could. *Is it enough?* Cautiously, he explored her skull beneath the weight of tangled hair and found a knot. Tegan flinched and finally, finally opened her eyes. At first she only stared at him with an unseeing gaze, appearing not to understand.

When enlightenment dawned, she touched his cheek with a shaky hand. "You saved me."

"Barely," he bit out.

Now he should probably let go and feed her some meat, warm some water for her to drink, but his arms would not unlock. He could only hold her even closer, his breath coming in ragged gasps. The weakness overwhelming him had no peer. Even when the odds were bad, he didn't let the prospect of failure prevent him from taking action.

"I'm sorry."

He fisted one hand in her hair. "Please. Don't ever go again where I can't find you."

"I didn't mean to. The light wanes so fast here. You know, it's different on the mainland. There's more time where the sun hangs in the sky, orange and yellow, then the dark sort of ripens."

Was she mad? To be talking of the sun and the mainland when he felt this, like a hole had opened inside him that might never be filled. Provoked, he shook her shoulder to be sure he had her full attention. "Listen, healer. Don't *ever* go where I can't find you," he said again.

"I won't." But her tone made him feel like growling, and she didn't smell contrite.

He snapped his teeth once and then swallowed hard, his throat thick with unspent rage and Uroch scolding. But if he unleashed it in his native tongue, she wouldn't understand, and she must. "If you go," he said deliberately, each word an angry bite, "I will follow."

Now she stared up at him, eyes wide and dark and slightly fearful.

Good.

"By go, you mean . . ."

"Yes. I have a mission, healer. It is more important than my life. If you go where I can't find you, I can't . . . I can't . . ." Yielding to that raging tide, he tipped his head back to snarl at the ceiling, a string of Uroch that she probably couldn't translate. "I will follow. Understand? I will not mind anymore what else is lost, if you are."

Tegan shivered, a little sob escaping her. "You're saying if

I'm careless, I'll doom your people. Because I'm *that* important to you."

"Yes." Szarok set his jaw, angry all over again.

Because it *was* true, and part of him hated that it was, as if he'd turned down the wrong path without knowing, and now it was all darkness and thorns behind him, with no way back. He imagined bringing this human before the People and saying, *This is the one who holds my heart-bond.* There would be only shock, blame, and questions, so many questions, not least how the vanguard could grant his deepest trust to the enemy. It was impossible for so many reasons.

But most of all, because of—

"I won't go where you can't find me," she said softly. "I'll take care."

Some of the sting went away because it seemed she understood at last. Chastened, she tried to move away, and this time he let go, a conscious choice. He looked away as she put on the baggy uniform that comprised their sole change of clothes. She didn't come back to bed afterward, instead kneeling before the stove.

"Eat something." He passed the cooked meat to her without meeting her gaze.

"I'm sorry for scaring you."

Part of him realized he should comfort her instead of being like this, but his entire body, inside and out, ached with the throb of a sore that wouldn't heal. The old ones had suffered that way, every step a misery, and he had those memories, but this was the first time anything had left him so raw. With half his heart, he wanted her so close that she could never get away, and with the rest, he wanted to run until he couldn't see, hear, or smell her, and hope with desperate grief that this awful need went away.

I am turning from my purpose. There is one who waits. But the reminder didn't help.

"You're heartless," he muttered, as if she had nearly frozen to death intentionally.

"No." She came toward him on her knees, stopping short of contact. "I have a heart, and it's yours, but maybe you don't want it."

His rage collapsed in on itself, dwindling until the space between them seemed intolerable. With a resigned sigh, he put out his hand. She took it. And with her other, she ate the meat he had provided, reminding him again that she was kin. Exhaustion piled in then. His head must have weighed more than his whole body, for he tipped over and met the mattress. The crash hit hard, as if all of his strength followed his fury. He could only clutch her fingers. Dimly, he sensed cool hands on his cheeks, his head, but he couldn't respond.

Her voice sounded faint and fuzzy. "It's normal, reaction setting in. You'll feel better when you wake up."

There was nothing more until the lovely, familiar rumble of *wake and rise* brought him from sleep. Tegan had fresh fish waiting for him, and with a smile she watched him devour it. This morning he felt more balanced, slightly chagrined by his behavior the night before. But to his astonishment, she didn't refer to it. Instead she only pressed a kiss to the top of his head and acted as if she nursed no grievance. Such excess would have earned him a good pummeling from a Uroch partner, so perhaps being entangled with her wasn't *all* disadvantages.

"How do you feel?" he asked.

"Sore. I wish I had my bag, but . . ." She shrugged. "I miss my staff even more. I've gotten used to the support, and it makes a handy weapon."

"Did you clean your arm?"

"How . . ." Appearing to reconsider the question, she only nodded.

"Did the snow melt?"

"It didn't stay. The sun's bright again today, but I think we should skip the swimming lesson. We both need to rest."

"You can have vegetables. I'll hunt this afternoon."

"We should try signaling tonight." Tegan paused, her gaze on the distance between them. "I don't want anything else to go wrong, but the longer we're alone here, the more likely it is that we'll take risks. And . . . I can't be the reason you disappoint your people."

He understood why she tiptoed around the harsh truth. Humans and Uroch were only one year past a brutal war that would've ended in annihilation. The old hatreds ran so deep that anything could spark a renewed conflict. Sometimes he felt as if he ran along a road lined with broken blades, and only blood would mark his passing.

But . . . it was wrong to have set so much on her shoulders. "I was . . . not myself. Now that my mind is clear, I hope I would be strong enough to focus on my work and not on . . ." *Loss. Devastation.* There was a concept in his native tongue that encompassed a feeling of sorrow so complete that it meant, *My soul is weeping.* But even that translation didn't adequately express the broken anguish of wreckage that cratered one's entire being.

For a moment he feared that revelation would wound her, but instead she sighed a little and smelled of the sweetness of relief. "Thank you. Your task is too important. More than this."

It both pleased and hurt him that she understood. "Why are you so wise and good?"

She flattened her hand over her heart. "I'm not. But be sure of this: I've survived so much worse, and I'm stronger than I look. I won't ever give up. Sometimes the methods I choose may not seem the fiercest, but in my way, I am always resisting, always—"

"Who dares imply that you're not a warrior?" he snapped, greatly affronted.

Seeming amused, she touched his cheek. "Stand down. It

doesn't happen so much anymore. And look, you made me forget what I meant to say."

Sorry, he growled.

"Ah yes. It's this—even without me, your work must go on. And I can't bear to hurt you, but . . . even if . . ." She struggled to get the words out, eyes cast up. "You let go your memories, *I* will go on because I've fought too hard for too long. Even without you, I can heal the sick. I can keep learning." The tears streaming from her eyes whispered of great suffering, of wounds he couldn't see but only sense. "Know that doesn't diminish—"

"Stop," he said. "Please, don't keep last night's madness in your heart, for it shames me."

She cried, harder than he'd ever seen. But humans didn't show him their sorrow; they saw him as a monster, an enemy who preyed on weakness. The fact that she trusted him with the swollen horror of her naked, grieving face brightened him as if he'd swallowed the sun. Szarok patted her shoulder, relishing in the smell of her salt and the heat of her skin. She leaned into him and encircled his neck with her arms.

"I feel better about this now. Before, I thought we had to stop, because neither of us can afford to be weak. But if it makes us stronger, more resolved not to falter—"

"Then we carry on," he said tenderly. "And so we must, my Tegan, my treasure. It would break my heart if you turned from me now."

Better Than Elsewhere

James Morrow had never seen a snowstorm out at sea, and it would've been breathtaking if it hadn't also been cold as a witch's tit. He was helping Sung Ji scrape away ice as fast as it formed on deck, making it hazardous for the sailors. Millie was busy below with a constant rotation of coughs and complaints. He'd expected the crew to caterwaul about the alleged curse, but misery and peril stole all their spare energy.

It wasn't deep winter, though, so there was no ice in the water yet. According to Captain Advika, that was their saving grace. He'd thought life was hard marching with Company D, but he'd never sailed through darkness spackled white until his face froze and he couldn't get a proper breath. Sung Ji mocked him with exaggerated wheezing as they went to redo work they'd already finished once, twice, three times.

Will this night never end?

That evening Morrow didn't sleep, but in the morning, when light broke wide over the sea, it was misty but clearing, and he saw land in the distance. Not an island like Antecost or the skerries they'd been passing, but a proper mainland. Yet from the shape of the coast, he knew it wasn't the one they'd left behind. There would no Otterburn here, no Winterville or Soldier's Pond, definitely no Lorraine or Gaspard. He'd gone sailing once before, but only for a few days, and he'd never gone beyond the widening of the bay. Instead he'd crept into the ruins time and again, rescuing old-world stories when he could've been making his own.

Despite smothering sadness and fear for Tegan, he couldn't quell a spark of excitement. *I'm about to set foot somewhere entirely new.* Advika shouted at her men as they streamed toward the docks. Since every settlement was different, Morrow leaned forward, anxious for a glimpse of landfall. This town had people waiting, many wearing anxious frowns.

"What's this place called?" he asked Sung Ji.

"Peckinpaugh. It's one of the largest settlements on our winter run. But when the captain said we'd be gone a half a year, not all that time's on the open water. We usually winter in Baybridge, but this time I'm worried we won't make it before the big ice."

As the *Catalina* cruised toward port, Morrow asked, "Pardon my ignorance, but . . . the whole sea doesn't actually freeze . . . ?"

"The rivers do and parts of the bay, back toward Antecost. This far north, you get ice floes that obstruct the usual straits. And sometimes they make it near impossible to navigate the shoals, especially when the water's dark and murky. I don't know how many ships have gone down due to ice and the bones of another wreck."

Now that he knew a little more about the dangers that lay ahead, Morrow wondered how the rest of the voyage would go. There must be other settlements between Peckinpaugh and Baybridge, so how many and how much time could they make up? Between the trouble in Antecost, the ferocious storm, and Captain Advika's decision to turn back, the whole trade run might be in jeopardy.

Finally the ship eased up to the dock, and since people had been calling and waving for a while, a large group stood assembled. A couple of Advika's sailors surged forward, running down the gangplank toward lovers who seemed to be waiting. One sailor greeted a handsome man with a warm hug and a deep kiss while another of his fellows fought the crowd to reach a very pregnant woman. With the number waiting, there were already more people than lived in Rosemere. Morrow stared, incredulous. The very pregnant woman wasn't the only expectant mother in the crowd, either. The captain greeted one family with a glad smile.

"Farrell, Netta. How have you been?"

Netta smiled. She was a pretty woman with a round face, a pointed chin, and a dimple to the left of her mouth that flashed when she spoke. "Well enough, as you can see."

"Looks like there will be another Gwynne before much longer."

"I have some time yet," Netta protested.

Advika addressed the husband. "You should give your wife some peace, man. Four is enough, don't you think?"

Two small children clung to the woman's skirt, and a big-eyed girl around seven held her father's hand. Morrow could tell by her expression that she liked the look of the *Catalina*. He knelt, wishing he had a gift from Rosemere to offer her, but he hadn't realized part of the excitement of putting into port came from the anticipation of small children.

"Hello," he said. "I'm James. And you are?"

"Lucilla," she told him.

Before he could say more, the throng parted, making way, and a tall, silver-haired woman with brown skin stepped forward. "Whadda ya at, Advika? We were after our supplies almost two weeks ago." She spoke with broad vowels and a lilt that rang with unfamiliar charm.

The captain offered an apologetic smile. "It's been a rough run, Khamish. I'll tell you all about it over drinks as my men unload."

By then Morrow should have been exhausted, but he caught a second wind. He waved at the little girl and followed the other sailors. The town nestled on the shore against a wild fir forest, taller and older than all the trees on the Evergreen Isle combined.

Here the air smelled different, too, sharp and crisp, brine and the promise of more snow. These buildings clearly had survived from the old world. He'd seen the style before, usually in ruins, but here they'd shored them up with good patches to crumbling walls, and the roofs were a combination of earth tiles and metal sheets. The settlement seemed larger than Antecost and Rosemere combined, enormous by his standards.

Everywhere he looked, there were people. Some of the houses had faded signs proclaiming what kind of trade they did. They had old-world machines, too, but instead of letting them run to rust, they'd repurposed, so here a bright-blue motor wagon had been turned into a spot where children played, clambering in and out with giggles of delight; and there, something he couldn't identify had been hollowed out and somebody had planted flowers in it. There were no walls, either, and certainly no weapons, no signs that strife had ever touched this place.

He paused to examine some loom craft, beautiful scarves and overshirts in bright patterns. The woman selling them gazed at him with cheerful curiosity. "How's you getting on, me fine friend?"

Her accent resounded even stronger than the leader Captain Advika had spoken with. Morrow had questions, but it must be impolite to ask. So he said, "Just looking."

Evergreen Isle chits were probably worth nothing here, and he didn't think she'd offer something so fine in exchange for a story, the way he usually paid for food and lodging on the road.

"Good and soft," she practically sang. "Treated these lovelies better'n my own children." Her laughing eyes said this was a joke. "You'll need a bit o' something warm this far north."

Fascinated, he noticed that she contracted certain words like *than* and *of,* she dropped certain consonants, and she pronounced the *th* at the end of words like an *f.* He'd never encountered the like before, so he tried to keep her talking. Not difficult, since he had lots of questions about Peckinpaugh, un-related to accent.

"Come from away, did ya?"

He nodded. "I arrived on the *Catalina*."

"Ah, good ship, that. Where ya longs to?" She seemed to be curious about him, too, but he had no idea what she was asking.

"Pardon me?"

"Your home, boy." At least, he guessed that was what she meant, for it was so compacted that it sounded like *yr home by*.

"Rosemere, on the Evergreen Isle."

"G'wan!" That seemed like an exclamation of surprise. "Reckon I couldn't find that with a pencil *and* a map."

Since she seemed in no hurry to move him on, even if he wasn't buying her wares, he decided to inquire. "If you have a moment, I was wondering . . ."

"Yes, buddy?"

"Did you have much trouble before the War of the River?"

The weaver stared at him blankly.

Morrow realized he didn't even know what to call the old ones. Before, they had been known by several different names, town to town: *Freaks, Muties, Eaters,* and the list went on. "There was trouble in the south. . . ."

"Ay." She made a dismissive gesture. "It never travels this far north. They have all kind o' sorrows, or so I hear, but we mind our own business."

"So there are no Uroch here?" he said, astonished. "A long time ago people got sick and they changed and then—"

"'Tis a mauzy day, no?" The vendor seemed a little uncom-fortable now, as if she didn't want to give a history lesson instead of selling scarves.

"Never mind. I'm sorry for bothering you."

Morrow headed away from the stall, struggling with the pos-sibility that *any* land had emerged unscathed from old-world strug-gles. Life obviously lacked certain things, technology they could no longer produce or repair, but these folks weren't broken or wounded the way he'd seen on the other mainland. Quietly, he walked through town, wondering whom he should ask.

And then he saw it.

A white building, worn and ancient, with the word LIBRARY across the top. Apart from Rosemere, he'd never seen the like. Though he'd found books in the structural remains of such places, this one seemed to be intact. He practically ran for the door and burst inside, fearing to find waterlogged wreckage and burned bits and—

He almost wept.

This room smelled of old books, a trace musty, but mostly, he breathed in leather and polishing oil. Row on row of intact books, different colors and sizes, organized in a way he could scarcely imagine. This was the incarnation of a fantasy he'd never even dared to dream. A distinguished older man with white hair rose from behind a desk, offering a half bow.

"Seen a ghost, have ya?"

"I'm having a hard time," he confessed. "It's so overwhelming. I've never seen so many resources assembled in one place."

"We were lucky."

That felt almost like an invitation to ask for answers. "I don't understand how this place is so . . . untouched."

"I'm no historian, but . . . I'll explain if I can. Never were a lot o' us. For such a sprawlin' land, at our height, only half a million souls."

"Half a . . ." Morrow couldn't even complete the phrase for the weight of his wonder. This town must be a thousand strong, and it was the most enormous intact settlement he'd encountered.

"Not all in one city, o' course. Even back then, we were flung like copper pennies. I think . . . that's what saved us. When the trouble started in the south, it just . . . passed us by."

"It was worst in the largest settlements," Morrow agreed.

He had found artifacts from the old world that had filled in some of the gaps. Yellowed papers that told him some of how it all went so wrong, but he hadn't realized that things were radically different in the north. These weren't ruins as he understood them; people were still simply living here, maybe not as they had before, but better than elsewhere.

The librarian went on, "When the machines died, the rest of the world went quiet. We knew a lot about getting by, so we kept to ourselves and, during the worst, turned away ships by the dozen. Sometimes they burned 'em in the bay rather than let 'em touch ground."

"So you're prosperous and safe because you refused to offer help or sanctuary." Morrow didn't mean to sound so angry, since these crimes were long since past, but outrage twisted into a razor coil inside him.

The old man didn't offer any defense. This probably wasn't the first time an outsider asked *how* and *why*. He must be used to giving this explanation. "It's only been, oh, roundabouts fifteen years since we opened trade. 'Twas a right flutter when the first ship came in. So many tasties we hadn't eaten before." He smiled, a touch wistful.

Morrow made an effort to recover from his outburst, hoping he wouldn't be banished. "I'm sorry for my rudeness. Is it all right if I look around? I won't touch anything."

"O' course. And books are for reading. Just be delicate with 'em. For many of these, they're the only copies left in the world."

With that caution ringing in his ears, it was a wonder Morrow got up the courage to pull even a single volume off the shelf. And it did take him a while as he wandered the rows, reading titles with a slow, precise pleasure. There were books on how to keep bees and build aviaries, books with murderous phrases as their title and ones that sounded sweet as love. He eventually picked up a tome, enormous and weighty, bound in battered leather, dated from a time so long ago that it felt like holding history in his hands. He read the complete sonnets of William

Shakespeare for the first time. He'd read portions before, sometimes not even getting to finish a poem because the pages were damaged. But standing there in the Peckinpaugh library, he read them all, one by one, and when he finished the last, he realized tears were trickling down his cheeks.

> *Came there for cure, and this by that I prove:*
> *Love's fire heats water; water cools not love.*

Carefully, he replaced the massive volume on the shelf. While he'd read, his anger had cooled, and now that he knew this place housed such treasures, he couldn't even bring himself to hate the locals for safeguarding it. Though countless souls had died due to their course of determined self-preservation, they'd also saved a great many priceless relics. *I'm not sorry,* he thought. He had expected to explore more ruins, not to find so many thriving settlements. His father ought to see about commissioning a ship in Antecost and sending a crew along Captain Advika's route to expand trade potential for Rosemere.

By now it was quite late, so when he stepped out of the library, the old man locked up behind him. The street was dark, lit by lanterns hung at regular intervals. Even in smaller villages, there was usually a public house, and in Peckinpaugh, he found a whole row of them. They had interesting names like Crown and Barrel, Rose and Thorn, Gull's Roost. None of them were large, but they all seemed inviting and clean, so he chose the Rose at random and stepped in for a look.

The smell of sawdust, sweat, and ale drenched him in the first breath. Unlike many taverns, the patrons weren't all men. Male and female alike drank up after a long day. The room had two long tables with eight chairs each and then smaller tables nestled against the back wall. Since there were no vacancies and no familiar faces, he went along to the Roost to find a similar setup, only with one big table surrounded by smaller ones. At the center of the crowd, he spotted Millie, rosy-cheeked from drinking or the merry fire, or it might even have been the way the man next to her leaned close to whisper something in her ear.

Shock rooted his feet to the floor. At some point, he'd gotten *used* to the way she followed him and the way she gazed up at him with those eyes. But now she wasn't doing either of those things, and he finally noticed how ridiculously pretty she was. Her drinking mate put an arm around her shoulders, and she shoved him off with a smile and a joke.

Morrow dove through the crowd as if he'd been shot by an arrow. Instead of chairs, this pub had benches, so he shouldered between Millie and the ass who couldn't keep his hands to himself. He planted himself with a cheerful smile, as if he didn't realize this was rude. A chorus of colorful responses greeted his arrival: "'ow's it coming?" and "'ow's she cuttin'?"

"Fine," he said. "What're we drinking?"

"We offered to stand drinks for this pretty love." The man he'd interrupted gave him a flinty look.

"You're some crooked," said one of the others, flinging a handful of white shells.

They had the remnants of a meal on the table: what looked like boiled eggs and some kind of fish pie, judging by the smell. Morrow's stomach rumbled, and it had to be during a lull in the roaring laughter, so the men broke down. A short one shoved the leftovers toward him.

"You're just about gutfoundered. Have a scoff."

Millie leaned over. "He means, 'You're very hungry; eat something.'"

Something about her easy translation rubbed him the wrong way. "I knew that."

What was she doing while I was reading sonnets?

But the man on the other side of her pushed the food away. "Paid good coin for that. Why should I waste it on this skeet?"

An intake of breath told Morrow he'd just been insulted,

though he had no idea what that meant. But he forced a smile and lifted a hand to signal the owner. "I'll entertain your patrons for a bit of food and drink. Fair trade?"

As they usually did, the woman agreed. "No sad stories, mind. I don't want the old ones cryin' in their beer."

"So you're the storyteller." The fellow he'd aggravated seemed to have taken it personally, so he sneered the last word. "Tell us a story, then."

Since this was his bread and butter, he went to the hearth, where everyone had a good view of him. It didn't take long for the patrons to quiet. Quickly, he sorted through his repertoire and settled on a story with plenty of action and a dragon in disguise. At first the man next to Millie set out to heckle, and some of his friends encouraged it, but it wasn't the first time he'd won over an unfriendly crowd. When the princess chose the dragon instead of the knight and lived with him amid all that hoarded gold, the crowd went wild.

"Great yarn!"

"You've got a callin', b'y."

He smiled. "Storytelling is thirsty work."

People patted his back as he returned to Millie. The groping ass had sidled close to her again, but after a long moment she shifted to make room. The proprietor brought him a fish pie, some kind of fried bread topped with crispy bits of meat, and a huge tankard of amber liquid that smelled both yeasty and sweet.

"Many thanks."

After he took the first bite, Millie whispered, "I'd choose the dragon, too."

And Morrow wondered why that stung *so* much.

When You Alone Remain

Tegan stayed close to the tower for a few days after she nearly froze.

After the strange, early snow, she expected winter to settle in for a long stay, but the weather warmed enough to let them continue Szarok's swimming lessons. He complained all the way down to the shore, but he steadied as she explained about holding your breath, at least according to Uncle Walter. Funny how years later she still ached at the thought of him, and she couldn't decide if she hated the idea of him living well without her, or if that would be comforting. Or maybe the pain would only disappear if she knew for sure that he'd died.

Szarok studied her for a moment. "What's wrong?"

With anyone else, she would've donned a bright smile and rambled intellectual nonsense. It was absurd that others believed she was made entirely of altruistic desire and love of learning, but Tegan supposed if you played a role long enough, people accepted it, even when it defied credence. False reassurance faltered on her tongue, and she couldn't speak. The Uroch didn't judge things the same as humans, so in that reality she took refuge.

"My uncles." She hoped that would be enough of a prompt.

It took him a moment, likely because he had so many memories. But the fact that he could retrieve her confidence at all . . . Well, it resonated like winning a prize. "I've been thinking on that. Is it possible they went out to hunt and . . . something went wrong?"

"Sometimes they *did* scavenge," she admitted.

"Did they steal all the supplies as they vanished?"

"No. But they could have only taken a few things—"

"Tegan, my treasure, would you hear my candid thoughts?"

For a while she stared at the rippling water. Today it was chilly, with a bright sun, and it would be frigid in the dark. Soon the sea would be too cold even for a brief breathing or paddling lesson. Hard not to feel that their time was running out.

"Tell me," she said.

"They went to search for food . . . and they died. I don't believe they intended to abandon you. If they had, they would have taken your remaining provisions. It was easier to believe they did, because then you could blame them for leaving you vulnerable and kinless. You swallowed a pit of anger and never spat it out. Otherwise, it's too painful to admit that they died while you were sleeping, and you can't even fault them for it."

His words hammered home, relentless, chiseling away, until hurt spilled over her in a drowning wave. *This, this is why I don't ever tell the truth. Because people say true things back and it feels like dying.* Dropping to her knees, she gasped for breath. *I won't cry. I won't.*

Warm hands curved over hers where she dug her fingers into cold, packed sand. "I wish I could take this from you. Every hurt, every memory that left a scar. I would carry it all gladly."

"It doesn't work like that."

"Not for your people."

Unwillingly drawn, she asked, "Can it? If someone's not dying?"

"Yes."

"I'm intrigued, but . . . I don't wish for that. Terrible things made me who I am, and . . . I don't think I deserve to be unmade."

But there are still secrets you don't know.

He whispered in Uroch and cradled her close as the sea washed about their ankles. "Mourn for your uncles, or you will carry this pain always, like a blade lodged in your heart."

Tegan wept into his shoulder, sandy fingers on his arms. "For so long I thought it was their fault. That if they had taken me with them . . ."

The Wolves wouldn't have gotten me.

They were ignorant, violent, and territorial. Warring over ruined buildings and bits of salvage, it never occurred to them to cooperate or share. And unless you were physically strong, capable of fighting your way up the ranking hierarchy, you had no hope of being treated like anything but chattel. The Wolves took "survival of the fittest" to extremes and acknowledged no quality but brutality as a virtue. "Might makes right" encapsulated their credo, and living among them had been unmitigated hell.

"In all likelihood, you would be dead as well," he said softly.

"That might be better." With her defenses down, the truth slipped out, raw and awful.

She immediately tried to recoil, but his ears were too good and, as ever, he had his attention focused on her completely. Szarok eased her back and gazed into her face with the fiercest eyes she'd ever seen. He gave her a little shake.

"Why? Why would you ever say such a thing? Does your life mean so little to you?"

"You don't know what I had to do to hang on to it." Like vomit, she couldn't keep the words down, what she'd sworn never to speak of again. Nobody could understand if they hadn't lived it. There would only be disgust or horror or pity or some combination of the three, and if she saw that in his face—

I can't.

"Tell me." At that, she wrenched away, fully intending to throw herself into the sea, swim out so far that he couldn't follow. "Please."

The *please* moved her when all the orders, demands, and force could not. Tegan stumbled a few steps into the water, and she didn't look at him. He didn't follow, yet his caution registered as care, as it always had. Never once had he taken from her; he only made her want to give.

This time proved no exception.

Halting at first, and then as her words unleashed, she *told* him. How it was being taken, what she did to survive, the submission that made her scream endlessly inside her head rather than end up with a bloody smile carved into her throat, as happened to girls the Wolves deemed too much trouble. *They treated me like a thing; they used me. It didn't matter what I wanted.* They didn't usually hurt breeders, as they needed more warriors. So she said that aloud, and everything else, including how she'd hated the monsters they put inside her and how she provoked her captors just enough.

Just enough to lose them. So I didn't have to bring more of them into the world.

She was sobbing now, her voice ragged. "I am not kind. I am not sweet. I am not forgiving. I am *so glad* that your people rolled through and cleansed Gotham like a fire. I hope they all died in agony, every Wolf, every cub. But . . . this is not what I've shown everyone else. They wouldn't understand. I've been afraid for so long, and I say whatever people want to hear, the version of reality that will move them and make them want to help me. Sometimes they even act like it's *my* fault."

She remembered Deuce saying, *I would have fought until I died.* Like that was better. As if there was something *wrong* with surviving. A fresh wave of anger rocked through her. *I'm not sorry I broke her nose.* When Deuce took so long coming back to Soldier's Pond and worried her foster mother, Tegan got to hit her while pretending all that anger stemmed from concern. She told Szarok that, too, and ended her rant with a ferocious scream. She keened until her voice gave.

There. It's all out.

Afterward, Tegan buried her face in her hands. There was no sense of relief, only emptiness where all the poison had been. Residual nausea rolled through her in waves, and she hunched over, racked with dry heaves. The crunch of his feet on the sand whispered that he was close by, but he didn't touch her.

"You were right," he said.

"About what?" She swiped tears and snot from her face, wishing she could wash.

"Terrible things shaped you. I could say that I yearn to disembowel those who hurt you, but those kills rightfully belong to you. I'm sorry my people stole them." With a sigh, he shook his head. "Humans are remarkably stupid. It is best to kill an enemy outright, for if you torture them, they *will* return when they are stronger."

His reaction shocked her enough that she turned to look. Szarok evinced none of the emotional response she'd dreaded, no sympathy or even particular shock. She'd gotten better at reading him, so while he was clearly angry, this didn't seem to have changed anything. Her fists uncurled, and she took a deep breath as her sour stomach settled somewhat.

"That's it?" she said.

"Is there more?"

"I don't know. I thought . . ." *That you'd react like a human.*

"What? I can praise your great strength, if you wish. You are a queen, my Tegan. When you alone remain after your enemies fall, it only matters that you emerged victorious."

"I did," she whispered, tears starting again. "I waited. I watched for my opportunity, and I took it. In the end, *I* vanquished them."

"Not all battles are won with teeth and claws. Your wit is your greatest weapon."

In the end, she didn't ask if her confession altered the way he saw her. That question would insult both of them. When he took a step toward her, she ran two and fell into his arms. He rubbed his cheek against hers, the top of her head, the side of her throat, and the curve of her shoulder. Now that she understood what he was doing, it meant more; and she grasped the subtext. *You're still mine,* he said silently. *Still the closest of my kin.*

Stretching up, she cupped his face in her hands and kissed him. This belonged to the two of them alone, all sweetness and . . . learning. A long while later she eventually taught him those breath exercises, but it was more fun to do it mouth to mouth instead of in the water. He participated with enthusiasm, until they were both shivering with cold and excitement. Once he conquered his fear, Szarok progressed faster in the water than she did in language lessons. They curled up by the fire, and she tried her best, as it delighted him whenever she perfected a new phrase. Her more impressive failures earned sharp barks of laughter.

As the light faded, he rose.

"Hunting?" she asked.

He rested a hand briefly atop her head. "As I must, if we want to eat."

"Be careful." It was only a sliver of what she wanted to say, but it sufficed.

At nightfall, she tinkered with the crank-light and the glass shards. It wasn't far from the signal tower to the shore, so Tegan picked a path down the incline. No snow tonight—the sky was clear, a good night to be sailing. Mentally crossing her fingers, she flashed a signal repeatedly against the dark sky. For a ship to spot them, it would need to be passing at the right moment, and then it might not bother investigating. Eventually she gave up and headed home.

There was a little leftover seabird meat from the day before, and she grimaced at the congealed fat. The gamy taste didn't improve upon sitting, either. She also had part of a potato and a mouthful of seaweed. Long term, this diet couldn't sustain her, though she suspected fresh meat would do for Szarok. But the goats were getting harder to find, even for him, and the foxes were both nasty tasting and lousy with sinew and gristle. Tegan tried not to obsess over the challenges they faced with winter on the way, but her brain didn't easily relinquish worry.

Hours later she was bundled in bed when the door eased open. Even in the dim light, she recognized his silhouette. *Besides, who else would it be?* "Good hunting? Did you eat?"

Pausing, he seemed surprised that she was still awake. "Yes. I tied the birds up where the foxes can't get them. The cold will keep them fresh longer."

His tone alerted Tegan that something was wrong. "What happened?"

Without answering, he closed the door behind him and crossed to the stove. His movements in stoking the fire spoke of leashed frustration. Each jab threw sparks, highlighting his sharp features. When she considered how important he'd become, her stomach tightened at the idea that he couldn't talk to her, especially since he held the keys to her soul.

I told him everything. But he can't?

"Szarok . . . ?" It felt much later than usual, as if she'd waited halfway into the night, but it was harder to keep time in the dark.

"It feels like I scoured every inch of the island. I was looking for anything we could use to build . . ." He didn't finish the sentence.

"A boat?"

"Yes. But I don't know anything about their design, and even if I did, there isn't enough wood available."

Tegan nodded. There were no tall, solid trees, only stunted ones, reeds, grass, and scrub bushes. "You're worried about what's happening to your people."

This wasn't a new concern, but it must come at him in waves, as anxiety did.

"Even if we get back, I haven't *accomplished* anything, though

I learned everything I could about human customs. I've bitten my tongue, ignored slights that—" He bit off the last words, whatever they were.

"What can I do?"

"Nothing," he muttered.

Ignoring that denial as if it were a wall she could scale, Tegan left the bed and knelt behind him. When she flattened a palm on his back, he shivered. Since he didn't shake off her touch, she slipped her arms around him from behind and rested her cheek on his shoulder. He lowered his head and stared at the glowing embers in the stove. Just when she thought she should leave him be, he covered her hands with his. She didn't offer platitudes, and in a few moments he shifted so they could warm each other.

"Come to bed. Anything you have to say, I'll listen. But you're freezing. I know you're not a fool, so why were you wandering the night like you are?"

His expression brightened. "It's strange how happy I feel when you scold me."

Snuggling close to him, she pulled the furs around them. "I can do it more. Or you can talk to me. It's your turn anyway."

Szarok rested his head on her chest, making her feel . . . needed, as if in this moment she was the strong one. Tegan smiled at the top of his head, savoring that sensation.

"If life were a little easier here, I could just . . . stay. And not mind my people suffering. I hate that I forget sometimes; then it's even worse when I remember. That I'm happy with you."

"Because I'm the enemy?"

"Not mine. Never mine. But . . . in a way, yes."

"It makes sense. And"—she swallowed hard—"I'll never ask you to choose. I know you have an important job to do and—"

He touched her lips gently to still them. "Are you telling me what I want to hear? I don't care if you lie to everyone else in the world. Never to me. Understand?"

"Yes. And I'm not. From now until forever I'm saving all my truths for you."

Shifting slightly, he encircled her in his arms; the most reassuring sound in the world must be the thump of his heart. Tegan raised her face and kissed his chin, just as she had accidentally the day by the well. Probably it shouldn't make her so happy that the Uroch didn't use their mouths for kissing, but she never had, either, so for both of them, it seemed brand-new.

Normally she didn't touch him much before they slept. Though she trusted him, she could be skittish, and it seemed better to avoid misunderstandings. But tonight . . . everything seemed rather different, partly her prior confession and partially his vulnerability. She couldn't pin down the change, but . . . she couldn't sleep, either.

"You're breathing so fast," he whispered.

Tegan had no idea what to say. She closed her eyes; better to pretend this conversation wasn't happening. Then he kissed her chin with such exquisite care that she shivered. She meant to say something sweet, but only "I'm not scared" came out.

"Good. Try to sleep."

"I can't."

"Why not?" He sounded a little drowsy, a sign that he didn't share her restless energy, and . . . she wanted him to.

Even if that was unfair.

"I want a good-night kiss."

"Is that a custom you wish to teach me?" Szarok levered up on an elbow, eyes gleaming in the dark.

"If you care to learn."

"Yes."

That was her new favorite word, the beautiful simplicity of it. He rolled onto his side, facing her instead of holding her close. Tegan leaned in and brushed her lips against his, a soft little tease, when she needed more. But kissing was safe. It only ever felt good.

"That's it?" he asked, just as she had earlier.

"Did you want more?"

In response, he took her mouth and sucked on each lip in turn. She made the *more* sound deep in her throat, and his claws grazed her head, shoulders, spine. Never anything else, but tonight, she ached at his restraint. Tegan went after his tongue, unable to resist pressing closer.

"I don't think these good-night kisses are meant to make me sleep."

Maybe not.

"Sorry."

While she wanted more, she didn't know how to ask, or even *what*. She kissed him behind the ear and then tried to settle down. *What were we talking about?*

Oh.

Eventually she said, "I wish I could solve being stranded. But the only thing I can do is keep signaling."

At that, he kissed the top of her head as low-grade shivers curled through him. "You saved me. I don't want you to feel guilty."

"That's incidental. And you saved me, too. So . . . let's stop keeping score. If we're truly partners, it doesn't matter anyway."

Unholy Alliances

"Here," Szarok said.

He had been secretive for the last few days, returning to the tower later than usual. And now Tegan had the answer why. He'd carved her a new staff, possibly because she'd mentioned missing the old one. She hefted it and found it perfect for her height.

"Thank you."

"I made it out of the wood that you used to save our lives."

Her eyes widened. "You must've scoured the shoreline for ages."

"It was worth it if you're pleased."

Stretching up, she kissed him just below his ear. "I'll do my utmost never to lose it."

That gave her a pang, as she'd left her doctor's bag behind and in it, Dr. Wilson's precious anatomy book. *It's probably still on the* Catalina. But it felt strange to be separated from the medicines she had made her life's work and the tome that represented the power she'd accumulated through sheer stubborn effort, reading and memorizing late into the night. People respected her now because she could treat their sickness and patch up their wounds, but she wouldn't be satisfied until she lived up to the old man's expectations. That grumpy scientist had taken one look at her and decided she had great potential.

It was the first time Tegan had believed that she did, too.

"I'm going, then."

"Good hunting," she said.

They parted ways, and she headed down to the shore with the crank-light and a shard of glass. She *thought* the two together should reach farther, but it wasn't as if she'd tested the theory with what Dr. Wilson would call good science. For the past three nights she had signaled at regular intervals to be sure her flashes didn't get mistaken for natural phenomena. She carried on until her hands went numb from the cold and winding the light. Just before she gave up for the night, brightness flickered in response. Szarok was hunting—she didn't know where precisely—so she shouted, hoping the wind carried the sound to his sharp ears.

At first against the backdrop of darkness, it seemed as if a ghost light were drifting toward the shore, and then the shape of a small schooner clarified. *Definitely not the* Catalina. While the shallows might be possible for a ship this size, navigating the shoals would be dangerous. It looked like they had dropped anchor, so Tegan resumed signaling. An indistinct call echoed across the water, but she couldn't make out what they were saying. She yelled again, both for Szarok and for the boat she'd attracted.

It's probably the last before the big ice.

The light rocked closer, and she identified two men rowing toward shore. Impossible to tell anything about them, but she set down the crank-light and the shard of glass to grip her staff with both hands. Moments later the rescuers hauled the dinghy onto the stony beach. Each scrape of wood on sand rubbed her nerves raw. In Tegan's experience, everyone was a potential enemy until they proved otherwise.

"Ho there, castaway!" came the call as the larger man climbed out.

"Looking for a lift?" the other asked.

She nodded. "Wherever you're headed, any port will do."

"How long have you been here on your own, a little thing like you?" The sailor phrased it like a question, but it wasn't. Not really.

He ambled toward her, and the moon illuminated deep-set eyes and a hooked nose. They were both bundled against the cold, bulky with layers. *Stop,* she thought. *Don't come any closer.* The silent warning worked, or at least it seemed to, as the smaller one raised his head and inhaled sharply and then made a face.

"This place reeks. How do you stand it?"

"It's the seabirds. There are thousands of them, nesting."

The two men exchanged a look and then the bigger one said, "Well, time's wasting. Come along. We'll take good care of you."

"My friend will be along shortly," she said.

Her flesh crawled at the idea of climbing into a boat with these two, but the alternative was impossible. If she sent them away out of fear and the Uroch went to war, she could never face Szarok. *It doesn't matter if they're awful. I can protect myself.* Her grip tightened on the staff, and the smaller one appeared to notice. He nudged his companion.

"Even better." The tall one put on a smile that only made his face worse.

Soon Szarok came racing down the hill toward them. Since he hunted in his skin, he didn't have on much, despite the cold, and the cool starlight limned his features. The moment they identified him, the men drew weapons, one a firearm and the other a knife. Tegan ran to Szarok's side and held up a hand.

"There's no need. He's the vanguard, sent from the Uroch to human lands."

"I don't care what the hell he is. That thing's not getting on our ship." The big man spat to emphasize his point.

"You come on, love. We'll get you to safety, and once we make landfall, you can send someone back for . . . that." While the short man might not be as terrible as the large one, he echoed the same scorn.

"Then go about your business," Tegan said flatly. "And forget you saw our light. I won't leave without him."

The two traded another significant look, then they both laughed. "What madness is this? You think you're living a fairy tale, the beauty and her beast?"

Never mind, the small one is rotten, too.

After smacking his friend's shoulder, the tall man said, "I don't think you understand. You've wasted our time, kept us from our business. That means we can't just move along without getting something for our trouble."

"There's no salvage here." Tegan spoke around clenched teeth.

Beside her, Szarok remained still, breathing hard. He probably sensed the imminent escalation. Tegan shifted, gauging the distance between the gun and Szarok. The sailors had gotten too close to her; her staff was long enough to disarm. Once, Deuce had remarked that Tegan didn't like killing—probably because she was a healer—but . . . that preference sprang from her weapon of choice. It just wasn't *efficient* to bludgeon an enemy to death when she had trained slayers around who could dispatch opponents she incapacitated with one strike.

"Then you can make it up to us. Winter nights are long." This came from the short man.

She didn't wait for them to attack. That—that was enough. In a strike she'd learned from James, she slammed her staff against the gunman's arm. With a cry, he dropped the weapon, and she took out his knees. Her flurry of strikes smashed in succession: ankles, sternum, throat. The smaller man came at her with a knife, and Szarok was there. He disemboweled his enemy in a spatter of entrails that steamed in the frosty air. Tegan didn't ask him to finish her kill. She got the glass shard and carved the first sailor a crimson smile.

"We must be quick," he said without asking if she was all right.

She nodded. "There will be others on the ship. If we wrap up in some of their layers, they may not realize—"

"Until it's too late."

Swiftly, they cobbled together a basic disguise, and the moon cooperated, dodging behind a cloud. Neither of them knew how to row well, but they managed to limp toward the schooner. Close up, it was the strangest ship she'd ever seen, rusted in some spots as if it were metal, but the material was pale and sleek. Tegan guessed that the sailors had salvaged an old-world ship. Most of the ones she'd seen on the water were built in Antecost, based off simple, ancient designs.

"Have you ever seen anything like this?" she whispered.

Szarok shook his head.

As they got within ten feet, someone called, "Any trouble?"

"Not much." Szarok emulated the big one's voice.

"You all right? Sound kind of—"

"Please, no. I don't want to." Tegan whimpered as a distraction, and . . . it worked.

Wearing a broad smile, the sailor on watch peered over the side, and Szarok jerked him down, snapped his neck like dry kindling, and then dropped him into the water. Most probably she should have been alarmed by that, but instead that raw strength made her feel safe, because he'd never turn it against her, only their enemies.

Since the shore party had left the rusty ladder down, she went up first, as her face was unlikely to alarm anyone. However, the deck reeked of liquor and the rest of the crew seemed to be sound asleep. She hesitated only a second before deciding that the watchman set the tone for everyone else. At the prospect of a female captive, he didn't offer help. *No, he leaned over to inspect the merchandise.* Szarok didn't speak; he started the silent slaughter and she finished it, using the tiny knife that clicked out at the push of a button. Then they rolled the six corpses into the water. Tegan waited for regret, or even remorse, but it didn't come.

I tried to appeal to their better nature. It's not my fault they didn't have one.

"Let's check the stores," he said then.

But as she headed for the lower deck, a door banged open and someone opened fire. Tegan dove as the bullet speared into the wood behind her. *We left one alive. I should have remembered that the boss has his own room.* Holding on to her staff, she crawled toward cover, hoping the rocking of the waves would wreck his aim. In the darkness, it should have been even tougher to hit a moving target.

"Cowardly shit-heeled scum! You'll die even if I have to scuttle this whole damn ship," the captain shouted.

"Bad idea," she called back. "We can swim to shore, and if you follow, we'll kill you on dry land."

"It's a good way to die," Szarok agreed.

With some colorful cursing, the man slammed the cabin door. Szarok circled to her but again didn't ask if she was injured. That could register as indifference, but he'd smell it if she were hurt. So there was no point in wasting breath when they had a crisis unfolding.

"Best scenario, we make some kind of a deal. Because I don't really understand sea charts or how to sail this thing."

He inclined his head. "But he seems unlikely to come to terms, now that we've executed his crew."

"If the men are bad, they were probably following his lead," Tegan muttered.

From the sounds within, the sole survivor seemed to be building a barricade. The hull was hard and slick, the door made of the same material. It would take some serious force to break it down, and that was presuming there were no snares set. She made up her mind.

"Watch the door."

"Be careful," he said.

No questions, no delays. With that, she slipped away and

searched the ship. Tegan turned up a few weapons, none strong enough to kill through a wall or door. She gathered them up and threw them overboard. *If they aren't immediately useful, they can be turned against us later.* The lower deck was more of a storage area; this ship had been laid out differently than others she'd seen. Then Tegan stumbled on the biggest cache of old-world tech she'd ever encountered. Row upon row of tarnished metal, faded colors, and unidentifiable devices were piled against the wall.

Leverage.

By the great care with which all the articles had been cleaned and sorted, somebody must value this collection. Smiling, she picked up a square thing and carried it back to the cabin, where Szarok stood guard. He tilted his head, studying her discovery.

"What is it?"

She shrugged. "But I think it's important."

"Shall we find out?" He stepped to the side.

Tegan hammered on the cabin door with an upraised fist and then shouted, "I unearthed the most interesting junk just now. Wonder if it floats."

"Don't touch anything!"

"Too late." Enjoying herself, she described in loving detail what she was holding.

"Put that back! Do you idiots have any idea how much that's worth?" Sheer rage powered the captain's voice.

He must be tracking her movements, because his shouts became incoherent as she strolled toward the railing, hefting his valuable box. With a mental apology to the fish, she dropped it. A howl of pure fury echoed in reaction and then, judging by the crashes, it sounded like the captain might be wrecking his own cabin.

"Who's the real idiot?"

"You plan to goad him into a fight?" Szarok asked.

"Not quite."

Whistling, she returned to the door. "For every minute you

hide, I chuck something else into the sea. So sad. I'm guessing this is your life's work, too."

Silence.

Tegan shrugged and headed for the storage area. She only had to throw away two more articles before the door slammed open, and the captain stood, a weapon trained on Szarok. But she still had a third item, this one glimmering silver, cupped in her palm. The instant the asshole saw it, he lowered his weapon. He was a small man, slight, with a permanently windburned face and a salt-and-pepper beard.

"Let's make a deal," she said.

The captain curled his lip. "I don't bargain with murderers."

"So rape and pillage is where you draw the line? Good to know."

"What're you on about?" The wary tone didn't fool her; this shit bucket was easing the barrel of his gun back up in treacle-slow increments.

"We meant to parley for safe passage. Your crew tried to kill my friend and take me as plunder. And you *blame* us for not letting it happen? Sick."

"The last one standing gets to tell whatever story he wants," he snapped.

Tegan lifted a shoulder. "I don't particularly care if you believe me. The odds are in our favor. If I decide to stop talking, you join your precious artifacts in a watery grave."

A nasty smile curved his mouth, and she noticed the scar bisecting his left brow. "You'll be right behind me. I'll jump in the sea right now if you can tell me the difference between the jib and the mainsail."

I hate when morons manage to get it right.

"Then we've reached an impasse," Szarok said.

She nodded. "There's nothing stopping us from killing you, but we can't manage this vessel on our own. Truth be told, neither can you. Even knowing how, it's impossible for you to do all the work alone and reach port without any rest."

From the clench of his jaw, the captain agreed. "Maybe I'd rather die than come to terms with a beast and his bitch."

Szarok took a step. "So be it."

Much as she'd love to see this cretin's blood, she couldn't let it happen. But before she stopped Szarok, the captain stumbled back, his gaze locked on the claws and fangs advancing on him. With a little shudder, he put down his weapon, seeming nearly pissing scared.

"Don't be hasty. Let's talk a little more. That lot was worthless anyway. If we work together, I can get us all to port safely. How's that sound?"

"Fair deal," she said. "You keep the ship once we disembark, and I won't mess with your salvage. All you have to do is recruit a new crew. It'll be like this never happened."

"You'll forgive me if I don't shake your hand."

"Likewise. I'm Tegan. This is Szarok."

"Captain Piebald."

As they spoke, Szarok crept into the cabin behind and quietly gathered up the weapons. Tegan nudged the one on the deck toward him. By the time the captain noticed, all the guns were splashing over the side. If it was possible to die of a rage attack, she thought he might. He kicked at the wall and ranted for quite a while.

"Do you *know* how rare some of those guns were?"

She shrugged. "No. And I don't care, either."

"How close is the nearest port?" Szarok asked.

"Four days with a good wind." But the flicker of Piebald's eyes made Tegan wonder if he was lying.

Unfortunately, examining the charts wouldn't provide her an answer. The next few days would be tense, for damn sure, and she didn't look forward to sleeping in shifts and keeping an eye on this idiot at all times. *He might be planning to lead us into a trap, a port populated with his cohorts.* If they stayed alert, there had to be a way out, no matter how clever Piebald thought he was. *There's always a way out.*

"Time to pull up anchor," the captain was saying. "There's a good wind, so we can put some miles between us and this god-forsaken place."

"Where are we bound?" Szarok asked.

"Would you understand if I told you?" Then Piebald mumbled a slur Tegan hadn't heard since the war had ended, not even bothering to hide his prejudice.

She shivered, exhausted already, and the voyage hadn't even begun.

Pray to Your Gods

For a day and a half Szarok did not rest.

At times he closed his eyes and feigned sleep, but he smelled loathing and treachery on Piebald like the stench that clung to the human male, revealing that he hadn't washed in weeks. Even his beard advertised what he'd eaten for dinner, as if he saved the scraps for later. Everything about the captain made Szarok's flesh crawl.

The salty air stung his eyes and crusted on his skin. *So many firsts.* None of his people had ever journeyed so far, learned to swim, or crewed a sailing ship. Now he knew the names of ropes and pulleys, along with the different sails. When the wind was good, whatever that meant, the course did not need to be adjusted too often and the wheel could be set in the forward position. For the moment Piebald was holed up in his cabin, likely plotting against them.

"You'll get sick if you don't sleep," Tegan said.

Szarok didn't know if that was true. Historically, the People died young, but they didn't suffer from the same ailments that plagued humanity. But it was possible they would develop their own complications as time went on. Still, his eyes did burn, and a residual ache thrummed behind his ears. Constant wariness definitely took a toll.

"Come below for a while. I'll stand watch and make sure Piebald doesn't try anything."

Before Tegan, Szarok couldn't have imagined such complete trust in her kind. Yet he didn't hesitate, only followed her out of the biting wind and down to the storage area. The bed she had fashioned wasn't as warm or as comfortable as the nest they'd left behind, and sometimes the rolling waves churned the meat in his belly until he could scarcely keep it down. None of that qualified as conducive to peaceful slumber.

"Let me set the early warning system."

Clever healer.

In the mouth of the low-ceilinged, narrow stairwell, she tied a length of cord with some jangly metal bits. Piebald probably wouldn't be nimble or alert enough to avoid the trap. Then she returned and settled beside him. The pallet smelled of fish and brackish seawater, making him think it had been submerged at some point, but he didn't see how it could float.

Tegan settled with her back to the wall, facing the doorway. "Put your head in my lap."

"I don't think I can sleep that way."

"Oh. Well, if you'd rather not . . ."

Even if her tone hadn't revealed her disappointment, the spike in her scent would have. For some reason, she wanted this, and it was such a small matter. Szarok rolled onto his side, also with a view of the stairwell, and found it a surprisingly comfortable way to rest. Exhaustion gnawed at him with sharp teeth, until it became too much effort to keep his eyes open.

But once he shut them, other sensory input trickled in. It was never easy to tamp it all down—scents and sounds in particular—but water all around made everything worse. Then her fingers drifted down to his head, and she etched a pattern. Szarok focused on that, not the rocking of the ship or the unnerving howl of the wind. Focusing, he pictured the symbols she drew, until his mind settled.

"You coddle me," he said sleepily.

"A little."

"I like it."

Soon after, he dozed . . . and woke to find her in the same position, watchful and alert. Her staff lay nearby, and her hand was still gentle on his head. Szarok sat up and stretched. Neither of them had slept at the same time since they'd gotten on this hell-boat. The fear almost killed him in following her into the smaller craft and maneuvering across the chill and murky water to the larger ship that had awaited them.

I can swim, he reminded himself. *Memories won't kill me. Panic can.*

Yet horror still swept him in a dark tide as he recalled the water in his ears and mouth, sinking, choking, while the old ones shrieked in unison, dying a thousand times in his head. Unerringly, she found him in the dark and pressed against his side, as if she could drive away the dread with a touch.

It receded a little. Just enough.

"This will be over soon," she whispered.

"Did he come for us?"

"Not tonight. I think he's marshaling his strength."

Szarok nodded. "Two more days, provided he was telling the truth."

"He's definitely planning something." Tegan sighed, and the warmth of her breath fanned over him. Startling but not unpleasant. "I wish I could get a look at the charts, but he hasn't left the cabin unguarded, not even once."

"It makes me uneasy."

"Not knowing our destination? Or being unsure what he's hiding?"

He inclined his head. "Both. Any sliver of information could help us."

"It doesn't matter. He might be making for a port where everyone will try to kill us, but if so, we'll cut a path." Her mouth firmed.

"When you say such things, I forget."

"What?"

"That you're not Uroch."

"I'll take that as a compliment."

At some point, her open mind should stop surprising him, but each time she spoke kindly of his people, his heart opened to her a bit more. Moved, he rubbed his cheek against hers in a gesture of kinship. Pleasure curled through him when he breathed her in and her scent came back familiar, nearly Uroch from close contact.

"Get your lazy arses up here!" The shout from above interrupted further closeness.

Szarok emerged into a gray dawn, the sun only a frosty glimmer. When the light was dim, the details normally resolved into sharper clarity, but today fog misted over the water. This had the captain snarling unintelligible curses.

"We'll be lucky if we don't smash up on a 'berg," Piebald muttered.

The answer to his unspoken question loomed up, and the captain shouted orders in response to the jagged white ice. Szarok and Tegan worked feverishly in tandem to change course, but the side of the boat *scraped*, the sound striking him as if an enemy were close by and rubbing his blades together. He grasped the threat without a lengthy explanation. If the 'berg tore a hole in the hull, the hell-boat would take on water and they'd sink—and without an island nearby, there would be no surviving the wreck.

"Heave, you shit-birds!"

In response, Tegan hauled on the ropes and Szarok adjusted the sail. The schooner rocked, as if something massive had bumped it from below. Piebald swore in words so foul that Szarok didn't even recognize half of them. But there was clearly a problem.

"What's wrong?" Tegan asked.

"I'm not sure, but an orca just buzzed us. Normally it would be deeper this time of year or hunting near the coast. It's rare for them to surface so close to a ship."

Ahead of them a dark shape surfaced, enormous like a swimming skerry, then it dove, revealing a finned tail. *This creature could easily break this boat to bits or flip it.* Near paralyzed, Szarok watched it, but the sea beast didn't turn back, only raced onward. Yet something else slammed into the boat; the waves crashed all around and the vessel listed so hard that he fell. On his hands and knees, he scrambled toward Tegan and grabbed onto her. As she clung to the mast, she was *smiling.*

"Have you ever seen anything so magnificent?" Her eyes sparkled like the sun on agate.

Szarok didn't answer. He waited for orders from Piebald because while he didn't trust the man, he believed in his instincts for self-preservation. Another boom shook the ship, and this time the captain lost his grip on the wheel. Waves that didn't seem natural slopped over the sides, and he tried to control his fear.

"Another orca?" Szarok asked.

"Something's got them running scared."

As he watched, more of the massive sea beasts sped by, and the small schooner trembled in their wake. It was like cowering in the presence of giants. In his life, he had seen many things that would astonish the rest of the Uroch, but this memory, should he survive to pass it on, would remain a marvel among the People for generations to come.

"What could frighten anything that big?" Tegan wondered aloud.

"You best hope we don't find out." Piebald's grim tone penetrated her evident excitement, and she peered into the distance, probably scanning for threats.

Nothing in this sea-drenched world made sense. The smells

and sounds accumulated, but Szarok lacked the context to interpret the information. But he knew *one* thing for certain—something else was out there. Then a cold chill crawled over him that had nothing to do with the bitter wind . . . because the boat took another hit. This one, though, this one felt almost . . . playful. One strike, another, until it almost seemed like tapping.

"What I wouldn't give for more speed," the captain muttered.

Szarok tightened his hold on Tegan, but even he didn't know what he planned to do when the dark limbs rose from the water, boneless and horrible, with divots as big as dinner plates. His breath went as the appendages crawled over the side of the boat and wrapped around the second mast. Tegan's exhilaration evaporated, leaving her still and quiet against him. Whatever creature had ahold of them, it must be immense. The mast popped, the sail drooping in response. It didn't take much to imagine the boat flipping, going down, down, down.

He went light-headed at the prospect of dying in the water. Tegan's hands were so cold; she must be scared, too.

"What . . . ," she whispered, but she didn't finish the question.

"The Behemoth's got us," Piebald said. "Pray to your gods if you have any."

Szarok sent up a silent plea to his ancestors. The ship tilted hard, sending Piebald skidding toward the rail. Szarok didn't think, only reacted. In a reckless motion, he dove and caught the human by a wrist, just before he tumbled over the side.

As I did.

They locked eyes, and Szarok saw the man register how easily he could let go. *That's right. Your life is in my hands.* For a brief moment he considered letting the deep have Piebald. *No. We made a deal. And we need him.* So he hauled the human up and rolled him onto the relative safety of the deck. The captain wheezed out something that might have been a word of thanks.

Just then another orca skimmed by portside, and the creature's limbs lashed out, snagging its prey with a bizarre hook at the end. The whale let out a terrified sound, so shrill that Szarok doubted that the humans could hear the entirety. Then the attacker pulled its meal beneath the water, and the waves settled into their normal rhythm.

"It's gone," Tegan said.

The captain slapped a palm against his thigh. "It took the orca and let us be. But nobody will *ever* believe that we saw the Behemoth and lived to tell of it."

"What was that?"

"Giant of the deep. They're usually so far beneath the sea that we never even get a glimpse. I've seen pictures, heard accounts. But I never thought . . ." Piebald shook his head.

"What are the pictures like?" Tegan asked.

For the first time, the captain didn't seem like he wanted both their heads on a stick. Apparently he liked imparting information. "The ones I've seen are red and white . . . or deep purple. The beasts have eight arms and two tentacles, a long narrow head and a beak like a bird. Big ones are strong enough to sink a ship. Now and then a fishing vessel brings up a young one in their net. I've seen them for sale in the market."

"It sure knocked the ship around. I'll take a look below," Tegan said.

That seemed like a good idea. As she went down, Piebald inspected the mast and slammed a fist into his palm. "One good storm and we're done for. And the damage will slow our progress some, too."

"I have more bad news." Tegan emerged onto the deck, somber-faced.

"Let's hear it."

"We're taking on water. Seems to be a crack near—"

"Blast." The captain swore and ran off to check for himself.

"How fast is it filling up below?" Szarok asked.

"Right now just a trickle. But I suspect it will worsen, the longer we're in the water without the ability to repair it properly."

She was right.

Piebald tried, but the patch didn't hold. By nightfall they had to take shifts running buckets up to the deck to dump the water while the captain struggled with the ship alone. On the second day, the little schooner definitely sat lower in the water, and Szarok ached in ways he hadn't known he could. The combination of cold and exhaustion dragged on him, and Tegan was staggering. Neither of them had slept in . . . He couldn't remember. Even food and water came second to making sure the sea didn't suck them under. Each thump, each knock, had him searching the water for the whales or the Behemoth.

"You need to rest," he said as Tegan stumbled toward him.

The full bucket slopped water onto the stairs when he caught it. She only shook her head, accepting the empty pail he offered. "There's no time."

He pressed a hunk of salt fish into her hands. "Eat, at least. If you collapse, you'll leave me alone with Piebald."

Szarok growled a soft laugh when she crammed the dried meat into her mouth with a wicked scowl. While she might balk for her own sake, she'd never leave *him* to suffer. Sudden tightness in his chest stole his breath, and though they didn't have the time, he pulled her close and rubbed his cheek against hers.

Tegan let him hold her until the captain shouted from above, "Get moving, unless you want to find out where the Behemoth lives."

With a tired snarl, Szarok ran up the steps and to the railing, pouring out the water, and then he returned to trade with Tegan yet again. "How does it look down there?"

Weariness pinched her features, dark circles beneath her eyes. "Not good. I don't know if we can keep this up."

"We must," he said.

She seemed to take comfort in his certainty. Szarok ran until his arms burned and his legs quivered with exhaustion. But after a while, the pain faded into a sweet nothing. Numb, he plodded on as the water rose, and the schooner dipped farther below the water. They were still trudging, still bailing, when a massive crack split the silence. Szarok summoned a burst of reserve energy and sprinted to the deck, bucket in hand.

"What happened?" he demanded.

"We lost the second mast."

The captain stood, his shoulders slumped, staring at the pole sliding over the side. Since the human didn't try to rescue it, Szarok concluded there was no way to repair it. The mainsail remained undamaged, but the wind whipped over them like a dozen angry ancestral spirits. Between the leak and the loss of power, hope trickled away.

Perhaps . . . I won't see my people again.

That failure hit him harder than the buffeting gale that smelled of snow and salt. Tegan stumbled up behind him, her pounding heart audible to him beneath the other sounds. *She's terrified.* Somehow that realization gave him strength.

"How far out are we?" he asked.

Piebald scratched at his beard, such a foul facial feature, as he contemplated. "Thirty hours, at least."

"Then let's fight for every minute. I've never surrendered . . . and I never will. Not even to this deep-water devil."

"I can't do it alone," the captain warned. "It'll be tricky to maneuver with one mast."

Tegan raised her chin and squared her shoulders. "I'll handle the bailing. Somehow."

After a day and a half of icy hell, Piebald finally called, "Land ho!"

Szarok rushed to the railing to luxuriate in the craggy coastline, adorned with mossy rocks and trees growing high on the hills above. As the battered boat limped closer, down to a single functioning sail, the town proved unfamiliar. The weathered wood structures seemed older than other settlements, worn by the wind and rain until they all showed gray.

We're close enough now. We'll make it no matter what.

But this definitely wasn't Antecost or any mainland village Szarok had seen before. *Exactly how far did we come . . . ?* Tegan hobbled toward him, her small face chapped red but glowing. He'd rarely seen such pure triumph, and he must admit, their success against the odds made him feel like shouting to the skies.

"We're safe," she whispered.

Suddenly the captain smelled strange, sharp, a tang of—

And three things happened at once—Szarok turned, Tegan leapt, and Piebald fired the gun he was holding.

Killjoy

After the *Catalina* finished loading the supplies from Peckinpaugh bound for Baybridge, Captain Advika rushed the crew back on board.

Morrow wasn't eager to resume the journey with winter rolling in. But he couldn't give up hope that they'd find Tegan safe in some other port with an exciting story to tell. That possibility was the only thing that gave him the courage to greet a new day with a smile. If he accepted that she was forever gone, he'd take up drinking as his full-time occupation.

There were two more stops before Baybridge, and he realized he didn't entirely understand how Captain Advika benefited from transporting supplies. There must be payment involved, but since the settlements all seemed to use different currency, he couldn't figure out how she would profit, unless she accepted coin from all the towns and then spent the money in each port, as she needed it.

"You seem confused," the captain said.

As Sung Ji supervised their departure, Advika indulged Morrow's curiosity.

"A good question. There's a merchant house in Peckinpaugh, and they write me a letter of credit, good in the larger ports. The smaller settlements often pay in goods, so I keep a portion of the food or cloth that I transport. It saves me the cost of provisioning the ship, or if I have too much, I sell it for local currency and buy supplies that will be in demand elsewhere."

"That's fascinating," Morrow said.

"If I wanted, I have more than enough to build a fine house anywhere and eat well for the rest of my life, but I'd miss the call of the sea."

He nodded. "The promise of adventure is persuasive."

"That . . . and Sung Ji would never choose to settle down." Her dark gaze lingered on the first mate, the first time Morrow had realized they were more than captain and crew.

"Have you been together long?"

"Five years," she said, smiling.

Catching her eye, the first mate lifted a hand, and they swapped a look that made Morrow glance away. He excused himself to head below, ostensibly to check on Millie, but really more because his heart ached. She was in the infirmary, plucking splinters out of a sailor's hand. The way the fellow mooned at her, it wouldn't surprise Morrow if the numbskull had injured himself on purpose.

He waited outside, cross for reasons he couldn't name. "You're keeping busy," he said when her patient left.

"I'm glad there's been nothing serious. I don't know half of what I need to for this job."

"Tegan will be back."

Millie offered a measuring look but didn't dispute his claim. "I hope so. If you'll excuse me, I need to tidy up."

That was obviously a dismissal, and he might've protested if he hadn't spotted the cook pacing outside, cradling his hand. Either a cut or a burn, he guessed. So Morrow headed for the deck to make himself useful. Sung Ji always had plenty of work, even for an unskilled storyteller, tasks that required only the ability to follow instructions. At nightfall he was exhausted, and fell into his hammock with real gratitude.

The next day, around noon, a school of dolphins joined them, frolicking in the surrounding waves. As they leapt, seemingly attracted to the *Catalina*, Morrow leaned on the rail and bowed his head. *I was supposed to show you. Tegan, why aren't you here to see this?* The sheer joy of the aquatic display would have delighted her.

At some point, Millie joined him to watch the show. Without speaking, she linked her fingers through his, and they watched the twirling and leaping for quite some time. Eventually the dolphins got tired of pacing the ship and veered away. Morrow stared until he couldn't see a hint of their presence in the water.

"That was amazing," she said in a voice washed with wonder.

"They're playful creatures. I'm told they'll frolic right up to a moored boat, even let you swim with them." For once, he didn't feel inclined to elaborate or repeat one of the tales he knew, legends of seafolk and the like.

"I'd be afraid they would drown me."

"There are stories like that, too. For every happy ending, there's a dark one."

"You're a killjoy," she accused.

In his current mood, he couldn't argue. So he strode away and lost himself in work again, until his body hurt too much to think. Two more days passed like that, until the *Catalina* reached the next stop, Wild Cove. The community was small but spread out, rambling along the rugged coast. There didn't seem to be a town center, just gray wood houses dotted here and there. Even the dock where the *Catalina* came to rest had seen better days, and there was a broken pier half submerged in the water. A faded red building added the only surprising spark of color, though the rest of the landscape was breathtaking.

It was impossible to cling to sorrow in the face of such natural beauty. From the rolling green hills to the dark rock face, Morrow let the sights nourish him. As he disembarked, he admired the gleam of piled stones, water-slick, some striated in all hues of gray, from palest ash to darkest charcoal with whispers of heather and cream. With the winter-cast sky overhead, heavy with clouds, the water gleamed silver in contrast. Too cold for flowers, but a few plants still flourished. In the distance he made out a broken road, long abandoned and gone to ruin, and a white tower. Captain Advika fired off a round, presumably to signal the scattered locals that their supplies had arrived.

"Don't just gawp—start unloading," Sung Ji scolded. "If we're quick, we'll make Crow Head before nightfall."

"It's not far?" Morrow asked.

"Just a skosh north."

In terms of actual travel time, that could mean almost anything. Yet Morrow followed orders and set to hauling crates. Millie tried to help, but the sailors she had treated—and possibly ones she hadn't—kept snatching everything she picked up. That irritated him, but he clenched his jaw and kept at his assigned task until everything sat at the edge of the dock.

An elderly man with white hair and brown skin thanked the captain with a half bow and a firm handshake. "You made it just in time. I'll wager you've no time for a bite?"

Advika shook her head. "Two more ports and then we can rest."

"Then I won't keep you."

This was the shortest stop they'd made, but even so, with all the unloading, it was near sunset when they sailed. The sky blazed with unearthly hues, and when the stars came out, Morrow swore they were as big as his fist against the cobalt sky. In wonder he gazed up as the brightness intensified. And then he *ran*. Straight to Millie, and when she argued, he simply threw her over his shoulder. Once they reached the deck, he set her down.

"Stop complaining," he ordered. "Now look up."

Relief surged through him. She hadn't missed it—the sky and the stars and the sheer immensity of the beauty. Her voice drifted to silence; he drank her delight down like strong wine, and it left him odd and giddy. Millie let out a dreamy sigh.

"This is exactly why I wanted to travel. The world, James . . . The world is *so* big."

Morrow started. He couldn't recall if she'd ever said his name before, but it added to his quiet pleasure. For a few moments he just stood with the cold wind blowing and the starshine like shimmering ice overhead. Even the moon glowed magical with its faint halo. Silvered light rained down on her upturned face, rendering her so lovely that it left him speechless. Her mouth was full and sweetly curved, even more so when she smiled.

Like now.

"My ma says a ring around the moon means bad weather's on the way."

That prosaic observation broke the spell, and he looked away. *I'm not so unreliable. I'm not. My heart won't waver at a pretty face.* "Truly?"

"She says you know when the storm's coming by how many stars are caught in the circle of light." Millie raised a finger, counting them, and then her tone dropped, becoming ominous. "Four. In four days, we'll see if she's right."

Despite himself, he shivered. "You should be the storyteller."

"It may be nonsense, but . . . I hope we're safe in Baybridge by then." Her enjoyment undimmed by the prospect of bad fortune, she lingered on deck until she must have been freezing.

Eventually Morrow brought his best winter cloak and a mug of hot grog, because Millie showed no signs of wanting to get indoors. The sky had ripened to black by the time they reached Crow Head. Her teeth were chattering. Exasperated, he swept her up and carted her below. While he agreed that the sights were spectacular, she just lacked all sense of moderation.

"You do that a lot," she said mildly.

"What?"

"*Decide* things for me. Haul me about like a bag of oats."

A hot flush banished the frosty burn in his cheeks. "Sorry. I don't know why. I forget my words around you sometimes." And it had been happening more of late.

To his astonishment, she bobbed up from the infirmary

bunk and kissed him on the cheek. "That's the sweetest thing you've ever said to me."

Then she banished him with a gentle shove and shut the door in his face. Morrow stared at the rough wood for a few seconds before giving himself a little shake and heading for the lower deck, where it would be plenty warm, thanks to the number of men crammed into hammocks in an enclosed space. It also reeked of eggs, farts, and feet, but it was impossible to have an adventure without tolerating a measure of discomfort.

Just think of the next story.

In the morning, the crew made short work of unloading. This time, the townspeople were waiting with wagons, as the settlement was built on a rise with a rough track cut into the hillside leading away from the water. Rough-hewn cabins comprised the bulk of the village, no old-world relics to mar the scenery. It was easy to imagine that there had never been any monsters here, no bloodshed, either, just the harmonious union of land and sea.

Morrow shook his head as Advika chatted with the townies. *Amazing that she makes this run every year.* Most of these folk seemed young, surprisingly so, as he'd seen a lot of lined faces as they sailed. But nobody here looked older than his father. *How does that happen? Maybe there was a sickness. . . .*

Sung Ji seemed to understand his curiosity because he said, low, "There used to be a town with the same name farther inland, but a traveler brought the plague, and they all died. With so much land to settle, a few families migrated from Peckinpaugh, oh, ten years back? They mostly fish up this way, some whaling ships. Without goods from Antecost and Peckinpaugh, they wouldn't be thriving." The first mate gazed with obvious pride at Captain Advika, who had clasped the town leader's shoulder in a friendly gesture.

"She does important work," Morrow said.

Sung Ji nodded. "Not without its risks. There's the weather

and the ice, dangerous sea life, and don't forget the outlaw colonies. Those who don't fish or farm, just live by stealing from honest folks."

"Is that the main problem in the north? Not changed ones but human enemies?"

Whatever the first mate would've said, the captain beckoned and he hurried to her side. Still wondering, Morrow walked along the cliff overlooking the rocks below. *Not far from here, an entire town died of the plague. Nobody changed. So what was different . . . ?* When the signal came much later to return to the ship, he ran, not wanting to be stranded in Crow Head.

He was among the last to board, with Advika aiming a dire look in his direction. "Are you trying to screw up my schedule?"

Morrow shook his head quickly. "Sorry. I got distracted. The land around Crow Head is . . . haunting."

What an imprecise word. But maybe she had answers?

"They said everyone died in the original Crow Head . . . ," he started, then didn't know how to continue.

"You're wondering why? When there was so much trouble elsewhere."

Belatedly Morrow recalled that the captain hailed from the ruins, much farther south. "If you have answers, I'd welcome them."

"They didn't get the vaccine," she said quietly. "Supply lines were already breaking down when they did the drops. Only made things worse, from what I can see."

"Is there anywhere that the sickness didn't touch? Where it's like the old world and all the machines still run?" He had considered himself well educated, so to discover how relatively little he knew . . . it was humbling.

Advika lifted one shoulder, gazing out to sea. "Not that I've seen. But I haven't sailed around the whole world, either, my lad. Wouldn't that be a feat?"

"It would indeed."

"Did you know I have a sister?"

The non sequitur of a question surprised him. "You've never mentioned it before."

"She came out of the ruins with me. We've each got our own ships now, but she doesn't run supplies."

"Oh?" That piqued his interest.

"Passengers," she said with evident relish. "It's a marrying-ferry, more like. Often in these remote settlements, people can't find anybody to partner up with, so Devi suggests matches, delivers mail, and brings couples together. She makes a good living carrying folk back and forth with weddings on her ship. She only sails the warm months, though, so you'll meet her when we arrive in Baybridge, along with her wife, Evette."

"I'm looking forward to it."

The next two days were clear as they sailed north. But the third morning, as the *Catalina* drew closer to Baybridge, the wind kicked up. With a shudder, Morrow remembered how Millie had used her mother's method to predict a bad storm. By noon, freezing rain sleeted across the deck, making it a misery to breathe, let alone work. All the sailors bundled up, and Morrow toiled until his hands cracked and bled.

"I was afraid of this," Sung Ji shouted over the roar of the wind.

The ice on deck made it near impossible to keep his footing, so Morrow went after it with a scraper. *We survived before. And . . . the captain knows the way well.* He imagined her sister, Devi, waiting year after year, and it was some comfort to note she'd never yet been disappointed. The *Catalina* always pulled through.

In time they sailed through the storm, and lights glimmered along the coast. But when alarmed shouts went up from the rest of the crew, he realized he wasn't seeing the lamps of town. No, these bright flickers were moving *toward* them and at a cracking pace.

"Raiders!" Sung Ji sounded the alarm.

"Weapons ready." Advika strode along the still slippery deck, overseeing the sailors who took up positions with their rifles.

Morrow had read of historical ships rigged with weapons, but the *Catalina* ran for speed. If the enemy vessel had big guns . . . He shook his head against the thought. The other ship was small, but it seemed to have a lot of men. He ran toward the captain.

"I'm better with a blade, but I *can* shoot. Do you have any extra rifles below?"

"My cabin," answered Advika.

He raced for the weapon and checked it. *Good firing condition. How much ammo?* A box nearby addressed that question, so he grabbed it and dashed back to the bow, where he took up a position near Sung Ji. From the stern, Captain Advika was shouting strategy. When the enemy ship got within range, the *Catalina* crew opened fire, but bullets came back hot, spattering the deck and dropping the sailor beside him. Wood shrapnel peppered Morrow's arms, but he didn't flinch.

"They've come heavy!" Advika called.

No idea what that means.

Until the first orange sphere exploded on deck, sending flames everywhere. The damp wood smoldered, slow to burn, but another fireball slammed into the ship nearby. Sailors dove overboard to avoid the fire, preferring the wicked sea to fiery doom. *Millie. Where's Millie?* Eyes watering, Morrow staggered in search of the water buckets, but as he went, the other vessel rammed and dropped boarding gear.

The Catalina *may be lost.*

three

a crowd of stars

And bending down beside the glowing bars,
Murmur, a little sadly, how Love fled
And paced upon the mountains overhead
And hid his face amid a crowd of stars.
                    —William Butler Yeats, "When You Are Old"

Our Song Is Complete

Pain exploded in Tegan's shoulder. She hit the deck, rolling with Szarok beneath her. Two more bullets bit into the wood nearby. She knew it wasn't life-threatening. No vital organs there. But that awareness did nothing to mitigate the discomfort. Szarok snarled and shifted her aside. His speed astonished her. By the time Piebald had fired once and prepared for a second shot, he went down under a furious tackle.

"You dare," Szarok growled, angrier than she'd ever seen him.

"I was aiming for you," Piebald said.

"That changes nothing. I *saved* you."

"And I got your rotten arses back to port, as promised. The deal's done now, and I get to take revenge for what you did to my crew. They might've been worthless, but they were *mine*."

"Try." Even from across the deck, Tegan could see how hard Szarok shook the little man.

One sound squeaked out. "Huh?"

"You tried. And failed."

As Tegan struggled to her feet, Szarok ripped their enemy's throat out with his claws. As the body gushed blood, he hurled it into the sea and then ran toward her. "You shouldn't be moving. What's *wrong* with you? He could've killed you."

She couldn't muster a light tone and certainly couldn't shrug. "I was worried about what would happen to you. But we have more pressing problems."

The ship was heading top speed toward the dock, and she couldn't help with the ropes. Szarok seemed to realize this at the same moment, and he leapt to drop the sails and then the anchor. It was enough, eventually, to prevent a collision. Blood trickled down Tegan's back, and she was starting to feel light-headed.

"Come. I'll bring us to shore in the rowing boat."

"You're not afraid?"

At first he didn't answer, lowering the dinghy from where it was attached to the larger craft. "I am. I always am with this much water. But if my choice is between facing my fear and letting you suffer, there is no dilemma."

"I can climb down," she said.

In truth, she nearly fell twice, between her bad leg and the hurt blazing in her shoulder. But he caught her and held on, so they went tandem, and once they settled in the boat, he took up the oars, maneuvering with a speed and strength that probably would've impressed her under different conditions. There were a few fishermen on the dock as they clambered onto the boards, so Tegan straightened, fearing how they'd treat Szarok. To her surprise, they seemed surprised but not frightened. He received second and third looks but compared to how he had been greeted elsewhere, the interest registered as benign.

"Is there a healer in town?" Tegan asked.

A boy of around twelve answered, "Khamish. She knows about herbs and such."

"Show us the way, please," Szarok said.

The vanguard swept Tegan into his arms as if her legs were injured, but she didn't protest. She couldn't hang on to him because it hurt to move too much, pulling at the wound. The size of the settlement registered on her vaguely as she raced through town in his arms. Outside a whitewashed, well-kept cottage, the boy paused.

"Here. I have to get back to work now, or I'll have no supper."

"Thank you," she murmured, but he was already gone.

Szarok thumped on the door, his impatience growing with every moment that they received no answer. Tegan didn't know how long she could keep her head together, between the pain and the bright sparks dotting her vision. Her head listed to the side, and of course he noticed, because he saw, heard, and smelled everything, even when she didn't want him to. *No use pretending to be strong.*

"She's not home," he said.

"Better to ask forgiveness than permission."

"What?"

"Just something Dr. Wilson used to say. Let's go in if the door's open, and make use of her supplies. I can walk you through the treatment."

I hope.

It would be hard to picture a more horrified expression than the one currently facing her. "I'm no healer."

"You could be. Anyone can learn. And do you really want me to bleed to death while you argue over qualifications?" Though it probably wasn't that serious, the implicit threat galvanized Szarok into action.

Still cradling her close, he got the door open and stepped inside the cottage, larger than most houses she'd seen. *This is old-world construction.* The cook room was separate, and there were two rooms at the back for sleeping, both warmly decorated and inviting. They discovered this as Szarok carried her around in search of supplies.

Finally she said, "Let's check the cabinets. Back that way."

Her insight was rewarded with a fine cache of herbs and various healer's tools. Tegan pointed out what he would need, though she noticed his hands were shaking. With her good arm, she pulled him close and kissed his cheek. He stared at her for a moment, and then some of the tension left him.

"You can do this. I believe in you. First, wash your hands. We don't want Piebald's blood mixing with mine."

There was a deep basin with an attached pump. *Quite handy.* In many settlements, they shared a well and someone had to go in the morning with buckets to bring back the day's water. Szarok figured it out quickly and scrubbed up with more soap than he needed. Despite the pain, she smiled at how carefully he cleaned his claws.

"What now?"

She pointed out what he needed. Soon he had a small basin, yarrow powder, and goldenrod ointment set aside. "Help me get my shirt off."

Other than a little click in the back of his throat, he gave no sign that the request bothered him. That removal hurt so bad, she nearly passed out. Ears ringing, Tegan sat at the table, hunched forward, so he could inspect the wound.

"It's clotted," he said.

"That's good. It will probably bleed a little more as you work— nothing to worry about. You need to get the bullet out next."

"How?"

"Use that." She indicated the scalpel, but he couldn't hold it at the right angle to work.

"I can't do this. Maybe I should go look for this healer." Szarok took a step back, but she wrapped her fingers around his arm.

"Use your claws. You cleaned them properly, and it won't hurt any worse than metal."

"Tegan . . ."

"Trust me."

With a little shudder, he stepped behind her and sank one talon into her wound. She clenched her teeth so hard against the pain that she feared they might crack. But thankfully she didn't need to give him further instructions, while it was all she could do to stay conscious. He probed until he tapped metal and then he dug it out with as much delicacy as Dr. Wilson could have managed on his best day. Szarok flicked the bullet into the basin with a quiet sigh.

"How do I proceed from here?"

"That mixture there, with the herbs floating in it? Use it to thoroughly clean the wound. Irrigate it fully before moving on."

"Irrigate?"

"Pour some of the liquid inside. Let it run out. Blot away."

Seeming more confident, he followed her instructions. "Now?"

"We're almost done. Apply some ointment to the bandage. Sprinkle the powder over it. Then wrap my shoulder. Make sure the medicine ends up on top of the wound."

Five minutes later she still hurt like hell, but the medical care was complete. Now she'd just have to watch for drainage and infection. At the first signs of inflammation, she'd pack the wound with raw honey, provided she could find some here. *Wherever here is.* As she struggled back into her torn, bloody shirt, she heard the front door open.

Tegan stood and went to greet their hostess. A tall, brown-skinned woman stared at her, caught in the midst of taking off her boots. "What're ya at?" she demanded.

"I'm sorry for the intrusion. A boy at the docks guided us here, but you weren't in and . . ." Tegan summarized their misadventures, hoping for a sympathetic ear.

"That's some rough," Khamish said. "Ne'er let it be said that Peckinpaugh's an unkind quay. Did yer man care for ya?"

"Well enough. He's tidying up. Thanks for the supplies."

"Did ya have someplace to bide?"

"Not yet." She hated asking for charity, but everything she possessed was either in the Winterville cottage or in the infirmary on the *Catalina.*

"Then stay with me. If you crewed for Advika, yer the next thing to a friend for me. I just ask ya see anybody that's ailin' in return."

Brightening, she readily made that deal. "Done. It's a little tiring sometimes, but I don't turn people away who need help."

"Heard ya there. Peckinpaugh is full o' good folk."

Szarok emerged from the kitchen then, standing half in shadow. "Sorry we entered without asking. The situation was—"

"No worries. Come and meet me proper."

Tegan sensed his reticence, but he stepped into the fading light. Instead of a handshake, he made the little bow she noticed that he preferred with strangers. "Again, thank you."

"You're some odd-looking," Khamish said cheerfully.

Tegan restrained her urge to step in and start explaining. He was the vanguard of the Uroch, after all, and he had no need of her interference. Still, she chewed the inside of her lip, wishing this wouldn't end badly, hoping he didn't have to swallow yet another hurt.

"So are you," Szarok replied.

Khamish laughed. "I just dies at you. The years do for us all, and yet I'm some glad to have this face and those years."

Her good nature appeared to thaw him a bit. "Me too. I hail from a rare mainland tribe. We've never been this far north. So . . ."

"Welcome, b'y." Khamish clapped him on the shoulder.

"My thanks."

"Ya two smell wicked. Get pumping, and ya can have a bath. I still have some work in town, so I'll be back once I take care of yon boat."

Right, the abandoned schooner.

"Anyone who can fix it is welcome to it," Tegan said. "It's full of salvage, so that alone should make it worth the time."

"Raiders." Khamish practically spat the word.

That confirmed Tegan's suspicions. "But one mast is gone and there's a crack, so it'll probably need to be pulled out of the water for proper repairs."

"I know just the fellow."

"Nobody's been bailing for a while," she added. "You'll need to be quick to salvage it."

Without further conversation, Khamish hurried out.

It took quite a while to fill the tub in the proper bathing room. Tegan had never seen anything quite like it, at least not intact. There had been bits and pieces in the ruins, where she guessed at how something might work, but this tub was actually part of the room. She and Szarok took turns washing up, though she had to be careful with her bandage. Before she'd left, Khamish hadn't seemed to think anything about Szarok scrubbing her down, and Tegan preferred his touch to that of a kindly stranger.

She borrowed a comb, and he spent a long time working out the tangles. Sometimes it hurt, but he was gentle and patient. It had been so long since anyone had taken care of her. In Salvation, the Tuttles were kind, of course, but she didn't get to stay with them long, and life had taught her that farewells came just as she started feeling safe and loved.

Better not to let myself feel much of anything.

But she couldn't do that with him. Szarok had so much of her that it would be terrifying if she dwelled on it. Tegan closed her eyes, half dozing as he fiddled with her hair.

"How do you even know how to do that?" she asked.

"You're not the only one who enjoys learning." He'd teased her so before.

"Not funny." But she was smiling.

"Grooming is how all animals show that they're kin," he said then.

She considered the implications of that, and then the question came naturally. He'd said if she wondered, to ask. "Without hair, how do the Uroch—"

"Demonstrate that kinship?"

"Yes."

"Our skin requires tending. It's a great kindness to rub oil on a kinsman."

Tegan's heart dropped when she realized she had *never* done that for him. *I didn't know I was supposed to.* But that didn't change the fact that he had been deprived of something that would make him feel more at home. So she levered to her feet, despite the shriek from her shoulder, and went to the bathing room, where such things were likely to be. After some searching, Tegan found a tin of herb-scented oil. It might be meant for rubbing into sore muscles, but it should suffice.

"Give me your hands."

In answer to his inquiring look, she poured a little oil in her palms and rubbed them together to warm it. Then she took his left hand and smoothed with her thumbs. He stared at her with a strange, avid expression the entire time she massaged his palms and fingers, neatly avoiding the claws, and then working her way up his arm, each in turn.

Finally she got nervous and blurted, "Is something wrong?"

"No. It's just . . . it feels different when you do it. We use our palms and the heels of our hands. You're using your fingertips."

"Do you like it?"

"Yes. It's ours, but you've made it yours, too. Just like me."

With slippery fingers, she touched his cheek, and his eyes shimmered in that look. Just as he leaned down, the door banged open in a chilly breeze.

"That's handled. For now we best fire up a scoff and have a yarn."

Trying to hide her disappointment, Tegan smiled at Khamish, not entirely understanding the local dialect, but when the older woman started cooking, the meaning became clear. For the first time in forever, Tegan devoured a full meal of fry bread, poached fish, boiled greens, along with fruit and cheese to finish it off. She also drank two glasses of something strong, then her head went muzzy and she couldn't stop laughing.

She heard Khamish say, "Not much of a drinker, yer love. Get some rest."

Then she floated for a time, and a door closed behind them. Szarok laid her down with gentle hands, but she wouldn't let him go. She fisted her hands in his shirt until he whispered, "I'm not leaving. Just let me get ready."

Those words meant nothing, and she complained in a low mumble until he got into bed. His bare skin was deliciously hot, and she curled into him, half floating in a memory of their time on the isle. Warm breath stirred her hair.

"What am I to do with you?"

"Don't know for sure. Have some ideas."

"I wasn't really looking for an answer, my treasure." Soft growls of laughter spilled into her hair, making her smile in reflex, even with her eyes closed.

"I have a question."

"As I said before, ask."

"I know you remember . . . how the old ones considered us food. So I'm wondering, and I probably would never say anything if I wasn't a little, a little . . ." She waved her hand in a too-big-for-bed gesture and smacked him on the cheek.

Szarok took her hand and pressed a kiss into her palm, then tucked it safely against his chest. A little trill of pleasure rippled through her at that, and also when he sifted through her hair with his claws, dragging with just enough pressure to make her tingle.

"Jug-bit is what Millie calls it," he said.

"Yes. That."

"So you're wondering . . . ?"

"If I make you hungry." That was a blob of a question, floundering between them like some hideous sea monster.

He inhaled sharply, his hand stilling in her hair. "I wonder if you'll even recall asking."

"Who knows?"

"It doesn't matter. If I'm honest . . . yes. At first. Because the old ones found your folk meaty and delicious. So I have that echo. But now that we've Awakened, we understand it's wrong to eat things that can . . . communicate."

That answer roused her from the dreamy stupor that the liquor had left behind. Probably she should be terrified, unnerved over letting him wet his claws with her blood. But she was only faintly dizzy, sore, and . . . curious. Gently, Tegan traced the lines of his face in the dark, her fingertip gliding over sharp cheekbones and the line of his jaw, formed to accommodate a different sort of teeth.

"And now?"

"You make me hungry in an entirely different way," he whispered. "And that . . . is difficult. My people would say I've studied your kind too much in becoming the vanguard, lost some of what makes me Uroch."

"I'm sorry." Probably she should move away, but she'd just found the best position for her wound and—

I don't want to. He can go if he must. I won't.

His touch heated, and a flood of memories washed over her. At first she didn't understand what she was seeing, because it was her own face, again and again, at first awful and repugnant, and then later tinged with a warmth of affection that became beauty. *These are his memories,* she realized. *This is how he sees me.* When that profound gift ceased, she was crying and she couldn't stop.

"It's nothing that needs an apology. Though others may not understand, I have chosen you. And you said today, in one ridiculous leap, 'Beloved, I would die for you.' So each time my heart beats and yours answers, our song is complete."

I Am Here

P eckinpaugh was a revelation.
It was the largest settlement Tegan had ever set foot
in. As her wound healed, she and Szarok explored what
the place had to offer. In the mornings, she saw patients while
Khamish took care of town business. While she wasn't anything
so official as a mayor, governor, or chief, citizens looked to her
to settle disputes and for good advice.

"I reckon it's because I'm oldest," Khamish said when Tegan
asked at the breakfast the next day. "And before you ask, no. I'm
not telling."

"All right. Before, you said the *Catalina* passed through . . . ?"

"I did."

"Were they well?" Tegan wondered how Millie and James
were doing, now that she had some mental energy to spare.
Maybe it made her a bad person, but before, she could only focus
on their immediate survival.

"So far's I know. They came late and didn't bide long. Should
be in Baybridge by now, if they didn't run into trouble."

"I wish I'd completed the season with her, like I promised."

"Advika won't blame you. There's always another run. Until
there isn't." Khamish smiled over a plate of fry bread and then
wiped her mouth. "Ya know the deal by now. If anybody comes,
treat 'em."

"Got it," Tegan said.

In silence, Szarok helped her clean up the kitchen. Clearly something was troubling him, as he hadn't spoken a word yet today, just nods and subverbal sounds of acknowledgment that she understood from her Uroch lessons but only confused Khamish. She let it go until they finished the household work.

"What's wrong?"

He only shook his head. "Let me change your bandage."

While she considered arguing, it would serve no purpose. He'd talk when he was ready and not a moment before. But she definitely registered that he had a burden he was currently shouldering alone. He'd gone out by himself a couple of times while she was seeing patients, so maybe something had happened?

No point in guessing.

Tegan sat down and let him tend to her, asking fact-finding questions. "Is there any heat? Red streaks? Has it sealed properly?"

Szarok described what he saw and she nodded in satisfaction. "You did good work. It's healing just fine. When I can move my arm without so much pain, I'll start training the muscles to get back some range of motion."

As he finished wrapping the fresh cloth, someone knocked on the cottage door. She went to answer and Szarok hid, as usual. A young mother brought her baby girl in. When Tegan offered a smile, the other girl just stared. Tegan touched her face and then her hair, wondering if the braids had come undone.

"Is something the matter?"

"Ya are so young. I heard a proper doctor had come from away, but ya . . ." She didn't seem convinced Tegan could know much of anything.

"I've apprenticed with two different doctors," Tegan said quietly. "But it's up to you if you want me to examine your little one, or if you'd rather wait for Khamish."

As if on cue, the child let out a fretful wail. "She won't eat a bite, and just cries."

"Let me wash up and then I'll have a look."

After a thorough check, Tegan could report, "It's nothing serious. A touch of fever, probably brought on by teething. Soak a rag in this and let her chew on it. Give her this at bedtime. Once the tooth pops up, you'll both get some rest. Feel where it's pressing, here?" The baby clamped down on her finger and seemed like she meant to gum it off.

"S'what my ma said, but I was some worried."

"You wanted confirmation. What seems like a bit of nothing can turn terrifying so quick, especially when they're small."

Or old. How well I know it.

"Thank ya. My ma's the weaver hereabouts, so I brought some cloth. Is it enough?"

"Of course," she said automatically.

And then she saw how *much*, but the girl had already bundled up her baby and was heading out the door. Since arriving in Peckinpaugh, the weather had been more shade, then sun with wintry clouds hovering and frosty winds cutting through her ragged clothes. Tegan wished she had something fine and warm left from her foster mother's sewing kit, but those had been ruined long ago, with so much bloody wear.

"What will you do with that?" Szarok stepped out of the room they slept in, seeming as if he'd resolved some internal conflict.

Good. Maybe he'll share it soon.

Lifting the dark fabric, she unfolded it to show him. "There's enough to make me a jacket and you a new cloak."

"You know how?" he asked.

"Don't look so surprised. The mattress I made on the island would've been nicer if I'd had better supplies. My foster mother thought I should be able to put stitches in a shirt as well as people. I never got to her level, but I'm . . . competent."

That might be stretching it, but she *had* made clothing. Khamish had a sewing box with good needles and plenty of thread. Tegan would have to find a way to pay for what she used, along with their food and lodging. But so far the other woman wouldn't talk about recompense.

Trying to remember how Ma Tuttle had done it, she measured Szarok and wrote his numbers down; then she draped the thick brown fabric and checked her work. Before she could mark or cut, another patient came. This time Szarok only went into the kitchen. She saw two more people, elderly sisters, one with a persistent cough that might turn for the worse and the other with a wrenched arm from carrying things she shouldn't. They listened to her advice with great care and then paid her with a tin of sweet bread. She opened it immediately and crammed a slice into her mouth. Her eyes closed as the honey burst on her tongue.

"This is what you were born to do."

"Eat cake? How lucky I am." Licking her thumb, she grinned at him around a mouthful of deliciousness. "I'm untrained but willing to make this my life's work."

"Not precisely what I meant."

"Doctoring, then, you think?"

"I know. People come with heavy hearts and you lift them. Even if they're sick, they feel better after just *talking* to you."

Since she'd promised they all belonged to him, she offered a simple truth. "It's much easier to care a little for lots of people than to care greatly for one."

"Yes," he said.

From that simple word, Tegan knew he understood. A weight lifted and she went to him, wanting the kiss she had been denied days ago. She pressed into him until his heat became hers. He brought her closer still with the odd near embrace of his claws curved over her shoulders. For a long moment his gleaming gaze lingered on her upturned face, so intense that she shivered. Smiling, Tegan looped her arm around his neck. He was used to it and no longer recoiled; instead she got a nuzzle, cheek to cheek, cheek to throat.

She luxuriated in his closeness. "Scent-marking is nice. But so is breath-marking."

"Are you asking?"

"Do I have to?"

"Never," he whispered.

His lips met hers softly. As if it was a private ritual, he always kissed as she'd taught him that first time, first by playing, then sucking, and finally deepening with teases of tongue. He made a savoring sound in his throat, and he licked the sweetness from her lips.

"I didn't know you liked cake."

"Only when you eat it."

A hot flush blazed in her cheeks, and she hid her face against his shoulder. "Don't say things like that."

"Even when they're true?"

She mumbled an incomprehensible reply.

Szarok rested his cheek on the top of her head, slowly rubbing back and forth. "You smell of flowers. I will miss this."

At first the words seemed too impossible to make sense, and then she realized. *He's only saying that because—*

"You're leaving," she guessed.

"Yes."

"When?"

"Tomorrow. I found a ship heading to Antecost. It is the last before winter sets in."

Tegan closed her eyes. *I promised never to ask him to choose.*

"I'm so glad you can get back before the big ice, as they say up this way."

That's the right tone. People always leave. They go or they die. It's all the same.

I can bear this. I can.

Somehow the bullet hole in her shoulder didn't hurt as much anymore, compared to the white-hot blaze incinerating her heart.

She couldn't meet his gaze, so she resisted when he tried to peel her cheek away from his chest. *I'm not crying.*

"Tegan . . ." The way he said her name—it was all heartbreak and longing.

Resolutely, she willed the tears away, until they only tightened the back of her throat. She couldn't dig deep enough for a smile. "This is no surprise. You were never meant to stay with me. So I'm telling you, go in good heart tomorrow. Finish your work. Save your people."

"I wanted to stay until you healed, but—"

"There's no need. I'm fine. And you can't miss the last boat bound for Antecost."

"I've decided," he said gravely. "The lands there are plentiful. We can build without asking, and if the closest settlements choose not to trade with us, we will survive. I have learned a great deal on this journey, many things that will be useful."

"I'm glad," she said. "Y-you know how much I enjoy learning."

"Yes. But there is one thing I don't know . . . and cannot figure out, no matter how hard I puzzle over it."

She swallowed, staring at his chin. "What's that?"

"How I am to leave you. How I sail away without you. But those are basic questions. The more difficult ones are impossible."

"Like what?"

"How do I sleep without you next to me? How do I begin a new day if you are not there to say"—he growled *wake and rise* in Uroch—"so badly that it makes me smile? When I imagine the day that I no longer smell of you, I hurt so much that I might die."

"You're making it really tough for me to be strong," she got out.

"I don't think you ever promised me that. You promised me truth."

With a muffled sob, Tegan wrapped her good arm around him. "Would that make it better? If I said that being separated from you is worse than being shot?"

"Yes."

"I could . . ." This was impossible, but she had to offer. Otherwise she'd always regret not being brave enough. "Come with you?"

His heart leapt beneath her ear; she listened to the pounding rhythm for a while. His silence didn't hint at anything good.

Finally he said, "I wish you could. But my people won't understand. And I have . . . obligations. I will try to explain . . . us, but it would be dangerous for you to accompany me. They may see you as a corrupting influence or an obstacle to be removed."

"That makes sense." Her breath hitched as if she'd actually cried instead of swallowing all those tears. "If I'd have to leave you in Port-Mer anyway, I should stay here. I'll heal better with Khamish than on a ship."

"Clever healer," he said.

"Just practical."

Whatever else he might have said, another patient interrupted. There was a steady stream for the rest of the morning, so Tegan pulled herself together. In truth, the distraction helped her. Focusing on work meant she couldn't count down the hours, so the afternoon arrived in a flurry of snow before she realized where the time had gone. Szarok vanished, likely talking to the captain about his passage.

When Khamish returned at suppertime, Tegan had the meal ready. They ate without him, discussing the people she'd treated. "Some just wanted a gawp at ya. Made a good impression."

"I'm glad to hear it."

"Where's ya man at?"

"Not sure. He'll be along later."

Tegan worked feverishly on Szarok's cloak, since it had to be ready by morning. She pricked her fingers more than once, and the stitches were definitely not pretty. But before Khamish set aside her knitting for the night, she had his mantle finished. *Well, near enough to serve.* Tegan held it up and Khamish inspected it.

"Not bad. Should be warm, at least. I'm after some rest," the older woman said.

Though Tegan considered making an excuse to stay up later, waiting up wasted lamp oil and candle wax, so she left the sitting room as Khamish snuffed the flames. After washing her face, she climbed into bed alone, wondering if he was already on the ship, waiting to sail with the tide.

I'll never forgive him if he just goes, even if it's easier.

But as the night lengthened, Szarok slipped into the house. Tegan recognized his footfalls and the sharp coppery scent that meant he'd been hunting. He paused in the doorway without speaking. Since she said nothing, he turned and went, presumably, to rinse off. When he returned, he smelled of cool water and soap. Tegan pushed back the covers, resolved not to spend their last night away from him.

"Come to bed," she whispered.

It's the last time I'll say that.

Her heart clenched, but she still opened her arms to him. With only a brief hesitation, he came to her, so chill that his skin almost burned. "Sorry. The captain said I should provide my own meat, so I—"

"I know. Thank you for coming home."

One last time. It didn't matter that this was a borrowed room in a house belonging to a woman they'd only just met. The word still applied as long as they were together.

"That's the easy part."

"I know that, too."

She stroked his head, the soft skin behind his ear, and he nestled into her, shaking, but not entirely with cold. More than ever before, he touched her, too, firmly with his palms and delicately with his claws, as if he meant to memorize every curve and hollow. Tegan didn't suspect he had any hidden motive, but in time, that stroking made her squirm. Her breath came in little gasps, and he drank them down with his mouth, cool at first, and then warmed with friction, and finally hot as he rubbed it over her throat. Not kissing, not quite, but . . . stirring. He moved, and she did, and suddenly it went irresistible. Normally he stopped, but . . . tonight he didn't. Somewhere in the midst, a powerful feeling swept her and she cried into his shoulder.

"I have no words," he said.

"Me either."

In a frenzy of touching, they'd learned something without quite understanding it, and she wished with all her might that she had another night and another to figure out if that could be repeated. But there was only this night, this time, this moment. Tegan moved toward him, careful of her shoulder, and curved against him.

When he is gone—

No.

But her mouth wouldn't cooperate with her will; it spoke soft words, desperate ones. "I don't know what to do without you."

"Whatever you did before," he said.

"As if it's so simple."

Wish, hope, dream.

Study.

Yes, that was the answer. Books would save her again, as they had before. Perhaps she could learn more from Khamish and offer what she'd mastered as well. Trading knowledge seemed like the best possible cure for this awful, endless ache. She pictured all the people she could help, and it eased a little.

Szarok put a palm over her heart and took hers to cover his in turn. "You feel this? Ours is not a wordless song. If you listen, what do they say?"

I . . . am . . . here. Feeling ridiculous, she whispered the answer.

"Yes, my treasure. Listen when you miss me and know this is always true."

"I will. I promise. Your cloak is done. It's waiting in the other room."

"I'll wear it well." He kissed her one last time, touched her cheek gently. "Then . . . let's say farewell here. I cannot endure your sad face staring at me from the shore. I might swim back to you."

"Yes," she said.

He rewarded her with a kiss, deep and long and tasting of bittersweet. She didn't realize he'd kissed away her tears, but he must have. She licked the salt from his lips, and then marked him with her cheek. Face, throat, shoulder. *No matter where you are, you will always be mine. Yes?* But she couldn't bear to hear any other answer, so she hid the question deep in her heart.

It's getting light outside.

Tegan listened to the roar of her pulse in her ears, this grief overshadowing every loss, every parting, until she must surely crumple beneath that weight. And she counted the impossibility of it, even in her own heartbeat, now thumping a different song:

I can't.

I can't.

I can't.

On the fourth beat, her heart said:

I must.

And she let him go.

The Vanguard's Burden

S zarok sailed with the dawn tide.

He did so with an ache that blazed stronger as the crew put him to work as the lowliest among them. They didn't treat him as less than human, however, so that was something. At the end of a long day, he lay below, sick with the rocking of the ship and missing her. His days looped in quiet anguish. Until now he hadn't realized that silence could feel like screaming.

Though the days were long and cold, there were no threatening sea creatures, only boundless waves and inclement weather. He ate the meat he'd hunted outside Peckinpaugh, and counted himself lucky it was cold enough to keep it fresh. As it had been before Tegan, he hid his habits and spoke to no one, apart from the necessities.

The farther south they sailed, the easier their progress. Fair winds filled the sails, and they reached Antecost half a day ahead of schedule. The snow hadn't settled here yet, and he wondered how it was in Peckinpaugh. To finish his term of service, he helped unload the vessel, torn between a desperate desire to return to her and a wild anxiety that something dreadful might have happened in Appleton while he was away.

Hunting was already scarce.

It would be difficult to convince his people to travel such a long way on multiple boats. *Before it will be feasible, I must teach them to swim.* That seemed like an impossible task, and it hurt all over again. Those lessons with her shone in his memory with a terrible radiance, immutable by time or distance. A small part of him wished that they hadn't escaped the island—that a ship had never come—and then he couldn't be blamed or held responsible.

"You're alive!"

Startled, Szarok turned and came face-to-face with the village chief. If anyone had ever introduced them, he couldn't recall the man's name, but his voluminous facial hair made him instantly recognizable. He offered a wary half bow, as the last time Szarok had been in Port-Mer, they'd wanted to hang him. Yet this was the only route he'd found open to the south, and he had no idea how he'd get to Rosemere from here. Once he reached the Evergreen Isle, he trusted a boatman would ferry him across, no matter when he arrived, as the river never seemed to freeze.

"I'm so grateful to see you hale and whole," the man was saying.

"What?" That was nothing like he expected.

"We owe you an abject apology." Then the chief explained how the *Catalina* had returned to port with the men responsible for Malena's death and that he'd felt guilty ever since. "I hope you'll allow us to host a feast in your honor as a means to make amends."

"It's a kind thought," he said, "but there's no time."

The village chief tilted his head, a sympathetic light in his eyes despite the furrowed brow. "You have urgent matters pressing?"

While he suspected it wouldn't do any good to share his troubles with this human, Szarok decided it would do no harm, either. So he summarized his people's plight in Appleton and concluded with, "If you would truly aid me, I'd ask for a boat to carry me as far as Rosemere. I can make my own way from there."

"And what then?" the chief asked. "No, sir. This is no talk for the docks. We'll have you on a boat in the morning, if that's your choice, but you'll be my guest tonight."

"I will?"

Somewhat astounded, he followed the chief through town,

receiving nods and bows from villagers who seemed genuinely remorseful. The man stopped outside a large house, nearly double in height compared to the rest around it. Before he could follow the chief inside, a woman tapped his shoulder to draw his attention.

"Yes?"

She was an older woman with lines bracketing her mouth, her gray-streaked hair bundled at the back of her head. Human faces no longer troubled him, but sometimes he found it tough to tell them apart by looking at them. Their scents usually told a more interesting story. This female, for instance, had been baking up until recently. A yeasty smell wafted from her clothes in bright puffs, and she'd eaten fish for breakfast.

She rubbed her fingers together in a gesture unfamiliar to him. "I'm told the men who murdered my Malena tried to kill you as well."

"Yes." There seemed no point in elaboration since she already knew the gist of the story.

"I'm glad they didn't succeed. If you'll wait here a moment, I'd like to give you some fresh bread. My husband was part of the mob that . . . well. I'm just sorry, that's all."

Without waiting for a reply, she rushed off. Szarok didn't know if he should stand right there or go inside. Would the woman knock if she didn't find him? While he debated, the chief came out to see what was keeping him.

"Any trouble, sir?"

The formal address stunned him. While he'd heard it used for people of importance, he'd never been accorded that respect, even when they knew he came as the vanguard, the official ambassador for his people. "I . . . no. But there may be a visitor for me presently."

"Not a problem. My wife will see to it. I don't think we've met properly. I'm Byron Littleberry. You'll meet Carys when she brings refreshments."

Port-Mer hadn't struck him as especially hospitable last time. The shift made him nervous, but he didn't smell any signs of trouble. No fear sweat, no acrid tinge that suggested cloaked intentions. So he sat down gingerly on a padded chair and took in the paintings on the wall and the touches of nature in the dried flowers and herb bundles.

"Now then. As I understand it, you're looking for a place to settle?"

"Yes, sir." It seemed polite to reciprocate the respect he'd been given.

"Please, no. Littleberry is fine. Only my mother called me Byron, and she's been gone for twenty years."

The Uroch had less of a sense of time than humans, though he understood the concept. The People lived until they died, and that was that. But he wasn't sure what he should say in response, so he only nodded. He had been with Tegan too long, perhaps, because he'd grown used to her clarity. She never left him in any doubt of what she thought or felt. By contrast, other humans seemed even stranger.

"Littleberry, then," he said, as the man seemed to be waiting for . . . something.

"Excellent. Well, Antecost is much bigger than Rosemere. Better game, too. And . . . unlike Governor Morrow, we realize we don't own this land."

"So all that forest . . . ?"

"There aren't a lot of us, scattered among the villages. There're far more deer and salmon than we could ever eat. Trout and moose, too. So if you're looking for a home, Antecost will have you gladly. Tell us how many ships you need, and we'll send them for your people."

He couldn't speak. This offer seemed like a miracle, something so generous and good, that it must be a trap. But he couldn't smell one. Finally he got out, "Why?"

"We're told you fought for Malena. You confronted the men

who hurt her, just like she was one of yours. And such valor for a girl whose people treated you like we did? It shames me. If we don't make it right, my heart will never be at ease."

That isn't why, he wanted to say. But he barely remembered how that argument had gone, as they'd enraged him by threatening his healer. In the end, he had pronounced their guilt and been thrown at watery death as a result. *Is it wrong to accept this gratitude?*

"Since they hurt her, they would have harmed others," he said. "It had to be done."

Littleberry nodded. "If that's representative of how your people think, we'll be better for having you among us."

Such a small matter to hang our fates on. Like Millie Faraday's kindness. The People will honor Malena hereafter. He would see to it.

"Are you sure there won't be . . . problems?"

He shook his head. "I know we treated you poorly, but the word's spread like wildfire. To be honest, it feels like a heaven-sent chance to have you in port again. We'd only heard stories before, you see, and we let them poison our minds."

It was easy to imagine what travelers had said, given the atrocities that lingered in his mind and . . . occasionally tempted him. "Then I accept with great appreciation."

"Seal the deal?" Littleberry offered a handshake, and Szarok made a rare exception, not wanting to insult his benefactor.

A round woman with white hair and amber skin carried a tray into the room then. "Hello, I'm Carys. My, what big eyes you have." She gave a nervous laugh when her husband nudged her. "Sorry, just a little joke."

"I'm sorry, I don't understand."

"Oh, it's just a little thing from one of our books. I could—"

"No need," Littleberry cut in. "Thank you, dear. We have no time for children's stories."

Szarok avoided the sweet cakes and buns with seeds and dry fruit in them, though he did have some tea. Most human food barely qualified as such. If he ate too much of it, over time it left him dizzy and sick. But Littleberry didn't appear to notice his caution.

"Well, then. I'll just give you this parcel. It's from Malena's mother."

He understood that it was rude to refuse gifts, so he accepted the bundle of bread. "Thank her for me."

"Certainly. His manners are lovely," she added to her man in the softest whisper, probably thinking he couldn't hear.

That's some progress. Last time they called me "it."

"We'll speak later," the chief said.

With a final smile, she went out. The smell of her anxious interest lingered, but at least she didn't reek of fear. This would be a good place to build, more welcoming than the lands farther north. *Easier to travel here as well.*

"To answer you . . ." Szarok told the human about Appleton, the lack of resources and their inability to make good use of old-world salvage. He closed by estimating how many Uroch would be moving.

"So . . . ten ships, most like. It'll be cramped, even then. If you can get to the southern tip of the Evergreen Isle, that would be some help."

"The governor may not be pleased if we—"

"Let him complain. It'll be a day or two at most. I'll take responsibility if he argues."

"You're willing to take our side?" Szarok said, startled.

Littleberry nodded, his mustache bobbing in emphasis. "Our side. Exactly right. You're of Port-Mer now, and we'll look after you like our own."

"What about the other villages?"

"Those who have settled the cragged coast don't associate much with outsiders anyway. If they chose a spot where ships can't come in, there's a reason for it. But they don't bother us, and I'll ensure they don't make trouble for you and yours."

"Thank you," he said. "While I can get my people to the river, the isle may be difficult. It was hard enough to get our bravest warriors on the rafts, let alone—"

"I'll let the captains know. Mainland side of the river it is. That impacts the boats that can safely traverse the waters, but let me worry about that. When do you plan to move?" Littleberry seemed to understand his difficulties.

The deepest, coldest part of the year lay before them. After some thought, he answered, "We can last one more season with our stores. Spring will be better."

"Best not to rush," Littleberry agreed. "The weather will make the journey kinder on your folk, too. I'll send your boats by the first day of spring, you have my word."

I have much to teach them when I return.

The People had not done well in the cold, but since Awakening, their tolerance had increased. *We must improve our hunting and learn to do better dressed in other skins.* But such small adaptations shouldn't prove impossible, considering the odds they'd already overcome.

"I look forward to it," he said.

That night they feasted him as promised and there was plenty of meat. It was no hardship to eat it grilled or roasted. The Uroch had experimented with fire after they worked out how to keep the flame alive, but in the end his people decided it served better for offense than cooking, as meat tasted delicious as it was. There weren't many guests, but they all treated him with great courtesy, even if some shivered in his presence.

And in the morning he got on a boat where he did not need to work for his passage. Instead the sailors saluted him with two fingers and bobbed their heads when he went by. He handed the packet of bread to the captain, who had undertaken this trip so late in the year as a special favor to Littleberry. The woman smelled the gift and then beamed.

"My favorite! How did you know? I'll probably eat these in one night."

"Enjoy," he said.

As I wouldn't.

More than twenty villagers gathered to wave when the small craft set sail. Such sudden success should have filled him with brightness, but when he listened to his heart, he could not hear the song he'd promised. *I am here* shifted to *I am one.* He ignored the pain and tolerated the journey. Boats no longer made him sick; he just didn't like them.

And Szarok could share that truth with his people, enough to make them believe in the pilgrimage to Antecost, a place so fresh and pure that it came without memories, without ruins. The green expanse of trees and the soft singing of rivers . . . If his people learned to swim, they could enjoy fish as he did. Silently, he relinquished his dream of home tied to Rosemere.

We will go nowhere that we are not welcome.

The morning that the Evergreen Isle came into sight, he asked one quiet favor of the captain. "Sail past Rosemere to the south. I will carry myself to the mainland."

When he'd led the warriors to meet the Huntress, they all battled terror on the rafts. There would be a few left from that first landing, and he preferred not to delay in town. But the captain surprised him by shaking her head.

"I can sail downriver easy enough, but I won't leave you. Littleberry would have my hide. I'll drop anchor in the middle and have one of my men row you ashore on the other side."

True to her word, they sailed past the isle and onward, closer to Appleton. He must travel on land for a time, but she made it possible for him to get there faster by sending her men to deliver him safely to the mainland. They took him all the way to the shallows, so he bowed low when he climbed out. Sometimes kindness *did* beget kindness.

"Please thank the captain for me."

"See you in the spring," the sailor called.

He cocked his head. "Will you?"

"Aye. The captain's already volunteered to be among the ten ships."

"I'm glad to hear it."

But that was too lean a word for the choking relief that lifted some of this burden from his shoulders. He had never told anyone, not even his dear healer, how he struggled with the honor of being chosen. How he'd felt at hearing, *You carry all our hope and promise with you.*

"Good day," the other man shouted, already rowing away.

Cold water splashed over his feet as he stumbled ashore. The familiar mainland smells washed over him. Soon he would reach Appleton, a human settlement taken by the People before they realized they couldn't keep it . . . for a host of reasons.

Running alone seemed strange and alien. At first he focused on the silence, and then the world whispered to him as it had before: prey, enemies, traces of scent and faint echoes in the distance. *I lost this. But I found her.*

As if to outrun that thought, he added speed, pausing only to drink or hunt. Much quicker than he could've predicted, the ruins of Appleton loomed before him. There had been no human scent for days; they avoided his territory as if they would still be slain and eaten. He did spot a couple of Gulgur, but they were engaged in a mission no less critical than his own, so they only waved and passed by with their salvage wagon. Growls of greeting met him in the broken streets. Questions peppered him. *"Are you well?" "Did you find us a place?"* Everyone recognized him, so the tribe came in droves, so familiar and dear that his heart ached. And then it hurt more when a soft voice snarled, *"Welcome home."*

With a heavy heart, Szarok faced her, the mate his people had chosen for the vanguard.

The Day He Stopped Waiting

Flames hissed at the buckets of water emptied on them. Smoke rose and curled up into the darkness. But the noise from the burning ship didn't drown the cries of pain. *The other vessel rammed us so fast.* Morrow tried to fight his way toward lower deck access—Millie needed someone to protect her—but there were too many bodies in the way. *I'll have to cut a path. So be it.* The rifle he'd retrieved from the captain's cabin wouldn't do him much good in this scrum, so he drew his blade. Others had the same idea, forming a rough line of defense.

The raiders couldn't truly intend to sink the *Catalina*. It would be better if they could take it—and the cargo—intact. Captain Advika had skimmed up into the riggings and taken position with a rifle. As her weapon cracked, bodies fell. Down at the base of the mast, Sung Ji fought with twin knives, stabbing with a proficiency that reminded Morrow of the old days. He battled his way to them, a kick here, a slash there.

As Morrow reached the captain and first mate, a trio of invaders lined up in front of him. *Tch, cowards. They must be quaking in their boots.* Morrow swept his blade before him horizontally, scattering the men. He kicked the nearest over the railing and into the frigid waters below. The closer of the two remaining enemies slashed at him with a boot knife, but he parried and, with a twist, disarmed his opponent. *Been a while since I had a challenge.*

The other rushed him, cutlass upraised, while the first dove after his knife. He elbowed the would-be swordsman in the throat, and while he staggered, Morrow skewered him through the stomach. When he yanked his weapon free, blood slicked the blade. Red glazed the dying enemy from the flames nearby as Captain Advika shot him in the head. Morrow lifted his chin in thanks at the captain perched above, then he raced to aid Sung Ji, as Morrow's final opponent lunged at the first mate, knife in hand.

"Watch out," he called.

The first mate whirled and blocked a strike and kicked out, nearly breaking the man's kneecap. But more invaders, at least ten, pressed forward. Morrow didn't like the odds, until Advika dropped two in quick succession. Bodies and weapons hit the deck.

"Get those fires out," she shouted.

All around, the sailors who weren't defending hurried with buckets in a makeshift fire brigade. Morrow went after the knife-wielder currently advancing on Sung Ji. Morrow beckoned with his free hand, and the enemy raced toward him. In a lightning strike, he sliced the man's weapon arm, and his fingers lost strength with wrist tendons severed. His blade slipped from his hands and clattered away. Smiling, Morrow advanced and executed him in a neat slit of the throat.

Seven left.

Then a boom sounded nearby, and Morrow turned to spy Millie silhouetted in swirling smoke, backlit by the titian glow of fading flames. Shotgun braced firmly against her shoulder, she fired again and again, dropping three of the seven almost faster than he could track it. She took the bruising recoil without a flinch, and she fell back as they wheeled on her. Apparently without fear, Millie lofted the weapon for another go. Terrified for her, Morrow stabbed one of them in the back, Advika took out another, and Sung Ji did for a third.

Just one, last man standing.

No time to breathe. Or to scold her. The deck trembled beneath the hulking beast approaching, likely the raider captain. He stood nearly seven feet tall, bald as an egg, and scarred so that Morrow couldn't parse his features, except half his nose was missing. The giant clutched a boarding ax, big enough to hack through the mast. Morrow dodged the first lumbering swing, but the lummox had a free hand, and he clocked Morrow with an enormous fist. Ears ringing, he reeled back; Sung Ji caught him, and as the enemy lowered his head for a final charge, his body jerked. Advika shot him in the chest, and Millie took him through the back. The raider captain roared at the onslaught, but he still didn't go down. Sung Ji flung both knives and they each struck, shoulder and thigh. Millie finished him with another blast, though she didn't lower her weapon until he went down.

Finally.

"Clear the bodies," Captain Advika ordered.

Ignoring Morrow, Millie set to with Sung Ji, carrying corpses like it was her life's work. Though the ship was damaged and smoldering, it seemed to be intact. The sailors whooped as they boarded the enemy craft and fastened it to the *Catalina*. It would take a little longer to reach Baybridge, but they'd limp in as heroes.

Just like the old days.

"Any casualties?" Millie asked, once the deck was clear. A few men answered in the affirmative, and she gestured toward the lower deck. "I can't guarantee I'll be able to help as much as Dr. Tegan, but I'll do my best."

Morrow clenched his teeth as she led the injured sailors away. Once, she would've asked if he was all right, she would've gazed up at him like— Well, everything about her lately aggravated him plenty. Morrow swiped the sweat from his brow and succeeded in smearing the soot so that it came off on his palms.

With a sigh, he turned to Sung Ji. "What can I do?"

"You already did plenty on defense. Major repairs will keep until we dry-dock the *Catalina* for the winter."

Somehow Morrow stayed on deck and resisted the urge to check on Millie when every instinct urged him to reprimand her. *Where the devil did she find a shotgun, let alone know how to use it?* The first question answered itself—*probably the captain's quarters, same as me.* As for the latter, he had no clue. If she had any common sense, she would've stayed below, where it was safe. Angrily, he kicked at a charred crate and it collapsed into splinters. With a guilty glance around, he set to cleaning up the mess he'd made.

"Good of you to pitch in, storyteller." A sailor smiled at him in passing.

"It's my pleasure," he mumbled.

As he cleared the rubbish, Advika paused beside him. "You've a cool head in a crisis, James Morrow. You're a welcome addition to my crew."

"I can't guarantee how long I'll stay."

"You miss her," she said in a sorrowful tone.

He did. Of *course* he did, but just as with the blacksmith's wife, Clara, time had muted the feeling. With every fiber of his being, he still hoped Tegan was alive, but . . . the reunion wouldn't happen as he'd once so desired. Now he just wanted to see Tegan, laugh with her, and find out what the hell happened after she went over the railing. In time, he might come to accept that she was truly gone, along with Szarok, not just missing.

But today is not that day.

"She's my friend," he answered finally.

The captain studied him briefly, then she laughed. "We're both in a spot, aren't we?"

"What do you mean?"

"I've captured an enemy vessel intact. The right thing to do is offer it to Sung Ji since he's my first mate. That way, he can run his own ship and crew."

"But if you do, he might leave you." Morrow grasped her dilemma at once.

"It's not a tough choice. If he wants his own ship, I should make it possible. But I won't lie; it hurts something fierce to picture him moving on."

"You haven't had a chance to mention it yet?"

"I'm putting off the inevitable. Besides, there's work to be done." With that she went to inspect the stern, where most of the fire damage was centered.

For his part, Morrow worked alongside the crew until they reached Baybridge. The lights of town blazed against the dark like inviting little beacons, each house a flicker of hope. Though the docks were quiet at this hour, Advika's people made short work of leaping to the pier and roping the ship in. The enemy craft took some more doing, but eventually they had it under control, too. Exhausted, Morrow stumbled down the gangplank after the captain.

"Where does the crew bunk?" he called.

"Most have family here or a partner. You and Millie are welcome to come with Sung Ji and me to my sister's place. This way."

In the dark, Morrow couldn't discern many details about the town, except that it was sprawling. It was impossible *not* to notice the small figures hurrying in a group toward a brightly lit building. He followed them with his gaze until Sung Ji bumped him.

"The Gulgur have made it this far north?" Morrow asked, astonished.

The other man grinned. "They came with Devi last summer. Odd dialect, but no worse than what you hear over Peckinpaugh way. It's funny: they brought all manner of salvage, and they're obsessed with figuring out how things work. One of them got the old mill running. . . . Well, you probably don't care about that."

"No, local stories always interest me."

"I'll tell you more over a hot drink. Devi and Evette will be looking for us. For weeks now, actually." Sung Ji sighed a little and arched his back. "It'll be nice to sleep in a bed that doesn't roll around for a while."

"But you love the sea?"

"Definitely. Almost as much as our dear captain." Whistling cheerfully, he hurried to catch up with her.

As Morrow moved to do the same, Millie fell into step beside him. Her face was dirty, her eyes hollowed out with overwork. Yet there was also a spring in her step. He choked down a host of disagreeable words, entirely out of keeping with his character.

"You fought well," she said. "But I guess I should expect that, having read your stories."

Somehow it didn't feel like a compliment. He tried to breathe through the rising irritation. "So did you. Where did you learn to shoot?"

"My dad taught me. We didn't battle much in Otterburn, but before the tithes, we did encounter the occasional Mutie raid." She fixed her gaze on Sung Ji and Advika, some distance ahead, then she quickened her pace.

Deliberately, he walked faster, too. Since she was short, it would be near impossible for her to outpace him without running. "Did I do something wrong?"

No reason to let resentment simmer.

"Not at all," she said. "I just had a little case of hero worship before—that's all. I'm over that. But I guess maybe you miss it."

"What?"

"Me mooning over you while you stare into the distance, thinking of somebody else."

Well, that's clear enough. But it gave him a little pang to realize she no longer saw him as someone special. "I'm sorry."

Morrow didn't even know what he was apologizing for, really, but he had the unmistakable sense that he'd hurt her. In that case, the right thing was always to own up to it. She slowed a bit then, following the curve of the rocky road up the hill. Captain Advika glanced back to make sure they were still within her line of sight, but she didn't speak. Morrow watched as she curled her arm through Sung Ji's and he touched his head to hers, briefly.

"Don't."

"What?"

But she didn't answer. Millie broke into a bounding run and caught up to the other two and she didn't look back. He reached the warm house as Captain Advika opened the door. From inside came the excited chatter of women greeting one another after a long separation. He waited in the doorway for an invitation, not wanting to be rude. Devi resembled her sister quite a bit, though she looked somewhat younger, and she wore her hair longer. Evette was smaller than Millie and delightfully round, with hazel eyes and freckled skin.

"We've been so worried!" Devi hugged Advika again. "But it looks like you ran into trouble. You're all filthy and you reek of smoke."

"We'll tell you all about it, as long as you feed us."

"James, come in and close the door. You're letting the warm air out."

He flushed as the captain treated him like a wayward boy. Chastened, he followed instructions and settled at the long table that dominated the comfortable room. Cushions and a fine woven carpet went a long way to making this place seem like home. He admired the various souvenirs that lined the walls while Devi and Evette set food on the table.

Over a hearty meal of stew and bread, Advika performed the introductions and told their story between bites. Devi interjected now and then, mostly out of worry, Morrow thought, but then Evette would touch her on the arm to settle her down. Their bond seemed deep and true, and he wondered if they'd met as part of the marrying-ferry the captain mentioned before. For a story-teller, he didn't say much that night. Yet it was also a relief not to sing for his supper.

"When are you going to stop this nonsense?" Devi said finally.

Advika shrugged. "I have no idea. But it won't be this year. Baybridge needs me to take its goods south, or have you forgotten?"

Her sister sighed, as if this were an old argument. "I know. But you all must be exhausted. I'm sorry to keep you talking so late."

"I didn't mind," Millie said. "And everything was delicious."

"Reckon you're tired of pottage by now," Sung Ji put in.

"A bit," she admitted with an adorable smile.

Adorable. When did I start thinking that? Morrow stared until Millie shot him an awful look, her dimples disappearing into a scowl. He got to his feet and stretched, rubbing the bruise the raider captain's fist had left on his jaw. That, she noticed, and her aspect softened.

"You're hurt?"

"Nothing serious."

While the others cleared the table, she scolded him and forced him to sit back down so she could put some ointment on the mark. "You carry your own medical supplies now?"

"Not because I want to be a doctor," she snapped. "So don't think I'm trying to replace anybody. Just . . . in case. It's smart to be prepared."

"Nobody's arguing."

Her frown deepened. Millie wasn't gentle as she smeared the salve onto his jaw, and oh Lord above, for some reason, he just wanted to wrap his arms around her and tickle her. But that was no way to treat a cantankerous woman.

It took another hour to get everyone spot washed, the best they could do at this hour. Then came the question of where everyone would sleep. They whispered about it for a while, so Morrow finally said, "A pallet on the floor is fine by me. I can just roll beneath the table, if that's fine with everybody else."

"That's not the issue," said Devi. "We only have one spare room."

"Oh. Well, I'm sure Millie won't mind the floor, either. You can trust me not to pester her in the night."

At that, Millie snorted sharply. "That's for damn sure."

Everyone traded looks, but it was settled, and Devi passed out pillows and blankets before the two couples retired for the night. By this point, Morrow's bones were aching, so a comfortable nest near the fire seemed like heaven. He didn't undress, though, just rolled into his covers like a tunneling mouse.

"James . . . ," Millie whispered, just as he was about to drift off.

"Hm?"

"Do you truly not remember . . . ?"

"When we first saw each other?" Maybe it was because his mind was weary and wandering, but an image of her standing near the public house in Otterburn flashed into his head. Wide eyes watching their group in awed silence, and pretty as a spring flower in her blue dress. "Think . . . maybe it was when Company D came to Otterburn, seeking aid against the horde?"

"Yes!" Her delight startled him wide-awake.

Before he knew much of anything else, she'd crossed the distance between them, gazing down at him in the moonlight. *That face, those eyes. She's . . . breathtaking.* His heart kicked up a wild rhythm, and he couldn't quite get his breath.

She went on, softly, "I thought you didn't see me, that you never would. But me? I've been watching you all along. And it got lonely."

"I'm sorry," he whispered.

This time, he knew what for.

"You were the finest man I'd ever seen and I just . . . I know they say it doesn't happen, but when I *saw* you, I couldn't breathe. I couldn't move. And my heart just . . . went."

"Oh, Millie . . ."

"But then you opened your blasted mouth. *I've been here before,* you said. *But I didn't see anything worth staying for.* And you were looking right at me. And it felt like it was possible for somebody to break your heart without even speaking to you."

He winced. It got worse.

"Don't forget how you called my hometown 'a bit of an eyesore.'"

"No wonder you're angry," he mumbled.

She shook her head. "Not really. Not about that, anymore. I just . . . I wanted . . ."

Then she gave up on talking and kissed him.

Sorrow Came Calling

now covered the ground in a white carpet.

It had been a month since Szarok had left, and in that time, Tegan had been accepted as Khamish's new apprentice. While she felt uneasy, considering how her first two teachers had ended up, the woman knew so much about midwifery that she couldn't pass up the chance for . . . learning. Even framing the word in her mind summoned a burst of yearning. She missed him in a way that she hadn't known was possible, as if someone had carved her heart from her body and locked it away in a box.

"Come on now. No time to dawdle." Khamish emerged from her room, clean and ready to start the day.

"No breakfast?"

"We need to check on Mrs. Gwynne. She's near her time, and she had trouble with the last one. Her man won't know what to do with those three littles if anything goes wrong."

The pain receded. Keeping busy provided the best panacea for what ailed her. She gathered the new doctor's bag she'd traded for a couple of weeks back, and checked the medicines that Khamish had been kind enough to supply. *Everything's here.* It wasn't quite as comprehensive as the kit she'd left on the *Catalina*, but willing hands went a long way toward making up for that.

As they went out, she said, "You usually make patients come to you."

"So I do. But there are exceptions. If they're bedridden or ready to drop a baby in the street, it's best for me to do the walking."

Tegan had gotten used to the woman's accent, so it no longer registered as strong, though sometimes new expressions still puzzled her until she worked them out by context. Tegan hurried out behind Khamish and stepped in the footprints she made in the snow. From both necessity and convenience, she dressed like her new mentor as well: thick trousers, sturdy boots, under-blouse, vest with many pockets, and a heavy overcoat. Someone had knitted her a hat, scarf, and mittens in thanks for treating a child's putrid throat, and she bundled up, as the passing weeks brought winter stalking in like a hungry wolf.

Khamish maneuvered in the white like a dancer, long legs eating up the distance. Tegan struggled in her wake, but since she was determined, the older woman didn't arrive much before her. Mr. Gwynne was pacing on the porch, smelling of hops and fermented grain. Once, she didn't pay that much attention to people's scents, but time with Szarok had left her noting the details, so these days she almost always knew what they'd been eating or drinking.

"I'm so glad to see you." The man's relief was palpable as he rushed toward them. "She's inside with our oldest girl. I sent the babies to my sister."

"Is she having pains?" Khamish asked.

"I think so. When she started crying and cursing me, I ran."

Khamish muttered something Tegan felt sure was uncomplimentary. Louder, she said, "Stop drinking. It won't help."

"Yes, ma'am." He lowered his head in apparent remorse.

"Let's have a look, shall we?" Khamish opened the door and stepped inside.

The cottage was warm, and a woman's cries came from the

back room. Tegan went with her mentor to see how bad it was, but she didn't count on the wave of shock that iced her from head to toe. The smell and the weeping, it carried her back to *that* time and everything she'd done her best to forget. Tegan sucked in a breath, trying to conceal her tremors. It wasn't just the blood, but the woman's tearful face and the stink of her sweat, traces of copper, and the natal fluid soaking the bedcovers.

Khamish offered her a sharp look. "This is your first birthing?"

"Yes," she got out.

"Well, suck it up. Religious folk say women are cursed, and that's why we bleed and have to suffer. I call that nonsense, but I'll agree this is a poor natural design."

"Can you stop waxing philosophical while I'm dying?" Mrs. Gwynne shrieked.

The older woman laughed. "You're not; it just feels like you are. I'll wash up and be right back. Tegan, keep her calm."

Easier said than done. The nausea and terror came at her in waves like enemies determined to wear her down. Yet the little girl, no more than seven or eight, held her mother's hand bravely, and she remembered doing the same, whenever her mama had fallen ill. It got easier to breathe when she focused on the child.

"What's your name?" she asked.

"Lucilla."

"That's pretty. Are you happy you're getting a baby brother or sister?"

The girl made a face. "Not really. I wish they'd stop. We have enough already."

"Lucilla!" Mrs. Gwynne snapped.

"What? You told me it's wrong to lie."

Breathe. Just breathe.

Soon Tegan had her feelings under control, and she peeled off her cold-weather gear. Then she knelt and said, "If you don't mind, I'm going to make you a little more comfortable."

With Lucilla's help, she found fresh bedding and changed it so Mrs. Gwynne wasn't lying in the wet. Khamish came back as she got the patient settled, and she did the exam with quick precision. The older woman showed no sign of alarm as she concluded her check.

"It all looks good so far, but you're not quite ready to push. I know you'll hate hearing this, but it would probably go faster if you moved around."

"You're merciless," Mrs. Gwynne mumbled.

But she did struggle to her feet with Tegan's help. She supported the woman in pacing around the room, down the hall into the sitting area and back. They went fifteen times before the labor quickened and Khamish took another look. Her expression told Tegan that it was time for a baby to be born.

"Lucilla, love, take your father to your auntie's house. I'm afraid he's still drinking out there, and if he falls down in the snow . . ."

"He'll freeze," the girl finished. "Very well, I'm going."

"Should she be put in charge of him like that?" Tegan asked.

"If you're worried, you can walk with them. This isn't the first baby I've delivered. I thought you might want to see it, but I can manage on my own."

Quietly relieved, she set a hand on Lucilla's shoulder. "I'll make sure you get there safe and then come right back."

"I know the way . . . but thank you." The little girl's smile said she appreciated the extra care, even if it came from a stranger.

Tegan had the idea that she probably did a lot around the house and helped look after her younger siblings, too. The things Lucilla said didn't sound particularly childish, and Tegan understood all too well how that was. She couldn't remember a time in her life when there had been no fear, no threat looming, even . . . before.

She grabbed her winter clothes and layered up, then helped Lucilla do the same. As they came out, they caught Mr. Gwynne drinking on the porch. Startled, he chucked his cup of whatever into the snow beside the house. Lucilla only sighed. Tegan frowned at him.

"Is this any way to greet a new life? Come on. We're taking you to your sister's house."

"I want to stay," he protested.

"For what?" she demanded.

Lucilla tugged on his sleeve. "Daddy, don't be stubborn."

"I'm sorry, squirrel. Let's go then." With a tremulous sigh, he took his daughter's hand, but his gait was none too steady when he set out.

Muttering, Tegan propped him up on the other side, and Mr. Gwynne kept trying to veer off to see friends, or for "just a quick visit to the public house." So it took much longer than she expected to herd him across town. She'd never wrangled such a difficult man. Breathing hard, she finally dragged him to a well-built house with multiple stories.

"We're here," Lucilla said.

Tegan hauled him up the steps onto the porch and rapped on the door. The minute she let go of him, he staggered toward the street. Whatever he'd been drinking clearly had a long tail. She grabbed ahold of him and shoved him through the door as it opened. The brown-haired woman seemed startled until she recognized her brother.

"Oh, Farrell," she said, shaking her head.

"Will you look after him?" Tegan asked.

"Of course. I'm sorry he's troubled you. He doesn't cope well in tense situations."

"True," Lucilla said.

"Well, come in, all of you, and have a cuppa. It's some bitter out." Farrell Gwynne's sister beckoned, and Tegan stepped inside, not wanting to be rude.

But she didn't take off her coat. "I should probably get back. . . ."

But I don't want to.

I don't want to see a live baby that makes me think of my dead ones.

She'd told Deuce that she wanted to protect them, but nothing could've been further from the truth. While the Huntress might be a capable warrior, she was blind when it came to other people's hearts. If she'd ever been taken by force, maybe then she'd understand Tegan's hate. She had never shown it to anyone, until Szarok, never thought anyone would understand. *But he did.* His voice growled in her memory: *I don't care if you lie to everyone else in the world. Never to me. Understand?* Forced sweetness had been her sword and shield, but it was time to find new weapons, forged of honesty instead. She no longer feared that her truths might drive others away.

Making up her mind to face her fear, she turned for the door with a word of apology. In that moment, Mr. Gwynne stumbled and cracked his head on a table's edge. Head wounds usually looked worse than they were, so Tegan didn't panic over the profuse bleeding. Lucilla started crying, so her aunt comforted her.

"Do you have bandages? I'm sorry. I left my bag."

Presently they brought basic supplies, so she cleaned the wound and patched him up. The whole time, his sister scolded him for being an irresponsible arse. Once she finished, it seemed churlish to refuse the drink a third time.

So she stayed.

Eventually she said, "I should go."

"Must you?" Lucilla asked, all big eyes. "You're so nice. Won't you read us a story first so we don't worry about Ma?"

Twelve more wide eyes stared up at her, all innocence and appeal. Tegan couldn't resist, so she accepted an ancient storybook and read about a princess and a frog until the children passed out in a pile on the floor. Mr. Gwynne was snoring nearby in a chair, so the scene seemed much calmer than the rowdy house she'd entered earlier.

"You're a miracle worker," his sister said. "Between his littles and mine, me nerves . . . They got me drove."

"No trouble at all."

It was late by the time she headed back to the Gwynne place. Flurries of snow dropped on her skin in icy kisses. The house was mostly dark; she didn't knock, as Mrs. Gwynne could hardly answer and Khamish was likely to be busy. But instead of cries and commands from the back, there was only stillness and silence. She started when she registered Khamish just sitting in the front room, head bowed.

Her stomach tightened. "What happened?"

"It went bad," Khamish said softly. "She tore and bled, and I didn't have enough hands."

Oh. Oh no.

"The baby . . . ?"

"Stillborn, like the last."

Tears rising, Tegan dropped to her knees beside the older woman and took her hands. "Would it . . . Could we have saved her if I'd been here?" With all her heart, Tegan wished to hear a definite no.

But Khamish only sighed. "Hard to say. I don't think the baby was ever meant for this world, but Netta Gwynne? I don't know."

"Sorry. I'm *so* sorry. If I'd known, I wouldn't have gone. Mr. Gwynne wouldn't cooperate on the way, then he hurt his head, but I shouldn't have lingered with the children. This—"

"Is not your fault. When you hold people's lives in your hands, it's easy to take on guilt until you can't breathe for it. But if you'd stayed, maybe Mr. Gwynne and his wee girl would've frozen in the snow. Lucilla's a taking child, but she shouldn't be put in charge of her da."

Tegan recognized this for what it was, an attempt to clear her conscience, but the weight wouldn't go. "What should we do?" she asked, aching at the idea of crossing town again with such dreadful news.

"I've already washed and wrapped the bodies. Now we must notify the family."

"If they had other kin, they should be here. I don't understand why—"

"Mara, Mr. Gwynne's sister, is the only one. Netta's people passed early in life, and I half raised her." Khamish let out a sigh so long that almost sounded like a sob. "Some days I'm plain tired. Never thought I'd live to see this girl gone."

"Then . . . I'll go with you." It was the least she could do.

But the older woman shook her head. "Go on home. People will say wretched things in the shock of grief. I can bear it, but you shouldn't have to."

"No, I'll go."

No matter what Khamish said, Tegan didn't change her mind. For the second time, she trudged through the snow. They didn't speak, and she sucked in the cold air like it could numb her guilt. But the feeling only intensified as they went up the steps to the door. Khamish knocked, and Mara stood there wearing an expectant look.

"Who . . . Who's with Netta?"

"I'm sorry," Khamish said. "I truly am."

Mara crumpled against the doorframe, her head falling back. "Oh, Farrell. Whatever will you do?" After taking a few steadying breaths, she gathered herself. "I'll not wake them with such news. The morn is soon enough."

Heavily, Khamish nodded.

Tegan stopped listening to the words because they couldn't change anything. *I chose wrong. I chose the comfortable path. If I'd been there . . .* She didn't truly believe it would've come to a choice between two tragedies. Lucilla probably could've shepherded her father just fine. *I just preferred to go.*

Mara didn't offer tea. Eventually she shut the door on them, and Khamish led the way back to her cottage. The weighty silence lasted until they got inside.

"Hungry?"

Tegan shook her head.

"You can't starve because we lost today. This is the way of the world, me girl. Sometimes it's awful and it hurts like hell, but if you can't swallow the bitter down and keep moving, you can't call yourself a healer."

Tegan spoke through clenched teeth. "I can. I *have*. It's about all I know how to do."

"Now that just isn't true. You can mend a wound, soothe a sore heart, and I heard from Mara how sweet you were with those littles."

"I'm not sweet," she snapped.

"Not always. Nobody is. But a person isn't made of one or two colors like a tree."

Tegan had no reply for that. She didn't argue when Khamish put a bowl of soup in front of her. She cleaned the dish like her life depended on it. Afterward, she washed up and then went to the window to watch the snow falling. The inexorable flurry of white had already covered their footprints, leaving no trace that they'd come or gone.

"It's unnerving how fast it happens sometimes," said Khamish.

"The snow?"

"That . . . and dying. I'll carry it for a long time, how Netta said to me that we were waxing philosophical while she was dying. And I made light. Now she's gone."

For the first time, Tegan saw how her mentor was hurting. Her brave face crumpled, tears streaming for the young mother she'd half raised. She ran to Khamish and hugged her, eyes wet, but it didn't matter what she felt. Comforting others, that was something she knew how to do.

"She was well enough then. You treated her with nothing but kindness."

"I know. But let me be weak tonight. I'll pick up and carry on in the morning. You know Netta told me to look after her littles? I'm too old. I don't see how I can keep that promise."

The older woman cried and cried until Tegan feared she might be sick. Finally she put her to bed with a hot drink and then she read from an old book until her voice nearly gave. *I'm sorry,* she thought. *Because of me . . . Well, I'm just sorry.* That whole night, she lay with Khamish in bed like she had done before her mother had died, but she didn't sleep. Tegan listened to Khamish's heartbeat, but it only tapped out a basic rhythm. There were no words, like Szarok had promised.

Loneliness sang to her instead, and in the morning, sorrow came calling.

A Fire in Winter

When Tegan opened the door, Lucilla stood there with a basket in her hands. The smell of fresh roasted potatoes wafted from the wrapping cloth. She couldn't meet the girl's gaze as she stepped back to let her into the house. Her small face was tearstained and rosy with cold. The imprint her little feet had left in the snow seemed impossibly lonely.

"Come in," Tegan said.

"I have to go back and help Aunt Mara. My da isn't well."

"I'm sorry."

The girl ignored that. She'd probably heard it a lot already, and her mother hadn't been gone long. Tegan remembered how much she'd hated the words when they'd come from her uncles. Khamish came to the door then.

"Does he need treatment?"

"Reckon not. He just won't stop drinking."

"That's a type of sickness," Khamish said severely.

"Auntie told me to bring this for you in payment and to say we're having the funeral tomorrow. It's too cold for burying, so we're having a fire instead."

She's too young to carry such messages.

Khamish sighed. "Mara didn't need to send anything."

"People are already bringing food," Lucilla said. "I have to go now."

With that she turned and trekked back through the white,

hopping between trampled patches with silent concentration. Tegan watched until her small back vanished from sight, and then she stared at the branches of the tree that half shadowed the cottage, liberally frosted in ice. The contrast of dark and light soothed her aching heart.

Khamish touched her arm. "Come in from the cold. We'll make some nice soup with those potatoes and the herbs I've put by. How's your shoulder, by the way?"

"It seems to be healing well enough."

"I'll have a look."

Tegan lacked the energy to argue. While there was residual soreness, she thought it was forming a healthy scar. There was none of the burning that accompanied an infection, and Khamish had changed the bandages regularly after Szarok had left. Because it was better to be careful, she let the healer inspect the site.

"How does it look?" she asked.

"You've a pretty new scar."

"That's about what I expected."

"I imagine you've got many, most down where nobody can see." With that surprising pronouncement, Khamish went into the kitchen to put together a pot of soup.

Stunned, Tegan assisted, but the words played over in her mind, until she had to ask, "How do you know?"

The older woman dried her hands, seeming unsurprised by the question, or even curious why it had taken her so long to ask it. "After a while you get to recognize it. I see the same shadow on Advika, though she's got more years behind her."

"I know she's from the ruins, too."

Khamish nodded. "Reckon you two could share some stories, if you're inclined."

"Not usually," Tegan said.

"Advika neither. But sometimes it's good to know that somebody's walked your path before and they're all right somewhere down the road."

"Yes." She let out a breath. The vise that started tightening when she found out Mrs. Gwynne didn't make it loosened a little. "Why were you so willing to take me in, before?"

"Mostly I'm lonesome and you need teaching."

Stung, she said, "I've studied with two doctors already."

Khamish laughed. "Not like that, me duck. You already know plenty about treating ailments. I'm talking about your heart."

Tegan raised a brow, reluctantly amused. "You're teaching my heart."

"Not so much as you're learning to be true to yourself. But I'll play my part, too."

Talking to Khamish sometimes made her head ache—in a good way. If nothing else, her teacher kept her from dwelling on what couldn't be changed. She pretended to understand this cryptic comment and tidied up the kitchen after the soup had finished cooking. They ate a little for dinner, and late that night a patient came from three houses down with an upset stomach. Tegan handled it without waking the older woman, but the neighbor seemed reluctant to go home.

"Such a shame about Netta Gwynne," she said.

Since Tegan was in no mood for such a chat, she ended the visit quickly. Maybe it was a little rude to usher the woman out so fast, but she only had a little gas, and Tegan suspected she wanted firsthand gossip. *Is this what town life is like?* In Winterville they'd regarded Dr. Wilson with a combination of fear and reverence, so nobody ever stopped by with mild symptoms and a hankering to chat. The fact that he'd kept a Mutie named Timothy in the laboratory as part of his experiments had likely contributed to his isolation. Even after Tegan had joined him to assist with research, keeping others at a distance just seemed . . . natural. But even while traveling with Company D, she'd done the same thing.

Once the night went quiet, Tegan donned her jacket and

stepped outside to gaze up at the sky. It was ridiculous—she *knew* it was—but she couldn't stop herself from asking the silent question. *Are you out there? Are you well?* One month. Two months. Twelve. How long before she stopped whispering to the stars? And maybe she didn't really want to stop. Because if she did, it would be like accepting he was gone, forever-gone. The ice on the tree branches cracked and fell, spearing into the snow. In the silence, her heart pounded like thunder, and then she heard it, faint but unmistakable:

I. Am. Here.

Her pain eased enough to let her sleep. The next day, they carried the soup to the Gwynne household, but the family seemed to have moved. Khamish headed across town without asking any of the neighbors. She guessed they must be staying with Mr. Gwynne's sister. A crowd gathered in the front yard proved her right; the mourners had apparently gathered to accompany the family. Khamish set the food inside, and then she came out to where Tegan waited with the others.

Farrell Gwynne spotted Tegan and his face flushed. Letting go of Lucilla's hand, he lurched toward her and landed a vicious shove. Her bad leg gave, toppling her into a snowbank. Gwynne loomed over her with a face so devastated that she couldn't even blame him. So instead of fighting, she stayed down.

"You . . . Why did you . . . Better if I'd died instead of her. Why weren't you there?"

"I'm sorry," Tegan whispered.

The man's sister hauled him away with a whispered admonition about frightening the children. For a little longer she sat in the cold, feeling it trickle through her layers until it reached the skin. The icy air burned her lungs, and Tegan might have sat there forever if Lucilla hadn't come over to offer a small hand. When she didn't immediately take it, the girl shook her arm with impatient demand.

"Don't feel bad," she said.

Tegan struggled to her feet first, then she wrapped her mittened fingers around Lucilla's. "I'm trying not to."

"If you do, I have to, too. I begged you to stay."

Realization dawned then, and Tegan crouched, peering into the child's face. Big, haunted eyes stared back at her. In that moment she understood what she must say. And it had to be true. "Let's feel sad that she's gone, not because we did wrong."

The simple hiccup of a yes reminded Tegan of Szarok. On impulse, she scooped the girl up and set her on her hip. *I'm strong enough to carry her. I am.* Later, Lucilla would be asked to support her father and look after her brothers and sisters, but for today she deserved somebody who could hold her. Her dad and auntie both had their arms full. Without meaning to, Tegan caught Khamish's gaze, and the older woman smiled with her eyes.

More than half of Peckinpaugh turned out for the service. When she'd picked Lucilla up, she didn't realize she would be walking quite so far. Despite aching arms, she didn't regret it, even as they marched through town to a spot overlooking the sea. Someone had already built the pyre, and the bearers moved through the assembled mourners with the pine box that held Netta Gwynne and her youngest. Lucilla hid her face against Tegan's shoulder as Khamish stepped to the center.

There's no holy man?

Normally at such times, they read from a small, worn book. But Khamish only tipped her face to the sky and said, "Nobody who goes is ever gone. We don't understand why the spirits call as they do, but when our time comes, we each must answer. If Netta misses us, she'll visit in our dreams."

"In dreams," the rest echoed.

That seemed to be the cue. An older man came forward with a torch and he offered it to Farrell Gwynne, who shook his head fiercely and looked away. Khamish took it. The healer lit the pyre in multiple places, and the fire blazed up. They must have treated the wood to make it burn so hot. Tegan backed away, awed at the ferocious hunger of the flames; they flickered orange with white-hot flares. For a while everyone just stood, warmed by the ending of two lives, and the pillar of smoke rose up, pungent with pine and fir needles. Beneath the crackle of the flames, Tegan listened to the crash of the icy sea below.

What a lonely place.

"It's time," Khamish said.

"Good-bye, Ma." Among those gathered in grief, only Tegan heard Lucilla's whisper, and she cradled her closer in response.

The exodus began in twos and threes, townsfolk returning to their homes. Soon only a small group remained. Tegan glanced back at them in following Khamish toward the path that led away from the bluff. Ten men stood by, likely volunteers who had offered to keep the flames burning long and hot enough to finish the job properly. They had lots of chopped wood set by, so there would be a glow on the rise deep into the night.

"I'll take Lucilla home," she told Khamish.

"Go on then."

Their paths parted in the center of town. Only a few businesses remained open, two public houses and a general goods store. Tegan couldn't remember ever feeling part of anything like this before. In the ruins, it was impossible; with the Wolves, unthinkable; and then during the war, there was only endless passing through. She reached her destination with all the feeling gone in her arms. Lucilla slid down and lowered her eyes.

"You can come see me anytime," Tegan said.

That didn't win a smile, nor did she expect one. The girl nodded before trudging up the steps to where her aunt waited. Mara waved with all the weariness in the world. Tegan wished there was more she could do, but she'd made a deal with Lucilla. *Normal sadness, that's all.* Despite her thick boots, Tegan couldn't feel her feet. Her hip hurt from the fall, and so did her thigh, the old injury aggravated by the cold. To make matters worse, the wound on her shoulder throbbed like mad now that she wasn't holding

Lucilla. While she'd noticed the pull, a little pain seemed worth it. Yet now she ached in three places.

She was limping by the time she reached the cottage. The smell of mulled wine wafted out to her, more inviting than anything but Szarok's scent-marking. Inside, Khamish waited with two mugs, and she sprinkled some powder into Tegan's before passing it over.

"What's that?"

"A cure for what ails you."

That seemed like a good idea. She downed the drink without tasting it. "How awful."

"The medicine?"

"This whole day."

"You were good to Lucilla. She'll remember that."

"I lost my mother, too." Whatever she'd expected to blurt out, it wasn't that.

Khamish only nodded. Words were unnecessary in the right kind of silence. They ate a quiet meal of leftover soup and bread, and Tegan sighed as the medicine kicked in. Her pain thinned down first to an ache and then a gentle soreness. Afterward, she forced herself to wash the dishes. Though she hurt from old wounds, she imagined old age must be worse.

"You're a good girl." The healer sank into a chair with a tired sigh.

"I could be," she said.

I want to be.

Not just because it made people like her. Because it was right.

"Come, me duck. This is something you should learn."

To Tegan's surprise, it was nothing related to healing or midwifery. Khamish held up some yarn and fine long needles. Though Tegan had watched her knitting many nights before bed, she'd never yet seen anything finished come out of this work basket. There was just a long gray tube that coiled at the bottom like a snake.

That was the magic word.

Learn.

It started a fire in her chest, the best kind, carrying the memory of swimming lessons and speaking in Uroch on an island that reeked of wild birds. *Oh, Szarok,* she thought. *Those may have been the happiest days of my life.* Tegan pictured herself at Khamish's age, teaching another girl everything she knew, and it seemed . . . right, but also heartbreaking. *This could be my house someday.* With utter focus, she kept the tears in check and studied her teacher's hands. When the time came, she took the needles and reproduced the stitches with clumsy determination. She failed more than once and tried again, until at last Khamish said:

"Do you understand now?"

"It's like our work," she answered. "Trying is the important part."

"That, and it gives your heart and mind a rest. When you're working a pattern, you aren't thinking about what you did or should've done."

"Thank you. I did need to learn this." The loss binding her chest unraveled a little more.

One day I might take full breaths again.

One day.

She didn't regret a minute she'd spent with Szarok, not a single word or look. Once her mother had said, *Love is what makes the hurt worthwhile,* with a faraway look, and Tegan hadn't understood. Not then. But now, gazing down the years, she suspected her mama had been longing for her father, a man Tegan couldn't remember. He might have even died before she was born, because she'd only asked about him once. And now there could be no answers.

"You're most welcome."

"I'm wondering . . . why don't you ever finish anything you make?"

Khamish regarded her somberly. "A fortune-teller told me

long ago that when I finished my first scarf, that would be the day I died. I figure if I keep at it, I can live forever."

Tegan's eyes widened. "Truly?"

"No." The other woman broke out into delighted chuckles. "You're a gullible little thing. The knitting soothes me, but I'm too lazy to stop and start again. Plus, I'd have to find good homes for all the bits and bobs."

"Oh," she said, feeling foolish.

"You're looking done in. Sleep well."

Nodding gratefully, Tegan set her small section of knitting in the basket and stumbled down the hall to her bed. She slept the night through and woke feeling almost human. The sun was out, and there were patients to see. *Death comes for us all in time. Fear of it shouldn't keep us from living.*

For the next two months she learned from Khamish as the snow fell. Sickness came and went. She tended Lucilla through a fever and watched over her as she recovered. Sometimes, on clear days, she climbed to the top of the bluff and looked out over the gray and churning sea. This late in the year, no ships passed by, but she imagined them.

Carrying James and Millie and—

No.

Szarok would not be on board, sailing back to her. So she imagined him happy instead, and usually that was enough to make her heart sing, just for him. *I am here.* And again, *I am here.* As the weather warmed, Tegan made that pilgrimage until people watched and waved as she went through town. Some thought she must be waiting for a lover; she heard the whispers. Others said she was surely mourning for poor Netta Gwynne.

Yet no one ever asked or dug into her secrets. Sometimes Farrell Gwynne walked with her; they never spoke. He hadn't apologized for the shove, but she suspected he didn't even remember. The wildness of his grief had faded into terrible weariness that left him hollow, like a straw man that lost all its stuffing over a long winter.

That day, as they climbed, he turned to her with a tentative look, delicate as daybreak. "This morning I saw a blue jay."

Cautiously, she replied, "The trees are budding."

Quietly, while she worked and watched and *learned*, the snow had melted, leaving the world dark and fresh and ready for life to begin anew.

In her soul as with the weather, spring had come at last.

Exodus

y Uroch standards, Tcharr was unquestionably beautiful. *"You reek of humanity."*

At the moment she was also furious. Szarok didn't attempt to block the strike. As his head snapped back, he noted that she hadn't used her claws, so her fury had limits. Still, he tasted blood from where his fangs sliced the lining of his cheek. Spitting it out would be disrespectful, a sign that he didn't accept her rebuke, so he swallowed.

"You were gone too long," she snarled. *"Rroclaw whispers of war."*

"Apologies," he replied.

Rzika, the oldest of the People, stepped forward. One of the first to Awaken, she didn't have much time left, but she had seen to his training and chosen his mate with great care. Most Uroch formed their own heart-bonds, but since he had been elevated to vanguard, certain freedoms had been lost. As Tcharr was the strongest female, they must fortify the tribe together. She was also the obligation he'd mentioned to Tegan.

"Peace, consort." Rzika made a staying gesture at Tcharr by flourishing her claws, then addressed him. *"What news, vanguard?"*

After so long, it felt good to be surrounded by the familiar sounds and smells of home. The complex and layered scents told him volumes about how his people had fared in his absence, and not all of it good. Sour notes spoke of fear and pleading, probably with Rroclaw. As he swept the crowd, only a few would meet his gaze.

"I found our home," he growled.

Now he had everyone's attention. Cheers rose up, and he imagined Tegan's reaction to the cacophony of sound. Would she be frightened? Since he had been away, he understood how the noise could sound aggressive to untutored ears. A silent on-looker might suspect the People were plotting some vicious attack instead of celebrating.

"Where?"

"Tell us more."

So he did. In the plaza, he spoke of what he'd seen and survived, how he had learned to float in the hell-waters, and they stopped him.

"Liar!"

"From our earliest memories, we die in the wet. Always."

Tcharr snarled at the crowd, but Szarok only waited for them to calm with the composure that Rzika had beaten into him. *You must not rage. You are the vanguard. If the humans see your anger, they will fear you, and fear leads to violence. There will be no peace if you falter.* When his people quieted, he explained the plan.

"When spring comes, we march to the river. There will be boats waiting."

With imperturbable patience, he paused to allow the discussion that would be held, whether he willed it or not. Rzika lifted her chin, and though he had been free of her control for a while, her approval still warmed him. As consort, Tcharr was never required to learn tolerance, so she snapped her teeth at those still chattering.

Szarok had expected objections, and they came, fast and ferocious.

"It's probably a trap. The humans will drown us."

"Even if they don't betray us, the water will kill us before we reach the promised land."

That, too, ran its course. After a time, the People ran out of fear and excuses. The throng went silent, and Szarok praised them, as he had been taught.

"My thanks. But I know the People's hearts, and you are all too brave to let fear keep you from such a bountiful home."

He described the plenteous game and thick forests, clean water, and no human remains to taint the settlement. Szarok closed with, *"There will only be what we build. We have said that we only seek a fresh start, where we can live in peace and grow as a people. I have found it."*

Instead of more cheers, the silence after his speech was broken by the slow scrape of claws rubbing together. Rroclaw sauntered to the front, offering a calculated insult with such obvious disdain. *I am the vanguard. I may not repay discourtesy in kind.* Yet Szarok wished hard for thirty seconds of freedom to teach this mud-tooth some manners.

Rroclaw growled, *"How many of the People would you drown for a dream? These ruins are inhospitable, but there are better places nearby. We need only take them."*

"You would kill them in battle instead when we have signed treaties?"

"They traded on our ignorance of their ways. Don't you think they knew how impossible we would find it to sustain life here? We committed to slow death by starvation." Rroclaw lunged to back his words with force, but Tcharr checked him with claws at his throat.

The consort pressed, almost breaking skin. *"Move. Breathe. And we'll learn who speaks with proper reason."*

Physical challenges sometimes settled matters of truth, but Szarok couldn't let this issue go to a contest, especially not like this. Before he could intervene, Rzika knocked Tcharr's hand away. The oldest Uroch made an intimidating sound in the back of her throat.

"Enough. Come. There will be time to talk."

But Rroclaw whirled and shoved through the crowd, ignoring

the elder's cautioning words. Watching him go, Szarok acknowledged the likelihood that there would be conflict before the rest accepted that the journey must be undertaken. Fear of the unknown might discourage some, but past winter's end, he could teach others to swim.

It hurt him to see how his folk lived, curling up in ruined houses. They had no trades, apart from hunting; their repairs were basic and didn't hold through heavy snow. Once, some Gulgur had come to teach certain crafts, but they fled after Rroclaw's faction had harassed them. The other male had been considered as vanguard, but Rzika determined he lacked the necessary mental control, and Rroclaw had been angry ever since. He wanted to lead the People, but most understood that it would mean more war and possibly a return to atrocities they'd only begun to put behind them.

Szarok's own resting place was no better: sagging walls, holes in the roof, ruined furniture, and bits of vegetation growing inside. Tcharr and Rzika accompanied him; the two females talked long into the night about the offer he'd received in Port-Mer. Eventually they offered him some meat, but as he ate, he ached over how thin the People had become. Hunting parties ranged farther and farther from Appleton, competing with humans for their game. It would be better in the northern wilds, and he thought the villagers should be willing to sell some herd animals that the People could keep as food reserve. Though he didn't look forward to the journey, Szarok truly believed this to be the best solution, long term.

"I will support the exodus." Rzika finally rose with an audible popping of her joints. *"You must be weary?"*

Szarok made a sound of assent.

Once the elder had departed, Tcharr tilted her head at him and he smelled the heat of her intentions. *"Shall I stay?"*

He should want that. The People required him to.

He didn't.

The excuse flowed out before he could stop it. *"I would disappoint you."*

"Soon then, vanguard."

Alone at last, he curled into the nest of furs left from the last hunting season. Duty and obligation might choke him to death, for he felt the leather of the leash tightening on his throat. That night, Szarok slept poorly on his own; again and again he woke, reaching for a healer who wasn't there. As the days went by, her smell faded, until there was only his own scent on his skin. Each night, he made a new excuse for Tcharr, who eventually stopped asking when he told her that he wished for their offspring to be born safely in the promised land.

Apologies, consort. I do not want our children to be born at all.

Some while after he returned, Rzika presented Szarok's proposal to the assembled populace, but Rroclaw came with his own plan. *Pure chaos.* The debate raged on until deepest winter, but his proposal carried the day by a narrow margin. Rroclaw stormed off after the conclave ended, accepting defeat about as well as Szarok had expected.

Tcharr watched him go, her eyes narrowed. *"We will probably need to kill him."*

Szarok agreed.

It was unthinkable to execute someone for crimes he might commit. So as the winter wore on and snow fell thick on the ground, they prepared for the journey as best they could. Meat was scarce, and they ate most of what they had cured. In the heart of the icy worst, two younglings froze to death without passing memories. The People mourned by raking their claws across their chests and bearing new scars in honor of the fallen. If they had first shared their collective experiences, there would be no need to grieve at all.

"You're different." Tcharr often came to him, and it wasn't her fault that his heart had flown for someone else. So he tried not to show his silent yearning.

"Am I?"

"Not calm but sorrowing. Is it the ones we lost?"

"Yes," he said, hating himself.

"Grieve less. When we reach the promised land, humans will help us build proper homes. There will be plenty of wood for warming and all the meat we want."

"My thanks for believing. We need only endure a little more."

When the snow melted at last, the People were lean and hungry. Szarok led several hunts as the sun brightened and the grass greened, stockpiling for the trek. More than once, he nearly collapsed under the weight of Uroch hope, all resting on his shoulders. Then he pictured his healer's smile, her warm eyes, the sweetness of her sweat, and pushed on.

Rroclaw's warriors struck on the way back to Appleton. *Fifteen younglings, dying for no good cause.* Snarling with rage, Tcharr raced toward Rroclaw while Szarok tried to speak reason.

"This changes nothing. If you fight us, you become exiles. No tribe, no home. Reconsider, kinsmen. Kneel if you would live."

Six dropped to one knee, and Szarok shook with relief, even as he joined the hunters in battling Rroclaw's rebel eight. Most were too raw to have seen real combat; Szarok keened silently in cutting them down. The People should never use weapons, because they needed to remember how it felt to wet their claws with the blood of a kinsman. He lost one of his, but they prevailed, and then he rushed to Tcharr's aid. Rroclaw had her pinned, and he sank his talons into her chest. Bearing the pain, she flipped him and went for his throat. Szarok kicked him in the head and then gripped with his toe claws, holding the traitor still so Tcharr could finish him.

"Your weakness will destroy the People," Rroclaw gasped.

She ended him, and his blood gushed onto the ground. In counting, Szarok saw that they had fifteen left in total. He studied the six still kneeling.

"Will you follow me?"

"Yes," they snarled.

"Then rise and gather the game. This is done."

Tcharr refused his offer of support; she would probably bite a chunk out of him if he ever tried to carry her as he had his healer. With her palm pressed over the wound, she set the pace for their return to Appleton. Between his hunters and the rebels, they carried the meat back to the ruins to be prepared for travel. The news spread quickly about Rroclaw's fall, and while there was still some resistance, excitement spread among the People, too. Ordinarily, Szarok paid little attention to time, apart from the change of seasons, but as the days lengthened, he marked them because it was important to reach the river before the ships.

At last the morning of the great exodus dawned. The People gathered all the supplies and set out. Szarok led them at a pace that wouldn't weary the old or the young. Most human caravans gave them a wide berth, but he recognized one from their short acquaintance in the war. Trader Kelley surprised him by lifting a hand in greeting.

"Ho there, Uroch! Looks like your whole town's on the move."

Szarok nodded in the human way. Odd, he'd almost missed their strange speech. "We're bound for the northern wilds."

"A long journey, then. I'd offer to trade, but it looks like you've already got as much as you can carry."

"I appreciate the thought."

"Safe travels!"

"He seemed friendly enough," Rzika growled, once their group walked on.

"They are, mostly. And you can smell when they aren't."

Tcharr acknowledged this with a grunt. She was moving slowly, and he wished Tegan could examine her wound. But the consort snapped at him any time he tried to check, not that he knew much about healing. The People tended to recover well or die, not much variance in between. So he pretended he didn't notice Tcharr weakening; it only angered her.

Nine days after they left Appleton, the People arrived at the river. Since the weather was warm, they slept in the open, camped beneath the stars. The night after their arrival, the Gulgur who lived nearby investigated their fires, but once they learned the Uroch would be moving on, they didn't linger. For the next week, Szarok gave swimming lessons, and his heart ached.

If you were here, my treasure, would this be easier?

But even without his healer, the People learned. Not all, of course, but enough. The ones who mastered his teachings joined him in instructing others. As their confidence grew, others dared to strive harder. *Even if disaster strikes, we won't all perish.* That soothed much of the uncertainty, and he smiled to see the younglings splashing at the water's edge without fear.

On the eighth day, the promised ships arrived.

His people gazed in wonder, as they had only ever used the small boats on Rosemere or shoddy rafts of their own design. These were finely built in Antecost and crewed by those Littleberry had entrusted with this mission. He recognized the captain who had brought him just before the big ice, and he lifted a hand to her.

"Ahoy, Szarok! I see you're ready to travel. Have you explained what comes next?"

"They understand. I'll remain onshore until the last have been ferried aboard."

Amid much snarling excitement, the People went by rowing boat out to the larger ships. Rather than clog the river, they sailed off as they filled with passengers. The numbers on the riverbank dwindled, until only he, Rzika, and Tcharr remained. He escorted the females to the dinghy and climbed in last, relieved to be away. He'd feared that the mainlanders might take Uroch movement as a sign of impending hostility, but it appeared that the friendly Gulgur, along with John Kelley, had spread the word.

The first day on the water, his folk suffered, shivers and sickness. He'd warned them it would be bad, but the Uroch were fierce-hearted. By the time they reached Antecost, most had adapted. The People would never love the sea, but the drowning chains broke as they disembarked in Port-Mer.

Littleberry greeted him with a smiling face and an even more luxurious mustache. "There are more of you than I imagined. I had the men scout a site, six miles from here. If you agree it's a good location, we'll help you get started."

"This is more than I expected. By now your conscience should be clear."

The chief laughed. "The best way to rest easy is giving with a generous heart."

For the first time since the war, humans and Uroch mingled freely. His people wandered in Port-Mer, examining wares in the market and practicing their human-speak. Initially Szarok couldn't relax for fear of conflict, but since the villagers in Port-Mer had resolved to offer a warm welcome, many of them shared food and drink, not realizing his people wouldn't want most of what they had.

"They're so ugly," Tcharr growled.

"Careful." Rzika rapped the consort on the back of her head. *"Some of them may understand us."*

Only one, he thought. *And she is not with me.*

She may never be again.

The pain surprised him, so ferocious that it seemed as if he had been skewered through the heart. He breathed through it.

"Delicious!" A youngling devoured a fresh fish straight out of a fisherman's net, and Szarok growled in delight over his rare wonder.

For a bit longer he let them explore, but they needed to leave before the sun set. Finally he called, *"You'll be welcome here again, but we should move. We're nearly there."*

Those nearby ran through town, helping him gather the tribe, and once he had everyone, he followed Littleberry's scout. Since they were so close to the end of the journey, he walked quicker than he had on the mainland. His people had rested on the ships, and though some were still weak, they could manage a brisk pace for a short time, knowing what lay ahead.

"*So beautiful,*" Rzika marveled.

"*Yes.*"

The clean water and trees spoke to the People, and Szarok smelled the rising joy, tangible as a song. Younglings darted after prey, running back when they realized there was no urgency. The ground trembled with ripe scents, so much game. With every step, their delight rose to a crescendo that made him want to roar his triumph. At last the human stopped in a fine clearing, bounded by a fir grove, with sparkling water close by.

"This is a good place," he told the man. "Convey my thanks to Littleberry."

"Will do. I'll send a crew out tomorrow, and we'll get started on your village. Once you want us to step back, though, just say so. We only want to help."

"Understood."

When the human disappeared from sight, the People shouted their exultation, and then they set to exploring with confidence that grew with each step on this promised land.

I have done it, my treasure. We are home.

Bisected by equal measures of brightness and desire, Szarok listened for his love beneath the cheerful warble of birdsong. He remembered her scent and the softness of her hair, and then she whispered to him with each pump of his heart:

I am here.

The Sweetness of Home

Shock held Morrow still for a moment, and then the rightness of it cascaded over him like a sudden rain. He wrapped his arms around her and kissed Millie back with an intensity that surprised him. Her soft lips enticed him, and he sank into her with a heated shiver. One kiss turned into several small ones, and then a long, deep one. She hooked her tongue in a move that startled him every bit as much as it filled him with want.

Millie pulled back with a teasing look. "You didn't think you'd be *teaching* me or something silly like that? Maybe there's nothing worth staying for in Otterburn, but we found ways to entertain ourselves."

He kissed her chin. "I truly am sorry about that."

"It's past now."

Her quick forgiveness moved him. In his life, he'd only loved from a distance, so he understood exactly how she felt, and it made him ache that he'd bruised her heart that way. Settling her close to him, he breathed in the sweet scent of her hair. In retrospect, he had to shake his head at himself; he'd grown so accustomed to the idea of adoring Tegan from afar that he'd never even noticed when his feelings had shifted. But now he understood why he'd been so cross about Millie's dwindling attention, possessive when he had no right to be.

"I don't know what you see in me, unless you're mesmerized by my stories."

She laughed softly, settling her head against his chest. "Remember, I had no idea who you were the first time I saw you. So I didn't see a famous writer or even a member of Company D. You were all just strangers in town."

"It can be . . . tiresome," he said quietly, wondering why he had never realized it before.

"What can?"

"When I arrive in a new place, if they've heard of me, they say, 'Tell us a story,' before any greetings or introductions. Sometimes it feels as if I've ceased to be a person, and I'm only a collection of words, or worse, just a source of entertainment." Self-conscious, he avoided her gaze by firelight, knowing he sounded melancholic at best.

"Don't worry about that anymore. You're my man first, and so I'll tell anyone who asks." Nudging closer, she put her face next to his. "You *are*, aren't you?"

Laughing, he pulled her into his lap. "I'm slow but not ridiculous. I do wish I'd known how lovely it is to have someone like you sooner."

"That's such basic knowledge that I'm embarrassed for you," she told him pertly.

Morrow tickled her in response to that sass, and she squirmed with an abandon that led to other things. As he kissed the curve of her throat, she shivered and sighed. Then she pushed him away and combined their bedding. While he definitely wanted to be close to her, he also suspected she might be punishing him for being so sluggish at figuring things out.

"Is this wise?"

Millie opened her eyes at him in a look that no longer registered as innocent. *Dear lord*, he thought. *She's been teasing me for months.*

"It's practical," she replied. "We won't need to feed the fire as much if we're generating our own heat."

"Fine."

He muffled a groan as she snuggled into the pallet beside him and drew up the covers. All sorts of objections cluttered his head, but at base, he didn't really want to sleep alone. Morrow settled Millie against him and wrapped an arm around her. Since his mother had died, he couldn't remember sleeping with anyone. His father was kind enough, but distant, which was probably why he'd taken refuge in stories.

"Tell me something about young James," she whispered, settling in.

This . . . this is fantastic.

He wanted a lot more than sleep, but it was too soon. So he said, "I suppose I was lonely. The governor as my father meant I got a lot of respect, but the other children tended to be nervous when I wanted to play. I eventually stopped asking, and I just read instead."

Millie laughed. "Oh, you adorable dolt. *That's* your sad story?"

Stung, he muttered, "Stop laughing. And . . . my mother died when I was young."

"Of illness?"

"That's what I'm told. I don't remember."

Millie kissed his temple. "No wonder you're confused. For everyone else, the world is devastating and dangerous. For you, it's *lonely.*"

"Things were much worse outside Rosemere. I know that. I saw it when I went to the ruins on the other side of the river."

"But . . . my darling James, knowing isn't enough. For you, the ruins were an adventure. To someone else, it was a hell they couldn't escape, and they probably didn't even know it could be better elsewhere."

There's no doubt she means Tegan.

The words cracked his mind open with such force that he understood so many things now. *Too late for it to do any good now.* He squeezed his eyes shut. "I'm such a child."

"A little, perhaps. But it's also marvelous that you had a chance to be. Most of us didn't. You shouldn't regret the sweetness of your life or the richness of your luck."

"Thank you," he said.

"For what?"

"Saving me. Nobody's ever talked to me like this . . . and it's exactly what I need."

"Well, you are the governor's son." But she softened the sting with a kiss, and then another, until he no longer minded hearing such truths.

In the morning he woke to a foot in his ribs. "I thought you weren't going to bother her."

Cracking an eye open, he found Devi standing over him. He flushed. "I—"

"Didn't." Millie sighed as she rolled out of the blankets. "I am supremely unbothered. However, I'm wondering where we can stay for the winter. I don't imagine you want strangers on your floor for several months."

Evette turned from stirring the porridge and gestured with a wooden spoon. "It's not for our sake, dear. You'll soon tire of not having a room of your own. But the matter's much simpler if we're only seeking one spare, not two. Is that so?"

Morrow wouldn't have spoken so boldly, but it was endearing when Millie did. "Most definitely. I can help with cooking and cleaning for our keep."

As if I'd let you support me.

He scowled. "I'm sure I can find work as well."

Her smirk practically scraped his skin down to the raw nerves. "No doubt. Do you reckon they'd pay you to teach sword fighting? Or maybe storytelling . . . ?"

She thinks I'm useless.

It didn't cool his anger that she had a point. As he balled up a fist, Devi said soothingly, "Don't squabble before breakfast, little ones. You'll get indigestion."

"I'm not," Millie said in a placid tone. "But you know men and their pride."

Both Devi and Evette nodded, and the latter said knowingly, "Men."

Outnumbered and feeling it, he mumbled, "Where is Sung Ji?"

Devi laughed as she set bowls on the table. "You won't see him or Advika for a day or two. There's a limit to how much fun they can have on board a ship, so we just set food and water outside the door."

"Once they broke the bed," Evette added.

Morrow's whole face caught fire, but Millie gazed down the hall in wicked delight. "Say it's not so?" But her expression begged for confirmation.

Morrow bolted to his feet and donned his winter gear as fast as he could wrap up, unsure what was worse—that he'd soon be privy to some noisy bed games or this conversation about it. Either way, exploring Baybridge offered the least potential for additional humiliation. Engrossed in her chat, Millie showed no signs of wanting to follow him, as she used to.

"What about breakfast?" Devi asked.

"I'll find something. Good day, ladies."

With that, he hurried into the lightly falling snow. The village sprawled before him, built into the rolling hills above the water. Crisp and cold, the air smelled faintly of the sea, but there was also smoke from so many chimneys and a molten tang that reminded him of the smithy in Rosemere. Cottages lined the road down into town proper, most whitewashed and built of quarried stone, but others were weathered wood or even what looked like earthen brick, now grown over green, brown-turned in the season, and soon to be frosted white. It was too cold for an open market, but Morrow spied a large building that seemed to serve the same function, and there were more public houses than he'd seen even in Peckinpaugh.

Morrow walked until his chagrin had cooled, but that proved useful when he spotted a sign in the window that read SCHOOL TEACHER WANTED—INQUIRE WITHIN. A tinkling bell announced his entry. The shop smelled of dried herbs and camphor, but it was also deliciously warm. He stamped the wet off his boots and glanced around, intrigued by the oddments that had been bottled. An impressive selection of dead insects lined one shelf, and another seemed to be withered parts; he recognized the chicken feet, but the rest eluded him.

A small man came out from the back, two gray-caterpillar brows dancing above deep-set eyes. "What can I do for you?"

"I'm here about the job," Morrow said, trying not to stare.

"Ah yes. Have you taught children before?"

"No. But I'm highly lettered. I've even written—"

"Never mind then. In this line of work, it's more important to be kind than clever."

"How do you know I'm not both? And how many applicants have you had, anyway? The *Catalina* barely made it to port this late in the year." Aware he sounded contentious, he couldn't back off what might be the only suitable work in town.

"True, true. I'm Lionel Fairstone, the apothecary, also the administrator in charge of education in Baybridge. We have a three-room school, you know." Fairstone said this as if Morrow must realize it was impressive.

He did. Rosemere educated all the children at once while some settlements left learning to the parents. In those cases, the little ones rarely learned to read or write because there were animals to tend and hunt, endless washing, crops to cultivate, and work that never paused for dreaming. To one who loved books as he did, that seemed like a diabolical shame.

"So I would be working with two others. Then . . . ask me some questions, get a feel for my personality. And if you like what you learn, I could work on a trial basis under the supervision of my colleagues."

"You're well spoken," the other man admitted. "Very well, tell me about yourself."

So Morrow did. He spoke of Rosemere, growing up as the governor's son, the war down south and his role in Company D, and finally the adventures, losses, and gains that led him to Baybridge. By this point, his stomach was rumbling, so it seemed reasonable to accept Fairstone's offer of toast and tea. The administrator then quizzed him with some potential disciplinary situations to see how he'd handle them. At the end of the interview, Fairstone offered a hearty handshake.

"Welcome aboard, sir. You'll do well for our children. We can't pay much, but the job comes with room and board. There are three small cottages adjacent to the school."

"Perfect. But I feel I must be clear. . . . I'll likely be sailing in the spring. There's a girl my father must meet before I can formally offer her my heart."

"Then we'll take those four months gladly and hope that providence replaces you."

They talked a little longer, and then Morrow followed him out of the shop. Fairstone flipped the sign and wrote, BACK IN TEN MINUTES, then he led the way to the school for a short tour, as it was really just a house that had been repurposed for education. The teacher cottages were small, as stated, especially compared to his home on Rosemere, but as he turned in place, he imagined living here with Millie. There was a padded settee before the fireplace and a stove for cooking, and a room devoted just to washing up. People lived much worse in Otterburn, so she'd surely be delighted.

And I did this for us.

"It's all right if someone lives here with me?" It seemed best to check.

"The girl you mentioned before?"

He nodded.

"I have no objections. As long as you do your work reliably, your life is your own to arrange as you see fit."

"Thank you, sir. I'll report tomorrow, bright and early."

Morrow raced through town, slipping on the snow, and didn't pause for breath until he reached Devi and Evette's house. Unsure if he should knock, he rapped twice and ran in, at first wheezing too hard to get his news out. The women stared at him in alarm and pelted him with questions. But soon he shared his good tidings, and Devi poured homemade elderberry wine.

She raised her cup in a toast. "Well done, sir. In time I would've asked around, but you were too quick."

Millie caught Evette's eye and grinned. "Told you goading him would work."

He choked on his wine and spluttered, "You . . . you were *teasing* me? On purpose?'

"A little. But don't be glum; we've got a place to stay this winter. I'll keep it clean and have dinner on when you get home."

That sounded too lovely for him to sulk. So he drank until he shouldn't anymore, since he was starting a new job in the morning. Morrow did notice that neither Sung Ji nor Captain Advika emerged before he and Millie set out for their own house the next day. *What a sweet ring to those words.* When they arrived, someone had stocked the shelves with bread and cheese, dried meat, and various staples. Millie kissed him good-bye and shooed him out the door.

At first the children were obstreperous, but he quickly learned that if he could turn a lecture into a story, they focused much better. All told, holding their attention wasn't that much different from entertaining a bunch of drunken men. He found he liked it, and he especially enjoyed when a child's face lit with understanding. And at the end of each day, Millie waited for him, as promised, with a hot meal.

They made friends in town and visited often with Devi and

Evette, Advika and Sung Ji, over cheerful meals and silly games that James had never been invited to play, like Forfeits, Lookabout, Fox and Geese, but his favorite by far must have been Throwing the Smile, for the moment he locked eyes with Millie, she beamed like a beacon, and he *always* won. In truth, the winter months flew. It seemed as if he slept once, twice, snuggled up with this wondrous girl, and then suddenly the sun came back again.

On his last day at school, his students cried, and he did, too, though he pretended to have something in his eye. Millie had their bags packed, not that they had accumulated much. Most of it, they left in the cottage in case the next teacher could make use of it. Lionel Fairstone had a party for him at the Limping Dog, well attended by parents and pupils alike. People toasted him and spoke of gratitude and never once asked him to tell a story.

Here, I was more than the governor's studious son. I made my own way this time.

Afterward, Millie hugged him from behind, where he stood gazing out the cottage window at the darkened schoolhouse. "James . . . I'm happy here. And I know you are, too. We could just . . . stay."

Smiling, he shook his head.

"Why not?" She bristled and tugged on his arm until he faced her.

She thinks I mean to search for Tegan. Or spend my life on something else, perhaps salvaging old books, while she grows old waiting for me.

He cupped her face in his hands and kissed her softly; cheeks, chin, nose, brow, and finally lips, where he lingered long enough nearly to forget what he intended to say. "Because *you* must first come to Rosemere, and *I* must go to Winterville. Next year, if you want to come . . . and stay, maybe bring your parents with us, then I'll have no objections."

When Millie parsed his words, she pounced; they didn't sleep much that night.

In the morning they barely made the *Catalina* before it set sail. Millie headed for the infirmary with their things, and he made himself useful. As he helped the first mate, Morrow avoided Sung Ji's teasing gaze.

"Hope you celebrated well. There's not much privacy on board, and subbing as our medic, Millie's in great demand. The whole crew speaks so fondly of her gentle hands."

Part of Morrow's brain filled with lightning, but he choked it down. "How sad for them. Talking's all they'll ever get to do with her."

Sung Ji laughed, adjusting the sails. "You've got it bad, son."

"I know. But . . . you said subbing. Does that mean you think Dr. Tegan might come back to work someday?"

The other man shrugged. "The sea is a strange mistress. Sometimes she gives; sometimes she takes. Until I know for sure, I always wait and hope."

Love Never Leaves

As Tegan pinned the laundry to the line, Lucilla ran down the path toward her. Smiling, she caught the girl and lifted her for a proper hug. "You're late today."

"I came as soon as I could. Auntie Mara needs my help a lot."

"True." She kissed Lucilla's forehead and then set her down to finish her work.

The little girl handed her clothing from the basket piece by piece, until it was all drying beneath the warm sun. "You'll never guess what happened."

"Peter pulled your hair."

"He always does that."

"Ate your sticky bun?"

Lucilla sighed. "That, too. No, this is important."

"Oh. Sorry." She smothered a smile. "By all means, tell me."

"That ship you told me about . . . the *Catalina*? It's finally here!"

Stunned, Tegan dropped her basket. Without another word, she took off running, Lucilla close behind her. They raced to the docks, and she recognized the ship currently being unloaded. To a nearby dockworker's dismay, she climbed on top of a crate for a better look. Sure enough, she spotted Captain Advika and Sung Ji on deck, preparing to disembark.

Millie and James must be here, too.

She hopped down without regard for her weak leg and

pushed past the workers to dash up the gangplank. Until this moment, she hadn't realized how much she wanted to see all of them again. Good-byes had been such a permanent part of her existence that once someone went—or she did—she tried not to think of them again. Most days yearning seemed like another word for weakness. In her life, only one person ever lasted through her attempts to forget and cut him out.

"Are these your friends?" Lucilla asked.

"They are."

It's true.

She'd resisted roots like they might strangle her, but now happy tears ran down her cheeks. "Captain. Captain!"

The older woman whirled and then *sprinted* toward her, her smile giddy, eyes gleaming. She hugged Tegan, or vice versa, and then the first mate joined in. Soon everyone on deck was shouting, until James and Millie emerged from below. Morrow stopped cold and just . . . stared. Tegan smiled at him, tentatively, because this felt like the first meeting of a new life. The months had been good to him. With sun-kissed cheeks and sparkling eyes, James looked . . . happy, for want of a better word. He'd also put on muscle working aboard the ship. As for Millie, she, too, radiated joy, though her expression faded to shock on spotting Tegan.

"You're alive," James said hoarsely.

Captain Advika let go of her, and Sung Ji stepped back. In moments James had her in his arms, but it was a different sort of hug than he'd offered before. Hard to quantify the difference, but his hold was firm, and his touch didn't linger. He eased her to arm's length to scrutinize her.

"Last I checked." She smiled a bit.

"I'm sorry. I'm *so* sorry I didn't save you."

"That wasn't your role," she told him gently. "I never *wanted* you to save me. Mostly I wished to be someone people trusted to save herself."

A nod told her that he understood. "Still, I'm unspeakably relieved."

Next, Tegan turned to Millie and gave the girl a longer embrace; they'd set out together, after all, and she'd followed someone else into the sea. "I'm glad to see you both."

Beaming, Millie kissed her cheek. "You look well."

"I told you." Nudging James, Sung Ji seemed really pleased with himself.

James nodded. "Always wait and hope. That's my new motto."

"What happened?" Millie asked.

There was far too much mutual news to share while standing on the ship's deck, so Tegan picked up Lucilla, who was anxiously tugging on her sleeve. "When you have time, come to Khamish's place." She asked Advika, "You know where it is?"

"Certainly. James and Millie can go with you now. Once we wrap up here, Sung Ji and I will be along."

Tegan could tell everyone had so many questions, but she didn't mean to repeat the story. She led the way back to the dock, balancing Lucilla on her hip. Once they reached the street, she put her down and took her hand instead. The little girl was all big eyes, studying the strangers.

"Who's this?" Millie asked.

"Lucilla, ma'am."

"I just aged twenty years." Cheerfully, Millie locked arms with James.

Sending a message, Tegan suspected.

But it was unnecessary. No matter what James may have thought or wanted, she'd never seen him as more than a dear friend. Until Szarok, she'd suspected that she was incapable of forming such bonds. But he'd broken down walls she didn't even know existed, and when he marched out of the ruins of her heart's fortress, she sat among the fallen stones. Instead of weeping, she marveled at the breeze.

"I suppose you could say she's my apprentice. But she has a few years of studying with Khamish before she'll be able to travel with me."

Alarmed, the little girl wrapped her arms around Tegan's neck. "You're leaving?"

"Yes, love. There are friends I wish to see. But I'll return."

"Liar," said Lucilla. "People only go; they don't come back again."

For the first time since they'd left the *Catalina*, James spoke, and it was in a different tone than she'd ever heard from him. "You're being disrespectful, young miss." He tapped Lucilla lightly on the head, then went on, "Besides, my friend wouldn't lie. . . . She keeps her promises."

"How do you know?" Lucilla asked, startled out of an impending sulk.

Tegan regarded James with fresh approval. Whatever he'd been doing, it had transformed him from a good-hearted clown to a man worth taking seriously.

"I saw this woman dive over the rails of a ship into a stormy sea. And yet here she stands before me. Don't you think if she can survive that, she can survive anything?"

Yes. I can.

"Did you really do that?"

"As it happens, yes."

"Why?" Lucilla demanded.

"You'll have to wait for the captain and first mate before I start talking."

Though Lucilla protested, Tegan held firm. After they got to the cottage, she set the girl to helping Khamish prepare refreshments. Since the house was small, she spread a blanket on the grass in the shade and created a makeshift picnic. James and Millie offered to help, but she declined. Tegan rushed in and out, carrying food, so everything was ready when the last two guests arrived.

"You're a sight for sore eyes," the old healer exclaimed.

She and Advika hugged, and Sung Ji settled next to James, on the other side of Millie. Tegan chose a spot between Lucilla and Khamish, but the little girl soon squirmed into her lap.

As they ate, she told her story, punctuated with interjections from her rapt audience.

James feigned an angry stare. "You rescued the vanguard, eked out a living on a lonely isle, and then dispatched a band of ruffians. If that's not enough, you also commandeered their vessel, encountered a sea monster, and dealt handily with sudden yet inevitable betrayal."

She giggled at his summary. "When you put it that way, it *does* sound like quite an adventure."

One I can hold in my heart until it stops beating.

"Never say you encountered the Behemoth," Sung Ji breathed.

The first mate looked as if he wanted to pinch Tegan to make sure she was human and not a maritime chimera sent to steal their souls. Even Captain Advika seemed impressed, and she asked a whole bunch of questions about how the thing acted as it chased the whales. Tegan tried her best to recall but eventually admitted, "I was pretty terrified. You'd have to check with Szarok for more details. I'm sorry."

The quiet that fell over the group unnerved her. At last she prompted, "What?"

"Isn't he . . . ?" James wore a sorrowful, hangdog look.

That assumption startled a laugh out of her. "See, this is why you're the storyteller, not me. *I* got shot, not him. Received a new scar, too. He's fine. Once I healed a bit, he headed for Appleton by way of Rosemere to take care of his people."

"Oh. I had the impression that the two of you would never part," Millie said softly.

Tegan's smile tightened a little but didn't crack. "You were wrong."

James stepped into the breach; rescuing her had become a

habit he couldn't break, it seemed. Glancing around, he donned his storyteller demeanor like a colorful cloak. "You didn't corner the market on excitement. We fought off raiders."

While snuggling Lucilla, Tegan listened to their story, and it was quite late by the time everyone finished talking. Farrell Gwynne came looking for his little girl around that time, so Tegan sent her off, and the rest of their visitors took that as their cue to depart as well. Tegan cleaned up the picnic remnants and then fetched the knitting basket. She had her own tube, but some-day she might turn it into a scarf.

For the right person.

"You've got a faraway look in your eyes, me duck. Does that mean you're shipping out when the *Catalina* sails?"

"Will you be all right without me?"

The older woman laughed. "Did I build a fence around your life? Whatever you want, you should have it. I'll be fine. Lucilla will come, just as her mama did before her."

"As I told Lucilla earlier, I *will* be back. Because I was happy here."

"Was," Khamish repeated with a faint smile. "That means your heart is already gone."

A flood of warmth surged through her, remembering Szarok. "It's never really been here with me," she admitted softly. "But I've learned to live without."

"Ah." Just that. It was an acknowledgment but also a brief in-vitation to speak on, leaving the choice in Tegan's hands.

Where it always should be.

She spilled everything to Khamish and then finished with, "I'm not even sure why I'm telling you all this, except . . . that I want someone to know that I love him."

"You speak as if you'll never see Szarok again."

"Perhaps not. I don't know what the future holds. Part of me thinks I should stay where he left me and wait for him to come home."

Khamish was far too clever not to put the pieces together. "That's why you walk up to the bluff and watch the sea?"

"I suppose."

"It's your life. Do you *want* to spend it here?"

She thought about that long and hard as she washed the last of the dishes. In time she said, "No. Not now anyway. I'm not ready to settle down yet."

"Then sail with Advika. See other friends and heal the sick as you go. If your man's meant to find you again, he will."

"You put more faith in fate than me."

Khamish shrugged. "In my time I've seen stranger things. But . . . even if you do meet up, your path probably won't be smooth. Folks won't see the two of you together and think it's beautiful that you got past your differences."

"I know," she said. "But I'd rather climb a mountain with him every single day of my life than sit on a featherbed with anyone else."

"That's love, me duck. I'll keep a fire burning for you both here, and if he happens to come home while you're away, I'll tell him you've gone looking."

Tears came upon her like a spring storm, sudden and hard, and the healer stroked Tegan's hair as she wept. "You c-can't make that promise. Before, you said you're too old for that."

"Pish," said Khamish. "These bones are made of promises. To see Lucilla raised proper, I need to live at least another ten years or so."

"I'll be back before then."

"Then stop your bawling. That's what the knitting is for."

Half laughing and half crying, Tegan mopped her tears and worked on her own tube until she calmed enough to sleep. The next few days, she alternated between seeing patients and wrapping up her time in Peckinpaugh. On the fourth day, she was ready to travel. She gave hugs to Khamish and a sniffling Lucilla at the dock, but it did feel as if she'd left a sliver of herself behind as the *Catalina* caught the tide, sails billowing free.

"Well, this is a good feeling," Advika said, propping up beside her.

Sung Ji had the departure well in hand, so the captain was taking a break. Tegan smiled at her, waving madly at the ones she was leaving behind. It occurred to her then: *Khamish is a teacher who's survived me. Maybe the curse is broken.* Or maybe there never had been one at all. But thinking of Dr. Wilson reminded her—

"It is. But I need to ask you something . . . and I can't believe I forgot for so long."

"Have at it," Advika invited.

"Before, in Winterville, I studied with Dr. Wilson." She repeated his dying words as best she could remember them. "Does that mean anything to you?"

"Oh." The other woman's face went dreamy and distant. "He's the one who saved me, you know. He was working as a ship's doctor then, and he patched me up when they picked me up outside Saint City. I guess you could call him my first love." She slid a look at Sung Ji, who was too busy to notice her melancholy. "Not my last."

"Why didn't it work out?" Tegan asked. "If you don't mind."

"He was tired of the roving life, and I'd just begun. He was born to science folk in Winterville, and he learned all he could until his father passed. Then he took a notion to see the world . . . and found me. Later he wanted to settle down, but I didn't want to stay and he couldn't go. His bloodline was bred and buried there, he said, and he needed to help them deal with the mutant threat. But me . . . ? I wanted to see the world."

"He was widowed when I met him," Tegan said.

"I'm glad he found someone . . . and that he's at peace. Thank you for telling me." The captain broke her usual protocol and strode toward the first mate and took him in her arms right there on deck.

The sailors whooped, but Sung Ji shouted for them to get back to work. He aimed a confused look at Tegan, over Advika's shoulder, but she only pantomimed that he should keep holding the captain tight. *I guess when you truly love someone, you always do, at least a little. And it's hard to hear that they've gone.* But unless Advika was much older than she looked, Dr. Wilson must've been close to twenty years her senior.

Still less of an obstacle than a lasting love between human and Uroch.

Eventually the captain tired of the staring, and scolded her crew. Sung Ji came over to Tegan at the first chance. "Something happen?"

"I gave her some news I should've delivered long ago."

The first mate raised a brow. "Anything I should know?"

"Ask her."

Visibly disgruntled, he returned to work. It was a clear, warm day, with a sea like glass. The light wind aggravated the crew, and it took longer than usual to reach their next stop on the way south, which was Port-Mer in Antecost. At night Tegan didn't bother James and Millie when she saw them settled in the infirmary. She just got blankets and curled up on deck. Night after night she drifted off beneath a crowd of stars. A sliver of a poem James had read to her once bobbed like a fishing line in her mind, something about how love fled. But if she'd learned anything from Advika, it was that love never left. Not really. Not when it was true.

I am always there, she told the night. *Even if I am not beside you.*

The *Catalina* reached Port-Mer around noon the next day, successfully navigating the dangerous shoals. Anticipation percolated through her. Maybe nothing as drastic as raiders or sea beasts, but Tegan could use a little excitement. But the town looked more or less the same, and she remembered how a girl named Malena had died the last time she'd passed through. That dimmed her sunny mood.

Yet the village chief, Little-something, greeted the captain like an honored guest. "So good to see you, Captain. You're always welcome."

"Glad to hear it."

"Any news?" Advika asked.

Whatever he might've said, Tegan never discovered. For a lone Uroch—not one she recognized—raced into town, snarling in their native tongue. From his flourish of claws, alarm drove his urgency, nothing more. The others clearly had no idea what he was saying, but drawing on lessons that seemed so long ago now, she puzzled out the gist.

"A healer. Please! We need a healer. The consort is deathly ill."

For All Things a Season

J udging by the runner's agitation, there was no time for questions. A sailor brought Tegan's medical bag, now augmented with supplies she'd acquired in Peckinpaugh. She had Dr. Wilson's precious book again, but she'd replaced her old staff permanently with the one Szarok had crafted for her. With it in hand, she followed the scout to the stable, where she borrowed a sturdy pony. She wasn't a good rider, but better that she jostled for a few miles than try to keep up with the Uroch moving at top speed.

The flight through the forest gave her no time to wonder. Within the hour, she reached the settlement, and it was wondrous. Though they'd just begun, the houses that had been built integrated beautifully with the surrounding woodlands. Most of the People seemed to be living in tents for the moment, but it was obvious the Uroch had, at last, found their permanent home. Tegan dismounted and a youngling took the pony's reins.

"*This way*," the messenger snarled.

Heart pounding wildly, she followed him to the largest of the homes, a three-room structure built of split logs. Inside, she smelled infection and herbed smoke. Despite the warmth of the day, a fire blazed in the hearth. There were three people present, two females, including the one prone on a pallet, and . . . him. Her gaze locked on Szarok; the situation was too dire for a smile, but pleasure overwhelmed her just the same. In their time apart, his sharp features had drawn even tighter, etched at chin and jaw, thin mouth, golden eyes. . . . She catalogued his face like a treasure she meant to auction.

It's fate, she thought. *Khamish was right.*

Without needing to look for him, here he was. And in need of a healer, too. Her smile brightened by degrees, despite the circumstances.

"I give greetings," she said in passable Uroch.

The elder started. Yellow eyes searched her, and then the female offered a half bow, reminiscent of Szarok's early days. *"Save the consort, please."*

She nodded, but before she could reply, Szarok spoke. *"Leave us, Rzika. The healer needs to work."*

From the look of her, the Uroch female had been ailing for a while. Briskly, Tegan sterilized her hands and then checked the wound. *Infected, as I thought.* The consort must be uncommonly strong to have fought for so long. As Tegan set out her supplies, she had to ask.

"Who is she?"

That wasn't what she truly wanted to know. Other questions fought for supremacy. *How have you been? Did you think of me?* Her hands shook a little until she controlled them. *No, I can't think of that. The patient needs me.* Szarok stood with his back to her, and she drank in even the forbidding line of his unyielding spine like he was a clear mountain spring that could quench her thirst. For a long moment he didn't speak.

When he did, his voice sounded rusty, as if he hadn't used human words since the day they'd parted. "My mate."

Those two words eviscerated her.

Her hands stilled on a bottle of dried comfrey. "I've been summoned to save your . . . ?" Tegan swallowed hard and breathed through sharp, shocking pain. *I had no idea you could be this cruel.* "Ah. Well, that is my job, after all."

She focused on her work then, because seeing him hurt too

much. The wound had gone putrid, so she had to cut away some dead flesh. Her patient snarled, but she seemed too deeply unconscious to suffer fully. It would be better if Tegan had maggots, but they weren't feasible for her med bag. The puncture wounds were deeply infected, though Uroch skin didn't show the same streaks as humans. Yet the stench was unmistakable, as was the material she expressed from the wound. Two separate abscesses had formed, and she worked feverishly. At first the Uroch female thrashed, but the longer Tegan prodded, the weaker she got.

Stitches would help nothing in this situation, as the wound needed to drain. At last Tegan finished and packed the wound with medicine to fight infection. Finally she brewed a tea and fed it to the sick Uroch in slow spoonfuls, one by one. Since the blend had a soporific quality, the patient settled. Her fever still seemed alarming, but there were temperature differentials, variations in Uroch and human physiology.

"That's all I can do for now." As Tegan packed her bag, Szarok cleaned up the mess. "I'll leave a supply of the tea for you. That, along with the medicine for the bandages, may be enough to save her, if she has a fighting spirit."

"She does," he said.

It hurt to breathe. *I never knew . . . never guessed. That I was just a distraction from his real life.*

"Good, then." Her motions were jerky as she turned toward the door.

"Tegan."

She clenched her fist on the handle of her bag so hard, it hurt. "Don't call my name like you know me. From this day on, we're strangers."

"Please stop."

"If there are complications, you can send for me. I won't be in Port-Mer long, though. I'm with the *Catalina* again, so I'll be sailing soon. You don't need to worry that . . . that I'll linger or make things awkward."

"What are you saying?" he demanded.

"I understand."

"What?"

"That I was a . . . a test. Or a game you were playing. Maybe you wanted to see if you could make a human feel something for you. Well, congratulations, your training was a complete success, vanguard."

With a snarl, he crossed the room and cupped her shoulders in his hands. "Not another word. If you think this is easy, you're mistaken. You force me to admit—*in her hearing*—that the consort means nothing to me? Will it comfort you to know that I'm like an animal in a trap? You are, and always will be, the one choice I ever freely made."

A sobbing breath escaped her, and she tried to break free of his hold, but not really, not ferociously. In the end she leaned into him while pain shook them like a fierce wind in summer trees. His arms encircled her, and his scent seduced her as it ever had. He smelled of springtime, pine woods, and salted leather. Szarok leaned his forehead against hers, breathing her in with equal alacrity, as if this moment must nourish him forever.

"I missed you." That admission wrenched from her, as painful as if each word was carved on her flesh with glass.

"As did I, my treasure." Trembling, he cupped her face in his hands, and she took wild joy in knowing that she still moved him like this.

But no matter how he felt, it wasn't right. It never could be. Not again. *Before, I couldn't guess what he meant by obligations.*

"Did you . . . Was she . . ." Tegan couldn't get the question out.

But she knew what answer she wanted. It didn't come.

"Yes," he said.

A lie of omission, then. How wretched of you to whisper that I can deceive the rest of the world, but not you. Never you.

If she had any pride, she would push away and go now. But since these moments must last a lifetime, she hoarded them. His heartbeat surged beneath her ear. "So she was waiting the whole time you were with me."

His flat tone chilled her. "She was selected as suitable for the vanguard. The People believe our children will be exceptional."

"So you're like royalty, the crown prince and princess of the Uroch."

"Not by choice." As if he couldn't help it, he rubbed his cheek against the top of her head. The familiar caress made her hands tighten on his arms. Slowly, Szarok tilted his forehead against hers, and for long moments they traded breaths, not quite kissing.

She wanted to.

But she couldn't forget the sick Uroch female shifting restlessly nearby. Her sense of morality hadn't slipped enough to let her do *this*.

When he leaned down to finish the gesture, scent-marking, she stepped back and shook her head. "Nobody gets to pick his fate. I'm not generous enough to wish you happy. But I hope she recovers fully and that you're . . . well."

Tears blinded her as she rushed out of the house. The messenger brought the pony, and she scrambled gracelessly onto its back. Fortunately the animal knew its way back to the stable, for Tegan wept the entire way, offering no guidance. By the time she reached Port-Mer, she had her emotions under control, but the evidence of distress couldn't be blotted away. Rather than worry the others, she returned the mount and walked aimlessly until the swelling subsided.

Since almost everyone was enjoying their time in port, the *Catalina* was nearly deserted when she went aboard. There were a few sailors on duty, responsible for the ship, but she skirted them and went to the infirmary to lie down. Tegan considered mixing herself a potion for sleep, but grief was its own narcotic, and she winked out without needing any help. Much later she woke to find Millie spooned up against her. James must have elected to sleep below, and the rocking of the ship told her that they had left Antecost.

Good. I won't go back again.

With fair winds and current, it was a short jaunt to Rosemere, but she had already decided that she wouldn't be continuing her journey. She'd spend some time with the people who loved her in Rosemere, and then eventually she would head back to Peckinpaugh to stay. Millie and James both tried to talk to her, but she avoided them, not easy in the confines of the *Catalina*.

What she needed most now was privacy and time to mourn. He might not be dead, but she must bury him in her heart all the same. With a soft sigh, she stared at the dried flower, pressed between the pages of her anatomy book. She'd taken this as a memento when Szarok had shown her the waterfall on Antecost. Tegan held it up to the wind, but in the end, she couldn't let it go. Not yet. She closed the book.

As they dropped anchor near the Evergreen Isle, she approached the captain. "Thank you for everything. I'm sorry Millie ended up doing most of my work."

"I'm just happy you're healthy and whole. You have friends here, I gather?"

"Old acquaintances anyway, who *could* be friends if I let them."

"Sometimes trusting people is the hardest thing in the world," the captain agreed.

"Safe travels," said Sung Ji.

She hugged them both and then found James and Millie ready to disembark also. Since they each had all their belongings, this couldn't be a shore visit. "What's this about . . . ?"

Millie danced a little in place, overflowing with delight. "I'm meeting the governor."

"He'll love you," Tegan said. "Then I'll wish you both much joy. But why don't you pop off for a visit and continue on? I know you wanted to see the world." Possibly it wasn't her business, but Tegan hated to think of Millie giving up her dreams for James.

The other girl leaned her head against his shoulder and said simply, "He *is* my world."

The exquisite, fearless honesty snatched her breath away. While she recovered, James shuffled in embarrassment. He dropped a kiss on Millie's temple. "We need to travel to Winterville, too."

They're serious, meeting families, getting permission. Even if she and Szarok had a future, there would be none of these sweet formalities. But she couldn't spend her life flinching away from things that made those she cared about happy. Tegan fixed a smile on her face like a painting and beckoned Millie toward the railing. Down the ladder, the sailor tasked with rowing them ashore waited. Nearby, the many boatmen of Rosemere queued up to transport the supplies Advika had brought from the north.

As the couple climbed into the boat after her, she asked, "Would it be possible for you to send my boxes to Peckinpaugh from the Winterville cottage? Khamish will look after everything until I'm ready to take up studying again."

"All that research should be saved," Millie said.

James nodded. "We'll take care of it."

On the pier, she parted company with James and Millie after more hugs. Her feet knew the way to the stone cottage built on the rise on the other side of town. Part of her wanted to chuck the staff Szarok had given her, but since it was the only proof of their time together, she held on to it instead. *No point in blaming the tool for the master's mistakes.* Really, that wasn't even the right word. He had never promised he would come back to her; she'd only hoped.

In the six months or so since she'd left, nothing much had changed. The plants and flowers were growing well. As she walked up, Deuce was tending them. Then she straightened and Tegan noted her enormous belly. *I take it back. Everything will be different now.* Deuce caught sight of her and waddled through the gate, one hand on her lower back.

"Just look at you," Tegan said. "I suppose I have to call you Breeder now."

Once, that would have made Deuce ball up a fist, but she only laughed. She was rounder than she had ever been, not just belly, but cheeks, shoulders, hips, and all. Soft living and good food had padded her out over whipcord muscle, but her pasty skin still hadn't taken on much color. Now she was pale and pink, progress of a sort, Tegan supposed. She suffered a hug from the pregnant Huntress and got nudged in the stomach by the unborn babe.

"Are you hungry? Fade's helping Edmund at the shop, but he'll be back later. Come in." Impatient as ever, Deuce herded Tegan into the house. "Tell me everything that's happened since I saw you. I'm a tad jealous. Sometimes it feels like my story is done while yours is just beginning."

Tegan said softly, "You got a lovely ending, though."

"True enough." She bustled around the cottage, fixing food Tegan hadn't requested. Right then it seemed she might never be hungry again.

Of course I'd give my heart to someone who can't keep it. Of course I would. Perhaps it was because she already hurt so much, and there was no barrier between old pain and new. But today old words bubbled up until she couldn't swallow them anymore.

"We're friends?" she asked then.

Deuce appeared startled by this question. "You're family to me, same as Momma Oaks and Edmund. After all we've been through together, you could say we're like sisters."

"To you."

"Huh?"

"That's how you feel. I've always pretended with you because if I didn't, you might turn on me."

"I have no idea what you're talking about."

Tegan let it all go in a rush, every grievance she carried, starting from the meeting in the ruins. "And then you said, 'I would have fought until I died.' Do you know how much that *hurt* me? How can I be like sisters with someone who said that?"

"I apologized, or I *think* I did." Confused, Deuce came over and sat down in the chair opposite. "But if I didn't say it enough or seem like I meant it, tell me how to make it right."

Tegan tipped her head back and sighed. "If I knew, I would. Mainly, I want to get closer to you, truly close, not me pretending nothing is wrong because it's easier. I'm done with that life."

"You want me to beg forgiveness outright? I'll do it, though it's hard to get up again."

At first Tegan thought she must be joking, but then Deuce plopped onto her knees. "You know I'm an idiot, and I had to learn so many things that other people came knowing. But I'm beyond sorry—you don't even know how much—but *especially* because I had no idea that there was trouble between you and me."

She'd rarely seen the Huntress cry, so maybe it was the baby influencing her, but Tegan couldn't keep her anger hot when she saw tears coursing down the other girl's cheeks. And once that core of anger dissipated, it surprised her how much affection lay beneath. No, she wasn't perfect, but maybe sisters didn't have to be. *I should have said something. I should've been braver.* Tegan came out of her chair and hugged Deuce as best she could around the belly.

"I forgive you. Truly, this time. Now you need to get up and calm down."

As Tegan helped her up, a gush of water hit the floor.

Deuce's eyes widened. "It's a couple of weeks early, but I've been cramping a bit for the last day or so. I didn't realize . . ."

She sighed. The problem with warrior women was that their pain threshold meant they had no idea how deep in labor they were. But she still reassured her patient. "A week or two won't matter." Tegan waited for the revulsion and horror, but none came. Instead she unpacked her supplies while giving instructions. "Get undressed. You can keep your shirt on. I need to wash up and then see how far you've progressed."

She arranged bedding on the floor and made Deuce comfortable, then she did the exam as Khamish had taught her. "Not quite there. It'll be an hour or two yet. You probably want your family here, but I won't leave you to fetch them."

A contraction hit the other girl hard, and she gripped Tegan's hand. "Fade . . . should be along shortly. He said . . . he'll be home for lunch."

"Breathe. Like this." Tegan demonstrated.

As predicted, her man returned a few minutes later. He staggered and clung to the doorway when he realized what was happening. But Tegan didn't let him panic.

"Get her family. Momma Oaks, for sure. Tell Edmund, too." If something went wrong, she wouldn't let Deuce end up like Netta Gwynne, wishing she could see her loved ones once more.

"I'll be right back," Fade said.

He raced out, leaving Tegan to mop the sweat from her friend's face. "You're going to be fine. It'll hurt like hell, but you've had worse."

"That's my line," she wheezed.

When Fade entered the cottage again, he had Momma Oaks and Edmund, along with Rex and Spence. The men poured some drinks and dragged the father-to-be outside while Momma Oaks settled in to assist Tegan. Every now and then she heard cursing from outside and the sound of someone being knocked around.

"Fade's scared," Deuce said somewhat unnecessarily.

"And he's not even doing any of the work," Momma Oaks muttered.

A few hours later, Tegan delivered a healthy boy for the happy couple. No excess bleeding, no complications. *Thank you, Khamish. I couldn't have done this without your teaching.*

"Well," she said then. "What are you going to name him?"

No Longer the Vanguard

or five days and nights Szarok tended Tcharr as instructed. She woke on the sixth morning, the infection subsiding, but she was thin and weak from her long struggle. It took another week before she could feed herself, but the settlement, simply named Olurra, or *our land*, celebrated with great abandon once it became clear the consort would live.

"You care for me with such devotion."

Szarok couldn't meet her gaze. If she pushed, he would speak of duty. Her eyes fell and her hand dropped away from his arm. *"Send Rzika to me."*

His joints groaned as he stepped into the arboreal sunlight. Even in spring, it was chilly, but not so much that it would cause his people harm. He found the elder teaching a group of young-lings, and he waited politely for her to finish the lesson. At the first opportunity, they scattered to run and hunt, no danger of humans deciding they had strayed too far and shooting them. As Littleberry had promised, they were welcome in Port-Mer. The other villages were a little skittish, but nobody had been unfriendly.

"We owe the humans much," Rzika said. *"I had my doubts, but they will make tolerable neighbors."* Her tone revealed a quiet loathing that no single kindness could dispel.

He inclined his head. *"Tcharr would see you."*

"How is she?"

"She'll mend."

Thanks to his healer. *No. Not mine anymore.* She said . . . ah, just the remembering seemed as if it would end him. When she went with her suffering eyes and tearful face, he took a wound that would neither kill him nor stop bleeding. *I have done everything I must.* But the weight of obligation never eased.

"You smell of sorrow."

Szarok snapped a look at the elder, but her mien was imperturbable. This was where he had learned his composure, after all. With that, she turned and made her way to the house that he would share with the consort once she recovered her strength. Their children would play in these woods, and when the time came, he'd pass his memories to them.

Every fiber of his being shouted no.

How much is enough?

For most of the day he helped with construction. They needed many more homes before winter. The Port-Mer crew had taught them everything, so now they felled the logs and worked on their own. *The People are building.* At least that aspect of Olurra gave him great joy, but this . . . this was no longer his private dream.

When he returned to the house, he found Rzika sitting outside. *"I give greetings."* She glanced up at him in the twilight, eyes hooded. *"Tcharr tells me that you tend her as a brother, not a mate."*

There was no point in subterfuge. Secretly he had wanted to broach this conversation for weeks but couldn't. Not while Tcharr lay ill. *"My heart does not move for her."*

"You understood how life would be when you became the vanguard."

"Yes," he said. *"But my control is imperfect. I do feel."*

The elder flourished her claws with a faint growl of acceptance. *"Who among the tribe has caught your eye? Do your duty first with Tcharr and have the one you truly desire later."*

"She is not of the People."

Rzika shot to her feet with a quickness that belied her age. Fiercely, she struck him twice, both times in the mouth. He swallowed the punishment.

"That human healer . . . she smelled of you as she left. Is she the one?"

"Yes," he said.

Prowling closer, Rzika sank her talons into the nape of his neck. *"This is madness, vanguard. Your place is here. There is far too much blood spilled between our people for such a union to flourish. You must know this. The People cleave to one another. To accept humanity as our neighbors, this is enough."*

He ignored her arguments and persisted, *"Not for me. I need my freedom."*

Realizing how serious he was, she responded in kind. The elder snarled, calling out to the tribe nearby. *"To me! The vanguard has lost his reason and his loyalty."*

If he'd ever doubted who held the real power, he didn't now. Within moments, Rzika had him bound and on his knees. She selected a tree branch and passed it to a sturdy male. *"This is for his sake. We must bring him back to us."*

"What's his crime?" a youngling growled.

"Forsaking the tribe. He is a traitor who would abandon his own people, turn from his destiny, and lie down with the enemy."

Goaded, Szarok shouted, *"This is how you made me."*

"Repent!"

The People spoke as one, and then the wood came down. Szarok lost count of how many times they struck him. Streaks of agony lined his back, his shoulders, his chest, his face. When the wielder tired, he passed the stick to someone else. Blood filled Szarok's mouth, and his eyes swelled so that he couldn't see. But no matter how much the pain rose, he never uttered a sound.

"Come back to us!" Rzika cried. *"What does it say of the People if the best of us cannot bear to stay? That a human has more worth than our consort in the vanguard's eyes?"*

"It doesn't matter what you do. There is no pain greater than living without her. If I cannot be free, I would rather die. Make it swift."

Snarls of shock reverberated through the crowd. *This is Rroclaw's retribution,* he thought as they renewed the onslaught. Szarok had known they wouldn't tolerate this love; it was why he'd rejected Tegan's offer to accompany him. She might be on the ground beside him if she had. Eventually they dragged him back to the house he shared with Tcharr and threw him down before her. Someone bound his wrists and shoved him back onto the pallet.

Rzika said, *"He is yours, as promised. Use him well."*

Szarok heard the shuffle of the elder's footsteps and then the closing door. He recoiled when Tcharr touched him, but she only mopped the blood from his eyes. Now he could see in slivers, her hovering face, still thin from her long illness. Tcharr let out a long breath.

"Am I so awful? That you must be beaten before you come to me?"

He tried to speak . . . and couldn't. Their gazes met and tangled. For another warrior, she would answer his every need. But her desire could find no home in him. Tcharr tried; she touched him in ways that should have roused him and brought him pleasure, but they only prompted him to twist away, silently begging her to stop.

"This is wrong," she said finally.

While he lay helpless, she went to the door and called for the elder. *"If you think children born of this will be happy, you must be mad. They will remember their sire's pain."*

Rzika sighed audibly. *"What else can I do? We cannot afford to lose him."*

Gathering his strength, Szarok rocked into a sitting position and spat blood. The females gasped, for it was the first time he had challenged their right to discipline him. With a few more swallows, he found his voice.

"You won't if you let me go. Let Tcharr choose who moves her heart.

With him, she can lead the People. You taught me to go forth among the humans, and so I have. Let me go again. This I promise: nothing I learn, nothing of mine will be lost. Instead of offspring, I will bring back memories. Before I die, I'll return and pass on all that I am to your younglings."

"An honorable offer," said Tcharr.

Sensing a chance of escape, he cared nothing for the pain. *"The People will gain much from my travel in the wider world. You should rejoice in how well you taught me, that I could love our enemy."*

Rzika snarled, but he recognized defeat in that sound. *"Go now, before I change my mind."*

"He can hardly move," Tcharr protested.

"I'll go to her if I must crawl." And so he did, until he found the wall near the door. With shaking hands, Szarok pulled himself upright.

When he staggered out of the house, a young male—by the scent of him—tried to stop him, but Rzika growled a protest. *"No one touch him. No one interfere. Szarok goes forth, no longer the vanguard, but simply a free heart of the People. He brought us to the promised land and fulfilled his destiny. Permit him to find his own fate from here, as we shall."*

The chorus of farewells barely penetrated his resolve. His eyes still didn't offer much help, just slices of light and shadow. The swelling would go down in time, however, and he could run to Port-Mer blind. *As I must.* He stumbled at first, holding on to trees and pausing for breath because his ribs ached as if they were banded in fire.

Darkness fell before he made it to Port-Mer. Here, it was less familiar, so with a lowered head, he asked a random human to guide him to Littleberry's house. It was a woman who did; she didn't speak much on the way, but she smelled of lavender. "Here you are," she said. "Take care of those wounds, mind."

I don't care about that. I have to find Tegan.

It's not too late.

It cannot be too late.

Littleberry's wife—he'd forgotten the female's name—answered his knock. "Oh, dear heaven. What happened? Were you robbed?"

"Your husband? Please." Szarok couldn't be sure his words were intelligible in her tongue, until she took his arm and led him inside.

"Wait just a moment. I'll get him . . . and a cold compress."

Soon he was sitting in the village chief's front room, his hands unbound, a damp cloth across his eyes. Littleberry let him rest for a while before speaking. "I won't ask what happened. Instead I'll ask why you've come."

Through bruised lips, Szarok made his request. "This isn't to make amends, but I'd count it as a personal favor, the last I'll ever request, if you could get me to Rosemere in the morning."

"You should heal first."

He shook his head so hard, his ears rung. "No. I can't. Please."

"No need to beg. In weather so clear, it's an easy wish."

"Thank you," he whispered.

Mrs. Littleberry must have drugged his tea because he slept like the dead, and he barely remembered the journey to Rosemere. His ribs still hurt when he got off the little boat, but he could see again at least. He drew up his hood in honor of the Evergreen Isle's brand of prejudice. Though Szarok wanted to run through town shouting for her, instinct warned him it would be a poor choice.

Where would she be?

After the war, she'd stayed at the governor's manor, but if he had a choice, he'd never see that particular human again. *Where? Where are you, my treasure?* Breathing in, he found no trace of her. Too much human stink, tradecraft, livestock. Growling in frustration, he prowled through town, where he garnered a few looks, but nobody questioned him. It seemed likely that her friend the Huntress would know where Tegan had gone.

But as he set forth, the wind whispered of her. He had found her seeking solace there once before. Szarok seized on her scent like a starving wolf and followed her, past the rose-wreathed cottage with its pale stone walls and all the way down to the water. He smelled her sadness before her saw her, a salt-tinge to her usual sweetness, and when he followed the bend in the land, relief nearly drowned him like hell-water—that she was still here, that she had not gone where he couldn't follow.

"Tegan," he said.

But she didn't turn. Her back stiffened. "Leave, stop haunting me. I want to hate you, and it maddens me that I can't. Your voice is everywhere, your warmth, your smell. . . ."

At once, he realized. *She thinks I'm not truly here.* There was no gain in being tentative, so he ran to her as fast as his battered body permitted. Claws on arms, he spun her. Her eyes widened as she took in his injuries, but when she tried to touch his bruised cheek, he clasped her hands.

"I don't need a healer. I came for you."

"What have you done?" she whispered, taking him in with darting glances, as if she feared he might vanish before her eyes.

Never in his life had he dreaded anything so much as the possibility that she might say it was too late. *You will never be a stranger to me.* Abandoning all pride, he dropped to his knees before her and bowed his head. In a desperate rush, he told her everything.

"I have nothing now. I'm not the vanguard. I don't even know how many years I can offer you. But all I want in life is to be where you are."

For a long moment she destroyed him with her silence. And then she settled before him and stroked his cheek, throat, jaw, and the spot behind his ear. "Please, please, don't let this be a dream. My heart has broken a thousand times as I lay sleeping. You're truly free?"

"Yes," he said. "And I am forever yours, if you'll have me."

A sob burst out of her, and he drew her in. As her scent rolled over him, he shuddered with agonized desire. Her tears tasted of salt and he licked them as they fell, until she sought his mouth with hers. *Yes. Yes.* Her lips were as soft as he remembered. Some sweet fruit lingered on her tongue, and he fell into her with a hunger that could never be satiated. Tegan touched him with hands light as feathers, careful with his injuries, but just the feel of her blunt fingertips—that once made his flesh crawl—inverted pain and pleasure.

"Yes," she sang.

And he didn't know if it was an encouragement to kiss her more or an answer to his question. He gambled on both and sipped at her lower lip, until she made a sound that made his head go hot and fizzy. Soon he wouldn't be able to stop, and he didn't even know—they'd never discussed—but she made the decision for him, digging blunt nails into his shoulders in an unmistakable message. Their clothing shifted. When she curved above him, everything went white-hot. He shuddered as she *learned*, and then he discovered that their differences weren't absolute. Panting, he put his face in the curve of her shoulder while she moved.

Afterward he held her, or she rocked him. Either way, they tangled together in the sunshine, falling back in the long grass. The sky smiled overhead, blue unbounded. Probably he should mind that they'd given no thought to privacy, but nobody had interrupted them, and he had love in his arms again. Szarok nuzzled her cheek, throat, shoulder, though she smelled thoroughly of him already. But the fact that she had stopped him from scent-marking before, back in Olurra, throbbed like an unhealed wound.

She is mine, and I am hers. Always, always, always. The world made no sense any other way.

"Did you really say you'd rather die than live without me?"

"Yes," he said.

"You are my heart," she growled.

Then she hid her face, for she hated doing anything badly, and her throat wasn't shaped to form all the right sounds. *"It's enough that you try, my treasure."* He kissed the top of her head and breathed her in. "I've promised to learn much and bring that knowledge back to the People."

"I like the way you think. As it happens, I could use an apprentice. A girl in Peckinpaugh holds promise, but she's young yet." From the sun-bright scent of her to her open smile, Tegan wore happiness like a floral crown.

"My people would benefit greatly if I learned of medicine," he murmured, thoughtful.

She stroked his back in long sweeps, delicious enough to distract him from her words, so she had to ask twice. "Enough to make them truly forgive your defection?"

He lifted a shoulder, inviting more contact. *It will never be enough.* "The deal is struck. If they always consider me lost, I'll count it a fair trade for being with you."

She kissed him for that. Oddly delicious, telling the truth. "Should I chastise you for lying when you said I shouldn't?"

"I never did. You simply didn't ask if I had a mate. And . . ." He struggled with how to put it, the human words dancing out of reach. "It was a formality. We never—"

"Did what we have?" she supplied.

"Yes."

"Then I suppose I'll forgive you. They punished you quite a lot already."

"My tribe knows of you. Will you tell your loved ones about me?" If she preferred to hide their heart-bond, it would sting. But he could bear anything for her.

"Of course. Khamish already knows. You are mine, no matter what anyone says."

"I love you," he said.

Only those words would suffice for the universe that burned in his spirit, solely for her. It sounded better in his tongue, so he snarled, *"My heart beats for you."* When Tegan responded, *"You are my meat and drink,"* he nearly died of pleasure.

But she added, "And I, you," just in case he had any doubts.

There were none. He was all brightness, all yearning. *"My beloved, thank you for waiting."*

"About your apprenticeship," she whispered, shifting toward him. "See? My shoulder has healed just fine."

Thus invited, he checked the scar on her back. "It matches this one." With his cheek, he nuzzled both warrior marks, shoulder and thigh, proof of her great strength. "You are my queen."

"My dearest love, I probably should've made you grovel more, but I'm done pretending. I don't care where we are, or what we do, as long as we're together."

Happy Endings

The governor of the Evergreen Isle had been alone a long time. Never had Morrow understood this better than when he brought Millie to the quiet house he'd fled, time and again. She wore a clean dress, freshly pressed by the public house owner. Yet as she stepped over the threshold, her fingers trembled in his.

"Don't worry. He won't eat you."

Her pretty eyes filled with tears. "You know he can't possibly approve. I'm nobody."

"You're my love," he told her. "And besides, you're also the girl who saved the free territories with her kindness."

She groaned. "Don't start that again."

But at least she was smiling when they entered his father's sanctuary, a room filled with books that had quietly taught Morrow that it was safer in those pages and safer to fix his heart on people who would never ask anything of him. Never tease, never tussle, never challenge. Now more than ever, he grasped that books should be part of his life, not the depth and breadth of it.

"James?" The elder Morrow rose from his reading chair, setting the volume aside with great care. "I didn't realize you were back."

They'd quarreled before he got his father to agree to donate some provisions to cover his passage on Advika's ship. The question, *When are you going to settle down?*, had lingered between them. At least now he had an answer.

"I'd like you to meet Millie Faraday."

She bobbed before his father like an acorn in a river. "My pleasure, sir."

"Likewise. This is such a surprise. James doesn't bring friends home often."

Morrow almost laughed, as he could count on one hand the people in Rosemere he'd identify as such. "Once her parents grant permission, I intend to marry her."

His father seemed amused. "You don't ask my blessing, I see."

"You're welcome to give it," he said. "But it won't change my plans, either way."

Horrified, Millie elbowed him in the side. "*James.*"

"Don't mind him. He's taken the idea that I'll respect him more if he challenges my authority. And he's not entirely wrong." Taking Millie's arm, the governor led her out of the sitting room and down the hall to the dining table. "Let's have lunch and get to know each other. Are you sure you want this rascal of mine?"

Visibly relieved, she chuckled. "Dead certain, sir. I've had my eye on him for ages now. It just took him a while to look back."

"Please don't hold it against him."

Stunned, Morrow watched them for a moment and then hurried to catch up. The housekeeper brought luncheon, and by the time the meal finished, Millie had his father eating out of the palm of her pretty hand. She told him all about their adventures and how Morrow had taught school in Baybridge. His cheeks flushed before she paused in singing his praises.

Afterward, the housekeeper took Millie to freshen up, leaving him alone with his father. "You got over the healer?"

Once, he would've been offended by the question, as if his

feelings were flotsam. "It was only a crush," he said softly. "Boys are prone to them."

"And now you're a man." That wasn't a question. The governor patted his shoulder with an approving look. "Proud of you, son. I like her. Seems as if she'll be the making of you."

"She has been," he admitted.

"What are your plans?"

"Winterville, first, and then I think we'll be going back to Baybridge. You should come," he said impulsively. "Don't let this house become your tomb."

When he saw the rejection forming on his father's face, he wondered why he'd bothered. But the words never came; they died on his lips, and then he cocked his head, seeming pensive. "Maybe," he answered at last. "Someone else might breathe new life into this place."

Surprised yet elated, Morrow put out his hand for a shake, but his father hauled him in for a rare, back-pounding hug. "This is the first time in forever I feel like you've actually come home."

If he's trying, I will, too.

"It would probably help my case if you travel with us to Winterville."

"You're worried they'll turn you down?" his father asked.

"A little. I hope they're willing to relocate to Baybridge, so I don't have to separate Millie from her family. They moved once already for her, so maybe it isn't a long shot."

"Then . . . when do we leave?"

The next day, for the first time in Morrow's memory, the governor packed a bag and prepared to leave the Evergreen Isle. They hailed a boatman, who ferried them to the mainland, but he had so many questions. "Who shall we ask if there's trouble?"

His father shrugged. "You work it out."

Over the next two weeks, he saw a side of his father he hadn't known existed. Morrow had thought he'd have to teach him everything about surviving in the wild, but he started the campfire without supervision and he even knew how to set snares overnight. They traveled slowly, so by the time they reached Winterville, spring flourished all around, the flowers ripening into fruit.

Like Otterburn, Winterville was an eyesore, and he traded a look with Millie that ended in a secret smile. Her step gained a skip the closer they came to her family home. The weathered wood had seen better days, and the man tending to a garden outside looked equally tired. But when he spotted Millie, he dropped his hoe and ran for her. She went into his arms for a spin, and Morrow watched them, his heart in his throat.

I have to convince them.

"Stop, Da. *Stop* now. I'm like to choke."

"You're a sight for sore eyes." She got another hug before her da noticed he had two interested onlookers.

Blushing, Millie brought him into the conversation by word and gesture. "My father, Harmon Faraday. This is my man, James. He's come to get your permission to spark me."

"Is that so?" An ice-cold gaze skimmed him up and down.

"And I'm James's father. If we're to be in-laws, I thought we should meet." The former governor offered a handshake, along with all of his best manners, making Morrow grateful.

"This is so sudden," Mr. Faraday muttered. "Let me call my wife."

The worst of Morrow's nerves melted away. When Millie took his hand and smiled at him, he knew it would be all right. And it was.

A week later they negotiated transport with John Kelley's trade caravan. His wagons were light, so his father and Millie's parents rode while they walked. It was a slow trek to the river, but he was in no hurry. The only thing that troubled him was that she didn't want to sleep in his arms with her folks close by. She kept whispering, "Once we're settled," like that was a magic phrase or something. He contemplated telling Mr. and Mrs. Faraday, whom he was supposed to call Ma and Da, about their winter in Baybridge, but that would probably just create more problems. Still, he sulked.

Millie coaxed him out of it.

A month after they'd first left Rosemere, they returned. It felt like a homecoming of sorts, and to his astonishment, Devi and Evette were moored off the isle, picking up passengers. One fellow had been corresponding with a gentleman in Peckinpaugh, and now he was ready to head north to meet his potential partner.

This seemed like providence, so he turned to Millie. "How would you like to wed on the marrying-ferry?"

Their families had questions and objections, but one by one, he laid them to rest. *This is our perfect ending.* And no matter the resistance, he wouldn't budge, and soon Millie joined him in insisting on a wedding at sea. *Well, on the river, anyway.*

"Ho, there!" Devi called as she rowed her boat to shore. "We're leaving on the morrow, but I could make room for a few more."

"I *am* the Morrow," his father said.

He shook his head over the awful joke, but Millie earned points by laughing. Her parents chuckled, too. Thus, it was settled. After spending one last night at the governor's manor, their group would emigrate permanently, Baybridge-bound. Millie went with their family while Morrow went to pay a farewell call. It didn't seem as if it had been that long, but Deuce and Fade's baby had already grown quite a lot.

"Look how strong he is," Fade said as the boy wrapped his fist around his thumb.

Morrow nodded. "A real warrior."

Deuce brought drinks, seeming well recovered from the birth. "You've got a particular look about you."

"That's because I'm here to say farewell," he said.

She sighed. "You and Tegan, both. She just boarded a ship. I don't reckon either of you will be back to stay. Am I wrong?"

He shook his head. "I won't rule out a visit, but I'm taking my father north, too."

"What about Rosemere?" Fade asked, plainly shocked.

"Maybe Edmund is interested in being governor?" he suggested, only half in jest.

Deuce paused with her cup in midair; then she snapped her fingers. "No. Momma Oaks."

"Whatever's best for the town." Her mother was certainly kind and wise. She'd make a warmer leader than his father.

"Maybe when the baby's older, we'll make a trip," Fade said.

Deuce nodded, taking young Karl from his father. "Please stay safe."

They named him after Longshot, he realized. He'd never met the man, but Deuce had told him about the mentor she'd lost in Salvation. Evidently Longshot had been a trader who'd saved her life more than once. It seemed fitting that she'd made her firstborn his namesake.

After lunch, Morrow went to the mansion for the last time. Mrs. Faraday had his father laughing so hard with one of her colorful expressions that tears were running down his cheeks. Millie turned to him, and it actually twisted his heart in his chest, how happy he was to see her. *Don't ever leave me,* he thought.

A restful night passed, and in the morning Millie donned her finest dress. Morrow took care with his appearance, too. His father lingered a little over the things his mother had loved, but Morrow guided him firmly out of the cold, quiet house and into the spring sunshine.

"You don't need anything from here," he said softly.

The once-governor of the Evergreen Isle lifted his face and smiled. "Untrue. But as long as I have you, the rest can pass away."

It took several trips to get everything the Faradays wanted to take ferried out to Devi's ship, smaller than the *Catalina* but no less elegant. It had clearly been built in Antecost, and it was, somewhat hilariously, called the *Love Boat*. Morrow showed his expanded family where to wait, but his father wanted a word with Devi about the journey, and Mrs. Faraday was a gregarious soul, so she went to chat with the other passengers.

"That woman never met a stranger," Mr. Faraday said fondly.

Maybe one day I'll be brave enough to call him Da.

Once we're married.

For ten years or so.

"Millie takes after her, I think."

The other man nodded. "If you hurt her, I'll break both your legs and drop you down a hole so deep, nobody will ever find you," he said. "Her happiness matters more than my life. Since her brother died, I can't say no to that girl. That's why I let her go chasing off with a healer I barely knew. You understand?"

Morrow gulped before answering, "Yes, sir."

"Attention, happy couples! I'm the captain of the *Love Boat*, and if you've come aboard to partner up, assemble front and center."

With a final nod to Mr. Faraday, Morrow went to claim Millie. Three other couples joined them, but he was surprised to spot Tegan by the railing, snuggled against Szarok like the wooden nesting dolls his mother had treasured. They were the only things of hers that he had packed, amid all those possessions that had owned his father for so many years. Even the books, he'd left behind. Because he'd meant it when he said he only needed Millie to feel whole. Once, it would've hurt to see Tegan of the Staff so close to someone else, but nobody who registered how the Uroch held her could doubt that she was beyond precious to him.

A few other passengers shot them skeptical or downright hostile looks. *They don't have an easy road ahead, but this is right.* With a half smile for an old friend, he gave his full attention to Devi.

"Take your love's hand now, and repeat after me. 'You are my rock and my shelter. I promise to turn to you always, from this day forward. I choose you as my partner and my love. Until my last breath, so I do swear.'"

Despite speaking the words in unison, they still hit him hard. He faced Millie on Devi's instruction. "Now kiss your dear ones like you mean it."

Before he could move, Millie jumped into his arms and planted such a deep kiss on him that Morrow felt vaguely surprised that his hair didn't catch fire. Eventually he pulled back. "Our family's watching."

She shrugged. "They know what comes next."

As the boat set off, the party went into full swing. He congratulated the other couples while he tracked Millie's movements with his gaze. The crew passed around drinks—and didn't have any, he noticed, but his father and Millie's parents definitely made merry. From across the deck, he admired how fast his wife made friends. She learned all the other couple's names within an hour and had invitations to visit within two.

Finally he worked up the nerve to join Tegan, still tucked beneath Szarok's chin like she belonged there. "You didn't want to make it official?"

"We already spoke all the words we need," Szarok said.

Though Morrow was no threat—and had just married the love of his life—the Uroch still radiated a quiet menace, like he might growl if anyone got too close to Tegan. Instead of bothering him, that only made him smile. "Then what're you doing on the *Love Boat*?"

"I don't want to work," Tegan told him with a bashful smile. "This trip is just for us."

"Ah, I wondered. You haven't met Devi before?"

She shook her head. "Advika told me about her, though. So when she arrived—"

"You leapt at the chance. Understood. What will you do now?"

Tegan raised her eyes skyward as if for inspiration. "Everything? But that's no answer. So . . . travel. Help people. Likely stumble into more adventures." She traded a secret look with Szarok and said, "Above all, we'll learn. And when we're ready, I suspect we'll often call Peckinpaugh home, other times Olurra."

That's the Uroch settlement on Antecost, James recalled.

"That sounds exciting. Send a letter with Devi now and then, won't you?"

"Definitely," Tegan said.

"I'm off, then."

Pleasure radiated from the Uroch at the promise of Morrow's imminent departure. Szarok nuzzled Tegan's cheek, and she lifted her face with such palpable pleasure that Morrow blushed and looked away. But as he turned to find his wife, Tegan's soft voice stayed him. "Thank you for teaching me to fight, for believing that I could. Be happy, James."

"I will," he promised.

It was one he could surely keep.

Morrow tapped the pen against his brow, frustrated. Working as a schoolmaster didn't leave him much time for writing, but he'd promised to finish this up before the thaw, so Devi could take it south to Peckinpaugh, where he'd last had word from Tegan and Szarok. Grumbling beneath his breath, he reread the line aloud. *No. Terrible.* He couldn't capture the bittersweet beauty of their forbidden romance in bloom, though he was doing his level best to encapsulate the story as Tegan had described. He scratched out what he'd written and tried again. *All wishes fulfilled, they leaned close for a final—*

"James!" Millie sounded impatient. A furtive glance at the clock told him why.

"Yes, my dear?"

His wife seemed to be on the verge of scolding him soundly. "The twins want you to come and play. Stop scribbling already."

With a final flourish of the pen, he scrawled, *Happy endings write themselves anyway, while life—and love—waits for no man.* Then he closed the book for good.

Thank you for reading this FEIWEL AND FRIENDS book.
The Friends who made

VANGUARD

possible are:

Jean Feiwel, PUBLISHER
Liz Szabla, ASSOCIATE PUBLISHER
Rich Deas, SENIOR CREATIVE DIRECTOR
Holly West, EDITOR
Alexei Esikoff, SENIOR MANAGING EDITOR
Kim Waymer, SENIOR PRODUCTION MANAGER
Anna Roberto, EDITOR
Christine Barcellona, ASSOCIATE EDITOR
Kat Brzozowski, EDITOR
Anna Poon, ASSISTANT EDITOR
Emily Settle, ADMINISTRATIVE ASSISTANT
Ilana Worrell, PRODUCTION EDITOR

Follow us on Facebook or visit us online at
fiercereads.com.

OUR BOOKS ARE FRIENDS FOR LIFE